Acclaim for Richard Mabry, MD

"Packed with thrills, *Stress Test* is a lightning-paced read that you'll read in one breath."

— Tess Gerritsen, *New York Times*
best-selling author of *Last to Die*

"Original and profound. I found the Christian message engaging and fascinating, and the story a thrill-a-minute."

— Michael Palmer, *New York Times*
best-selling author of *Oath of
Office*, regarding *Stress Test*

"Sirens, scalpels, and the business end of a revolver—*Stress Test* offers Code 3 action and a prescription for hope."

— Candace Calvert, best-selling
author of *Code Triage* and *Trauma
Plan*

"Vintage Mabry. *Heart Failure* weaves an intricate plot of mystery and suspense that will leave you guessing until the final page."

— Billy Coffey, author of *When
Mockingbirds Sing*

"*Stress Test* comes with a warning: Prepare to stop life until you finish the last page."

— Diann Mills, author of *The Chase*
and *The Survivor*

"Recurring legal, medical, and romantic thrills. Diagnosis: Pure entertainment."

— James Scott Bell, award-winning
suspense author

"Mabry's latest provides fast-paced, edge-of-your-seat action and suspense. His medical knowledge is evident in the realistic and detailed characters and scenes."

— *RT Book Reviews*, 4 1/2 star review
of *Stress Test*

"The plot moves along with plenty of action and empathy, and there's suspense and suspicion enough to keep readers zipping to the last pages."

— *Publishers Weekly* review of
Stress Test

HEART
FAILURE

HEART FAILURE

RICHARD L. MABRY, MD

THOMAS NELSON

Since 1798

NASHVILLE DALLAS MEXICO CITY RIO DE JANEIRO

Published in Nashville, Tennessee, by Thomas Nelson. Thomas Nelson is a registered trademark of Thomas Nelson, Inc.

Published in association with the literary agency of WordServe Literary Group, Ltd., 10152 S. Knoll Circle, Highlands Ranch, CO 80130. www .wordserveliterary.com.

Thomas Nelson, Inc., titles may be purchased in bulk for educational, business, fund-raising, or sales promotional use. For information, please e-mail SpecialMarkets@ThomasNelson.com.

Publisher's Note: This novel is a work of fiction. Names, characters, places, and incidents are either products of the author's imagination or used fictitiously. All characters are fictional, and any similarity to people living or dead is purely coincidental.

Scripture quotations are taken from the King James Version of the Bible and the New American Standard Bible®, © The Lockman Foundation 1960, 1962, 1963, 1968, 1971, 1972, 1973, 1975, 1977, 1995. Used by permission.

Library of Congress Cataloging-in-Publication Data

Mabry, Richard L.
  Heart failure / Richard L. Mabry.
     pages cm
  ISBN 978-1-4016-8710-6 (Trade Paper)
  I. Title.
  PS3613.A2H43 2013
  813'.6—dc23   2013015672

Printed in the United States of America

13 14 15 16 17 RRD 6 5 4 3 2 1

This novel is dedicated to the pastors, staff, and my fellow members at Stonebriar Community Church.

ONE

ADAM DAVIDSON AND DR. CARRIE MARKHAM STROLLED OUT THE doors of the Starplex Cinema into the warm darkness of the springtime evening. As they made their way through the few cars left on the parking lot, Adam's right hand found Carrie's left. She took it and squeezed, and his heart seemed to skip a beat. His fingers explored until they felt the outline of the diamond ring he'd placed there only a week ago.

She leaned in to briefly rest her head on his shoulder. "I never thought I could be this happy."

"Me either." And if he had his way, this was how it would be for the rest of their lives. Two people in love, enjoying their small-town lives, their only worry what movie to see on their regular Saturday night date.

A loud noise in the distance made them both stop. Then Adam saw a shower of color on the horizon, about where the ballpark would be. "Fireworks show. The Titans must have won." *Get a grip, Adam. Stop jumping at every noise. You're safe.*

When Adam first met Carrie eight months ago, she was fragile and hurting, as skittish as a baby deer, still bearing the scars from the death of her husband almost two years earlier. Her only interest seemed to be her medical practice. But, little by little, he'd seen her start to smile, to laugh, and eventually to love.

Carrie had restored the smile to Adam's life as well. He still had his own problems, even though he hadn't revealed them to her. He hoped he would never have to. But having her in his life made him certain that the life he now lived, so long as he lived it with her, would be all he ever wanted.

These things were supposed to take time, but in just a few short months each of them had decided that the other was the person needed to fill the hole in their lives. The culmination had come with Adam's proposal and Carrie's acceptance last week. They hadn't set a wedding date yet, but for now Adam was content to watch Carrie plan and bask in the glow of their shared happiness.

The couple reached Adam's car and climbed in, but hadn't yet fastened their seat belts when Carrie said, "I think a chocolate— No, make that a hot fudge sundae." She leaned back in the passenger seat of Adam's little Subaru. "That would . . ."

As she was talking Adam saw a dark SUV approach from his right, moving at a snail's pace. When the vehicle was directly in front of Adam's Forester, its side window came down to reveal the glint of light on metal as the driver's hand extended outward.

Adam's next action was reflexive. If he was wrong, he could

apologize. But if he was right—He was already moving when he heard the shots.

The impact of Adam's arm across her shoulder pushed her down until her head was below the level of the car's dashboard. Then Carrie heard it—a flat crack, followed by two more in rapid succession. Muffled thuds sounded above her, and she pictured bullets boring into the headrests at the place where her head and Adam's had been seconds ago. Carrie cringed against an expected shower of glass, but only a few tiny pieces sprinkled down on her.

The faint ringing in her ears after the shots didn't mask the screech of tires and roar of an engine. When the noise subsided, all that remained was the rapid thud of her heartbeat echoing in her ears.

Carrie huddled with her head down, her breath cut off as much by fear as by the pressure of Adam's body atop hers, a human shield. She felt his soft breath in her ear as he whispered, "Are you all right?"

"I . . . I think so. How about you?"

"I'm okay." The pressure holding her down lessened. "Stay down until I tell you it's safe." Carrie turned her head to catch a glimpse of Adam peering cautiously over the dashboard.

Her heart threatened to jump out of her chest while her mind wrestled with what just happened. After a seeming eternity, Adam bent down and said in a hushed tone, "I think they've gone. You can sit up."

Carrie raised her head barely enough to peer through the damaged windshield. When nothing moved in her field of vision, she eased upward to perch on the edge of her seat. A few cars were still on the lot of the theater after the last Saturday night show, probably the vehicles of employees closing down for the night. There hadn't been many people in the movie theater.

"Are you sure you're not hurt?" Adam's voice, full of concern, brought Carrie back to the moment. He brushed a bit of glass from her seat with a handkerchief, then tossed it onto the floor of the car.

Carrie unfolded from her crouched position and eased farther onto the seat. "Scared, is all," she said. "You okay?"

"Not a scratch."

He reached across to hug her, and she turned to find shelter in his arms. They stayed that way for a long moment, and the trembling inside her slowly eased. "What . . . what was that about?"

"Nothing for you to worry about." Adam's voice and manner were calm, and Carrie felt comforted by his very presence. Then, as suddenly as the turn of a page, he released her and swung around to face forward in the driver's seat. His next words were terse, clipped. "We have to get out of here." He reached for the ignition, key in hand.

"Wait a minute!" Carrie pulled her cell phone from her purse and held it out to him. "We can't leave. We need to call 911."

Adam took her arm, a bit more firmly than necessary, and pushed the phone away. He shook his head. "No!"

She flinched at the negative response and the tone in which Adam delivered it. "Why? Someone shot at us. We should call the police."

Adam's voice was quiet, his words terse. "Look, I don't have time to explain. Let's go."

What's the matter with him? She took a deep breath and let it out slowly. Twice she started to speak. Twice she stopped.

Adam turned the key and reached for the gearshift lever.

Carrie saw his jaw clench. She was terrified, but Adam wasn't so much scared as—she searched for the right word—he was *cold* and determined. The sudden change frightened her. "If this was a drive-by, we need to report it. Maybe the police can catch them before they kill someone."

"Just let me handle this," Adam said. "Right now, let's get out of here. I want you someplace safe."

Although Adam's voice was low, there was an intensity to his words that Carrie had never heard before. "You have to trust me," he said. "There are things you don't know, things that make it dangerous for me to deal with the police right now." He pointed to her seat belt. "Buckle up and let's leave. I'll explain soon."

Carrie wanted to argue, but she could see it was no use. She put away her phone and fastened her seat belt.

The lights on the theater marquee went out. In the distance a siren sounded, faint at first but growing louder. "We're out of here," Adam said. He put the car in gear and eased out of the parking lot, peering through the starred windshield to navigate the dark streets.

Carrie studied Adam as he drove. Most men would be shaking after such a close encounter with death. But he wasn't. Why would that be? Was he used to being shot at? She shook her head. That was plain silly.

She thought she knew him—after all, they were engaged.

Carrie glanced at him again. Maybe she didn't know Adam as well as she'd thought. That scared her even more than what they'd just experienced.

They rode in silence for a few moments, and during that time Carrie recreated the shooting in her mind. Then something clicked—something she hadn't realized until then. She turned to Adam. "You pushed me down before the shots were fired. You didn't react to the shots. You knew they were coming."

Adam glanced at her but didn't respond.

Carrie thought about it once more. "I'm sure of it. You shoved me below the dashboard, then I heard three shots. How did you know what was about to happen?"

He continued to peer into the night. "I was backed into the parking space so I had a good view of the cars moving down the aisle in front of us. A black SUV pulled even with us, and the barrel of a pistol came out the driver's side window. That was when I pushed you down."

"Lucky you saw it."

Adam shook his head. "Luck had nothing to do with it. I'm always watching."

His response made her shiver. She hugged herself and sat silent for the balance of the trip.

When they slowed for the turn into Carrie's driveway, Adam said, "Is there room in your garage for my car?"

"I suppose so. Why?"

"I don't want to leave it at the curb or in the driveway where someone can see it. Open the garage and let me pull in. We'll talk once we're safely in your house."

Carrie found the garage remote on her key ring and raised the door. When they were inside the house, with the garage door closed, she took a seat on the living room sofa. Adam went through the small house, drawing drapes, closing blinds, and making sure all the doors and windows were locked.

Finally he returned to where Carrie waited. He started to sit beside her on the sofa, apparently thought better of it, and sank into a chair. "I've wrestled with this all the way home. I thought I was finally safe, but maybe I'm not. I know what I'm going to tell you may change things between us, but you deserve an explanation."

That was the understatement of the year. Thirty minutes ago she and Adam were a newly engaged couple, winding down an enjoyable evening. By now they should be feeding each other ice cream like two lovebirds, talking seriously and making plans about their future together. But instead . . . "Yes," she said, "you owe me an explanation, a big one. So explain."

"Let me say this first. What I'm about to tell you started long before I met you. My life has changed in the past eight months. I'm different, and it's because of you. I'm . . ." Adam leaned toward her. He clenched and unclenched his fists. "To begin with, Adam Davidson isn't my real name."

TWO

"TO BEGIN WITH, ADAM DAVIDSON ISN'T MY REAL NAME." IT seemed to Adam as though all the air went out of the room as soon as those words were out of his mouth.

Carrie took a deep breath. "What do you mean?"

Adam swallowed . . . hard. Then, like a diver finally deciding to plunge off the high board, he said, "My real name is Keith Branson. I'm on the run. If the wrong people find me, I'm a dead man." He swallowed again. "I hope and pray I'm wrong, but what happened tonight may mean they've found me."

He watched emotions trace across Carrie's face like words running across an electronic billboard: puzzlement, disbelief, fear, anger. The ache in his heart grew with every passing second.

He'd thought maybe he'd finally found safety. He'd hoped he'd never have to share this information with her. But his hopes were dashed when the bullets flew through the windshield.

Maybe he'd never be safe. And now he'd brought Carrie into it. He had to tell her, no matter the cost to their relationship. He loved her too much to let her keep believing the lie.

"What have you done? Are you running from the police?" She almost shouted the next words. "What's going on?"

"Long story," Adam said. "First, I'm not running from the police. But I'm not who you think I am either. I'm not a paralegal, although I'm working as one. I'm a lawyer, and I'm running away from some very bad men—men who want to kill me."

"If you're hiding from criminals, wouldn't the police protect you?"

"Maybe, maybe not. But that would mean letting them know my real identity. And no matter how the police may try to keep it confidential, somehow that information is going to leak out. It has before. If it reaches the wrong ears . . . I'm dead." He shook his head. "Of course, it may already be too late."

The color drained from Carrie's face. She snatched a ragged breath. In a low voice she said, "Let me get this straight. You're telling me you're living here under a false identity. But it's not because you've done anything wrong."

"Right, I—"

Carrie continued as though Adam hadn't spoken. "When you didn't want to call the police after someone shot at us, I thought maybe you had a bunch of unpaid tickets, unpaid alimony, something like that." Her voice rose with every word. "But now you tell me you're hiding from someone who might kill you?"

"Yes," he said. "Now can I explain?"

"Go ahead. I want to know everything, Adam. Or should I call you Keith?" She clenched her fists. "Or is there another name for me to learn?"

He took a deep breath through his nose, let it out through his mouth. Repeated the process. *Be calm. You fouled up, but maybe you can salvage things.* "Please, call me Adam. I came here for a fresh start, and that's when I became Adam. That's when I met you. That's when I fell in love with you."

"If you're in love with me, why didn't you tell me the truth?" Carrie lowered her voice to a quiet tone that pierced Adam's heart more than any shout could. "Why did you—no, why did *we* almost have to die before you told me about your past? Why did it take a shooting to make you tell me that everything I know about you is a lie?"

"When I first met you, I told you the same story I'd told before, in so many other places. It had become a habit, a way of life for me. Then when we got to know each other, after we fell in love, I didn't want to spoil things by telling you the truth." His mouth was dry, his throat threatened to close off his words, but he didn't want to interrupt his story by asking for water. "I was wrong to keep all this from you. I admit it. I've been agonizing since you accepted my proposal, wondering when and how I'd break the news to you."

For a moment Adam couldn't read her expression. Then her words removed any doubt. She was hurt—hurt deeply. "And you think now is the time?"

"What happened tonight may mean that the people who've been hunting me for so long have found me." He looked down. "I'm sorry I waited, but I have to tell you the truth now. I love you too much to keep it a secret any longer."

"You say you love me, yet you hid your past from me. It took a *shooting* to change your mind. That doesn't sound like love to me."

Adam felt like one of the early Christians, the ones whose limbs were tied to horses that literally pulled them apart. "I admit it. I've put off doing this. I was afraid, because telling you who I am . . ." He took a deep breath, then another. There was a catch in his voice when he spoke again. "I love you, Carrie. More than I've loved anyone in my life."

Carrie hugged herself like a woman trapped in a deep freeze. "So what happened tonight? Was someone trying to kill you?"

"I can't be totally sure. Maybe someone's found me, maybe it was a random drive-by shooting. But I know one thing for sure. If my true identity gets out, even in the most innocent fashion, Charlie DeLuca will find me and try to kill me . . . and you too, once he discovers that I love you."

Carrie's expression shifted from puzzled to terrified. "So just being with you puts my life in danger?" She almost whispered the next words. "How could you do this to me? Were you using me? Did being part of a couple let you blend in to the population?"

"No! Absolutely not."

Carrie turned away from him and stared at the opposite wall. "What are you going to do next?"

"Tomorrow morning I'll call the police and tell them I found my car parked at the curb with three bullet holes in the windshield. I'll do my best to make them believe this was a case of malicious mischief. I can't have them digging too deeply into my identity. Because if they do, I might as well pack up and get out of town."

Her back still to Adam, Carrie said, "What if the police want to talk to me about the shooting?"

"They won't. Not if I tell it the way I've described." Adam

rose and began pacing. "Believe me, more than anything I want to keep you out of this."

Carrie spun to face Adam. When she spoke, her tone was cold. "I think you'd better go."

Adam stood, then stopped. "Carrie, I'm really sorry. I hope you can forgive me." He looked directly into Carrie's eyes. "I meant the things I said when I proposed. I still mean them. I love you."

For Adam time froze as Carrie stared, first at him, then at the ring on her finger, then back at him. Finally she put both hands in front of her, and Adam's heart dropped when he saw the twisting motion she made.

"Carrie, please don't—"

She took two steps toward him and held out her hand, the engagement ring in her open palm. "I don't know what to think right now. But it doesn't seem right for me to keep wearing this. I don't know whether I love you, or fear you, or feel sorry for you, or . . . I don't know." She shook her head. Tears streaked her cheeks.

Adam took the ring and noticed that her hand, like his, was trembling. He couldn't let it end this way. He had to make it right. "Carrie, please, we need to talk again. Will you call me?"

"I don't know." Carrie shook her head. "I honestly don't know."

———————————— ⌁ ————————————

Carrie listened to the hum of the motor as the garage door closed. She wasn't sure whether it was closing a chapter in her life or opening the door to an entirely different one. She was tempted to go to the window and peep through the blinds to watch Adam drive away. Maybe she should do that, a visual punctuation mark to the end of their relationship. But she wasn't sure she wanted it to end. She wasn't sure about anything anymore.

She took out her cell phone and punched in a number she knew like her own. It was late, but she needed to talk with someone. No, not just someone—to Julie.

The phone rang four times before a sleepy female voice said, "Yates residence."

"Julie, it's Carrie. I'm so sorry for calling—"

The voice dropped to a whisper. "No problem. Let me take this into the living room. I don't want to wake Barry."

Carrie had been pacing when she placed the call. Now she slumped into an easy chair and dangled her legs over the arm, unconsciously assuming the posture she'd taken so many years ago when she was a high school student chatting on the phone for hours on end with her best friend.

"Okay, now I can talk," Julie said. "What's up?"

"I'm sorry for calling so late, but I had to talk with someone. I was almost killed tonight."

"Are you okay?"

"I'm fine, just shaken."

"What happened?"

"Someone shot at the car where Adam and I were sitting. They missed, but my world's been turned upside down."

"I don't doubt it," Julie said. "I mean, having someone take a shot at you—"

"There's more. It's Adam. He's not the person I thought he was."

Who did I think he was? Carrie thought back to her first meeting with Adam, and it made her heart ache. A little more than eight months earlier, she was talking with friends in the foyer after church when a man she knew slightly approached. "Excuse me, Carrie. This is Adam. He's new in town, and I'm trying to introduce him around."

The man called Adam was prototypically "tall, dark, and handsome": a bit over six feet tall, olive complexion, brown hair with a slight wave, guileless gray eyes. He told her his name was Adam Davidson. He was a paralegal, recently out of a messy divorce, looking to start over in a new location. They exchanged handshakes and phone numbers, and Carrie forgot about it until he called the next day . . . and the next. Finally she agreed to show him around town. Then they had lunch at a restaurant she liked. Lunches led to dinners, and soon Carrie realized she was no longer a tour guide. She and Adam were dating—and getting more serious with each date.

During that time he was never anything but attentive, charming, and apparently taken with her. And she'd felt the same way. He listened to her talk about her late husband. She cried on his shoulder. And she experienced something she never thought she'd have again—love.

Carrie forced herself back to the present. "I don't know if I should tell you . . ." She snatched a deep breath, afraid for Adam, yet feeling the desperate need for her friend's assurances.

"What is it? This sounds ominous."

"You have to promise not to tell a soul, not even Barry."

"Okay . . ."

Carrie tightened her grip on the phone. "I've already told you that someone took a shot at Adam's car after we left the last show at the movies. Well, Adam refused to call the police to report it. When I pressed him, he told me his real name wasn't

Adam Davidson. He's on the run—not from the law but from what he calls bad men. And it's critical that his true identity be kept a secret."

"He called them bad men. So does that make him a *good* man?" Julie asked.

"I don't know. What really hurts is that he's been lying to me! I feel as though I've been part of a play, and I'm only now getting to know the actor playing opposite me," Carrie said. "I'm confused."

"So . . ." Julie hesitated, and Carrie could tell she was treading lightly. "So is the engagement still on?"

"I gave him back the ring. Now I don't know what I'm going to do."

"You have to answer one question: do you love him?"

Carrie shook her head, even though there was no one to see it. "I love Adam . . . or thought I did. But now I don't know who Adam is." She glanced at the clock. "It's late. I need to let you go. I wish we could get together to talk about this. You always help."

"Barry's going to be in Dallas soon, maybe next week. Why don't I plan to go with him? We can meet somewhere halfway between Dallas and Jameson. I'll give you a call and set it up."

"Thanks, Julie."

"And in the meantime," her friend said, "pray about it."

"I'm not sure I can," Carrie said. "I—"

"I know. Some well-meaning people told you that if you prayed hard enough, John wouldn't die. But he did. That doesn't mean you have to stop praying. God doesn't always answer prayers the way we want, but He sees the big picture. And He loves you."

Carrie didn't respond.

"I'll call you soon," was all Julie said.

Later, as Carrie lay in bed, she stared upward into the dark and wondered if Julie was right. Maybe prayer would help. Even if God didn't answer, it might help get this burden off her shoulders. Of course, since John's death, her belief in the power of prayer had gone downhill. But it was worth a try. She began, "God, I don't know what to do. Please give me wisdom to deal with this." But soon she found herself on a familiar track, wondering why her prayers for her husband hadn't been answered. Grief mixed with anger boiled up yet again, stirring a pain that was always there, just under the surface. Finally she rolled over, buried her head in the pillow, and sobbed herself to sleep.

The first thing Sunday morning, Adam dug out his phone directory and looked up the non-emergency number for the Jameson Police Department. "This is Adam Davidson. I left my car parked at the curb in front of my apartment last night, and when I came out this morning, I discovered three bullet holes in the windshield."

After Adam gave the necessary information, the man on the other end of the line asked him to stay where he was and meet the patrolman who'd be there soon.

"How soon?"

"Maybe an hour. Maybe a bit longer."

Adam didn't argue. He knew that complaints like this didn't carry a sense of urgency like those where the caller was in immediate danger. Besides, he could use the time to make another phone call.

He didn't have to look up this number. Several times

Adam had started to program it into his cell phone's speed dial, but for the sake of security, he decided to store it only in his memory. The call was answered on the second ring.

"Branson."

The voice brought an image to Adam's mind and a smile to his lips—an image of a man who looked like a slightly stockier, slightly older version of himself. "Dave, it's me."

"Keith?"

"You mean Adam."

"Sorry, old habits die hard." A door closed softly in the background. "Okay, what's up?"

"Someone shot at me last night. Might be a random drive-by, but I can't risk thinking that way. I have to assume I was the target."

Adam envisioned his older brother rubbing his chin, a sure sign he was thinking. "So I guess you're about to leave again. Adam, are you sure you want to live the rest of your life this way? Always on the run, always looking over your shoulder. Changing names and locations so often that you sometimes wake up wondering who you are, where you are."

"No, I'm not going to run anymore," Adam said. "You forget, I'm in love. I just asked Carrie to marry me, and if she'll still have me, I'm prepared to stay and fight."

"You're sure?"

Was he sure? He'd spent most of the night thinking about that question. "Yes. I'm convinced God brought Carrie into my life to complete it." He sipped from the mug at his elbow and grimaced when he found the coffee had gone cold.

"Does she know who you are? And does she understand the situation?"

"Not the whole story, but enough. Last night I told her that Adam Davidson isn't my real name and that I'm on the run from some dangerous people."

"And what did she say?"

"About what you'd expect. She's angry, hurt, confused. Besides all that, she realizes she's in danger by being close to me." The simple act of saying the words made Adam's throat tighten, a lump that all the coffee in the world couldn't wash away.

The silence on the other end of the line dragged on so long Adam thought they'd been disconnected. Then Dave said, "Where do you go from here?"

"I'm not sure yet. A lot depends on Carrie, I guess. If I stay, I put both of us in danger. If I go, I lose her." David felt tears forming. *Stop that. Real men don't cry. Or maybe they do if they've really fouled up and possibly lost the woman they love.*

"Are you praying about it?" David asked.

"Of course. I've prayed every day since I left Chicago. Sometimes it's the only thing that's kept me going."

Before Dave could respond, Adam heard the doorbell. "Gotta go. Police are here to take a report on the shooting."

Even after leaving his original identity, Adam had always been truthful with law officers. Not only was it part of his nature, it was an obligation. As a lawyer he'd been an officer of the court—still was, although his license was in his original name—sworn to uphold the law, cooperate with authorities, never withhold pertinent information. Now what he was about to tell the policeman at the door would be an outright lie. *And so it begins.*

Adam wondered where it would end.

THREE

CARRIE AWOKE ON SUNDAY MORNING TO A GRAY WORLD. SHEETS of rain beat against her windowpane, matching her mood. Maybe this was a good day to stay in bed. She burrowed deeper into the covers and thought about the changes in her life.

The shooting in the movie parking lot had shaken her. Then Adam's revelation turned her world upside down. She didn't really want to go to church. She wanted to hide her head, block out the world. But church was a habit she'd acquired years ago, and Carrie knew that ultimately she'd leave the safety of her bed and get dressed. Duty or desire, it made no difference. Church was on her agenda today.

She visited the coffee pot, then set about getting ready to face the world. As she did, she took stock of herself in the mirror. Her blond hair was cut in a no-nonsense short style that framed a face others told her was attractive. Her green eyes saw things clearly without the need for glasses, although obviously they had been unable to penetrate Adam's disguise. She was an attractive professional, still in the prime of life. But after John's death she'd put up an invisible fence that might as well have had warning signs on it. *I've been hurt. I'm healing, but I'm still vulnerable. Stay away.*

When she met him, she'd opened the gate and let Adam in. In hindsight that was probably a huge mistake, one with which she'd have to deal. And now her world had changed again. Her ringless finger felt peculiar. Even more peculiar was a morning without the usual call from Adam, a day without a lunch or dinner date. She'd adjusted before. She'd do it again. Carrie wiped away the tears that formed in the corners of her eyes. Maybe church would help, maybe not.

She slipped into a simple green dress, gulped the last of her coffee, and grabbed an umbrella. *Ready or not, world, here I come. But be aware. The gate is closed again.*

The organ was sounding the final notes of the prelude when Carrie slipped into the half-filled sanctuary. She stowed her umbrella under her seat and tried to put her mind in neutral. Maybe the service would calm her heart. Maybe it would help her find the answers to the questions nipping at the edges of her thoughts like a pack of wild dogs. She hoped so.

Carrie found it hard to focus on the service. She went through the motions, but her concentration kept slipping. She sang the hymns without letting the lyrics sink in. She stood for the reading of the Scripture, but the words washed over her like waves on a beach. There was no comfort there. And through it all, her emotions were all over the place.

She alternated between anger at Adam for the lies he'd told and disgust at herself for believing them. Carrie revisited her sorrow for John's death and the part she might have played in it. She was wracked with pain thinking of her short time with John, snatched from her after only five years of marriage. Her heart ached as she realized the perfect life she'd envisioned with Adam was now disappearing as well, replaced by a situation that was dangerous at best and fatal at worst.

Carrie considered slipping out during the offertory, but then the pastor stepped to the pulpit and it was too late for her to move without attracting attention. The preacher seemed to stare straight into her soul, and his first words tied her stomach in knots. "Let not your heart be troubled."

The Scripture should have made Carrie relax, but instead it gave her the sensation of being trapped in an elevator in free fall. In an instant she was transported back to a scene from almost two years ago, a scene she'd never forget but wished she could. Her mind's eye saw the same pastor, the same pulpit. But this time there was a bronze casket at the front of the church, banked on either side by floral tributes that assaulted her nostrils with a sickly sweet scent.

Instead of her current seat in one of the back rows, Carrie was in the front row, with John's sister and her husband on one side, John's mother and father on the other. Carrie's parents hadn't bothered to come. Even the death of their son-in-law couldn't bridge the rift between them and Carrie, the chasm that developed when she embraced Christianity in her first year of medical school.

That day the pastor had read that same Scripture: "Let not your heart be troubled." She supposed the message he brought was one of comfort and hope, but other than the opening verses from the Bible, Carrie couldn't recall a single word he spoke.

There'd been music and words of tribute from a couple of friends. But all Carrie could think about during the entire service was, *We should have had decades together, but all we had was five years. It was such a freak thing—a punctured coronary artery during a routine procedure. I'm a doctor—why couldn't I save him?* She squeezed her eyes shut to hold back tears. What did she do wrong? Why did God let it happen? Why?

The swelling notes of the organ brought Carrie back to the present. She'd apparently stood at the proper time. She'd managed to bow her head with the rest of the congregation for the closing prayer. As she joined the crowd filing out, she thought about the morning's Scripture passage. "Let not your heart be troubled." The words brought a wry, mirthless smile to her lips. *Sorry, God. I can't help it. My heart's been troubled too long.*

———————————————⌇—————————————————

Carrie was halfway home, driving on automatic pilot, when the ring of her cell phone interrupted her thoughts. She pulled into the parking area of a nearly deserted strip shopping center and dug the phone from her purse. The Emergency Room was calling.

"Dr. Markham," she answered.

"This is Doris in the ER. We have an elderly man here with severe dyspnea. He says he's seen Dr. Avery in your group, but not for at least a year. You're on call, but do you want us to try Dr. Avery?"

"No, I'll see him. Get an EKG and chest film. Oh, and draw some blood chemistries and a CBC. I'll be there in ten minutes." Carrie laid her cell phone on the seat behind her and aimed her Prius toward the hospital. She kept her eyes focused on the road, but her mind wasn't on the hospital or the patient waiting there for her. It was on Adam—her relationship with him, the secret he'd told her, their future together . . . if they had one.

She wondered if there was any way out of this living nightmare. She'd have to talk with Adam again. There were too many questions still unanswered. But she dreaded their next conversation. What could she say? She still didn't know what she should do. She'd thought she loved Adam, but who, really, was Adam Davidson?

Carrie was still debating her next move when she pulled into the hospital parking lot. *Enough of that.* She plunged through the double doors of the Emergency Room, ready to immerse herself in the practice of medicine. Her personal life could go on hold for a bit.

The patient's name was Gus Elsik. He lay propped on the gurney in a full sitting position, struggling to breathe despite the oxygen mask on his face. The sheet had slipped to expose one swollen ankle. Carrie noted the distended neck veins. The diagnosis was already pretty clear to her, but she'd go through the necessary steps to be certain.

The patient was obviously in no condition to talk, so Carrie addressed her questions to the woman in a blouse and jeans who stood beside the gurney, fresh lines of worry adding to the ones that creased her face already.

"I'm Dr. Markham. What happened?"

"My father's having trouble breathing."

"Is this a new thing?"

The woman shook her head. "No, I took him to the clinic last year when he was having the same kind of trouble, just not as severe. He saw Dr. Avery, who said it was some kind of problem with his heart. The doctor gave him some pills, but after he started feeling better, Daddy stopped taking them."

"And when did he start getting short of breath?"

"It's been going on for a couple of weeks. Maybe more. When it got to where he couldn't walk from his room—he stays with us—when he couldn't walk from his bedroom to the dining room without resting to catch his breath, I insisted that we come here."

Gus's other symptoms confirmed Carrie's diagnosis: swelling of the feet and ankles, moist cough, waking up at night short of breath, having to sit upright to breathe. "What you have," she said to Gus, "is congestive heart failure. I'm going to admit you to the hospital, do some tests, and start treatment. I'll contact Dr. Avery. He'll see you tomorrow and follow up."

Gus's daughter asked, "Is it serious?"

"It's serious, but I've seen worse. We should be able to get this under control with some medications to get rid of the excess fluid and improve the heart function."

"What . . . did . . . you . . . call . . . it?" Gus asked, a gasp for air separating each word.

"Congestive heart failure. But don't let the words scare you. We're going to keep your heart going for a good while yet." She encouraged him with a smile and a pat on his shoulder.

As she sat at the nurse's station to write orders, Carrie thought about heart failure. There was the kind Gus developed, the kind that medications could help. Then there was what she was feeling right now: the heart pain, the anguish, the emotional turmoil that no amount of medicine would improve. That was the worst kind of heart failure.

A Scripture verse popped unbidden into her head. She

didn't recall the source—somewhere in the Old Testament—and she wasn't sure of the exact quotation, but the gist was that God promised to give a new heart. *You didn't give my husband a new one, God, so that's one strike. I don't know about Adam's heart. And I'm still waiting for my new heart.*

As soon as the clock in his kitchen showed eight a.m. on Monday, Adam dialed the law office where he worked. He hoped Brittany, the receptionist, wasn't running late. He had a lot to do, but the first thing was to square his absence with his employers.

He was about to hang up when there was a click on the line and he heard, "Hartley and Evans, may I help you?"

"Brittany, this is Adam."

"Where are you? Are you okay?"

"That's why I'm calling," Adam said. "Somebody decided to shoot up my car during the night. I've got to arrange to repair the damage, get a rental car, all that stuff. Would you tell . . . ?" Who? Bruce Hartley was the senior lawyer in the two-person firm. But it wasn't always possible to predict how Bruce would react. The other partner, Janice Evans, was the better choice. "Would you tell Janice what's happened? I'll get there as soon as I can."

Adam's next call was to his insurance agent. He expected to leave a message, then waste most of the morning waiting for a call back. Instead, the agent was at his desk and proved both sympathetic and extremely helpful. When he found out Adam's car was drivable, he told him where to take it to have the damage repaired. He even arranged for a rental car to be delivered there.

By mid-morning, Adam pulled into the lot that served the two-story building owned and occupied by Hartley and Evans, Attorneys at Law. He parked his black Toyota Corolla rental in his assigned slot, tugged his briefcase from the passenger seat, and headed for the front door.

The briefcase was a constant reminder of Adam's journey. Along the way he'd parted with his expensive Halliburton case, a gift from his ex-wife. He couldn't recall into which river he'd tossed the brushed aluminum status symbol, a gesture to further separate himself from a life he could no longer live. Then, after Bruce Hartley suggested that the grocery bag in which he carried his lunch and a few files wasn't appropriate for a member of their staff, Adam found a scuffed leather briefcase in a pawnshop in town. It was this case that he now parked next to his desk before he slipped into his chair.

Bruce Hartley paused opposite Adam's open doorway. Adam had heard Brittany describe Hartley as "sixty-one, going on forty." The lawyer had a receding hairline that he tried to disguise with an expensive haircut, and a bulging waistline that custom-tailored suits did little to hide. Hartley was just out of marriage number two or three—Adam couldn't recall which—and rumor had it he was already looking for the next Mrs. Hartley, although why anyone would put up with the man's unpredictable moods was hard to imagine.

Hartley looked pointedly at his watch, then hurried on down the hall. Adam didn't know whether Janice Evans had passed on his reason for being late, but evidently Hartley didn't consider his employee's tardiness worthy of comment.

Adam was going through the phone message slips on his desk when Evans stopped by. Janice Evans was a decade younger than Hartley, and to Adam's way of thinking, the more level-headed, intelligent, and talented of the two lawyers.

She wore a tasteful wedding and engagement ring set on the appropriate finger. Tiny pearl earrings were Evans's only other jewelry. Her perfectly styled ash-blond hair fell short of her shoulders. She wore designer glasses over gray eyes that seemed to see everything. He was no expert on women's clothes, but Adam was willing to bet that Evans's pants suit had a well-known label and cost several times more than his off-the-rack suit.

"Sorry to hear about your car," she said. "Get things wrapped up?"

Adam smiled up at her. "Yep. It's in the shop getting a new windshield and having the headrests redone."

"What did the police say?"

"Not much, actually. My own theory is that it was some high school kids with a gun, deciding to use my car for target practice." *How many more times am I going to have to tell this?*

"Well, be careful." Evans nodded once and retreated to her office.

A few minutes later Brittany eased up to Adam's desk and handed him several file folders.

"Anything urgent?" Adam asked as she shuffled through the stack.

"No. Usual stuff. But we missed you. The coffee you make is so much better than what I brew."

"Glad you like my touch," Adam said. "And unless someone shoots out my windshield again, I'll be in tomorrow to brew it for you." *That is, unless I'm dead.*

FOUR

CARRIE STOOD BEHIND HER DESK AND RAMMED HER ARMS INTO the sleeves of a fresh white coat. Why did the laundry think so much starch was needed for a professional look? Sometimes she thought the deliveryman should just stand her coats in a corner of her office instead of hanging them in her closet.

Carrie was trying to open the side pocket to admit her stethoscope when her nurse, Lila, stuck her head in the office door.

"And a very happy Monday to us all." Lila was a middle-aged divorcee, a bottle blonde, who still acted as if she were in her twenties. Today she looked as though she'd bitten the lime, only to reach for the tequila and find someone had hidden it.

"Party a bit too much over the weekend?" Carrie asked.

"Nope, didn't party enough. I had at least another day's worth of fun planned, but I turned around and it was time to start another week." Lila eased into a chair, crossed her legs, and looked up at Carrie, who now struggled to button her white coat. "How about you?"

There were two ways to get news spread throughout the twelve-doctor, multispecialty clinic where Carrie worked: put a notice on the bulletin board or tell Lila. Carrie chose not to go either route. "Pretty routine." She checked her pockets, lifted her gaze to Lila, and smiled. "Let's get on with it."

Lila stood and gave a mock cheer. "Once more the Rushton Clinic moves into high gear."

The clinic's official name was Jameson Medical Associates, but everyone called it the Rushton Clinic after Dr. Phil Rushton, the managing partner. He'd put together the group of physicians, helped work out a system for dividing profits and sharing expenses, made the administrative decisions most doctors were happy to avoid, and still found time to be the foremost cardiac surgeon in the region.

Carrie was one of two internal medicine specialists in the group. Her training was as good or better than that of the other internist, Thad Avery, and their practice sizes were about equal. She had no quarrel with the arrangement except for occasions when Phil Rushton's actions made her grit her teeth. She was ready to see her first patient when a secretary hurried up. "The Emergency Room called. Mr. Berringer was brought in earlier by ambulance. Heart problems. The ER doc wants to know if you'd like to see him."

Lila, now quite professional, said, "I'll let patients know you've had an emergency. They can wait or we'll reschedule. Go ahead."

Carrie walked through the breezeway that connected the clinic with the hospital, then made her way to the ER. The charge nurse handed her a chart and pointed to a curtained cubicle.

Carrie flipped through the pages, noting the history of weakness, blurred vision, and a sense of palpitations, culminating in a fainting spell. The ER doctor had already ordered blood work, and the report was on the chart. Carrie scanned the figures, stopping when her eyes lit on the potassium level: 2.6 mEq/ml—definitely a contributory factor, and something that should be corrected as quickly as possible.

She pulled aside the curtains and took in the scene. "Mr. Berringer, what's going on?"

The older man, pale and sweating, turned his head slightly toward her. The oxygen mask on his face added a hollow timbre to his voice. "I wish I knew, Doctor." He opened his lips to say more, but instead closed his eyes, apparently spent by the effort.

Carrie turned to Berringer's wife, who stood beside the gurney, alternately blotting beads of perspiration from her husband's forehead and stroking his hand. "Mrs. Berringer, is your husband taking any medications other than the ones you told the emergency room doctor about?"

"Dr. Markham, they're all medicines you prescribed. Don't you have the list there?"

Carrie smiled at her and said gently, "Let's pretend I don't."

The woman frowned. "You know about the heart pills and the cholesterol medicine. And, of course, there are those little tiny pink pills, but I don't think they count. They're just water pills of some kind."

Carrie tried not to grind her teeth. "Do those little pink pills have a long name that's shortened to some letters?"

"Oh, yes." The woman's face brightened. "I remember. HCZT or HTCZ or something like that."

Hydrochlorothiazide, or HCTZ, was a diuretic given to patients with high blood pressure, but it also could deplete potassium levels in the body. And when this occurred in patients who'd taken an overdose of digitalis, the combination had the potential to be lethal.

Soon Carrie was able to put together the story. Henry Berringer refused to be "one of those people who use little pillboxes" to tell him if he'd taken his medicine on that particular day, choosing instead to rely on his memory. Apparently, for the past several days he'd taken his pills two or three times a day. The resulting digitalis overdose at first manifested itself as nausea and lack of appetite. He complained of seeing a yellow halo around lights, something he blamed on his early cataracts. But when he fainted in the living room, his wife called 911. His pulse was fifty and irregular when the paramedics arrived.

"You've taken too much of some of your medicine," Carrie said to Mr. Berringer. "We need to make sure that doesn't happen again. In the meantime we're going to do some things to reverse the effects of that overdose."

Mrs. Berringer looked so relieved that Carrie thought she might burst into tears. "Thank you, Doctor," she mouthed as Carried slipped through the curtains with a promise to be back as soon as she could.

Carrie spent the next several hours shuttling between the clinic and the ER. Finally, thanks to atropine, Digibind, and intravenous potassium, Mr. Berringer's heart rate and rhythm were approaching normal levels. Carrie thought it would be best to watch him for a bit longer, and since he had a disturbance of cardiac rhythm and might have sustained heart muscle damage, there was no problem getting approval for his admission to the hospital's medicine floor. If serial EKGs and cardiac enzymes showed no further problems, she'd let him go home—but with a lecture about his need to become "one of those people who uses pillboxes." That was far better than becoming "one of those people who didn't take their medicine properly and died as a result."

Carrie was walking through the ER on her way back to her office when paramedic Rob Cole stopped her. "Dr. Markham, what's the latest on the man we brought in with the digitalis toxicity?"

"He's out of the woods," Carrie responded. "Good pickup on the diagnosis, by the way. He'd also taken too much HCTZ, so his potassium was in the cellar."

"Ouch. I noticed the atropine we gave him in the ambulance wasn't enough to get him straightened out. Glad he's doing better now."

"Thank you for asking."

Carrie turned away and had taken a step when Rob said, "Dr. Markham?"

She stopped and looked back at him. "Yes?"

He frowned and looked away. "Never mind. I'll ask another time."

As she traversed the enclosed breezeway that connected Centennial Hospital with the building that housed the Rushton Clinic, Carrie wondered what else Rob wanted to say. It seemed to her that, more and more, Rob went out of his way to run into her, sometimes in the ER when he and his partner dropped off a patient, occasionally in the cafeteria, once or twice in the halls.

It was flattering that he seemed to want to be around her. Rob was a little younger than Carrie, possessed of good looks that had all the nurses talking—wavy black hair, deep brown eyes, sparkling white teeth. There was no question he was what some of the staff would call "a hunk."

Get a grip, she told herself. *Stop wondering if Rob is coming on to you. This isn't junior high.* She looked at her bare finger and wondered if she'd acted hastily in giving back Adam's ring. Until thirty-six hours ago, Carrie was sure she was in love with Adam Davidson. But what about this new Adam? And what about their future? With the old Adam, it seemed certain and secure. Now it was uncertain and dangerous.

It was obvious that Mrs. Berringer loved her husband. She was right beside him in the ER, putting into practice her vow to love him in sickness and in health. Carrie had been ready to make that vow and more to Adam, but now was she really prepared to be with him "for better or for worse"? Especially if "worse" meant running from someone trying to take his life . . . and hers along with it? That was the question she had to answer. She was hurt at his deception, but it ate at her that if she really loved him, she wouldn't be running away when Adam needed her.

Carrie leaned against the wooden handrail that ran the length of the breezeway, pulled out her cell phone, then paused with her finger over the keys. She closed her eyes for a moment and tried to prepare for the call she was about to make. She at least needed to listen to his whole story. She'd set up another meeting with him. After that? She'd wait and see.

As hesitant as a child climbing onto a jungle gym for the first time, she pushed the speed-dial button.

When Adam felt the buzz of his cell phone in his pocket, he experienced the epitome of "mixed emotions." The display showed that the call came from Carrie—and she'd be calling for one of two reasons: to give him a chance to explain, or tell him to get out of her life and stay out.

"I'm glad you called," he said, hoping that her next words wouldn't make him a liar.

"Adam, I don't have long to talk. We need to finish our last conversation. But I want to meet somewhere safe. I don't want to be a target again."

Adam ran through the choices. He figured his apartment was out. If the gunman had found his car, he'd no doubt located where Adam lived as well. And there was no way he would lead a potential killer to Carrie's home. "How about the law firm where I work? Everyone is out of there by five—five thirty at the latest unless something unusual is going on."

"Is it safe?"

"I'm not sure any place is safe anymore, but this seems the best option. I'll leave the building with everyone else and drive around a bit to lose anyone who might be following me. Then I'll park a block away and come in the back door."

"So what do I do?"

Adam thought for a bit. "Hopefully the shooter doesn't know your car. The lot's well lit. Park right by the entrance and call me on my cell as soon as you get there. Hurry inside, and I'll double lock the doors behind you."

Carrie hesitated. If she said no to that idea, he wasn't sure what he'd do next. But finally he heard the rush of a long exhalation. "Fine. I'll be there as soon after six as I can make it."

"Thanks," Adam said. "I appreciate—" He stopped talking when he heard a click. Carrie had already ended the call. He stared at the dead phone, his heart sinking. He prayed their relationship wasn't broken beyond repair.

Outside the clinic exam room, Carrie scanned the information on her next patient. George Harris, age sixty-two, complaining of swollen feet and ankles. A number of diagnostic possibilities ran through her head, disorders like "congestive heart failure" and "deep vein thrombosis." That was what she liked about her internal medicine practice. Every day there were new challenges. Well, time to tackle this one.

She tapped on the door and stepped inside. The older man perched on the edge of the exam table had silver hair combed straight back. Blue eyes twinkled behind steel-rimmed glasses. He was already wearing an exam gown—Lila had seen to that— but he wore it with the same dignity as though it were a white tie and tails.

"Mr. Harris, I'm Dr. Markham. How can we help you today?"

"Frankly, I think I'm fine. But my daughter seems to have a different idea."

There was a distinct British accent there. Carrie checked the address on the man's papers and confirmed that he was local. Then the younger woman sitting in the corner spoke up and solved the mystery. "My father-in-law recently came to the United States to live with us. He says nothing is wrong, but we don't believe it's normal that his feet and ankles are so swollen."

Carrie eased onto the rolling stool, positioned it midway between patient and daughter, and looked first to one and then the other. "Suppose we get a little more history. Mr. Harris, when did you first notice this?"

As the story unfolded, Carrie mentally laid aside several possible diagnoses until only one stood as the prime suspect. Mr. Harris worked in Great Britain for years in an electronics manufacturing plant. His job had been to solder and weld various components, and although provisions were made to avoid inhalation of the fumes from his work, he and many of his fellow workers had hated the respirators, disliked the noise of the exhaust fans, so they plied their trade without them at every opportunity. And as a result, he now presented to Carrie with the consequences of decades of inhaling cadmium-laced fumes: facial puffiness, swollen ankles and feet, protruding belly. Why? Because his kidneys were failing, causing the loss of a protein called albumin from the body, with resultant accumulation of tissue fluid in these areas.

"We're going to start by checking some lab work," Carrie said when she'd finished her exam. "Lila will help you with that. I'd like to see you back again tomorrow, when we can go over the results and talk about treatment."

Carrie had just finished dictating her note when Lila appeared in the doorway of the cubicle. "Urinalysis and metabolic profile are cooking, but you don't seem to have any doubt about the diagnosis."

"No, I'm sure we're dealing with nephrotic syndrome. That poor family is about to have its life turned upside down."

Special diet, medications to control blood pressure, regular trips to the dialysis lab. Carrie closed her eyes and balled her fists. *God, why do You let these things happen?*

Then again, why was God letting Adam break her heart? And why did God let good men like John die because a seemingly simple medical procedure went horribly wrong? As she headed for the next exam room, it was all Carrie could do to focus on the patient inside. She worked to put aside her situation with Adam. She struggled to stop thinking about the way her husband's life had ended . . . and the role she played in that terrible event. Carrie thought she might pause and pray for help and guidance but quickly dismissed the idea. That avenue had been closed for quite a while.

As Carrie pulled into the law office parking lot, her heart thudded against her chest wall. It wasn't only the potential danger that pushed her adrenaline level sky-high. It was the very real possibility that tonight Adam might tell her something that would fracture their relationship forever. She loved him—that was clear to her. But how much could that love withstand?

She was about to find out.

The law offices occupied a small, two-story building. Adam had told her that the bottom floor contained offices, the upper story a conference room and law library. She punched his speed-dial number on her phone.

"Carrie?"

"I'm here."

"I'm unlocking the door now," Adam said.

She hurried the few steps from her car to the front entrance where Adam waited. They stepped into a reception area where a low-wattage light burned. The burgundy carpet was soft under her feet. Tasteful drapes of burgundy and tan framed the windows. Several upholstered chairs were situated along the walls. A cherry wood desk and chair faced outward from one corner, and behind it two lateral file cabinets of the same material flanked a door that probably led into a business office.

Adam pointed. "My office is back there."

Carrie walked down a hall lit dimly by security lights. In Adam's office, he flipped the light switch and gestured her to one of the two chairs across from his desk. He took the other and turned it sideways to face her. Adam seemed to have aged overnight. His face was haggard and his eyes were red-rimmed, accented by dark circles beneath them. Carrie almost felt sorry for him—almost. She recalled the love she'd felt for him—still felt. She wondered what her emotions would be after she learned more of his story.

Carrie nodded at Adam, as though to say, "It's your turn."

"Okay. Let's hear the rest of it."

Adam leaned toward her and she saw him struggle to keep his voice calm. Though they were alone in the building, he spoke in a quiet voice. "Thank you," he said. "For meeting me . . . for giving me another chance."

Carrie shook her head. "I should at least hear the whole story. I owe you that much."

He moved as if to reach for her hand, then pulled back and let his own hands rest on the arms of his chair. "As I told you, I started life as Keith Branson. I went to law school at John Marshall in Chicago. While I was in school, I met a woman who worked in her father's law office. She seemed perfect, and I fell hard for her. After a relatively short engagement, Bella and I were married. When I graduated, her father, Charlie DeLuca, took me into his practice."

Carrie nodded but said nothing. She didn't want to stop the flow of his narrative.

Adam went on to tell about an idyllic first year of marriage. But soon he discovered his father-in-law's practice had a shady side. Charlie not only defended some of the biggest criminals in Chicago, he played a key role in laundering huge sums of money, was a cut-out in several narcotics rings, and acted as an advisor, if not a partner, for a group that controlled most of the prostitution in that part of the state.

Beads of sweat dotted Adam's brow. "I finally told Bella what I'd found out about her father's law practice—that it was part of a criminal enterprise—and that I wanted no part in it. She laughed and said, in effect, 'The money's good. Keep your mouth shut.'"

"But you didn't," Carrie said.

"I couldn't. I tried, but it was harder with each day that passed. Sometimes the arguments lasted well into the night. Then Bella told me she was pregnant."

Despite herself, Carrie caught her breath. Did Adam have a child?

"I was overjoyed," Adam continued. "But Bella didn't share my feelings. She wasn't ready for motherhood. She told me she was going to visit a friend. She came back in a week and told me she'd lost the baby. It wasn't long before I found out that actually she'd had an abortion. That was the last straw for me."

"What did you do?"

Adam squeezed his eyes shut for a moment, as if he could

drive away the images that plagued him. "I put together a detailed file to be used against my father-in-law and his associates. When I had everything ready, I contacted the District Attorney and said I was prepared to testify before a Grand Jury and at any resulting trial. In return, I wanted protection."

"Obviously, they said yes."

Adam nodded. "I told my wife and father-in-law that I needed some time away, packed a suitcase, and left. The next time I saw them was at his trial."

The DA assured Adam that the U.S. Marshalls Service would keep him safe until after the trial. He was ferried back to Chicago from Milwaukee to testify before the Grand Jury. After that, the marshalls moved him from city to city, always under a new name, until finally he came back to Chicago to testify at his father-in-law's trial. The process had been a slow one—two years, in fact. And as each day passed, Adam wondered if he'd made the right choice.

"What about your wife?" Carrie asked.

"Once she learned what I had done, she filed for no-fault divorce—in Illinois it's called 'irreconcilable differences.' My absence sped up the process. Before I returned for her father's trial, the divorce was final."

"And your father-in-law?"

"The jury convicted him of a whole laundry list of crimes. He ended up with a total sentence of thirty years. He should have gotten even more."

"So you're safe now. Why not resume your true identity? Why not go back to Chicago?"

Adam laughed without mirth. "My life wouldn't be worth ten cents. Charlie DeLuca was part of a big organization, not to mention his family members and people who owed him favors. As soon as his sentence was handed down, I'm certain the word went out to kill me."

Carrie thought about this. "What brought you here to Jameson eight months ago, then?"

"After the trial one of the places the Witness Security Program—it's usually shortened to WITSEC—had me working in was an office supply store in a small town in Iowa. One day a guy showed up with my picture, asking if anyone at work knew me. Apparently no one cared for the guy's attitude, so they told him they had no idea what he was talking about. But the more I thought about it, the more convinced I was that my new identity wasn't all that secret. After all, WITSEC has a lot of moving parts, and all Charlie DeLuca's family, or hired gun, or whoever had to do was spread around enough money and they'd find me. It was time to find somewhere else, but this time, on my own."

"So the program didn't move you here?"

"No, I moved myself. No one knows where I am now . . . or, at least, I thought that was true. But if that shooting Saturday night wasn't random, someone's found me, and until I know for sure, I don't want to talk with the police."

"Why?"

"When I was working in Charlie DeLuca's office, I learned he had contacts with cops on the take in police departments from California to New York. There's no reason to think that doesn't include Texas."

Carrie was shaking her head before he stopped talking. "Why didn't you choose a large town, like Dallas? Surely it would be easier to get lost there."

"It is, but it's also more likely that organized crime has a bigger presence in a large city than in someplace like Jameson. I'm close enough to Dallas to enjoy the benefits, but a smaller place like Jameson seemed a lot safer."

"So you haven't told anyone where you are?"

"Just one man. He's a marshall, but this move is totally off the books. Besides, I'd trust Dave with my life."

Carrie frowned. "Why?"

"He's my older brother. He's David Branson, Jr."

Carrie thought about the story she'd heard. It revealed an Adam who had the moral fiber to do the right thing, even if it meant losing his identity, his family . . . and perhaps his life. True, he should have told her the story before asking her to marry him, but she could see by the pain in his eyes as he told the story how much it cost him to reveal it now. This wasn't the Adam she thought she knew, but what she'd heard did nothing to erase her love for him.

Carrie was ready to say something to Adam when the crash of breaking glass made them both bolt from their chairs and hurry toward the front of the building. A large hole ringed with shards was all that remained of the plate glass window in the reception area. Smaller pieces of glass littered the carpet like diamonds. The drapes, one area of carpet, and two of the upholstered chairs in the room were on fire, sending tongues of flame licking outward, threatening a larger blaze. Wisps of acrid black smoke stung Carrie's eyes and seared her lungs.

"Are you okay?" Adam yelled.

Carrie stifled her coughing long enough to say, "Just fighting the smoke. Is there a fire extinguisher here?"

"It's in the hall," Adam said. "I'll get it. Call the fire department."

As Carrie dialed 911, her first thought was for their safety. But her second was that despite Adam's insistence on not being involved with the police, now he'd have to be. She wondered how he'd handle their questions—and where it might go from there.

FIVE

ADAM HAD THE FIRE EXTINGUISHED BY THE TIME THE FIRE DEPART-
ment arrived, but the firemen spent another fifteen or twenty
minutes making sure there were no areas that might burst into
flames later.

The police arrived at almost the same time as the firemen.
Facing them wasn't exactly what Adam wanted, but there was
nothing to be done about it. He'd simply have to put the most
innocent face he could on the incident.

The patrolman taking Adam's statement asked him, "Any
idea why someone might have done this?"

Adam knew how this worked. He expected the question,
and had his answer ready. "There are two lawyers who work
here. The most likely explanation is that someone didn't like
the way one of the attorneys handled his case."

"Any recent cases handled by the firm that could have triggered this?"

"I don't know of any, but you should ask the lawyers. One of them should be here soon."

The patrolman looked at his notes. "When this call came in and you gave your name, the computer kicked out a recent report you made about vandalism to your car. Think someone's out to get you?"

Adam struggled to maintain a calm demeanor. "I doubt it. That was a simple case of vandalism. I don't think there's a connection here."

The questioning went on in that vein for what seemed like an hour, although when he glanced at his watch Adam found it had taken only twelve minutes. When it seemed the questions were coming to an end, the patrolman turned to Carrie and asked, "Anything to add, ma'am?"

Adam tried to send her a silent message. *Please don't say anything about what I've told you. Please.*

Carrie's face was smudged with soot, her blond hair was a mess, her green eyes were red-rimmed. She was the perfect picture of "let's get this over with so I can go home." She gave the patrolman a shy smile. "No, I have no idea who could have done this. Adam and I had some things to discuss, and we needed a quiet place to do it." She grimaced as she looked around. "Unfortunately, this wasn't it."

Adam breathed a sigh of relief when Janice Evans walked in. Now maybe the police and firemen would direct their questions to her. Before he could introduce Evans to Carrie, the attorney strode over and held out her hand. "Janice Evans. You must be Dr. Markham. Adam has mentioned you."

"I wish we could have met under better circumstances," Carrie said.

"It happens," Evans replied. "Sorry you were involved."

The policeman's first question to Evans was, "Any dissatisfied clients who might have done this?"

Her response was a calm shrug. "Sooner or later, someone decides his lawyer didn't do right by him. Some of them send nasty letters. A few file complaints with the bar association. But I must say I've never had one go quite this far." She grimaced as she turned to look at the damage. "After you're through talking with me, I'll call a client who's a general contractor. Maybe I can convince him to board up the window tonight." She nodded toward Carrie. "Adam, why don't you take Dr. Markham home? Come back here afterward so we can talk about keeping the practice running tomorrow."

"I have my car, thanks." Carrie nodded once to Evans, once to Adam, before she hurried toward the door.

"I'll see you out," Adam said, hurrying after her.

Carrie beeped her car unlocked and was inside it before Adam reached her. He stood there, wondering what Carrie's response would be to her second brush with danger in such a short period of time. Surely it couldn't be good.

Carrie lowered the car window. "Yes?"

He wasn't sure what to make of her tone, but the look on her face conveyed a desire to leave more strongly than any words could. He wanted to hold her, beg her to stay, assure her that his goal was to keep her safe, but she started the engine and looked ready to drive away.

"Carrie, I'm so sorry. I hate to leave things like this. We still have a lot to talk about."

"When? How? Each time we get together someone tries to kill you—and me in the bargain."

"Would you like me to follow you home to be sure you get inside safely?"

"I don't think that would make me any safer." Was that a faint smile, or a grimace? "Look, Adam. I want to hear more of your story, and we'll figure out a way to do it. But right now I'm going to head home, where I'll lock all the doors, take a long shower, and try to sleep."

"When can I see you again? Will you call me?"

"Eventually, but give me awhile to think about all this." Carrie rolled up her window and put the car in reverse.

Adam watched her taillights fade into the distance, and his heart went with her.

Okay, God. Please don't take her from me. Help me out here. What do I do next?

"After you finish with this next patient, Dr. Rushton wants to see you in his office."

"Thanks, Lila. Tell him it won't be too long."

Carrie paused outside the exam room. Why did Phil Rushton want to see her? It couldn't be that he wanted her to do a pre-op evaluation on his patient. He routinely asked the other internist in the clinic, Thad Avery, to do that. Was there some problem? Phil was a confirmed nitpicker. And although things had been quiet between them since John's death, there had been a few differences of opinion between her and Phil in the past—situations where tempers almost reached the boiling point.

Phil Rushton was an excellent surgeon. But Carrie didn't particularly admire him as a person. He had divested himself of his wife and two children as quickly as possible after completing his residency training. Now, other than surgery, he had little else to occupy his time. True, he didn't always lord his status over his colleagues, but he wasn't above using his position as chief operating officer of the clinic to snoop and pry. She wondered what he had in mind this time. Whatever it was, she had an uneasy feeling that it wouldn't be good.

Carrie finished with her patient and made her way down the hall toward Phil's office. The door of an exam room opened, and Carrie stopped to let one of the nurses, holding a handful of papers, exit with a middle-aged man.

The nurse and patient came toward Carrie. When they were abreast of her, the man stopped and looked Carrie full in the face, his eyes narrowed in a frown that made her take a step back. She swallowed twice. "Hello, Mr. McDonald." He didn't reply, just stood silent, fixing her with that look before he turned to follow the nurse. *If looks could kill . . .*

It had been over a year since Calvin McDonald's wife died. Was he still angry about her death? Or angry with Carrie about the part she played? Carrie hurried on, trying to put the encounter out of her mind, as she had others that preceded it.

Phil occupied a corner office in the clinic, bigger in size and more expensively furnished than anyone else's. It even had its own door leading directly outside, so he could come and go without anyone—patients or colleagues—being the wiser.

Carrie tapped on the closed door and received a curt, "Come." She'd always hated that response, since it came out sounding like, "I'm terribly busy, but if you must, I grant you permission to enter."

She opened the door, took a step into the room, and raised

her eyebrows in silent question. Phil looked up from his desk. "Come in. Close the door. Have a seat." He turned his attention back to the papers in his hand.

Phil Rushton was anything but a commanding picture. He was short, chunky, almost bald, and spoke in a high voice that reminded her of the lab experiment in high school where the students all inhaled helium. But he made up for what he lacked in appearance by a manner that said to all concerned, "I'm not just anybody—I'm *somebody*—and don't you forget it."

Carrie hitched one of the patient chairs closer to the desk, smoothed her skirt across the back of her thighs, and sat. Phil's attention was back on the paper in front of him, scribbling notes in the margin.

As she waited, Carrie looked around her. The walls of Phil's office were covered with diplomas and certificates that testified to the status he'd achieved: BS with honors from Northwestern University, MD degree and selection to Alpha Omega Alpha at the University of Chicago's Pritzker School of Medicine, chief resident in cardiothoracic surgery at Rush University Medical Center. He'd gone on to receive award after award while in practice. She'd heard the term before, even used it—this was his "I love me" wall.

After a moment she said, "You wanted to see me?"

Phil sighed gently, capped his gold-plated fountain pen, then dropped it on the desk. "Yes, Carrie. I sent for you." Phil leaned back and steepled his hands, displaying the long, manicured fingers that could do magic on the human heart in surgery. "I heard that you were one of the victims of a firebomb attack last night. What was that about?"

"Where did you hear that?" she blurted.

"At the hospital when I was on rounds," Phil replied in a cool voice. "I repeat—what was that about?"

Carrie bit back a retort. The question was valid, she guessed, although the manner in which it was asked was a bit demeaning. So typical of Phil. She took a deep breath. "My friend Adam and I went to his office so we could have some privacy while we talked. That's why I was there." Her words came faster than she intended. "One of the lawyers said she thought it was most likely a disgruntled client of the law firm, trying to exact some sort of revenge. The police seemed to agree." Just talking about it sent a chill down her spine, but she hurried on. "And, although you didn't ask, I wasn't harmed. Only shaken."

Phil leaned forward and fixed her with an earnest expression. "That was going to be my next question, Carrie. I'm glad you weren't hurt." He picked up his pen and began twirling it. "And you weren't involved in this? It had nothing to do with you or, for example, an unhappy patient?"

Carrie hadn't given serious consideration to the possibility. Surely the attack was meant for Adam, not her. But she wondered for a moment if Phil's eyes, eyes the color of winter rain, were seeing something that she missed. Then she thought of another pair of eyes, eyes that fixed her with a malevolent glare. Could a patient, Mr. McDonald or some other, go to this length to harm her? She'd have to think about that a bit. She hoped this was just Phil being Phil, making the moment melodramatic.

Carrie struggled to keep her tone even. "So far as I can see, the episode didn't have anything to do with me, except to scare me half to death. Now, are you through? I have patients to see."

Phil's voice softened slightly, but his eyes still seemed to probe her. "Carrie, I have to ask uncomfortable questions. It's part of my job as the clinic's managing partner."

No, it wasn't. Not this way, anyway. Could Phil be fishing for what her employment contract called "questionable behavior," trying to get rid of her? She wouldn't put it past him. *Stop it. You're being paranoid.*

Carrie stood up. "Sorry, but it still makes me uncomfortable to talk about the incident. Is that all?"

Phil rose and offered his hand across the desk. His smile was faint. She couldn't tell if it was sincere. "Carrie, we all know the stress you've been under since John's death. If there's anything I can do to help you . . ."

Phil let the sentence die.

"Nothing, but thank you." She drew in a deep breath. "Now, if you'll excuse me, I have patients to see."

Phil nodded, eased into his chair, and picked up his pen once more, effectively dismissing her.

As Carrie closed the door she decided that even if Phil weren't the senior member of the group, he'd still be in charge. The other doctors in the group would see to that. Sure, the clinic was in business to heal the sick, but to keep it going took money. And Phil Rushton generated a lot of money for the group. She hoped she'd never reach the point where she practiced medicine solely for the monetary rewards.

Going into medicine was a response to a call Carrie felt just as strongly as a call to ministry. Actually, it *was* her ministry, a ministry of healing. But Adam was trying to heal, in a manner of speaking, and so far she had done nothing to help him.

Sure, she was hurt because he'd lied to her, but she could see why he did it. She'd been about to let him back into her life, about to forgive him, when that firebomb came through the window. And what did she do? She ran away again. What did that make her?

Her next patient was an elderly gentleman. His appearance brought several descriptions to her mind: thin as a rail, pale as a ghost. The smile he gave her was the very definition of "putting on a brave front." His wife sat beside him, their hands touching.

Carrie smiled back at them. "Mr. Atkinson," she said, "I have your test results, and there's good news. The treatment seems to be working. Your blood count is much better. I think the leukemia is headed for remission."

Atkinson's face relaxed. Tears streaked his wife's cheeks. They both spoke at once. "Thank God." "Oh, Doctor, that's wonderful."

First Atkinson, then his wife moved forward to wrap Carrie in warm hugs. She luxuriated in the moment. Phil could have his certificates and awards, the satisfaction of pulling in the largest share of clinic income. But this was her reward. This was what she'd been called to do. This was why she practiced medicine.

———————————⌇———————————

Adam suffered through a restless night. He'd told Janice Evans he'd be there in the morning. After all, she had no idea the firebomb was meant for him. But weren't two attempts on his life enough to send him on his way, leaving Jameson and his would-be murderer behind? Not if the woman he loved was here, and that was exactly the case. He couldn't leave Carrie—not if there was any way to salvage their relationship.

He kept one eye on the rearview mirror as he drove to work. One of the schemes he'd turned over in his mind during the restless night was getting a gun. Dave had urged him to acquire one when he went into the Witness Security Program—even offered to help—but Adam refused. He couldn't bring himself to do it then, and he couldn't do it now. Maybe there was another way.

Twice he started to call Carrie, twice he pulled his hand away from his cell phone as though it were a fiery coal. No, she said she'd call. All he could do was wait.

The law office smelled of smoke. A large piece of plywood covered the front window. The burned chairs were gone, an empty spot where their replacements would sit. Workmen were on their knees, removing the damaged section of carpet. Despite all that, Hartley and Evans, attorneys at law, were open for business. No matter what else might happen, the legal machine continued to grind.

Adam slogged through the day, one ear tuned to his cell phone, waiting for a ring announcing a call from Carrie. But there was nothing.

"Would you take these papers over to the District Clerk's office? They need to be there by the end of business today." Bruce Hartley tossed a manila envelope onto Adam's desk. "Better hurry. They're about to close."

Adam looked at his watch. "I'm on my way. Then I'll head home. See you tomorrow." He shoved the envelope into his battered briefcase.

He was almost to the door when Bruce said, "By the way, was your girlfriend with you last night when someone lobbed that Molotov cocktail through the window?"

Adam paused with his hand on the knob. "Yes." He'd learned long ago never to give more information than was required.

"No danger of her suing us, is there?"

"Nope. But thanks for your concern."

Adam went out the door, leaving Bruce to decipher whether the last remark represented sarcasm or a sincere thanks. *If I were back practicing law, I'd run rings around him in court.*

During his short walk to the courthouse, Adam kept his head on a swivel. Every stranger was a potential threat. Each open window in the downtown area hid a sniper. Soon he was back at the building that housed the law offices of Hartley and Evans. Adam paused in the parking lot and scanned the rows of cars still there. Where was his car? Had it been stolen? Then it dawned on him. It was in the shop, getting a new windshield and having the damaged front seats repaired. He located his black Toyota Corolla rental and used the remote to unlock the doors.

He hadn't heard from Carrie yet. Should he call her? No, he was determined to give her some time to process everything. In the meantime, he'd run some errands. If he hadn't heard from her later this evening, maybe he'd call.

Adam was almost to the cleaners when he noticed that the blue SUV behind him looked familiar. Had it been sitting near his car in the parking lot when he left?

When Adam first entered the Witness Security Program, Dave had given him some rudimentary lessons on how to handle a tail. He put them into practice now, changing lanes, turning without signaling, jumping green lights and running through the last second of yellow lights. Finally, just before he was ready to take a short segment the wrong way on a one-way street, Adam looked in the rearview mirror and saw that he was clear.

He spotted a parking garage and wheeled sharply into it. The time dragged, but Adam forced himself to sit for ten minutes before he started the car and nosed back into traffic. It took him another five minutes of deke and dodge before he was certain he'd lost his tail . . . if there had been one in the first place.

Adam's brain hadn't been idle while he sat in hiding. He headed for the facility from which his rental car had come. Once there, his car safely lost in a sea of other returns, he entered an office staffed by a single clerk with a phone to his ear and two lines blinking. The clerk hung up and looked at Adam expectantly.

Adam put his rental paperwork on the counter. "I know you're really slammed, but this car's running pretty rough. I'm afraid the last renter put some cheap gas into it before turning it in."

The clerk frowned at the telephone with its blinking buttons. "I'm sorry. Why don't we put you in another vehicle?"

Adam had given this some thought. Jameson was a typical midsized north Texas town. The vast majority of vehicles on the street were either pickups or SUVs. "Sure." Adam paused as though considering a fresh idea. "How about a pickup?"

Adam had barely finished speaking when the clerk pulled a set of keys from a drawer and pushed them toward him. "No problem. Got a Ford F-150, and I'll let you have it for the same price as the car you're driving. Slot 18A. Enjoy."

By now, new calls had added more blinking buttons to the phone. When the young man picked up the handset and took the next call, Adam eased the rental papers he'd been ready to give the clerk back into his pocket. Apparently the person on the other end of the phone had a significant bone to pick with the car rental company and had the clerk's full attention. During the heated exchange that followed, Adam hurried out the door.

Great. Now the rental company's paperwork showed his previous car, while he was driving the most common vehicle in the city.

A shiny black pickup waited for Adam in 18A. Perfect. He tossed his briefcase inside, adjusted the mirror and seat, and headed out of the lot. He still had to run those errands. After that, if Carrie agreed to see him, he needed a safe place for them to meet.

He didn't want to bring Carrie to his apartment for a variety of reasons, not the least of which was that the shooter probably knew where he lived. After the incident with the fire-bomb, it was obvious that the law office wasn't safe. And under no circumstances did Adam want to lead his stalker to Carrie's house. He needed a safe base of operation, not only a place to meet Carrie, but somewhere he could relax without fearing he'd be murdered in his sleep.

He'd check into a motel, and he had the perfect location in mind. He'd need to pick up clothes and toiletries from his apartment. Maybe if he parked a block away, went through alleys and used the back entrance, he could avoid detection. Not now, though. He'd postpone that until after dark.

Adam needed cash, so his first stop was an ATM, where he withdrew the daily maximum from his account. No problem there. Adam had one more stop to make. Then he'd be ready to go to ground.

After his next errand he climbed into his new pickup and

took a roundabout route to one of the motels that ringed the outer part of the city. The one he chose wasn't part of a chain, but a small, family-owned motel that featured a row of cabins set back from the highway. He checked in and paid cash for three days.

When he filled out his registration, Adam put down a fictitious address and transposed two digits of his license plate. He entered *Ford* for his last name. Adam thought a moment before adding the first name *Edward*, figuring the clerk was too young to remember the Yankee pitcher Whitey Ford.

Once in his room, Adam used the prepaid cell phone he'd just purchased to call Carrie. She answered on the first ring. "Carrie, it's me, Adam." He took a deep breath. "I know I said I'd wait for you to call, but I can't wait any longer. Can you meet me at the Rancho Motel after dark?"

"Adam, I don't—"

"I'm in a motel for a reason," he hurried on. "I'm staying away from my apartment for now. There are parking areas in both front and back of a row of cabins. Park in the back, close to the breezeway where the ice machine is. Then walk straight through and turn left. I'm in cabin six."

The silence stretched on. Adam was about to say something more when Carrie said, "Okay."

"One more thing," Adam said. "Be careful as you drive here. Try to make sure you aren't followed."

Adam's call had caught Carrie in her car, sitting in the doctor's parking lot after hospital rounds. She'd ended the call, and within seconds her phone rang again.

"Carrie, it's Julie. Can you talk now?"

"Sure. I'm glad you called. Are we still going to meet for lunch?"

"That's why I'm calling. Barry and I are going to be in Dallas tomorrow. Will that work?"

"Of course. I need some face time with you." Talking with her best friend had always helped Carrie put things in perspective. "Tell you what. I can arrange to get away a little after eleven, and my first afternoon patient isn't until two."

They settled on a restaurant halfway between Dallas and Jameson. Carrie wondered if she should warn Julie to be certain she wasn't followed, then dismissed the idea as paranoid.

As Carrie drove out of the parking lot, something she'd heard in med school crossed her mind. *Just because you're paranoid doesn't mean they aren't out to get you.* Maybe it wasn't paranoid to be careful—not if someone was trying to kill Adam . . . and her.

SIX

ADAM JUMPED UP FROM HIS CHAIR WHEN HE HEARD THE TAP ON the door of Rancho Motel's cabin six. "Adam?" a small voice called.

He opened the door and waved Carrie inside. They exchanged an awkward hug, but when Adam made a motion to kiss her, Carrie pulled back, disguising the movement by tucking a strand of hair behind her ear. His heart sank.

Carrie settled into the room's only chair. "Do you think this is a safe place to meet?"

Adam eased onto the bed and sat with his back against the headboard. He'd asked himself the same question. "It's the safest place I could think of."

"Why didn't your caller ID show up on my phone when you called?" Carrie asked. "What I got was 'private call.'"

"I went to Best Buy and bought a prepaid cell phone. People, especially those on the wrong side of the law, call them 'throwaways.' I'll give you the number before you leave. From now on, use that when you call me."

"Why?"

"I understand that it's possible to locate a cell phone, even when it's not being used, by triangulating the cell towers it accesses. I don't know how sophisticated this guy who's after me really is or how much technology he has available, but I decided there was no reason to give him a way to pinpoint my location."

Carrie said, "Well, I can see that you're taking this seriously. But what's your next move? That is, if you don't mind telling me."

For maybe the hundredth time Adam regretted thinking he could get by without sharing his past with Carrie. But he couldn't change that. He leaned back against the headboard and closed his eyes. "I'm not sure what to do. Ordinarily I'd pack up and run again. But that would mean leaving you, and I can't do that."

"But if you stay, you're not safe. Right?" she said.

"You saw what's happened already. Does that seem safe to you?"

"What I can't understand is, if DeLuca went to prison, why is this still happening?"

"A connected mob guy can put out a hit whether or not he's behind bars," Adam said. "You can bet that's exactly the message that went out before the prison door closed on Charlie DeLuca."

"So that's why you were in the Witness Protection Program," Carrie said.

"Witness Security Program," Adam corrected. "But, yes. No one knows where I am except my brother."

"Why Jameson? Why here?"

Adam forced a smile. "My grandmother grew up here. She went north and married my grandfather, but as a child I heard lots of stories about Texas, and specifically about Jameson, which was just a wide place in the road when she left. I looked it up on the Internet and found it had changed. Like the story of the three bears—not too large, not too small, but just right."

"So you essentially slipped away from federal protection? Would they take you back?"

"I left the program because there were too many ways DeLuca's people could find me. I don't see why it would be any safer for me to go back now."

"How did you get a job here?" Carrie asked.

"All it took was a couple of forged references and an obvious good grasp of the practice of law. It's not hard to be a paralegal when you're already an attorney." A faint smile crossed Adam's face. "Besides, Bruce Hartley got me cheap, and that's just his style."

"What about me—or maybe I should say, what about us? Was that all part of your cover?"

Adam was shaking his head while she was still talking. "Absolutely not. My first week here, when I slipped into the Jameson Community Church and saw you in the congregation, I knew I had to meet you."

"So when we were introduced that Sunday morning after church, it wasn't an accident?"

"No. Until I saw you, I never put much stock in that 'love at first sight' stuff. You changed my mind, right then and there. And the more I got to know you, the more certain I was that love was real." He took a deep breath, swallowed twice, and said, "Carrie, I loved you then. I still love you."

Carrie turned her head and wiped at her eyes. A long moment passed before she finally spoke, and when she did her voice was fragile, as though it was ready to crack. "When John died, I thought I'd never love anyone again. Life had lost its color. But I met you, and it didn't take long for me to think you'd come into my life to fill the hole that was there. I started to live again."

"I wasn't trying to—"

Carrie shook her head. "You did exactly what was needed. You let me talk about John. You dried my tears and let me lean on your shoulder. You gave me your love. And the gray turned to a rainbow again."

Adam's heart swelled.

"You introduced yourself as Adam. Then I found out you're really Keith. You may even have other names. But that doesn't matter. I've decided that what matters is I'm not ready to lose you. I love you, and I want us to be together."

Hope rose in Adam's chest. "Does that mean our engagement is on?" he asked. "Are you ready to wear the ring again?"

Carrie rose and moved to the window. She stared into the night for a long time before speaking. "Let's leave it at 'I love you' for now. We can talk about our future when all this is settled."

"So where do we go from here?" Adam asked. "You know the choices I have. What do you want me to do?"

Carrie turned from the window and looked into Adam's eyes. "I don't know what to tell you. All I know is that we're in this together."

Adam crossed the room and put his arms around her. They hugged and kissed, this time with the passion that had marked their relationship earlier.

When Carrie finally pulled away she looked at her watch. "I need to go. Give me your new cell phone number. I'll call you tomorrow."

Carrie entered the number into her phone, then moved toward the door, where she turned to face him. "Should I keep calling you Adam?"

He nodded. "You have to, in order to keep my identity a secret. Is that going to be a problem?"

"No. You're still the man I fell in love with. That's all that matters." She kissed him once more. "Good night. Be careful."

All through a night marked by tossing, turning, and brief periods of fitful sleep, Carrie pondered her situation and weighed the choices facing her and Adam. Her dreams were filled with flashbacks of John's death interspersed with vivid scenes of a gunman bursting into the church and shooting Adam dead during their wedding. She woke in a mass of tangled, sweat-soaked bedclothes.

Over a quick breakfast of coffee and toast, she considered her options and found none of them good. Driving on automatic pilot to the clinic, her mind was a muddle. Now it was time to go to work, to put everything else aside. Her patients deserved her full attention, and that was what they'd get.

She stood outside the exam room where her first patient waited when a familiar voice made her turn. Phil Rushton said, "Carrie, glad I ran into you. Do you have plans for lunch?"

Carrie made a conscious effort not to show her surprise. What was going on? Phil Rushton didn't ask colleagues to lunch. It was generally held that he didn't ever stop for lunch. He went straight from the operating room to his clinic so he could see his post-ops, evaluate possible preoperative patients sent to him by his colleagues, and do the hundred and one things involved in a busy and successful specialty surgical practice.

There was definitely something going on here—but she wasn't sure what it was. One explanation was that Phil was interested in her as something other than a colleague. But that didn't ring true with her. Phil rarely did anything that didn't benefit him, directly or indirectly. Once more Carrie wondered if he was angling to get her out of the clinic. She'd noticed some time ago that he favored the clinic's other internist, Thad Avery. Maybe Phil or Thad wanted to replace her on the clinic staff with a friend of theirs. Whatever the reason, she'd better tread carefully.

"I'm sorry, but I have a luncheon date."

"With that boyfriend of yours?"

"Actually, no." *As though it's any business of yours.* "I'm meeting a woman who's been my best friend for years."

"Can you cancel it?" Phil said. Was that a smile on his face? Unbelievable. "There's a little hole-in-the-wall café down the street. The food is great, but it seems no one's discovered it yet, so it's quiet. Just the place for us to talk privately."

Talk privately, as in break bad news? Carrie liked this less and less. "Phil, I—"

"Dr. Markham!"

Carrie's nurse, Lila, came speed walking down the hall toward her. Something was definitely wrong. Lila didn't hurry for anything except the direst of emergencies. "What?" Carrie said.

"The EMTs just brought Mrs. Lambert into the ER. Chest pain, syncope, shock—probably a coronary. The ER doc's with her now, but they need you there stat!"

"I'm on my way." Carrie turned to Phil with an "I'm sorry" look, then hurried away, glad for the interruption, but worried about her elderly patient who appeared to be having her third coronary event in the past two years.

As she walked briskly through the enclosed breezeway that connected the clinic with the hospital, Carrie thought about what lay ahead of her. She wondered if this was the heart attack that might be the final one for Mrs. Lambert. Well, not if Carrie could do something to prevent it.

There had been a time when Carrie prayed for her patients. Then John died. She hadn't offered up many prayers since then, but this seemed to be the time for one.

God, I know the ultimate result isn't in my hands, but in Yours. Please use me to restore Mrs. Lambert to health. The doors to the hospital were straight ahead of her. Time to see if she, or God, or the two of them together could keep her patient alive.

Carrie pushed through the double swinging doors into the confusion of the Emergency Room. Her eyes swept left and right as she hurried to her patient's side. If one ignored the sounds that formed a constant background—beeps and voices and the clatter of balky gurney wheels—and focused instead on all the moving parts, they'd see staff going about their business in an efficient manner, with no outward hint of the inward adrenaline rush some of them undoubtedly felt.

"Dr. Markham, your patient is over there." An ER nurse, whose name danced outside of Carrie's memory, indicated a cubicle surrounded by drawn curtains that moved like sails in the wind from the activity going on behind them.

"Thanks, Jane," Carrie said, thankful that the right name had come to her just in time.

She drew aside the curtains and saw what she'd expected. An ER doctor alternately focused on the green lines of a heart monitor and the lab slips in his hand. An elderly lady, thin and pale, lay motionless on the wheeled stretcher. Oxygen flowed into a clear plastic mask that covered her lower face. IVs dripped into both arms. Her vital signs, constantly displayed on yet another monitor, showed a blood pressure that was low but adequate.

"I'm here," Carrie said to the other doctor. "Fill me in."

He did so in a few sentences, using the medical-speak only a professional would understand. "If you don't need me, I've got an ER full of patients. But call if I can help." He slid through the curtains and was gone.

As Carrie moved to her side, the woman on the stretcher opened her eyes, blinked, and squinted in recognition. "Dr. Markham. Am I dying?" Her voice was weak, and the effort of speaking seemed to exhaust her.

Carrie patted her hand. "Mrs. Lambert, you've had another heart attack—a pretty big one, according to what I see. We need to do a cardiac angiogram to see how to handle this."

Mrs. Lambert breathed out through pursed lips, then took in a deep breath. "So, another stent?"

"I'm—"

"It depends on what the angiogram shows. You may need an operation to supply more blood to your heart."

Carrie whirled to identify the speaker. Actually, his voice was easily identifiable to her—she'd heard it only minutes ago—but she couldn't believe Phil Rushton would try to claim the case without speaking to her first. "Phil, what—"

At that moment a man and woman in hospital scrubs pushed into the already crowded space and positioned themselves at the head and foot of the gurney. The woman spoke to Mrs. Lambert. "We're going to take you for an X-ray study of your heart." They busied themselves with changing from the wall oxygen supply to a tank under the gurney. The male member of the team unplugged the monitors, and in a moment they wheeled Mrs. Lambert away.

Carrie glared at Phil. "Can you tell me what's going on? And why you're taking over my patient without consulting me?"

Phil made a palms-out gesture. "Carrie, this is Mrs. Lambert's third infarction. I have no doubt that both her EKG and enzymes will confirm that it's a major one. Her daughter called the clinic right after you left and asked if I'd take charge of her case if she needed surgery. She gave me most of the history I need. We'll see what the angiogram shows, but I'm willing to bet that this time stents won't do it. Your patient will need bypass surgery. Now, unless you want to try to talk her and her daughter into going somewhere else, I think you'll agree I'm a good choice to do the operation. And the sooner we get to it, the better."

He was right, of course. Mrs. Lambert was a prime candidate for what medical professionals called a "cabbage." Not the leafy vegetable. She needed a coronary artery bypass graft, a procedure that bore the acronym CABG. Carrie had to admit the probable need for such surgery crossed her mind as she hurried to the ER. Mrs. Lambert shouldn't suffer because Carrie had her feelings ruffled. She shrugged. "Let's head for the angiography suite. I want to see what the angio shows."

"Are you sure you want to go back there?" Phil said. "After what happened to John—"

"I'll be fine," Carrie snapped. "I've been going to the angio suite since two weeks after John died. I'll be the first to admit it wasn't easy at first, but I did it." She turned on her heel and said over her shoulder, "I promise I won't break down, if that's what's bothering you. Now, are you coming?"

As Carrie hurried down the corridor, she wondered about the man matching her stride for stride. Professionally he was as competent as they came. She'd trust her life to Phil. Actually she'd trusted her husband's life to him. She might have assigned some blame to Phil in John's death, but now that some time had passed she realized he'd done all he could. The question that continued to plague her was whether she had done all she could as well.

SEVEN

PHIL WAS RIGHT, OF COURSE. THE ANGIOGRAM SHOWED ALMOST total blockage of Mrs. Lambert's left anterior descending and left circumflex coronary arteries. In layman's terms, blood flow to the major portion of the heart muscle was cut off. "I'll talk with Mrs. Lambert and her daughter," Phil said.

Carrie knew she'd been dismissed, but she couldn't simply disappear. She'd cared for Mrs. Lambert through two other heart attacks and thought she'd formed a bond with the woman. Even if the daughter asked Phil Rushton to take over the case, Carrie felt an obligation to be there. "I want to go with you when you talk with them. She's my patient too." *At least for now.*

She stood by as Phil explained the procedure to Mrs. Lambert and obtained her permission for the surgery. No problem, the woman said. She knew how close to death she'd come—how close she still was. If surgery was what was needed, she was ready.

Carrie's heart melted when Mrs. Lambert looked at her and said, "Dr. Markham, would you pray for me?" Carrie nodded her assent, afraid to speak. *I'll try, but my prayers haven't been too successful lately.* She squeezed Mrs. Lambert's hand and followed Phil out of the room.

They found the daughter, Mrs. Stinson, in the waiting room. Despite her earlier frustration about the call to Phil Rushton, Carrie sympathized with this harried, middle-aged woman who wore worry lines on her face like a combat badge. Mildred Lambert had lived with her daughter and son-in-law since her husband died over a year ago.

Carrie and Phil took two vacant chairs that flanked Mrs. Stinson. There was no one else within earshot, so this was as good a place as any to have the talk. "Your mother has had another heart attack," Carrie began. "And this was a big one— almost fatal. So Dr. Rushton needs to perform surgery."

Phil explained that Mrs. Lambert needed more blood flow to the heart, so he'd take a vein from her leg and hook it up to take the place of the clogged arteries. "We call it a bypass graft."

"Is it risky?" Mrs. Stinson's voice was weak, and now tears flowed freely.

"Of course," Phil said, and went on to explain the potential risks. "But it's necessary surgery. Without it, your mother would almost certainly die."

Mrs. Stinson turned for the first time to Carrie, an unspoken question in her eyes.

Carrie nodded. "I agree."

A secretary came over to the group and handed Phil a clipboard. He glanced at it. "We have the op permit signed. Now I have to get ready." He rose and hurried away.

"Is Mother strong enough . . . ?" Mrs. Stinson let the words trail off.

"We believe so. The anesthesiologist is excellent. Dr. Rushton is the best heart surgeon around. The whole team is extremely competent. Your mother is in good hands." Carrie found herself reaching for Mrs. Stinson's hand. "I have to get back to the clinic. Dr. Rushton will see you as soon as the surgery is over, and I'll be back this evening. Is there anything I can do for you now?"

Mrs. Stinson blinked away tears. "Just keep us in your prayers."

Carrie nodded and left the room. She looked at her watch and decided that if she hurried, she could finish seeing her patients and still be on time for lunch with Julie. In the hallway, she heard someone calling her name. Carrie turned to see Rob Cole trotting toward her. "Dr. Markham, I'm glad I caught you."

"Rob, I really have to get back to the clinic. What's so important?"

"I wondered about Mrs. Lambert."

"Did you and your partner have that call?"

"Right. Her EKG showed a massive MI. Did she make it?"

"So far. And you were right—she had a myocardial infarction. Dr. Rushton is doing a CABG right now."

"Well, she's in good hands," Rob said. He ducked his head, and Carrie thought he looked about fourteen years old when he did. "Um, I know that you're a doctor and I'm only an EMT, but I was wondering if you'd like to have a cup of coffee together sometime."

Carrie put her hand on his arm. "Rob, I'm flattered, but I'm involved with someone else. Thank you, though."

Rob was a good-looking young man who'd just asked her out. And Phil, despite his usual demeanor, had sent some signals of interest as well. Some women probably would be thrilled to have that much attention, but Carrie wasn't one of them. No matter what had happened, she wanted to honor her commitment to Adam.

She thought about the ring she'd given back. Did she regret that action? No. Although she was in love with Adam, Carrie didn't think they could move forward until they were no longer in danger. She only wished she knew when that might be.

Carrie and Julie had decided to meet at a restaurant in the Galleria, a large shopping center north of Dallas. Julie was already at a table toward the back, and the sight of her friend made Carrie's face light up.

Julie jumped up and met Carrie halfway to the table. The two friends hugged.

"I'm sorry I'm late," Carrie said. "Things were crazy this morning." She took the chair next to Julie and tossed her purse onto the vacant one beside her.

"No problem," Julie said. "Catch your breath, get something to drink, and we can talk." She sipped her iced tea. "Afterward, I have orders from Barry to check out the Nordstrom here. He agreed to pay for our lunch if I brought home something frilly." She raised an eyebrow.

Carrie grinned. In a few minutes the two friends were chatting as though no time had passed since they were last together.

The waitress served salads, and for a moment the two women nibbled, although neither seemed as interested in eating as talking. Finally Julie said, "Now for the reason we're here, I guess. The last time we talked, someone had taken a shot at you, after which you discovered your fiancé wasn't who you thought."

"I've found out even more since then," Carrie said. She leaned forward and laid out all she'd learned from Adam. "The real question isn't whether I love him—despite everything, I still do—but what we're going to do to get out of this mess."

"I don't suppose you've talked with anyone else about the situation," Julie said.

"Who would I tell? My parents pretty much washed their hands of me when I became a Christian my first year in med school. I don't have any siblings—you're the sister I never had." Carrie leaned across the table. "You're my best friend."

"Even though we were both in love with Billy Kiker in the third grade?"

"Even then," Carrie said, and laughed for what seemed the first time in weeks.

Julie took a forkful of salad. "Why didn't Adam tell you all this before he asked you to marry him?"

Carrie put down her fork. "He admits he probably should have, but he thought he'd made a clean start in Jameson and hoped he could get by without revealing his past."

"And you can forgive him for that?"

"When I think about how supportive Adam's been, when I realize how wonderful it's been to have him in my life—yes. He taught me how to smile again, Julie. When he and I first met, I was a wreck, mainly because of what happened to John."

"Stop it! John had a cardiac problem that no one, not even a great diagnostician like you, could have noticed. And even though the odds of a complication like the one he experienced are slim, that doesn't mean it can't happen . . . even with the best possible medical care." She reached to pat Carrie's hand. "You have to accept that."

Carrie inhaled, taking a moment to compose herself. "I know. And I'm making progress there." She took a swallow of tea. "The guilt about John's death isn't as bad as it was, although there are still triggers. But now I'm really frightened for Adam. The shooting, the firebomb, someone trying to kill him—and my life is in danger as well."

"Why doesn't he go to the police?"

"He says there's a possibility someone there might leak his true identity. I don't think it matters anymore, but he won't listen." She drained the tea from her glass, but her throat remained dry. "It's frustrating to feel so helpless. I don't know what's going to happen next."

Julie rattled the ice cubes in her glass, and the waitress appeared with a pitcher for refills. After she left, both women added sweetener to their glasses and drank. Then Julie said, "How would you like this to end?"

Carrie didn't answer at once. When she did, her voice was almost a whisper. "What do I want? I want all the danger to go away—right now, without our having to do anything. Just *poof.*" She opened her fist like a magician making a coin disappear.

"Neither possible nor realistic," Julie said. "What is both possible and realistic is that you give Adam your support and help him find out who is after him."

"Even if doing that puts me in danger?"

"Crossing the street puts you in danger. Driving to the grocery puts you in danger. Eating in the hospital cafeteria puts you in danger. And the reward for any of those doesn't approach what you'll get from having Adam in your life. You love him. Period."

Carrie shoved her plate aside. "And that's it? That's all I can do? Julie, I feel so helpless. I need to *do* something."

"Isn't that typical of a doctor? You always want to be in control." Julie pointed her finger at her friend. "You can't control this. You can brainstorm, you can do what Adam asks, but the main thing you can do is pray . . . for him, for you, for the whole situation."

"I . . ." Carrie's throat tightened. She couldn't get the words out.

"I know, sometimes praying is hard, especially if you haven't done it for a while. But there's no magic formula. Just talk to God. He's been listening all the time. All you have to do is make it a two-way conversation."

Adam could hear the argument in his head as clearly as if there were someone standing beside him making the case. "Leave town." "Don't go to work." "Hide." And to each suggestion, his answer was the same: a resounding, "No." To this point, his response had been to run, but this time he'd stand and fight.

He wasn't going to run, because to do so would mean leaving Carrie behind. Yet, if he stayed, he needed this job—not just for the salary, although that was essential, but because to step away from it would invite the very questions he'd tried to avoid. "Why did Adam do that? Is there something strange about him?" If he simply kept doing what he'd been doing, surely he'd think of a way out of all this.

Was it time to move past his principles and get a gun? No, he wasn't ready to take that step. He'd figure a way out of this without resorting to violence. Of course, if it came to defending Carrie . . . For now he'd stick with the actions he'd already taken to avoid a would-be shooter.

Adam was at his computer, scanning through LexisNexis for a legal opinion to back up some research, when he felt the buzz of his cell phone in his pocket. This was the new one, the one with a number only Carrie knew.

Although Hartley and Evans provided Adam with his own office, they'd been careful to emphasize the firm's open door policy. The attorneys would close their doors only when client privacy required it. Otherwise, everyone's door was to remain open, to promote ease of interaction in the office. It was nice in principle, but Adam needed privacy for this call.

He slid the phone out of his pocket, turned his chair away from the doorway, and whispered, "Carrie?"

"Adam, why are you whispering?"

"I don't want anyone to hear this conversation." He lowered the phone to his lap, effectively hiding it behind the edge of his desk as Janice Evans walked by and gave him a friendly finger wave. He waited until she was past to raise the phone to his ear once more in time to hear Carrie say, "So that's what I've decided."

"I'm sorry. I had to put the phone down. One of the attorneys just walked by. What was that?"

There was no mistaking the exasperation in Carrie's voice. "Maybe we'd better talk another time."

"Carrie, I'm sorry. I can call you in a couple of hours from outside the office."

"By then I'll be up to my eyebrows in patients."

"How about tonight?"

An eternity passed before she replied. "Your motel. Seven o'clock. I'll take the same precautions I did last night. Gotta go now."

"I really—" Adam heard a click. He had no idea what Carrie wanted to say, and he'd have to wait another five hours to find out. But surely she wouldn't agree to a face-to-face meeting again if she wanted him out of her life. Or would she?

"You're sure a popular person."

Adam snapped out of his reverie to see Brittany standing in the doorway of his office, one hand poised on her hip. She probably didn't realize her pose was provocative. Adam figured she'd been practicing those mannerisms for so long they were automatic by now. Brittany was an attractive young redhead who acknowledged that her life's ambition was to latch onto a handsome lawyer with a great income and a bright future. Since, as far as she knew, Adam didn't fit that description, she'd been pleasant but not seductive to him—thank goodness.

"Why am I popular?" he asked.

"Someone called for you this morning. You were out at the time. They asked if you were usually the one who closed up the office. I told them 'sometimes.'"

Adam's heart raced, wondering if the hit would be in the parking lot this time. He'd have to figure out a way to avoid that. "Did they give a name? Say why they wanted to know?"

"Nope. Just got the information, thanked me, and hung up."

Adam shrugged. "Probably nothing, but thanks."

"Well, I thought you'd like a heads-up."

"Thanks." *I'll be watching for him . . . the same way you'd watch for a snake when you're in the woods.*

Brittany swung away and headed for the coffee machine.

Was this another way to let Adam know the stalker had found him? He'd heard that some killers got a perverse sort of pleasure out of letting their victims know they were about to die. Then again there could be a perfectly innocent explanation for the call. But Adam doubted it.

In Adam's mind there was no question of whether the stalker would strike again. The only unknown was when and where . . . and who would be harmed or killed in the process. Here at the office, he'd have to be constantly on his guard. But outside? What else could he do that might give him a bit of breathing room?

He'd moved to a motel, mainly so he could get a good night's sleep without worrying about another firebomb or bullet. He'd switched to a different vehicle, but he realized that the anonymity that gave him would be short-lived. How long would these advantages last? What was the reflex he studied in college biology? Fight or flight. Some animals did one or the other reflexively. Only man made a choice. But what was his?

He needed wisdom that was beyond his own power. So he did the thing that had become as natural to him as breathing, the thing that had kept him sane during the last two years. He bowed his head and prayed.

EIGHT

CARRIE CHECKED HER WATCH—HALF PAST FIVE. IF SHE DIDN'T drag her feet on her hospital rounds, she should be able to get home, relax in a hot bath for a bit, then get ready to see Adam. The more she thought about it, the more she agreed with her best friend's advice. How had Julie put it? There was risk to everything in life, even crossing the street. She had to consider not just the worst possible outcome, but the best.

Carrie didn't want to lose Adam—no matter what. She still loved him—that much was becoming increasingly clear to her—and whatever it took, she was going to help him find out who wanted to kill him, then neutralize them. Together they'd put a stop to it. The reward was worth the risk.

She quickened her pace through the hospital corridors and soon was in the surgical ICU at Mrs. Lambert's bedside. The figure lying there didn't resemble the woman Carrie had seen so many times in her office. There she had been alert, animated, happy to be alive. Now she lay still as a wax mannequin, unmoving and pale. A ventilator controlled her breathing. IV lines and monitor wires were everywhere. But she'd survived the surgery, and that was important.

A quick scan of the chart showed stable vital signs and initial lab values that were no cause for worry. Phil's operative note, although brief, indicated that the procedure went off without a hitch, with the patient tolerating the surgery as well as could be expected for her age and condition. There was no need for Carrie to add either orders or a progress note. Her patient was unresponsive, so conversation was neither necessary nor possible. Moving on to the waiting room to face her family, on the other hand, took a bit of willpower.

If Carrie had any doubt that she'd been replaced in the mind of Mrs. Lambert's family as the primary caregiver, the reception she received in the waiting area removed it. Mrs. Stinson was polite, yet more distant than she'd been earlier. Yes, Dr. Rushton had been by. No, there was nothing Carrie could do, no questions she could answer. Almost as an afterthought, Mrs. Stinson added, "We've talked it over, and we'd like Dr. Avery to take over Mother's care after she leaves the hospital. Dr. Rushton said that would be okay with you. I hope you don't mind?"

Carrie swallowed the retort that was on her lips. "Of course not. The records are already at the clinic, so it's just a matter of your making future appointments with Dr. Avery." She shook hands with the woman, although it was the last thing she wanted to do, then beat what she hoped was a dignified retreat.

As she stepped out of the elevator, Carrie's first thought,

born of habit, was to retrace her steps back to the clinic. But she needed to save time, so she turned in the opposite direction, intending to reach her car by exiting through the Emergency Room. The door there emptied into the common parking area close to where she'd left her car that morning. As she hurried through the ER, her thoughts turned to her meeting with Adam. He would probably—

"Dr. Markham." Doris, the ER charge nurse, bustled up to Carrie and touched her sleeve. "I know you're not on call, but we need your help."

Carrie fought the urge to pull away. She didn't want to get caught, not now. "I'm in sort of a hurry to leave."

"This should only take a minute," Doris said. "The EMTs just brought in an elderly black man who collapsed on the street downtown. Erin thought she'd seen you with him in the ER a few weeks ago."

Carrie looked at her watch. She really needed to go. Then again . . .

"The man's comatose," Doris said. "He has no ID. There's no one with him. We don't even know how to contact his family, so if you recognize him that would really help."

Carrie took a deep breath. "Where is he?"

In a few moments Carrie looked down at a familiar face. She knew Garvin Burnett, knew him well. Mr. Burnett's visits to her office had always turned into prolonged sessions where he talked and she listened. Apparently she was the only person who would sit still long enough to do that for him.

Mr. Burnett was in his early eighties. He had lived at Meadowbrook Acres for some years, clinging fiercely to his independence. He never called it a retirement home, never referred to it as anything but a place where the population all happened to be well up in years.

She'd asked him once about his family, but he shook his head. "No family. But I don't need anyone. I'm fine on my own." When she broached the subject of moving to a section in Meadowbrook where he could get help if he needed it, Burnett bristled. "When I can't take care of myself, that'll be the time to pull the plug on me."

Two EMTs stood beside Mr. Burnett's stretcher. One scribbled on a clipboard, the other adjusted the man's oxygen mask. Carrie turned to Doris, who had taken up station at the foot of the stretcher. "You were right. He is a patient of mine. His name is Garvin Burnett," she said. "How did he end up here?"

The first EMT spoke up. "Got a call that a man had been acting crazy, then collapsed on the sidewalk at Fourth and Mizell. Witnesses told us he had a convulsion right before we got there. Nobody knew him, nobody saw anything else."

Carrie gazed down at the unconscious man. An IV was running, oxygen flowed into a mask over Mr. Burnett's face. The monitor showed his blood pressure to be low, although not at shock levels. Quickly, she ran through the differential diagnosis. Then her memory dredged up the most important fact. The reason she'd seen Burnett in the Emergency Room previously was his diabetes. He had labile, type I diabetes, controlled with some difficulty by daily insulin injections.

Carrie turned to the lead EMT. "He's diabetic. When you picked him up, did you check his blood sugar with your meter?"

"Part of the routine. His blood glucose was so low it was almost off the chart. We gave him glucagon and followed it with 50 percent dextrose, but he never came around."

"Labs back yet?" Carrie asked.

Doris spoke up. "Ordered them stat when he hit the ER, but they aren't back yet. We catheterized him but there was hardly any urine in the bladder."

Carrie nodded. The bladder probably emptied with his convulsion—so much for a urine glucose and ketone. "Okay. My first thought was that his blood sugar plummeted—too much insulin, no food, whatever—and it caused his convulsion and loss of consciousness. But that should respond to the treatment he got from the EMTs. There has to be something else. Let's start looking."

John Sullivan, the ER physician on duty, entered the cubicle. "Carrie, thanks for looking in on him. If you want to give me his medical history, we can take it from here. I imagine you're in a hurry to leave."

Carrie thought about Adam. She should probably take a moment to call him. But before she could act on it, she glanced at the monitor displaying Burnett's vital signs, and warning bells went off in her head. "Thanks, John, but I think I'll stick around for a bit."

Although he was neurologically intact when she examined him initially, Burnett's pupils even then were the least bit sluggish in their response to light. Now his blood pressure was going up and his pulse was dropping. She watched his chest rise and fall, his respirations getting a bit ragged. Cushing's triad. Increased intracranial pressure.

"We need to get him to radiology for a stat MRI of his head," Carrie said to Doris.

Two hours later Mr. Burnett was in surgery, and the answers to the puzzle were clear. The elderly man had wandered away from Meadowbrook Acres, apparently suffered hypoglycemic shock, convulsed, and hit his head on the curb. Although his blood sugar and chemistries had righted themselves with the treatment rendered by the EMTs, the MRI Carrie ordered confirmed her clinical suspicion of a skull fracture with formation of a subdural hematoma—a collection of blood pressing on the brain.

The hospital social worker, working with the staff of Meadowbrook Acres, verified that Mr. Burnett had no family. Carrie and a neurosurgeon certified the operation as an emergency, their signatures on the operative permit substituting for that of Burnett or his next of kin. Tomorrow, if Burnett lived through the surgery, the hunt would begin for a facility to which he could eventually be transferred for long-term care. The sadness already in Carrie's heart because of Burnett's condition mounted as she realized this episode spelled the end to the proud man's independence.

It was fully dark when she finally walked out of the Emergency Room entrance and headed for her car. Her watch showed almost nine o'clock. As she climbed into the driver's seat, Carrie rummaged in her purse and retrieved her cell phone. She scanned the display, dreading what she'd see. Sure enough, there were five missed calls, all from what was shown as "Private Number." No matter what the display showed, she knew what the number represented and who the caller was. It was Adam, on his throwaway phone.

Adam left a message the first two times his call to Carrie's cell rolled over to voice mail. When each subsequent call did the same thing, he ended them without speaking. For what seemed like the hundredth time, he parted the blinds in his motel room and gazed out. The parking lot was as it had been just moments before when he'd last looked—dark, almost deserted.

He hoped Carrie hadn't gotten cold feet. Adam needed to talk with her. He wanted . . . no, he needed to see her.

Of course, Carrie might have changed her mind. She might be coming to tell him she never wanted to see him again. If that were the case, he'd leave Jameson and find another town, try to start life all over . . . again. But how many times could he do that? Coming to Jameson had turned out to be the best thing he'd done since he began his journey. He didn't want to leave. Adam was determined that the shooter couldn't make him do so—but Carrie might.

He checked the time—eight thirty. There was probably a logical explanation for why Carrie was so late. After all, she was a doctor, he told himself. Doctors got caught on emergencies, and she probably didn't have time to call. No reason to worry . . . yet.

But despite his rationalization, worry was exactly what Adam did. He loved Carrie, and the thought that she might have fallen prey to the gunman who'd been stalking him, once it popped into his head, was almost more than he could stand.

As darkness fell outside, Adam had kept the light off in the room. No real reason, he supposed, but somehow he felt better in the dark—safer, perhaps. He pressed the button on his digital watch to illuminate the numbers. Eight forty-eight.

Should he call again? No, he'd left two messages, and if she looked at her cell phone Carrie would see she'd had multiple missed calls from him. *Just trust her, Adam.*

He tried to still the panic rising in his chest.

———————————/\/\————————————

It was two hours past the time she'd told Adam she'd come to his motel room. Carrie wondered if he'd still be there. Might he have taken her failure to appear as an indication that she wanted him out of her life? Maybe he was at his apartment right now, packing, loading his car, about to drop out of sight again.

Carrie punched in the number of Adam's new cell phone. On the first ring an electronic voice repeated the phone number and invited her to leave a message. "Adam, it's Carrie. I'm on my way. I'll explain when I get there."

She wanted this to be a face-to-face conversation. Carrie needed to apologize, explain. She'd tell him what she'd told him before, but now it would carry an additional message— she loved him with all her heart, and she was ready to stand with him in his fight to uncover the identity of his attacker and bring him to justice.

Carrie started her car and pulled out of the hospital parking lot. She'd printed the directions to the Rancho Motel before her first visit, but that paper was at home. Check the address on her iPhone? No, that would waste time when she could be driving. She thought she could find it, and after a couple of false turns, she did.

She parked in the back of the units as before, sneaked through the circle of light spilling onto the Coke machine and ice dispenser, and walked along the front row of doors, looking for Adam's room. She thought it was number six, but she wasn't totally certain.

She turned and scanned the parking lot. A few cars were scattered about, but none that she recognized as the black Toyota rental she'd seen Adam driving. Carrie walked back and forth in front of the units, watching for a light in a room, maybe even someone peeking out from between drawn curtains. But the darkness was unbroken.

Carrie pulled her cell phone from her pocket and pressed Redial. Even if Adam didn't answer, she might hear the ring inside one of the rooms. But no sound reached her ears. Again, the call rolled to voice mail on the first ring. Either he was on the phone or had his phone turned off.

She scanned the area one more time. All the windows were dark. The parking slots in front of all the units in the row were empty. She drew the only conclusion she could— Adam was gone.

Where now? How about his apartment? Maybe he'd gone back there for more clothes, something he forgot.

She climbed into her car and started out for The Villas. Adam's apartment was in a complex of four-plexes occupied primarily by young urban professionals. She found it easily enough, but now, with her brain racing a mile a minute, all the numbers seemed to be hiding from her in the dark.

Carrie exited her car and looked around, her confidence boosted only slightly by the container of Mace in her shoulder bag. She unzipped the purse and let her right hand rest gently on the metal cylinder. The lights were on in the apartment, and from behind the door she could hear classical music playing softly. Carrie found the bell and pushed it. Faintly, the first notes of the Westminster chimes sounded inside.

There appeared to be no response at first—no sound of footsteps, no change in the music, no voices. She poised her finger over the bell, ready to push it again, when the peephole darkened. Carrie moved so that her face was directly in the field of view of the person inside. "Adam?" she almost whispered. Then the door opened.

A young man who looked barely out of high school stood in the doorway. He wore faded jeans and a blue T-shirt with DHS written on it. His feet were bare. "Yes?"

Who was this? Adam didn't have a roommate. "I . . . I must have the wrong apartment," Carrie said. "I'm sorry to disturb you."

"Who did you want?" Neither his voice nor his manner displayed any annoyance at having a stranger ring his bell. "I've only been here a few weeks, but I know a lot of the people in the units around me."

"Adam Davidson," Carrie said.

"Oh, you're one unit off." He smiled. "They all look alike in the dark, don't they?" The young man stepped onto the porch and pointed to the next four-plex. "This is 402. He's in 302."

Carrie thanked him and hurried away. She ignored the sidewalk and crossed the lawn directly to the next unit. The front window was dark. She heard no sounds inside. Had Adam already left? Or could he be at her house, waiting for her to finally appear? Carrie took a deep breath, squared her shoulders, and pushed the bell.

When there was no response, Carrie rang again . . . and again. Finally convinced that the unit was empty, she trudged back to her car. Where could he have gone? The next place to look was her house. Maybe he'd gone there, looking for her after she failed to keep their rendezvous.

By now she had the car moving, heading toward her house, driving almost by instinct. If he wasn't at her place, either he'd left town or his stalker had caught up with him. She could picture Adam, lying in some dark place, bleeding from a gunshot wound, his attacker standing over him smirking.

As she neared her house, she slowed and looked around the neighborhood. His car was nowhere to be seen. She parked in the driveway, checked all around the house, including the backyard. No Adam.

Should she stay here and wait for him to call? Logic told her that was wise, but her instincts cried out for her to do something . . . anything. She'd try the motel once more. Carrie shuddered as she drove, praying for safety for Adam . . . and for her. *God, keep him safe until I can find him. And when I do, I won't let him go again.*

NINE

ADAM LOOKED AT HIS CELL PHONE, WONDERING IF HE SHOULD TRY to call Carrie again. Then he noticed that the display was dark. He'd let his battery run down. He hurried to the parking lot and found the sack with the box his phone had come in. The first charger he dug out was the one for his car. Fair enough. He needed to be doing something anyway. He plugged in his phone and set it on the seat next to him. Then he started his pickup and began to drive toward Carrie's house.

In a few moments a tone from his cell phone got his attention. Someone was sending a text.

He pulled to the side of the road and looked at the phone. "Blocked Number" showed on the caller ID. He scanned the message and his mouth went dry. The words were typical texting, abbreviated but easily understood. He read them quickly at first, then again, more carefully. "DR MRKHM N ACCIDENT. N SRGRY NOW CENT HOSP. COME QUICK."

He didn't bother wondering who sent the message, what the circumstances were. Carrie had been in an accident and was in surgery at Centennial Hospital. He needed to get there quickly. Adam put the pickup in gear and sped through the night, leaning forward as though he could make the vehicle go faster by doing so.

Adam's phone lay on the seat beside him. A beep made him look at the display. Missed calls. Voice mail. He ignored them. They were probably from the ER, someone with more details about Carrie's condition. He didn't want to take the time to answer. Besides, it might be bad news. And he couldn't stand that right now.

The Rancho Motel was normally fifteen minutes away from Centennial Medical Center. Adam made it in nine. He skidded into the ER parking area and took the first open slot he found, one marked for "Patient Unloading."

He threw the selector into park, turned the key, and paused to whisper, "Please, God. Please let her be all right. I'll do anything—" He slammed the door of his vehicle and sprinted toward the ER's sliding glass doors. Suddenly, to his left, bright lights flared and the engine of a powerful vehicle roared. He glanced in that direction just before a white sedan barreled toward him. Reflexes carried Adam, rolling, to his right and back. He stopped when he was tucked under the front bumper of a car. The vehicle sheltering him rocked and a loud noise assaulted his ears as the pursuing car grazed the front fender just inches away.

Either this was a trap, or someone was taking advantage of Carrie's accident to catch him unaware. Adam rolled out and ran toward his pickup. At the end of the row, the white sedan skidded into a turn, ready to come back for another try at him.

In his pickup, he started the engine and rammed the gearshift into reverse, burning rubber as he backed out of the parking space. Adam turned the wheel, slammed the selector into drive, and stomped hard on the accelerator. He didn't take the time to fasten his seat belt. The sedan was right behind him now.

At the last minute, Adam slammed on the brakes and cut the steering wheel of the pickup sharply to the right. He skidded into one of the parking aisles, barely missing cars right and left. A glance in the rearview mirror showed a flash of white going down the main aisle he'd just vacated.

He had to get out of here. Where was the exit? Adam slowed and began turning randomly right, left, left again, right, until he spotted an arrow and the welcome word "Exit." He screamed out of the parking lot, turned onto the main street that fronted the hospital, and floored the accelerator.

After a number of twists and turns, during which Adam finally took the time to fasten his seat belt, he was in a residential neighborhood. He remembered this one. It was full of streets that dead-ended, interspersed with speed bumps to keep motorists from racing through. Unfortunately, that was what Adam had to do right now. He navigated by dead reckoning, enduring bump after bump, grateful for his vehicle's heavy-duty suspension.

There'd been no headlights behind him for several minutes now. He spotted a house that was dark, with a vacant driveway leading to a closed garage door. He stopped, backed into the drive, killed his lights and engine, and hunched low in his seat. The few streetlights in the subdivision were low-powered, yellowish ones, casting eerie shadows but making Adam almost invisible as he sat there.

He waited—one minute, two, five—and finally decided his attacker had given up the chase. When his pulse had slowed almost to normal, Adam started the engine and drove away, keeping his lights off until he was back on a main street. Two blocks away, he stopped the pickup in the parking lot of a strip mall. He was pretty sure this had been a trap, but what if Carrie had really been in an accident? Adam dialed her cell phone. After three rings, she answered, and relief washed over him.

"Carrie, where are you?"

"I'm in the parking lot of your motel. I've been looking for you everywhere, but I finally came back here. Where have you been? Why weren't you in the room?"

"The battery on my phone went dead, so I missed your call. While the phone was recharging, I got a text telling me you'd been in an accident. At the hospital parking lot, someone tried to run me down. When I managed to get back in the pickup, they tried to ram me from behind. I finally lost them, but the sequence of events started me thinking, and what I've decided isn't pretty."

"What do you mean?"

"First, there's no question that the killer knows you and I have been seeing each other. And that you're important to me—important enough for me to drop everything and rush to the hospital if I thought you were hurt."

"So he's been watching you longer than a few days," Carrie said.

"Right."

"What's next?" Carrie asked.

"We need to meet. Stay right where you are. But keep your car doors locked and the motor running. And if anything looks suspicious, get out of there."

"Adam, this is scary," Carrie said.

And getting scarier every minute. Adam ended the conversation and pulled out into traffic, his eyes flicking every few seconds to the rearview mirror. Suddenly every car behind him carried a potential murderer.

He wondered if he'd ever feel safe again.

Carrie was parked at the end of the row behind the Rancho Motel, not far from a red Dodge, the only other vehicle in sight. When she saw headlights approaching, she pressed the start button of her Prius and put her hand on the gearshift. Her foot hovered over the accelerator. A black pickup pulled in beside her, the door opened and closed, and Adam tapped on her window.

She unlocked the door, and Adam slid inside. His kiss was quick but heartfelt. The next words came out in an urgent hiss. "Lock the door again."

Carrie swallowed twice. Her heart was hammering. "Adam, you frightened me."

"Sorry, but we have to take precautions."

"Where's your car? I didn't see a black Toyota in the lot."

"I guess I didn't tell you. I changed it for that Ford pickup." He turned until he was facing her across the front seat of her car. "Why didn't you meet me here like we'd arranged?"

"I'm sorry, but I had an emergency I couldn't leave." She explained a bit about what happened.

Adam took almost no time to respond. "I understand." His face was hidden in the dark, but his words conveyed his feelings quite well. "You care about your patients. That's one of the things I love about you."

A car wheeled into the lot, and Adam stopped talking as it pulled into a space at the end of the row and turned off its lights. Carrie hunched her shoulders against an invisible bullet. She wondered if it was true a person never heard the shot that ended their life. She hoped she wasn't about to find out.

Two doors slammed, and a young couple joined hands and walked slowly to one of the unit doors. Beside her, Adam let out a big breath, and Carrie realized she'd been holding hers as well.

"We'd better get inside," Adam said.

Carrie's senses were on high alert as she scurried through the semidarkness beside Adam. She heaved a sigh and dropped into the room's only chair while he closed and locked the door.

Adam perched on the edge of the bed. "Here's the big question," he said. "How did the person who sent the text get the number of this new cell phone? No one knows it except you. I haven't even called my brother to give it to him."

Carrie's answer came without hesitation. "I haven't told anyone."

"I'll accept that," Adam said. "But what if someone had access to your cell phone? Whoever texted me, and I have to assume it was the killer, must have thought, 'This was the last number dialed on her cell phone.' It was a pretty good bet that your last call would have been to me. When would you have made that call? And who had access to your cell phone after that?"

When had she called him last? They'd talked while she was on her way back after lunch with Julie. Where had her phone been since then? "After we talked I put my phone in my pocket. Sometimes I get text messages or calls from the hospital."

"Was it there the rest of the afternoon?"

Carrie started to say yes, but then she stopped. "No. I was seeing that patient in the ER, and while I was bending over his gurney, my phone almost dropped out of my pocket. I gave it to the nurse to stow in a locker in the break room, along with my purse."

"Was it locked up?"

"It's supposed to be." She thought back and felt a chill down her spine. "When I went to pick up the purse, the locker was unlocked."

"So for an hour or two, anyone going through the ER could have had access to it."

"I can't believe someone on the ER staff would do this," Carrie said.

"Not just the ER staff. It could have been someone pretending to be a patient or family member. Almost anyone could have walked through the ER and slipped into that room. It would only take a matter of a minute or two to identify your purse and check the call log on your phone."

"Would they know where to look?" Carrie asked.

"I'll bet I could find the nurses' locker room inside three minutes," Adam said. "And even if the locker was secured, you can open those things with a bent paper clip." He shook his head. "No, the list of suspects is pretty large."

Carrie couldn't help it. She got up and walked to the window, where she peered through a slit in the blinds. The parking lot was dark and still, but there could be a killer out there somewhere—a killer who had marked Adam for death.

"Let's talk about what I have to do next," Adam said.

Carrie was still at the window with her back to Adam, so he couldn't see her face, but her next words, the very tone, left no doubt of her feelings. "Not just you—we. I'm with you on this. Neither of us is going to be safe until we identify the attacker and see that he's locked up."

"You know this could put you in danger," Adam said.

"I'm already in danger," Carrie said. She turned to face him. "Besides . . . I love you."

Hearing the words made Adam's heart sing. His happiness was fleeting, though, because he knew what he had to do. And it broke his heart.

"I love you too—more than I can say. And that just makes this harder."

"What do you mean?"

"Whoever the shooter is, the driving force behind him has got to be Charlie DeLuca. I could stumble around here for weeks trying to figure out the identity of the person trying to kill me yet never succeed. And the fact that the caller got my number from your phone . . ." He shuddered. "They're involving you in this entirely too much. I'm going to go directly to Charlie."

"I don't understand."

But Adam did. He was through running. He needed to go

out and meet the challenge head-on. He needed to confront Charlie DeLuca once and for all—not just for his own safety, but for Carrie's.

Adam walked across the room to the window, where Carrie had turned back to stare into the night. He embraced her from behind. They stood that way for a moment, then she turned and kissed him, a kiss that made his decision even more difficult. "I don't want to go into details," he said. "Even with you. I have to leave town. Let's leave it at that. If people ask, you can simply say, 'He left. I don't know where he's gone or when he'll be back.' That's the safest thing for you."

Carrie's expression melted Adam's heart: a frown, a hurt look, tears. He took her hands in his. "Just trust me," he said. "Give me two weeks. That's all I'm asking."

"Two weeks?"

"Maybe less, certainly no more than that. And I'll call you as often as I can." Adam unlocked the door. "Now, I want you to drive straight home. I'll follow you and make sure you get into your house safely."

The hurt in Carrie's voice was obvious. "If you love me, why can't you share your plans with me? Why won't you tell me?"

"When I went into the Witness Security Program, one of the marshalls took me aside and warned me about telling people my plans . . . even people I trust. 'What they don't know, they can't tell,' was how he put it. You're better off not knowing."

⎯⎯⎯⎯⎯⎯⎯⎯⎯⎯⎯⎯⎯⎯⎯⎯⎯⎯⎯⎯⎯⎯

Adam insisted on seeing Carrie safely inside her home. Not until he was sure there was no intruder hiding anywhere did he say, "Lock the doors. Keep the blinds and drapes closed. I'll sit out front until I'm sure you're settled."

Carrie did as he'd asked. When she heard his motor fire up, she moved to the window, pulled back the curtain, and watched Adam's pickup disappear around the corner. She still couldn't understand what had happened. She wanted to help him out of this mess. And now he was gone. She wanted to contribute, but how could she when he was leaving her behind? Carrie had never felt so powerless, so frustrated.

As his taillights faded into the darkness, she turned away from the front window and slumped into a chair in the living room. Carrie reached for the lamp beside her, then drew back her hand. No, she'd sit here in the dark. It was a better setting for her to ponder what might happen next.

Where was Adam going? Would he come back? *God knows.* She marveled at the truth of that off-hand thought. She had no idea where Adam was going or what he'd do when he got there. But God did. And all she could do was trust Him.

That was when the tears started—first a few at the corners of her eyes, then a trickle down her cheeks, and finally the floodgates opened, and sobs accompanied it all. Carrie buried her face in her hands and let the tears come. She cried for the loss of her husband. She cried for the danger to Adam. She cried for the relationship with her parents that disappeared when she became a Christian. And she cried for herself, for turning loose of the only Anchor in her life that ever really held her secure.

Her prayer was silent at first, then continued as a whisper, and finally ended with words that echoed through the empty room. "God, I've pushed You away. I've blamed You for things that You didn't cause. I've found fault when You didn't respond to my prayers the way I thought You should. I've tried to be self-sufficient, to do it all without You. And it doesn't work. Please show me what to do. Please help me find the way. And bring Adam back safely. Please. Please. Please."

TEN

DESPITE KNOWING THAT DAVE MIGHT TRY TO TALK HIM OUT OF HIS idea, Adam dialed his brother soon after arriving home that evening. The conversation went about as he expected, but in the end Dave agreed to help. "I'll accept that you won't tell me everything you have in mind, but give me a call after you're on the road. I don't want you to do anything foolish."

"Have I ever done anything without thinking it through?" Adam asked.

"Lots of times, but we won't go into that now," Dave said.

Adam spent a restless night, turning over facts and suppositions, looking for puzzle pieces to fit together and failing at every turn, wondering how best to handle things at the end of his journey.

The next morning he rolled out of bed when he smelled coffee brewing, grateful for his habit of setting the automatic coffeemaker each evening. He'd just poured his first cup when the doorbell rang. He looked at his watch. Who could it be at seven thirty in the morning? Surely last night's call hadn't produced results already. And if Carrie needed something, she'd phone. Whatever it was, he might as well meet it head-on.

At the door, he peeked through one of the pair of glass side panels and saw a tall, middle-aged man standing patiently on the tiny porch. His visitor wore a tan, western-cut suit, and his leathered face was topped by a straw Stetson. Adam couldn't see his feet, but he'd be willing to bet they were shod in boots. Whoever this man was, he was certainly a son of the Southwest.

Adam opened the door on the chain and said, "Yes? Can I help you?"

The man reached inside his coat, and Adam tensed. Maybe if he threw himself to the floor, the first shot would miss. He could slam the door shut, lock it, and sprint for the back door.

The stranger pulled out a leather badge wallet, flipped it open, and said, "Keith . . . or should I say, Adam? I'm Sam Westerman, U.S. Marshalls Service out of Fort Worth. Your brother, Dave, said you needed some help. He asked me to drop by and lend a hand."

Still wary, Adam said, "Sam, I hope you won't mind if I seem extra suspicious, but did my brother give you anything to tell me?"

"You mean, like your first car was a Ford, your first dog was a mongrel, and your first girlfriend was named Ann?"

Adam relaxed for the first time in days. He undid the security chain and opened the door. "Come in. The coffee's ready. Let's sit down and talk."

Adam had most of it worked out by the time he walked in the door of Hartley and Evans, LLP, the next morning. He tried to use bits and pieces of the truth as a foundation for his fiction. For instance, it was true that his parents were dead. It was true that he had one sibling, a brother. Even his destination wasn't total fiction. But beyond that, the story was a construction of half-truths and downright lies. Adam thought he could pull it off. And if things didn't play out as he'd planned, he'd simply have to wing it.

Brittany was at her desk, sipping from a steaming cup in her right hand, blowing on the nails of her left. A capped bottle of nail polish was centered on her desk.

"Change your mind about the color of your polish?" Adam asked, his smile leaving no doubt that he was joking.

"Just some repair work," Brittany said, frowning as she inspected her hands. "I was going to get an early start on these papers, but I chipped a nail. And since one of my prime duties is to dress up the place, I figured I should take care of that before things got too busy."

"Are you saying I don't bring class to the office?" Adam asked.

"You're okay, but you really should dress more like Mr. Hartley. One look at him, those custom-tailored suits and designer ties, and our clients know they've got a winner."

Adam took silent exception. All the external trappings in the world couldn't disguise Hartley's true self—he was a poorer-than-average lawyer reacting to a midlife crisis with a series of women. But there was no need to argue the point. "Speaking of the bosses, is either one of them in?"

Brittany put down her coffee and tested the nail. Satisfied that it was dry, she stowed the polish in a desk drawer and pointed down the hall. "Mr. Hartley's in court this morning. Mrs. Evans is in her office. She said she was going to work on a brief, and no one was to disturb her."

"I'll chance it," Adam said, and strode away.

In keeping with the office's policy, Janice Evans's door was open. She was bent over a law book, looking up from time to time to make notes on a yellow legal pad. Adam tapped on the jamb.

Evans didn't look up. "Unless the president or the chief justice wants me, I'm busy."

"Sorry, I'm neither. But I need to speak with you."

Evans frowned, then said, "Come on in. I know you well enough to be certain you wouldn't interrupt me if this weren't important." She leaned back and rested her hands on the open law book in front of her. "What's up?"

Adam adopted a properly somber expression. "I got a call last night from my brother."

"You told us you were an orphan and an only child."

"Yes, my parents are dead. And I told you I didn't have any siblings, because for all practical purposes, I don't. We've been estranged for the better part of ten years. But I got a call last night that my brother's in advanced-stage renal failure. The doctors say only a kidney transplant can save him. And since I'm his only living kin, they want to test me to see if I can be the donor."

"Can the testing be done here? Or in one of the large cities in the area? Dallas maybe?"

"Probably," Adam said, "but if the match is good, they want to do the surgery immediately. It's easier if I go there."

"Where is 'there'?"

Adam took a deep breath. "The surgery would be done at Duke University Medical Center, but right now my brother's at the Federal Medical Center in Butner, North Carolina."

Evans frowned. "Butner. That name's familiar. Why does it ring a bell?"

"Because there's also a Federal Prison in Butner. That's where my brother's serving thirty to life for murder." He waited what he considered a proper interval before adding, "That's why we're estranged."

Carrie exited her car on Wednesday morning, squared her shoulders, and marched across the parking lot toward the clinic entrance. Her task was simple, yet harder than anything she'd ever been asked to do. She knew that every time she told the story of Adam's departure, not only would it cause her real pain, but she'd also have to project an air of shame, as though his leaving represented a failure on her part.

As the glass doors into the clinic slid to the side with a soft *whoosh*, she prepared to face the day. She made it as far as her office without more interaction with clinic staff than perfunctory exchanges of "good morning." Carrie dropped her purse into her desk drawer, shrugged into a fresh white coat, and looked at the top of her desk. As always, her schedule was centered on the blotter—a busy day, but that was good. It might keep her mind off Adam.

Carrie shuffled through the reports, noted the phone

messages, and decided there was nothing there that couldn't wait. Technically, she had no patients in the hospital, but even though others had taken over their care, she wanted to drop by and see Mrs. Lambert and Mr. Burnett. Lila met her in the hall, but after a quick, and she hoped normal, greeting, Carrie hurried on.

Phil's note on Mrs. Lambert's chart was, as always, brief and to the point. "POD #1. Doing well." Post-op day one. Had it been less than twenty-four hours since Carrie stood in the ER and watched while Phil took over the care of her patient? She'd thought she was unhappy then. But since that time things had gone increasingly downhill in Carrie's life.

Mrs. Lambert's family wasn't in the waiting room—apparently they'd been sent home to get some rest.

Mr. Burnett was also in the surgical ICU, his condition satisfactory after his craniotomy last night. He hadn't regained consciousness. Carrie knew that when he did, the news of what lay ahead of him would be devastating to the old man. She made a courtesy note on his chart, asking the social worker to page her if she needed assistance from Carrie in getting him into a rehab facility.

It was pretty much a certainty that Mr. Burnett would be unable to go back to independent living. When he fell, the severe head injury changed his life forever. Carrie could identify with that. Her life had changed as well. And she had no idea what would happen as a result.

———————⎯⎯⎯⎯⎯⎯⎯⎯⎯⎯⎯⎯⎯⎯⎯⎯⎯⎯⎯⎯⎯

Some of it had been difficult for Adam, some easier than he'd imagined. Bruce Hartley came in shortly after lunch. Janice

Evans quickly buttonholed the senior partner and they disappeared into her office, where they remained, the door firmly closed, for an hour. When they emerged, Bruce stuck his head through Adam's door and said, "Can I see you in my office?" The tone was pleasant enough, but Adam knew that following Bruce was mandatory, not optional.

Once Adam was seated in Hartley's office, the lawyer leaned back and clasped his hands behind his head. "Janice explained your situation to me, and we're sympathetic. You've been an invaluable asset in the few months since you joined us. We recognize your need to go, but the office has to keep running."

Adam felt his gut tighten. He had to go, whether on good terms or bad, but his employers accepting his story would give credibility to his leaving town. "I—"

Hartley put up his hand to stop Adam. "As it happens, last week I interviewed a woman who recently moved to the area. She's an experienced paralegal, and she's looking for work. I called her, and she's agreed to take over your position on a temporary basis." He pursed his lips. "If you're back and able to resume work in two weeks, we'll give her a good recommendation and help her get a job elsewhere in Jameson. If you're not, then . . ." He let the words trail off and made a palms-up gesture, as though no one could blame him for the action that followed.

Adam shrugged. "I understand," he said. In two weeks, maybe less, he'd have done what he needed to do. Depending on what followed, he'd be back or it wouldn't matter.

After that it was simple. His apartment rent was paid for another three weeks. No need to forward his mail. He never got any. Adam exchanged his rental car for his newly repaired vehicle, tolerating the good-natured kidding about staying away from gunfire in the future. He cashed a check at his bank and told the teller, a notorious gossip, his story about a sick brother who needed one of his kidneys.

The next day his alarm went off at six a.m. A breakfast of buttered toast and coffee was almost more than his stomach could stand. By seven he was ready to go. He loaded two suitcases into the back of his little SUV, took one last look around the apartment, and walked out the back door, locking it after him. It was time for the most important trip of his life.

He plugged the GPS system he'd bought into the cigarette lighter and called up the destination he'd programmed into it the night before. In the cup holder of his Forester were a bottle of cold water and a travel mug of hot coffee. On the seat beside him, his prepaid cell phone lay next to a folded map of the United States. Adam slipped on a pair of sunglasses and pulled away from the curb in front of his apartment. A robotic voice warned him of a "left turn in two hundred feet." He eased the car into the left lane, clicked on his blinker, and tightened his grip on the wheel.

By now, Adam executed avoidance maneuvers like a pro, ignoring repeated demands from the GPS to "when possible, make a legal U-turn." When he was certain he wasn't being followed, he got back on track to his destination. He had no idea what was ahead. He wasn't even certain this was his best course of action. But it was the best he could do. Directions for the drive were coming from the GPS system, but Adam prayed that God would direct his actions.

The first question came at noon.

Carrie was sitting at her desk thumbing through a professional journal and munching on a sandwich Lila brought her from the food court. What was it? Tuna? Ham? It might as well be cardboard. But she had to eat.

She had gone through the same thing after John's death. She had no appetite. Food had no taste. Time dragged by, marked by painful memories of the past and fears of what the future might hold. Would Adam's departure prove to be as hard as John's death? Both almost killed her.

Phil Rushton, a white coat covering his dress shirt and muted tie, tapped on the frame of her open door. "Got a sec?"

Carrie washed down a bite of sandwich—it turned out to be grilled cheese—with a swallow of Diet Coke. She blotted her lips with a paper napkin. "Sure, come on in."

Phil eased into one of the chairs across the desk from Carrie. "You shouldn't gulp your food like that. You'll get an ulcer."

"I've been doing this since my second year of premed. If it hasn't burned a hole in my duodenum by now, I don't think it will." She laid aside the remains of her sandwich. "What's up?"

Phil sat down and crossed his legs, revealing navy over-the-calf socks above black wingtip shoes. "Just checking on how you're doing. I don't want you to burn yourself out. It seems that every time I look up, you're in the office or ER, even when you're not on call. You need some time away."

Carrie decided to say what she was thinking. "Phil, how is that different from what you do? Both of us spend a lot of time practicing our profession, but I guess that's our choice, isn't it?"

Phil nodded. "Touché. And I must admit that you're not burying yourself in your work as much since you began going out with Adam." He looked down at her hand. "I hadn't noticed until now. You're not wearing your ring anymore. Is something going on?"

Carrie was acutely aware of her bare left hand. "I don't want to discuss that." She looked straight at Phil. "Adam's left town. I don't know whether he's coming back or not."

"Why did he leave? Where has he gone?"

"I don't know," Carrie said. She reached up to dab at the corner of her eyes, a gesture that wasn't fake. Just the mention of Adam's departure was enough to bring her to the verge of tears.

Phil rose. "Well, I'm sorry to hear that. You know you're very special to everyone here. If there's anything I can do . . ." He let the words hang for a moment, then turned and left the room.

Carrie leaned back and tried to ignore the urge to cry. She replayed Adam's leaving once more. Was he in danger? Would he be back? Or had she lost the love of her life for yet a second time?

For reasons she couldn't fully explain, Carrie swiveled her chair and reached into the bookcase behind her desk to retrieve a dusty, leather-bound volume. She laid it on top of the journal she'd been reading and opened it to the front page. The ink was fading, but the words were still clear: "To Carrie. Let this be a lamp unto your feet, a light unto your path. Corrine Nichols."

Carrie hadn't thought of that sweet lady in years. But maybe the gift she'd given to a medical student just starting on her Christian pilgrimage was what Carrie needed right now as she struggled to hold on to the spark of faith that flickered within her. She let the book fall open and ran her finger down the pages, looking for direction in a life that was rapidly sinking into despair.

Adam squinted into the sun and reached into his pocket for his sunglasses. His journey took him eastward, and that meant each morning he had to drive into the sun. Couldn't be helped. The quicker he reached his destination, the quicker he could start his search for the puzzle piece he needed. He planned to use every available hour of daylight.

He'd spent last night in a Holiday Inn just west of the Texas-Arkansas border. Their "free buffet breakfast" of juice, Danish, and coffee was about all he could tolerate—not because it was so bad, but because the butterflies that took up residence in his stomach when he started the journey were still fluttering furiously.

Adam intended to call Carrie last night, but by the time he arrived at the motel, he was too tired to do anything but shower and fall into bed. He didn't want to try phoning her during the day—cell coverage was sometimes spotty where he was, and if he did get through, she was hard to reach between patients. Besides, leaving a message for her would be worse than no call at all. No, right now he'd concentrate on his driving. He'd phone her tonight for sure.

The eighteen-wheelers speeding eastward on Interstate 20 made using his cruise control impossible. Instead, Adam guided his little SUV along, speeding up and slowing down, passing and being passed, always careful to stay under the speed limit. The last thing he needed was a traffic stop.

As the driving became automatic, Adam let some of the thoughts he'd suppressed surface. Why had he thought this harebrained scheme would work anyway? The smart thing would have been to pack up and leave town for good, strike out for a new city and bury himself there. Leaving the relative security of the Witness Security Program had probably been a mistake. On the other hand, it had brought Carrie into his life. And for that, he was eternally grateful.

Would this work? Could he—? No matter. Adam had to set short-term goals and not look beyond them. First, leave Jameson. Make sure the story got out, one that was believable but left him an option to return. Then make this drive. When he reached his final destination, call Dave and ask for his help in the last stage of the plan. Despite the promise he'd made, Adam hadn't called Dave. Why? Because if he revealed the final step of this scheme too soon, he knew his brother would surely try to talk him out of it.

And if this failed? He didn't want to think about that possibility.

The plan had to work.

ELEVEN

CARRIE WAS IN HER KITCHEN, ABOUT TO MICROWAVE A TV DINNER, when her cell phone rang. Once she recognized the caller, all thoughts of food left her. She dropped into a chair and breathed a silent "thank You" to God.

"Adam, is that really you?"

"Yes. It's so good to hear your voice. You'll never know how much I miss you."

"Oh, but I do, because I miss you even more." Carrie had a million questions, but they all fled her brain like dandelion fluff in a strong wind. She asked the one that remained topmost in her thoughts. "Are you all right?"

"Fine. Just tired. But only a few more days to go."

"Where are you?"

"I'm just east of—" Static filled the line, then everything went quiet.

Carrie looked at her phone display. "Call failed." Was it the fault of her phone? No, she had good reception. The problem must be with Adam's phone. Maybe a battery, perhaps poor cell phone reception where he was. She waited a couple of minutes for him to call back. When he didn't, she dialed his number—first his regular cell phone, then the throwaway phone he'd bought—but all she got was a mechanical voice saying, "Your call cannot be completed."

At that moment, what Carrie wanted most was to throw something, to vent her frustration with cell phones, cell phone towers, cell phone service providers, and everyone associated with the mass communication industry. Instead, she took a deep breath. It had been good to hear his voice and know he was doing well. That would have to be enough for now.

Before she returned to her food preparation, she murmured a brief prayer. *God, please keep him safe. Bring him back. Please . . .*

"Lila, I'll be ready to start seeing patients in a few minutes." Carrie scanned the list of morning appointments. Nothing unusual there. She decided that she might have time to finish reading the medical journal article that had caught her eye yesterday.

She started digging through the stack on her desk, but before she could put her hands on the right one, her phone rang—not the primary number, but her back line. She didn't give that number out to a lot of people, but one of them was Adam. Maybe . . .

She lifted the receiver. "Hello?"

"Dr. Markham?"

The voice wasn't Adam's. It wasn't even a man calling. Disappointment replaced hope in Carrie's mind. "Yes. Who's this?"

"This is Doris, in the ER. Your patient, Mrs. Cartwright, is here, complaining of weakness, nausea, sweating. May be the flu—lot of that going around—but I thought I should give you a call. Do you want me to have the ER doctor look at her, or do you want to come over?"

The fact that Shelly Cartwright had come to the ER in the first place worried Carrie. The woman wasn't a complainer. Her husband was in Afghanistan. The couple had a three-year-old son, an unexpected blessing that came while they were in their late thirties, but as far as Carrie could tell, Shelly was doing a good job of handling the stress of being both mother and father during Todd's deployment. This must be something bad if it sent her to the ER.

"Dr. Markham?" Doris's voice carried a hint of impatience.

"I'll come over to see her. In the meantime, let's get some labs going." She rattled off the tests she needed, including a blood count to look for anemia and a blood sugar to check for low or high values. She added potassium, since a deficiency could contribute to weakness. "I'm on my way."

When Carrie pulled back the curtains around the ER cubicle, she was taken aback by what she saw. The woman on the gurney looked nothing like the vivacious brunette with whom Carrie spoke at church only a few weeks ago.

Doris moved to the other side of the gurney and reached down to pat Shelly's hand. The nurse might have a gruff exterior, but Carrie knew better.

"Shelly, what's wrong?" Carrie asked.

"I feel so silly being here, but I kept getting weaker and weaker."

The history Carrie obtained was of the fairly sudden onset of weakness, sweating, slight nausea. "When did this start?"

"About an hour . . . maybe an hour and a half ago."

"Did you do anything for it?"

"I lay down, drank some Coke, but nothing helped."

"Any pain?"

"No, nothing. I just felt like I was going to pass out . . . still do."

Carrie looked across the gurney and checked the monitor again. Blood pressure had dropped a bit, pulse had gotten a little faster in the past few minutes. Cardiogram complex on the monitor didn't look quite right—maybe hypokalemia?

"Labs back yet?" Carrie asked.

"Not yet," Doris said. "I'll see what's holding them up."

"Just a sec."

Doris turned, a puzzled look on her face.

"Let's hook her up and do a full EKG."

Without question, Doris grabbed the apparatus and began attaching the leads.

In a moment Carrie was looking at the paper strip spewing from the EKG machine. "That explains it."

"What?" Shelly asked.

Carrie held up the wide strip with the full EKG tracing. "You were hooked up to a cardiac monitor that only gives a partial picture of your heart's activity. This is a complete one, and it confirms my suspicion. You're having a heart attack."

"But I don't have chest pain," Shelly said in a "this can't be happening" tone.

"Almost half of women who have heart attacks don't have chest pain," Carrie said. "But we know what the problem is, and we'll take care of you."

And that's what they did. Oxygen. Aspirin under the tongue. Amiodarone. A beta-blocker. A call to the interventional radiologist, and soon Shelly was on her way to the X-ray suite for a coronary angiogram.

While Carrie waited for the results, she asked Doris if she knew who was caring for Shelly's son. "Sorry, I don't know. Why don't you ask the EMTs who brought her in. Rob and Bill are still here. They're on break in the cafeteria."

Carrie found the two EMTs in a corner, sipping coffee and swapping stories. She didn't make the connection between name and person until the one with his back to her turned, and she saw it was Rob Cole. This might be awkward. Well, she needed the information.

"Dr. Markham, come join us," Rob called.

Bill slapped Rob on the shoulder and grinned. "Yeah, I'm tired of this guy's company."

Carrie pulled up a chair, declined their offer of something to drink, and got right to the reason for her visit. "You guys did the pickup on Shelly Cartwright?"

"Yeah," Bill said. "She was having second thoughts about calling 911 when we started to load her onto the gurney, but she was pale, her blood pressure was a little low, and the neighbor who was with her insisted that she should be seen by a doctor."

"So a neighbor was there," Carrie said. "Do you know if she's taking care of Shelly's son?"

"That's right," Rob said. "The woman's sort of a grand-mother type, and I got the impression she does that a lot when the mother has to go somewhere and can't take her son."

Carrie pushed back her chair. "Thanks. I'll have the social worker make contact with her. We need to be certain the little boy's taken care of until his mom is released."

Carrie was a dozen steps away when she heard, "Dr. Markham?"

Carrie turned to find Rob behind her. "Yes?"

"I . . . I wonder if you'd like to have dinner with me while your boyfriend's gone. I've been on my own before, and it's no fun."

"Thanks anyway, Rob, but I'll be fine until Adam gets back."

She turned to walk away, but apparently Rob wasn't through. "So where did he go? How long is he going to be gone?"

"Rob, I'm sorry. I have to get back to my patient." She turned and hurried away before the young man could say anything else. *Can't he take no for an answer?*

Adam dropped his suitcases and flipped the switch to illuminate the bedside lamp of his motel room. After making sure the door was double locked, he closed the blinds and pulled the heavy drapes together. Then he slumped onto the bed.

He closed his eyes and wondered how Carrie was doing. It frustrated him when his cell service failed earlier today, but at least he'd been able to tell her he was all right. In a bit, he'd call from the landline in his room, and they could talk as long as they wanted.

It had been a disappointment, but not a surprise, when Carrie said she wasn't ready to take back his ring. He wished she were wearing it now. On the other hand, if he did what might be necessary to protect her from Charlie DeLuca, there was a very real possibility Adam wouldn't be able to keep a wedding date anytime soon.

Well, it was too late to turn back. He should reach his destination tomorrow. Now there was another call to make, one that was critical to his mission. He dialed Dave's cell number, but the call, like the one that preceded it earlier in the day, went unanswered. Adam had already left one message. No need to leave another. He'd try again later.

Adam's grumbling stomach reminded him that he hadn't eaten since lunch. No problem—he'd seen signs for several fast food places nearby. One of them would probably be open late. He'd get a burger and malt, then call Carrie. After that, a shower and a good night's sleep.

He started to get up, then fell back onto the pillow. He was exhausted. He'd rest for a few minutes, maybe half an hour. Then he could be up and running.

Adam heeled off his shoes, pulled the spread over him, turned off the bedside lamp, and closed his eyes. After what seemed like only a few minutes, the ring of the phone brought him awake. He grumbled as he sat up and turned on the lamp. Adam snatched his cell phone from the bedside table, but the display was dark. His sleep-clouded mind finally cleared enough for him to realize that the ring came from the room's telephone.

Who could be calling? No one knew he was here. If this was a wrong number . . . He had to clear his throat twice before he could rasp out, "Hello?"

"This is Jeremy at the front desk. We were wondering if you planned to spend another night with us."

Why was this nut calling? Adam had just checked in less than an hour ago. He glanced at his watch and was startled to see it was twelve o'clock. The phone cord barely stretched to allow Adam to pull aside the drapes and peek through the slatted blinds. When he looked out he did a double take. It wasn't midnight-dark. It was noontime-bright. He'd slept for almost fourteen hours!

"I'm sorry. Yes, my plans have changed. I'll be staying one more day."

"Very good, sir. Fortunately we can accommodate you without your having to move. Have a good day."

Adam checked the display on his cell phone. No missed calls, no messages. A growling stomach reminded him that his last meal had been twenty-four hours ago. A cup of coffee brewed in the room's pot, with all the sugar and creamer available, would have to hold him until he could make himself presentable. After twenty minutes, showered, clean-shaven, dressed in clean clothes, he headed for the Denny's near the motel.

An hour later Adam was back in his room, his hunger satisfied and his mind working at full throttle again. He microwaved the coffee that remained in the carafe and added sugar packets he'd picked up from the restaurant. Coffee in one hand, his cell phone in the other, he sat on the edge of his bed and punched in Dave's number.

What if his brother still didn't answer? What if he was undercover, or somewhere with no cell reception, or . . . After the fifth ring Adam was about to end the call when he heard, "Branson here."

"Dave, it's me."

"Keith?"

"You mean Adam."

"Sorry. I may never get the name right as long as you keep changing it." There was a slight pause. "Where are you? And whose phone are you using? The display on my cell shows private number."

"I'm at an Econolodge in Creedmore, North Carolina," Adam said. "Where are you?"

"I've been undercover down here along the Rio Grande. Had my cell phone off for a couple of days." Adam heard a door close. "That should give me a little privacy. Now, what are you doing in North Carolina? Did you change your mind about running away?"

"Actually, just the opposite." Adam swiveled around to lie back on the bed, propped against the headboard. "I know it sounds crazy, but I need to see Charlie DeLuca."

"You're right. It does sound crazy. But why?"

"I want to talk to Charlie face-to-face and try to convince him to call off his shooter."

"That's not going to work, Adam." Dave used the same tone he'd used years before when he gave sage older-brother advice. "And even if he says he'll do it, what makes you think he'll keep his word?"

"If that doesn't work, then I've got an offer I'm pretty sure he'll take."

"And that is . . . ?"

Adam drained the coffee in his cup, but the lump in his throat didn't move. "I'll make him a deal."

"What can you offer Charlie?"

"His freedom. If he'll call off whoever's been targeting Carrie and me, I'll contact the DA and recant my testimony. Without me, the case falls apart and he walks."

"That's insane," Dave said. "Not only would you be returning a criminal to society, you'd be admitting to perjury. In effect, you're offering to take Charlie's place in prison."

"I know." Adam thought once more about what was at stake here. "When there was someone trying to kill me, I was willing to take the heat. But Carrie's in it now. And I'll do anything to make her safe again . . . and I can't think of any other way to do it."

"So that's why you're there in . . . whatever the name is."

"Creedmore. Yes. The Butner Correctional Facility, where Charlie DeLuca's serving his sentence, is a fifteen-minute drive from where I am now. I need you to use your contacts in law enforcement to get me access to him. Can you do that?"

Dave's sigh came through loud and clear. "I'm still going to try to talk you out of this, you know. But yeah, give me half an hour to make some phone calls. Give me your number and I'll call you back."

It was actually closer to an hour before Dave called again. Adam spent the time pacing the floor, his mind running in circles, trying to take the rough edges off his scheme. His mind threw up objections, then tried to tear them down. At the end of an hour, there were still some holes he might have to patch on the fly.

"Yes?"

Dave sounded almost sad, but then again, that was to be expected, given the circumstances. "I have the information for you."

"Let me get a pencil."

"You won't need it. I think you can remember this," Dave said. "The good news is that you or anyone else can visit Charlie DeLuca any time. But there's bad news that goes with it."

TWELVE

A COUPLE OF US ARE GOING OUT FOR LUNCH TODAY," LILA SAID from the door of Carrie's office. "Want to go?"

A polite "No, thanks" was on Carrie's lips, but she held it back. Since Adam left, she'd lived her life like a hermit. Breakfast at home with the newspaper, lunch spent at her desk reading medical journals while munching on a sandwich one of the nurses brought from the hospital, a frozen dinner defrosted and eaten in front of the TV each evening. This was how she behaved after John died, except that sometimes she forgot completely about eating. Why not get out? "Sure. And I'll drive."

There were four of them in the group: Lila, two other clinic nurses, and Carrie. For the first few minutes in the car, Carrie's presence inhibited conversation somewhat, but before they reached the restaurant they'd chosen—a barbecue place nearby—the group was chatting freely.

The food was good, the company even better, and by the time they'd cleaned all the barbecue sauce off their fingertips and gone through the "I had that so I owe this" division of the bill, Carrie felt as though she'd had a respite from her worries.

As she drove back to the clinic, she looked in the rearview mirror and did a double take. There was a dark blue Ford Crown Victoria behind her. Ordinarily, this wouldn't have been a cause for concern, but Carrie recalled seeing it following her car on the way to the restaurant. She struggled to recall the maneuvers to confirm if she was being tailed. She sped up. The Ford stayed with her. She slowed down and changed lanes. The Ford did the same. She made random right and left turns until Lila asked, "Dr. Markham, are you okay? Do you want me to drive? This isn't the way to the clinic."

Carrie looked back and the Ford was nowhere in sight. Maybe it had just been a coincidence. "Sorry. I was thinking about something else." Lila gave her a worried look but said nothing.

When the women exited the car in the clinic parking lot, Carrie felt a familiar tingle between her shoulder blades. She huddled in the center of the group as they moved toward the clinic doors and didn't relax until she was safely inside. Carrie wasn't sure how much longer she could stand it.

Adam, hurry home. We have to bring this to an end.

———————————————— ⋀ ————————————————

Adam supposed he could drive to Chicago, but there was no need. Charlie DeLuca was there, but he wasn't going to listen to Adam . . . or anyone else.

Charlie DeLuca was buried in the family plot in one of the

nicer suburbs of metropolitan Chicago. He'd experienced a heart attack while in the Butner Federal Correctional Institution, and that was where DeLuca died before he could be moved elsewhere for treatment.

Adam trusted his brother but still felt he had to confirm the information. He dug out his laptop, logged on to the free WiFi the motel offered, and after a few minutes found a tiny obituary from one of the Chicago newspapers. Yes, Charlie DeLuca was dead.

Why hadn't Adam done such a computer search long ago? Why had he just learned the news now? After a moment's thought Adam recognized the reason: from the moment the jury returned a guilty verdict, he'd worked to put Charlie DeLuca out of his mind. The man had been given a sentence that should have guaranteed he'd die in prison, and that was exactly what he'd done.

Adam should have felt relief, but instead the news raised another problem for him to solve. If DeLuca's death occurred several months earlier, why was someone still trying to kill Adam? It made no sense. But the persistent attempts told him one thing—he had to stop the killer another way. And that sent him to a totally different plan, one that left him with mixed emotions at best.

In a few minutes Adam was packed and ready to leave. The desk clerk surprised him by deleting the charge for a second day. "You just missed check-out time by a couple of hours. The maids are still working, and we'll have that room rented by sundown."

He smiled at the unexpected gesture. "Thanks. If I'm back in North Carolina, I'll stay with you again."

As he headed west, back to Jameson, Adam began work on a new plan. This one might not work either, but it was the best he could do. It would require one slight side trip on his journey, but the timing seemed right. And the thought of what he'd do there caused his pulse to quicken. On the one hand, what he was about to do frightened him. On the other, if this worked, both Adam and Carrie might be out from under the shadow of his would-be killer once and for all. Then again, if his plan misfired, he could end up in prison.

Carrie rolled over and squinted at her bedside clock. If she was going to attend church today, she should get up. Of course, that was a big "if." A gentle rain was falling outside, making this a perfect day to pull the covers over her head and sleep in.

She wasn't on call this weekend. The only people who'd look for her at church today were those wanting to ask questions about Adam's absence. Those questions hadn't slowed this week, but she'd finally reached the point where she could answer them almost without conscious thought. *I don't know where he's gone. I don't know why he left. I don't know when he'll be back.* All true and all resulting in a tug at her heart that was almost physically painful.

Adam hadn't called again since their phone conversation was terminated by a tenuous cell phone connection. Carrie had been tempted to try calling him but wasn't sure if he'd have cell reception or if he'd be able to talk. No, she had to trust him. He said he'd stay in touch.

Carrie lay in bed and let the events of the past few weeks unreel in her mind. She felt as though she were on an emotional and spiritual roller coaster. She'd prayed for strength and courage but still felt weak and afraid. Now her lips moved silently. *God, I know You're in control of all things. But I can't help it . . . I'm scared.*

Carrie's prayer was interrupted by the insistent ring of her bedside phone. She'd just been wishing Adam would call back. Could this be him? Even though she knew she shouldn't get her hopes up, she answered the call with more than a little anticipation. "Dr. Markham."

"Carrie, this is Adam."

She flung the covers off, swung her feet over the side of the bed and slid them into slippers. "Adam, I'm so glad to hear from you. Where are you? Is everything all right? When—"

"Easy. I love you. I've missed you, more than I can say."

"I love you too. What—"

"Look, we have lots to talk about when I get back, but I wanted to call and let you know that I'm on my way to Jameson. I should be there late tonight. We can talk tomorrow."

"Are you okay?" Carrie asked.

"I'm fine. But the situation has changed. That's one of the things we need to discuss."

Carrie took in what seemed like half the air in the room, then let it out slowly. "Is . . . is this call safe? I didn't check the caller ID. Are you using—"

"No need for any of that. I realized I've been going about this the wrong way all along. I thought I could protect us both by hiding. I was wrong. And I'm tired of running away."

"What's changed?" she asked.

"I'll tell you when I get back. I had a plan to stop the threats on my life at the source, but now I see they're going to continue no matter what I might do. So I intend to face the would-be killer head on."

"So I don't have to say I don't know where you are?"

"If anyone asks, you can say I called, I've been out of town because of a family emergency, but I'm coming back now."

She ran fingers through her hair. "I don't understand."

Carrie heard the sound of a horn in the background. "Look, I've got to drive, and traffic's heavy on the Interstate," Adam said. "I have to make one stop, then I'm headed home. It will be really late when I get into town."

"I don't care how late it is. I want to see you tonight."

"Okay. I'll phone when I get near your house. I can park a couple of blocks away and go through the alleys, then knock on your back door."

"I thought you were through hiding."

"I am," Adam said. "But I'm not going to lead the person who's after me to your doorstep either. When I face him, I'll choose the place—and it won't be anywhere near you."

After the call ended, Carrie slipped into a robe and headed for the kitchen to have her first cup of coffee and throw together some breakfast.

A few minutes ago she'd been ready to blow off church. No more. Church was exactly where she wanted to be this morning.

———————— ∿ ————————

As he drove, Adam considered how Charlie DeLuca's death had changed things. He'd hoped he could get Charlie to call off the killer. But Charlie was dead, yet the attacks continued. It seemed to Adam his only remaining option was to identify the potential killer, whoever he was, and neutralize him.

Maybe Carrie had been right. Maybe it was time to go to the police. But what, exactly, could he tell them? *Someone shot at me. Oh, that report I filed about finding the bullet holes in my windshield? I lied about that. Sorry. And somebody threw a Molotov cocktail through a window of the building I was in. How do I know it was meant for me? I just do. But you have to believe me. Somebody even tried to run me over in the hospital parking lot. Did anyone see it? Well, no. But surely you know I'm telling the truth.*

No, this was his best option. It wasn't great, and he didn't really know if he could carry it off, but he didn't see an alternative. So now he needed to buy a gun.

As he rolled through East Texas, he kept an eye on the roadside signs, watching for the right exit. Finally he saw a billboard telling him where to turn for the First Monday Trade Days. Soon he was guiding his car through the streets of Canton, Texas, looking for a place to park. He found a lot where he traded five dollars for a slot into which he jammed his little Forester.

Since moving to Jameson, Adam had heard about First Monday Trade Days in Canton. The activity didn't actually take place on the first Monday of each month, but rather on the weekend before that day. Since today was the Sunday before the first Monday, Adam was in luck. Although he could undoubtedly find a flea market elsewhere this weekend, one that offered what he needed, he figured Canton would have the best selection.

Adam picked up a map and studied it. Among the stalls where people sold everything from antiques to woodcraft were a number selling guns. But where should he begin? The choices ranged from gun dealers displaying a big inventory in open-air stalls to individuals with a few guns and knives laid out on plain folding tables. While Adam was considering his choices he discovered another option, one the map didn't show.

Adam jumped when a man approached him and said in a low voice, "Looking to buy a handgun?" He shook his head and walked away. After a couple of these encounters, he realized this was the way some individuals operated, choosing to sell a few pistols on a roving basis rather than pay the rental for a fixed space and deal with the paperwork required of a licensed dealer.

Now that he was confronted with so many choices, Adam regretted his lack of preparation. He wanted a dependable handgun, small enough to be carried easily, effective at short range. But did he want a revolver, a semiautomatic, what? He had no idea.

His work in the law office had familiarized him with Texas's "concealed carry" laws. A carry permit would require that he pass a firearms training course. It would also require a more extensive computer background search than he was prepared to undergo. Adam Davidson wasn't a convicted felon, but then again the identity he'd set up for himself when he struck out on his own might not hold up to intense scrutiny. After a few conversations Adam decided his best course of action was to buy a gun from a private dealer, one who didn't fill out the sale form regular dealers used. He could worry about the matter of a carry permit later.

After a number of fruitless stops, he wandered up to a small table tended by an older man wearing a plaid shirt and jeans and lighting one cigarette off the butt of the previous one.

Adam looked through the man's small stock of pistols, but in the end threw up his hands in both disgust and perplexity. "I'm sorry. I just don't know."

"Why don't you tell me what you want, son?"

Why not? Adam gave him the story he'd developed as he went from stall to stall: his wife was being stalked by a former boyfriend, and he wanted a weapon to give her—small enough to carry in a pocket or purse but with adequate stopping power. He didn't mind a used pistol, so long as it was in good condition and reliable.

The man took the cigarette from his mouth long enough to point a nicotine-stained finger toward a small food stand about a hundred feet away. "See that tall, weather-beaten looking man at the table drinking coffee? That's the Colonel. See if he'll sell you that pistol his wife had."

Adam thanked the man and headed toward the food stand. It sounded a bit unusual, but the whole day had been unusual. Might as well give it a try.

The man at the table was leathery and lean. His white hair was the only indication of his age. He wore starched khakis, a white dress shirt open at the neck, and shined engineer's boots. He looked up when Adam approached. "Yes?"

"Sir, my name is Adam Davidson." Adam extended his hand, and the man took it in a grip that was firm without making it a contest of wills.

"Sam Johnson," the man replied. "Most people call me Colonel." He gestured to the other chair at the table. "What can I do for you?"

Adam eased into the chair, then told the same story he'd

given the last gun dealer. "He said to ask you if you'd sell me your wife's gun. I wasn't sure what he meant, but I figured it was worth walking a hundred feet to talk with you."

Johnson took a sip of coffee, leaned back, and ran his gaze over Adam's face. Then he tapped the shoebox at his elbow. "I come here every month and bring this. So far I haven't been able to do anything about it. I can't bring myself to be one of those guys who walks the grounds and asks perfect strangers, 'You want to buy a gun?' Guess I've been waiting for the right person. Maybe that's you."

Adam wasn't sure where this was going, but he was curious to know more about the man's story. "I take it there's something special about the gun."

"It was my wife's." Johnson lifted the lid of the box. "Ruger semiautomatic SR9C, mint condition." The man looked into the middle distance and smiled. "Right after we were married, I told her a woman alone—and she was alone a lot of the time when I was deployed—a woman alone needed to protect herself. I bought this. Taught her how to use it."

"You said it *was* your wife's."

"She died six months ago." The man looked away and blinked hard.

"I'm sorry for your loss," Adam said.

"I'm still getting rid of some things," Johnson said. "This is one of them." He shoved the box toward Adam.

The gun showed evidence of care. No scratches marred a black finish that shone with gun oil. The pistol was probably six inches long. Adam lifted it and found that it fit neatly in his hand.

"Weighs about a pound and a half," Johnson said. "It looks like a toy, but one pull of that trigger can leave a man just as dead as if he'd been shot with a .357 Magnum."

The enormity of the step he was taking wasn't lost on Adam. Then he thought of Carrie, and his resolve strengthened. "I guess it's what I need."

"That model can accept either of two magazines. This one's got the smaller one, ten rounds. That enough for you?"

"That will be fine," Adam said. "If ten rounds isn't enough, I might as well throw it at them."

"You're right about that." Johnson leaned back and crossed his legs. "If you don't mind my asking, do you know how to use one of these?"

Actually, Adam didn't, but he thought he could figure it out. "If you mean where's the safety, how do I eject the magazine, stuff like that—no. But I can learn. After that it's a matter of point and pull the trigger, isn't it?"

"Pretty much." Sam took the gun from Adam and spent a few minutes showing him the mechanics of the Ruger. Then he carefully replaced it in the box. "One word of warning. It's something everyone who carries a gun should know. Don't pull it out unless you're prepared to use it. And if you shoot, aim for the torso—the center of the mass. Trying to hit an arm or a leg? That's not going to happen." He paused, apparently considering his words. "I guess what I'm asking you is whether you're prepared to kill someone."

Adam had thought about this for the last hundred miles of his journey. He had his answer ready. "Yes, sir. I am."

"Son, I retired from the army as a bird colonel. Never got the star because I wouldn't play their games. In thirty years I learned to read people pretty well and pretty fast." Johnson uncrossed his legs and recrossed them the other way.

Adam wondered what was coming next. Was Johnson about to back out? There was no way he could have any idea what Adam had in mind, was there?

"I think you're a good man. I doubt that you'll be using this to hold up a convenience store." Johnson took another sip of coffee. "Whatever trouble makes you need this, I hope it helps." He shoved the shoebox toward Adam. "Three hundred cash, including a box of 9 millimeter ammo."

Adam unfolded three hundred dollar bills from his diminishing roll and laid them on the table. He rose and picked up the shoebox. "Thanks."

"As a good citizen, I should remind you that you're supposed to take the class and get a carry permit for that pistol." Johnson unfolded himself from the chair like a carpenter's rule. He stuck out his hand. "Good luck, son."

Adam started back toward his car. He'd need all the luck he could get.

Carrie let the noontime buzz of the café wash over her, providing an auditory backdrop for her deep thoughts. Her Coke sat forgotten, its bubbles rising slowly to the surface. The sight and smell of her Reuben sandwich failed to tempt her. She idly munched on a potato chip and replayed her morning in church.

As she expected, there'd been questions about Adam. After a couple of them she had the new answer down pat: *He had to leave town in a hurry because of a family emergency.*

That's why no one knew any details. He called me this morning. Things are okay now, and he'll be back tomorrow.

The sermon? Not the best she'd ever heard, but then again, how much attention had she paid? Her mind had been on Adam. She could hardly wait to see him. She was anxious to hear about his trip. The electronic strains of Beethoven's "Fifth Symphony" cut through the chatter and clatter around her. Carrie picked up her cell and saw that the caller was Lila.

"Dr. Markham, I'm so glad you picked up." Lila's voice was breathless, and Carrie had the impression the woman was on the verge of tears. This was a far cry from the breezy, self-assured nurse with whom she worked every day.

"Lila, what's wrong?"

"It's my mother. She's in the ER, and they've called Dr. Avery to see her. But I really wish you'd come."

Carrie stared at her plate as though the sandwich and chips had just materialized there, surprising her with their presence. She raised a hand and beckoned a passing waitress. Carrie handed over her VISA card, pointed to the plate, and mouthed, "To-go box." There was no way she could fail to respond to Lila's plea. "I'll have them cancel the call to Dr. Avery. What's the problem? I need to tell the ER doctor what I want done while I'm in transit."

The relief in Lila's voice was obvious. "Mom complained of a severe headache this morning. I keep a blood pressure cuff at home to check my own pressure, so I decided to take hers." Her voice broke and the panic returned. "It was two twenty over one fifteen!"

"That's high, but we can get it down. What has the ER doctor done so far?"

Lila's deep breath whistled in Carrie's ear. "They drew some blood, ran an EKG, which I haven't seen, and gave her IV labetalol."

"Beta-blocker. Good choice," Carrie said. The waitress appeared with the check, plus a to-go box and a Styrofoam cup for Carrie's drink. She nodded her thanks. "That's pretty standard. Is her pressure coming down?"

"Yes. Of course, I realize they want it to come down slowly. It's not that. It's what the ER doctor wants to do now."

"Go on." Carrie snugged the cell phone between her ear and shoulder while she added a tip and signed the check.

"He wants to admit her and start a workup for pheochromocytoma."

Pheochromocytoma, a benign tumor of the adrenal gland, was certainly one of the causes to be considered in cases of chronic hypertension, but its incidence was estimated at about one per one thousand cases. And this wasn't chronic. The last time Carrie examined Lila's mother, Mrs. James had mild elevation of her blood pressure—not enough to merit medication, but sufficient to get her a lecture on the need for weight loss. The reported blood pressure now was certainly high, but it was too soon to jump to a workup for pheochromocytoma.

A phrase Carrie had first learned in medical school popped into her mind. She smiled the first time she heard it, but the wisdom behind the words was soon evident to her. Now she frequently repeated the words to medical students when discussing a differential diagnosis: *When you hear hoof beats, think horses, not zebras.* She picked up her food. "You're right. I think that's a bit radical. I'll call the ER right now and be there in fifteen minutes."

Carrie disconnected the call, then pushed the speed-dial button for the ER as she strode out of the café to her car, her lunch in hand. When the nurse answered, she said, "This is Dr. Markham. My nurse, Lila, is there with her mother, Mrs. James. Please call Dr. Avery and tell him not to come out. She's my patient and I'm on my way to take care of the situation. And let the ER doctor know too." She'd give him the horses and zebras talk later—in private.

———————————— ⎍⎍ ————————————

Carrie pulled away from her parking spot, looked in her rear-view mirror, and went cold all over. A dark blue Ford Crown Victoria had dropped into traffic right behind her. Well, she didn't have time to do the deke and dodge thing now. She headed for the hospital. Let them follow her. There should be enough people around to discourage an attack when she arrived, and maybe she could get one of the security guards to walk her to her car when she left. Right now she had to forget about her own safety and focus on Lila's mother.

After she entered the ER, Carrie picked up Mrs. James's chart at the nurse's desk and did a bit of mental arithmetic. Almost an hour had elapsed since Jeff Clanton, the ER doctor, began treating Mrs. James. In that time the woman had received an initial IV dose of a beta-blocker, following which an IV drip delivered more of the drug in a controlled fashion.

The treatment seemed to be working. Carrie headed for the curtained cubicle where Lila's mother lay and saw Jeff Clanton on a course designed to intercept her. Since he was the ER doctor on duty, that might explain some of this. Jeff was a recent graduate of one of the lesser-known medical schools in the south. He'd applied to three family practice residencies but hadn't been accepted at any of them. That wasn't totally uncommon—competition was pretty fierce at some institutions. One told Jeff they'd take him next year, so he was working here both to make a living and get experience until that slot opened up. To this point, Carrie hadn't had any problems with his performance. Jeff seemed anxious to profit from his time in the ER, and this seemed like a chance for her to do a little mentoring.

"Blood pressure's coming down nicely," Carrie said to Jeff as the two doctors stood at Mrs. James's bedside. "What do you think caused the hypertension?"

The ER doctor looked embarrassed. He inclined his head toward the curtains surrounding the ER cubicle. "Uh, think we should step outside?"

"Not at all," Carrie said. "Mrs. James is a retired LVN, and her daughter, Lila, is my clinic nurse. They're used to hearing doctors discuss cases, and I think they need to hear this. Besides, I have a question I want to ask our patient, and I think her answer may surprise you."

"Okay." He cleared his throat. "She says her blood pressure's always been high, but she wasn't on any medication. I took that to mean that this was a sudden spike. To me, that suggested an adrenal tumor, so I asked Dr. Avery—" He paused and gave her an apologetic look. "I would have called you, but he's on call— Anyway, I suggested a pheochromocytoma workup."

Carrie clamped down on her back teeth. *Be cool. He's just out of med school.* "What's the first thing you think of when you encounter a patient with a sudden rise in blood pressure?"

"Several things. Eclampsia, of course—but she's not pregnant. Renal disease, but her BUN and creatinine came back normal. She drinks two cups of coffee a day, no energy drinks, no Cokes. And her only medication is a hormone preparation. That leaves something like an adrenal tumor suddenly becoming active. I know it's unusual, but I think we should rule it out."

Carrie nodded. Jeff was right so far, but there was another possibility, one Carrie herself might not have considered had she not encountered it a year or so before. She turned back to her patient. "Mrs. James, what medicines do you take?"

The woman thought about that for a few seconds. "Just my hormone pill, like he said."

"What other pills—not prescriptions, just pills—what others do you take? What did you take today?"

"Well, you told me I had to lose weight, so I went to the health food store on Friday and got a bottle of weight loss pills."

Carrie glanced at Lila, and she saw her nurse's expression change as the light dawned.

"And did you take one of those today?" Carrie asked.

"Actually, the first one didn't seem to have much effect, so I took two yesterday. This morning I decided to try three. I mean, they're natural, so I don't see how they could be bad for me." She turned to Lila. "I think they're in my purse."

Lila opened the satchel-like purse slung over her shoulder, rummaged for a minute, and extracted a white bottle with a purple and white label that read, "Bitter Orange."

Understanding lit up the younger doctor's face. "I should have asked about nonprescription drugs."

"You don't use the word 'drugs.' You don't say 'medication' or 'prescription.' You ask if they're taking any pills, whether they got them from the doctor or bought them over the counter. You ask what they took today—this day, not regularly."

He nodded. "I—"

"It's okay," Carrie said. "We'll talk about it later. Right now, let's titrate that blood pressure down to a safe level."

Almost two hours later Carrie was ready to leave the hospital. She'd arranged to admit Mrs. James overnight for observation in order to taper the dose of the beta-blocker medication and observe for any heart damage from the episode. Dr. Clanton had learned a valuable lesson about horses and zebras. And Lila couldn't thank Carrie enough for coming to the hospital when she wasn't on call.

"No problem," Carrie reassured her. And it wasn't. Her time in the ER certainly had been more productive and more satisfying than a Sunday afternoon nap.

Carrie almost forgot the blue Ford that followed her to the hospital—almost, but not totally. She found a security guard in the Emergency Room waiting area and approached him. "Would you mind walking me to my car?"

It was a strange request, since it was broad daylight, but the guard either was used to such appeals or was unusually patient. In either case, he rose, giving her neither a puzzled look nor furrowed brow, and accompanied Carrie to her car, one hand on his holstered weapon, his head moving from side to side as though expecting trouble. She wasn't sure if he really believed her or was putting on a show, but in either case she welcomed his presence.

At her car Carrie thanked the guard and prepared to climb in. But just before she slid behind the wheel, she scanned the parking lot and saw a tall man, wearing a Stetson, leaning against the fender of a blue car three rows ahead of her. He was dressed in a suit and tie, and his manner was anything but threatening. He smiled and began walking toward her.

Carrie looked around. The security guard was almost back to his post. She was about to start running toward safety when she heard a soft voice with a definite drawl say, "Dr. Markham?"

The stranger wasn't hurrying, but rather ambled along as though he had all the time in the world. She found herself rooted to the spot, wondering if a scream would get the guard's attention in time.

The man tipped his hat. "There hasn't been a good time to introduce myself," he said. He reached into his pocket and showed her a leather wallet with a badge inside it. "Sam Westerman, U.S. Marshalls Service. I was asked to keep an eye on you while your . . . er, your friend is out of town."

Carrie wasn't sure how she felt—grateful that Adam was trying, in his own way, to keep her safe or angry that he hadn't bothered to mention it to her. "Thank you. I appreciate it," she said.

After Westerman touched the brim of his hat and ambled away, Carrie climbed into her car. As she pulled into her driveway, Carrie waved to the blue Ford behind her. *Thanks, Mr. Westerman. Thanks, Adam.* She decided she wasn't angry. In a few hours she'd see Adam again. That was enough.

THIRTEEN

IT WAS ALMOST MIDNIGHT WHEN CARRIE HEARD THE TAP AT HER kitchen door. She'd been sitting at the table, a cold cup of coffee in front of her, for almost half an hour. She peeked through the curtains and saw Adam standing on the porch. Carrie opened the door and held out her arms. In a single gesture Adam embraced her and kicked the door shut behind him. Then he kissed her in a way that affirmed his love much more than words could.

"I'm so glad you're back, Carrie said.

"Me too. I've missed you," Adam said. He pointed to the coffee cup. "Is there more of that? I've been subsisting on some of the worst swill imaginable, using it to wash down stale service-station pastries."

In a moment they were settled at the kitchen table with fresh cups before them. Adam reached across to take Carrie's hand. "I have a lot to tell you."

"Such as why you left without telling me more than a bare minimum?" Carrie said. "We're in this together. I never felt so left out and helpless."

"I recognize that," Adam said. "But—"

"Speaking of not knowing, why didn't you tell me about Sam Westerman?"

Adam looked genuinely puzzled. "I didn't? It was on my list to cover in that first phone call." Then the light appeared to dawn. "Oh, that was when our cell phone connection fizzled. After that it must have slipped my mind."

Carrie sighed but squeezed his hand. "Never mind. Tell me about your trip. Where did you go? What did you do?"

"I decided to go to the prison where Charlie DeLuca was held, get in to see him some way or other, and see if I could reason with him. I'd beg him to call off his shooter. And if he wouldn't budge, I'd offer to recant my testimony if he'd promise to leave you alone."

"No!" The word seemed to jump out of Carrie's mouth. Tears threatened to spill from her eyes. "If you did that, you'd go to jail for perjury. I know you were willing to do it for me, but I can't let you."

"Don't worry. It's not going to happen. Charlie DeLuca's dead."

"And you had nothing to do with it?"

Adam shook his head. "No, he had a fatal heart attack about six months ago."

"Wait. If he's been dead for six months, and the last attack came less than two weeks ago, who's trying to kill you?" Carrie said.

"I asked myself the same question," Adam said. "I see two possibilities. Either the order to kill me didn't die with Charlie, or . . ."

"Or what," Carrie said.

"Or the attacks weren't aimed at me. Maybe you were the target."

"I don't—" Carrie stopped. She thought about the patients and families who, for one reason or another, bore a grudge against her. Perhaps Adam was right. "I need to think about that." She looked into his eyes. "Are you willing to go to the police now?"

"And tell them what? No, I'm going to do this myself. I have to make the shooter show himself. What I'd like to do is capture him, but I've got to be ready to defend myself."

"What do you mean?"

He leaned closer to her and lowered his voice. "I have a gun."

Carrie clutched his arm. "I've heard you say before that guns can get turned on their owners. Won't this get you shot?"

"We're already being shot at. I promise I'll only use it to protect myself, or to hold the shooter captive while we call the police."

The discussion went back and forth until eventually she said, "I give up. You're going to do what you want. But please be careful."

"Let's talk about it at dinner," Adam said.

Carrie agreed to meet him at a local steak house the next night. "In the meantime, please be careful."

Adam patted his pocket. "I've been careful for two years. Now I'm prepared."

In his car after breakfast, Adam thought about his next move. He'd called Bruce Hartley last night and related his prepared story, ending with his readiness to return to work.

Hartley seemed a bit taken aback by Adam's call. "Uh, I wasn't expecting to hear from you this soon. I mean, Janice and I need to talk. That is . . . Why don't you come in about ten tomorrow and we'll discuss it?"

Adam had plenty of time to run a couple of errands before meeting with Hartley. First he planned to stop at a store that sold police equipment. He was a civilian, but he figured they'd take his money as quickly as that of a member of the law enforcement community. He needed a holster for his pistol. He could wear one on his belt, concealed by a suit coat or a sports shirt with the tails out. Or he could get an ankle holster to keep the gun out of sight but readily accessible no matter what he wore. That might be an even better choice.

As he drove, Adam considered another problem—getting a concealed carry permit for the gun. It was legal in Texas to carry a handgun but only with a permit. Before the application could be submitted, the gun owner had to complete a mandated course of instruction. That was no problem. Adam was anxious to learn.

But signing up for a course and a carry permit would subject his identity to the scrutiny of a full background check by the Texas Department of Public Safety. With what Sam Johnson had told him, maybe he could just go to a gun range—better still, drive into the country with a box of shells and some empty cans. After all, Adam wasn't planning a lot of long-distance shooting. Simple as one, two, three: get close to the target, point the gun at the main body mass, pull the trigger. He was hoping he wouldn't be doing any shooting, that the threat of the gun would be enough if he came face-to-face with his attacker. But if it came down to it, he was prepared to use the pistol.

As Adam pulled to a stop outside the store, he felt the weight of the gun in his inside coat pocket. The holster would be a step in the right direction. Learning how to use the gun, practicing with it, would be another. After that, it was a matter of unmasking the would-be killer and bringing him to justice . . . whatever it took to do it.

Adam expected to be greeted by a barrage of questions when he walked in the door of Hartley and Evans. Instead, Brittany waved and smiled but continued her conversation with whomever was on the other end of the phone line. Bruce Hartley emerged from the break room with a mug of coffee, beckoned Adam to get his own cup, then disappeared into his office, leaving the door open.

When Adam was settled, Hartley sipped his coffee, leaned back in his chair, and propped one foot on the bottom drawer of his desk. "So you're back quicker than I expected. Did the surgery go okay?"

Adam adopted what he hoped was a properly somber countenance. "I was too late. When I got there, they told me my brother had gone downhill so far that he was no longer a candidate for a kidney transplant. After he saw me he told them to take him off dialysis—said he'd gotten right with God and was ready to go."

"That's tough, man."

"We had a good visit, and he told me good-bye."

"I guess you'll be going back for the funeral."

"No, he didn't want a memorial. He wanted his body cremated and the ashes scattered in some woods not far from the prison. The chaplain said he'd see to it."

Adam could almost see Hartley decide how quickly he could shift gears from sympathy to business. Apparently it didn't take long. "So let's talk about your position."

"You said you were going to hire a temp. How's that working out so far?"

Hartley half turned to stare out the window of his office. "She's worked out very well. Matter of fact, on Friday we offered her a permanent position."

"After a week?"

"She was doing a good job, and we couldn't afford to be short staffed."

Adam clamped his jaws shut to hold back the comments that jumped to mind. He took a deep breath. "So where does that leave me?"

"Janice and I talked before we hired Mary—that's her name, the new paralegal. We decided that if you came back, we'd offer you the same deal we offered Mary."

If I came back? I told them two weeks. "And that is . . ."

"Go to work as a temp, same salary as before. If things go well, and we see there's enough work to keep two people busy, we'll make it permanent. Otherwise we'll give you a good recommendation."

A punch in the gut couldn't have taken Adam's breath away more effectively. True, he'd only worked there less than a year, but in that time he'd come to look on himself as an important part of the practice. Part of his new plan included returning not just to Jameson but to his job, resuming his usual schedule, making himself visible to his assailant. And, of course, he needed the income.

Adam didn't see any choice. "I'll take it. Are my things still in my old office?"

Hartley had the grace to look embarrassed. "Mary moved in there, so we boxed up your stuff and moved it into the storage room next door to her. I'll get a desk and computer in there by tomorrow. You can start then."

Both men rose. Hartley's right hand moved, but he didn't extend it. Just as well. Adam threw him a curt nod. "I'll be in tomorrow."

In the reception area an attractive brunette turned away from Brittany's desk as Adam walked by. She smiled and held out her hand. "You must be Adam. I'm Mary."

Adam forced a smile and took the proffered hand. "Adam Davidson. Pleasure to meet you."

She held his hand a second or two longer, and he had a vague sense that she was flirting with him. "Likewise," she said.

Adam watched Mary walk away, presumably to her office— his old office, but he'd have to get used to thinking of it in new terms. After Mary was gone Adam looked at Brittany and raised his eyebrows.

Brittany whispered, "There's more to that story than you know."

The woman's voice carried a mixture of amazement and anger. "Dr. Markham, I can't believe you'd charge me for that visit." The middle-aged woman sat primly on the edge of the chair opposite Carrie Markham's desk.

Carrie looked at the door of her office, hoping the office manager or someone who could help her with this argument might appear. She knew she had no chance to change the woman's mind, but was determined to be calm as she tried to explain yet again. "Mrs. Freemont, you came to the clinic, told the receptionist it was an emergency because you were having a heart attack."

"Yes, but it wasn't a heart attack. And it didn't take you long to find that out."

"On the contrary. I left the patient I was seeing to examine you. I took a history. We ran an EKG and some lab tests and found—"

"I know. I'm overweight. I drink too much coffee. I ate some spicy food. It made acid come back up into my esoph . . . whatever that thing is between my throat and stomach. But the pain was really bad. I was afraid I was going to die. I thought it was a heart attack."

Carrie forced a smile. "And I'm glad it wasn't your heart. But, like the grocer and the dry cleaner, we have to charge for services rendered. Of course, if you're indigent . . ."

Mrs. Freemont puffed out her chest like a pouter pigeon. "I'm by no means indigent." She clutched her purse tightly, a purse Carrie recognized as a Dooney & Bourke, well beyond her own price range.

"I'm sure we can work out an arrangement for you to handle the balance of the bill left after your insurance paid."

Mrs. Freemont was shaking her head before Carrie could finish the sentence. "It's not the money. It's the principle."

Carrie had heard this argument before, from Mrs. Freemont and others like her, and she knew that answer was far from the truth. *No, it's the money.* "I'm sorry. If you wish, you can talk with the clinic administrator. But the matter is out of my hands."

As the woman huffed out of her office, Carrie reflected that if looks could kill, she'd be lifeless on her office floor from hateful glares directed at her by Rose Freemont, Calvin McDonald, and a few other patients. And that thought triggered another one . . . one that made her catch her breath. Maybe Adam's alternative theory hadn't been too far off the mark. Maybe she *was* the target.

———————————————∿———————————————

Carrie peered over her menu at Adam, who seemed engrossed in the dinner choices the restaurant offered. "They didn't hold your job? You were gone a week, and they replaced you?"

"Hartley—he's the senior partner—he made it sound like it was strictly a business decision, and maybe it was. The practice has been getting pretty busy. But what he told me before I left was they were going to arrange for Mary—that's the new paralegal—to work for a couple of weeks while I was gone. He said if she worked out and they saw there was enough work for two, after I got back they'd add her full-time."

"But they didn't wait. And they didn't just add her. They gave her your position and stuck you in some out-of-the-way office."

The waiter came and took their orders. After he padded away, Carrie said, "So that's it? It's a done deal?"

Adam paused with bread in one hand, a knife bearing a pat of butter in the other. "Brittany, the receptionist, told me there was more to the story. So I bought her lunch, and she gave me the real scoop."

Carrie wanted to ask more about Brittany but decided to let that go for now. She began making circles on the tabletop with the condensation from her water glass. "So what's the 'real scoop'?"

"First of all, Mary's a looker. Mid- to late thirties, dark hair, a figure—"

Carrie raised an eyebrow that dared him to go on with his description. "Okay, no need to draw me a picture."

Adam looked over Carrie's shoulder. "No picture, but if you want a real-life snapshot, find an excuse to look behind you. She just came in."

Carrie eased her napkin out of her lap, then bent to pick it up. She gave a quick glance. "Black sheath with a white jacket over it?"

"Mm-hmm."

"Didn't get a good look, but from what I saw, I think you're right."

Adam murmured, "You're about to get a better view. She's coming over." He stood. "Mary, good to see you."

Carrie had always considered herself reasonably attractive: a nice face framed by blond hair and highlighted by green eyes. But at that moment she felt outclassed. Mary had carefully styled, shoulder-length black hair. Her blue eyes sparkled.

Her teeth were as white and perfect as the simple pearl choker she wore.

And Mary's voice matched her looks—slightly husky, definitely sultry, every word carrying an implied invitation. "Adam, I thought it was you."

"Mary Delkus, this is Dr. Carrie Markham."

Carrie stayed seated but held out her hand. "Nice to meet you."

"My pleasure," Mary said. She glanced up and frowned. "Well, I see they're serving our dinner, so I'd better get back. Doctor, nice to meet you. Adam, see you tomorrow." She turned and wended her way to a table where an older man rose and pulled out her chair.

"Well, I have to agree. She's a knockout," Carrie said. "Should I know the man she's with? He looks familiar."

"Uh-huh. That's Bruce Hartley. According to our receptionist, Mary lost no time getting close to him. Brittany says the woman must be handling a bunch of confidential files, because she spends a lot of time in Hartley's office . . . with the door closed."

"What did the other partner—what's her name? Evans? What did Mrs. Evans have to say about all this?"

"That's what surprises me. Janice Evans is a very sharp woman. Frankly, I don't know how Hartley got her to agree to the move, but somehow he did."

Their salads arrived, and they spent a few moments eating. After a couple of minutes, Carrie paused with a forkful of lettuce halfway to her mouth. "Seeing Mary with Bruce Hartley, I guess I know now how she got your position."

"Oh, give her the benefit of the doubt. Maybe she really needed the job. And Hartley says she's good at her work."

Carrie laid her fork carefully on her salad plate. "Men! All a woman has to do is bat her eyes, and you think she's the most innocent flower in creation. Believe me, the female of the species can be much deadlier than the male, as somebody once said."

In a moment the waiter returned and replaced their salad plates with their entrees. After a few bites Carrie said, "Adam, since you told me how long Charlie DeLuca's been dead, I've been rethinking the possibility that the attacks are aimed at me. Maybe you're right."

Adam frowned at Carrie's words. "When I mentioned it, you didn't think much of that theory. What made you change your mind?"

"You mean other than the fact that the first two attacks came when we were together?" Carrie sipped from her water glass. "I realized that it's not so far-fetched that an angry patient might try to hurt me . . . even kill me."

"Did something happen to bring about this change?"

Carrie nodded. "I had a visit from a hateful old woman, a patient of mine. She came to the clinic last month with chest pain and demanded immediate attention because she was having a heart attack. I dropped what I was doing to check her over. We discovered that what she had was chest pain from acid reflux."

They stopped talking as the waiter cleared their plates. They passed on dessert, asked for coffee. When the waiter was gone, Adam leaned forward and took Carrie's hand. "So you'd think the woman would be grateful."

"Nope," Carrie said. "When I gave her the news, I also told her she needed to lose weight, avoid all her favorite foods— caffeine, carbohydrates, carbonation, and chocolate—and take the medicine I prescribed. That didn't sit well with her, so now she's up in arms because she got a bill for my services. I mean, no heart attack, why should I charge her?"

"That's ridiculous."

"Nope, she was really livid when she left. And she's not the only one. For instance, there are the patients like—well, there's this man who brought his wife to the ER with pain in her abdomen. He apparently thought it was indigestion, but it turned out to be a perforated ulcer. By the time she came in, she was in shock. I made the diagnosis and got a surgeon to see her immediately, but she died on the operating table. The man hasn't said as much, but judging from the way he looks at me every time our paths cross, I'm pretty sure he blames me for her death, and he's pretty angry."

"But—"

"Here's our coffee. Let's just drink it and relax," Carrie said. She looked across the restaurant and saw Mary returning her gaze. "We can talk about this later, but not in such a public place."

In a few minutes the waiter came by. "Would you like more coffee?"

Adam exchanged glances with Carrie. He was ready to go, and apparently, so was she. "I think we're ready for the check."

Outside, Adam took Carrie's arm and steered her away from her car. "Get in mine. We need to talk some more."

"No. Let's go in mine. I have somewhere in mind, and it's better if we're in my car."

Carrie led Adam to her silver Prius parked a little distance away from his Subaru. She motioned him toward the driver's side. "Want to drive?"

"No, it's your car. Go ahead and drive."

In a moment the car rolled out of the restaurant parking lot. Carrie took a right at the first intersection. "Let me ask you a question," she said. "Where would you say the safest place is for me to park right now?"

Adam thought about that. "The police station?"

"No," Carrie said. "How long would we be there before someone came out and checked to see if there was a problem? Try again."

"Your house?"

Carrie shook her head. "Not out front. Too dark and relatively isolated. And not in the garage. We'd be essentially trapped in the house."

"So I guess you mean . . ."

"Yep, the hospital."

Adam shivered a bit. "Not exactly a scene of happy memories for me," he said. "Remember, someone tried to run me down there."

"We'll be fine. If anyone sees my car tonight, it belongs to a doctor who's come back to the hospital." Carrie wheeled the Prius into the parking lot nearest the Emergency Room. She chose a dark corner at the front. To their right, grass stretched like a calm black sea. To their left were probably a dozen or more empty spaces before the next car in the row, a huge, silver Hummer. Adam figured it belonged to some doctor who was more concerned with appearances than ecology.

She moved a lever and pushed a button to turn off the engine. "Now this is simply a doctor's car in the hospital parking lot. And we should have some privacy."

Adam half turned in his seat to face Carrie. "You were going to explain why the attacks could have been aimed at you."

"I've already told you about two of my patients who seem to hate me—truly hate me. I could name a half dozen more. That happens to everyone, even a doctor. And one of these people could be going a little crazy about it."

"I'll accept that the drive-by shooting could have been aimed at you. The same could go for the firebomb at my office. But what about someone setting me up and trying to ram my car right here?"

"I thought about that," Carrie said. "Let me ask you. If I wanted to hurt you, hurt you deeply, what would I do: hurt you or hurt someone you loved?"

"I guess—"

Adam never finished the sentence. Suddenly the driver's side window exploded and Adam heard two sharp cracks separated by a couple of seconds. His first thought was of Carrie. In a single motion, he unlatched his seat belt, lunged across the intervening space, and pulled her toward him, covering her body with his. Before the echoes of the shots had died, Adam called out, "Carrie. Are you okay?" When there was no answer, he said, "Carrie! Speak to me!"

Adam eased up and peered through the remains of the

driver's side window. Nothing moved. No one was visible in the dark parking lot. His hand went to his ankle holster, but he left the gun there. First, check on Carrie.

He bent down and touched her shoulder. "You can get up now."

Adam shook Carrie, gently at first, then more vigorously, but there was no response. He touched her head and his fingers came away wet. He held his hand in front of his face, but it was too dark to see. Nevertheless, he was sure—his hand was wet with Carrie's blood.

FOURTEEN

ADAM WAS OUT HIS DOOR IN A SECOND. HE SPRINTED AROUND the car. If the shooter was still out there, Adam was making himself a target, but he didn't care. All that mattered was Carrie. He opened the driver's side door and unlatched the seat belt that still held her, folded sideways toward the passenger side. He scooped her into his arms and ran for the ER doors that beckoned in the darkness. They seemed a mile away, but he covered the ground as fast as he could. Between ragged breaths, he shouted, "Help! She's been shot. Somebody help!"

At what appeared to be a loading dock for the emergency vehicles, a younger man emerged from between two parked ambulances and jogged toward Adam.

"I thought I heard gunshots. What's going on?" he called as he closed the gap between them.

Adam gulped air. "She's been shot," he said. "Help me get her inside."

As they approached the double glass doors, light-spill from inside showed Adam what his fingers had already told him: Carrie's face was covered with blood.

As soon as they were inside, the other man called to the woman behind the desk, "We need help. Stat. Dr. Markham's been shot!"

After that, things went almost too quickly for Adam to follow. Two men in hospital scrubs wheeled a gurney into the waiting room, took Carrie from Adam's arms, and gently laid her on the stretcher. A third man, wearing a navy golf shirt and dark slacks, charged through the outer doors, took in the scene, and went into action. Even without a white coat, his demeanor screamed, "I'm a doctor."

The doctor bent over Carrie. "She's breathing." He pried her eyelids apart. "Pupils equal." He put his fingers on her wrist and nodded. "Pulse is steady and firm." He cocked his head toward the doors. "Let's get her inside."

Adam started after them, but the doctor stopped him with a single shake of the head. "Get her signed in. After that the police are going to want to talk to you. If you wait out here, I'll let you know her condition as soon as I can."

The man who had helped him get Carrie inside was still standing by Adam. He touched him lightly on the shoulder. "Are you going to be all right?"

"I'm not sure. I'm more worried about Carrie . . . Dr. Markham."

"The doctor who took her into the ER is Dr. Rushton. He's a cardiac surgeon, not a neurosurgeon, but he's one of the senior staff. Believe me, he'll see that she gets the best of care."

Adam took in a big breath. "Thanks for your help."

"I'm a paramedic." He shrugged. "It's what I do." The man exchanged a few more words with Adam, then slipped out the double doors and was gone.

Carrie's first thought was that she must have overslept. She didn't recall hearing the alarm, and she wasn't sure what day it was, but there was a sense that she needed to get up, get out of bed right away. She'd be late to work.

She opened her eyes, blinked twice to clear the haze that clouded her vision, and discovered she wasn't in her bed. This wasn't even her room. Carrie turned a fraction to the right, but stopped as little men with hammers began a percussion concert inside her head.

"So you're awake."

The voice was familiar, even if the setting wasn't. Carrie cut her eyes to the right while keeping her head still and got a glimpse of Adam leaning over the rail on the side of her bed. In the background she heard phones ring, conversations in hushed tones, the squeak of rubber soles on waxed tile. She sniffed. Yes, there it was, faint in the background—a familiar, antiseptic scent. She was in a hospital.

"Adam—" She tried to clear her throat. "Adam," she croaked once more.

"Here." He ladled a spoonful of ice chips into her mouth. "Suck on these. The doctor says if you tolerate them, I can give you a few sips of water."

Doctor? She sucked on the ice, swallowed, and tried again. "How did I get here? The last thing I recall, we were sitting in my car in the hospital parking lot."

"Maybe I can help you remember."

Another familiar voice, one that seemed less out of place. Carrie managed to turn her head fractionally until she could see Phil Rushton standing beside Adam. "Phil, what's going on?"

This Phil was nothing like the cool, calm cardiac surgeon she knew. His eyes were red-rimmed. Faint stubble marked his face. He looked as though he'd been on an all-night bender. "You've been here a little less than six hours. He—" He nodded to indicate Adam. "He carried you into the ER about nine last night. You'd been shot."

Carrie did a quick mental inventory. Nothing hurt other than her head. She wiggled her hands and feet. "Shot! Where? How?"

Phil frowned, obviously unhappy at the memories of the event. "You were in your car in the parking lot when a gunshot through the driver's side window struck you in the head. The bullet plowed a furrow in your scalp. Of course, the wound bled profusely, as scalp injuries do."

"Did I have surgery?"

"No, you were lucky. The bullet followed the contour of the skull without entering it. It gave you a concussion, but nothing worse. Nothing that should cause lasting damage."

Carrie moved her left hand toward her head but stopped when she felt the tug of an IV line. She inched her right hand upward and felt a bandage on her head. "Did you . . . did you have to—?"

Phil managed a smile. "No, we didn't shave any of your hair, although the bullet burned a crease up there. I think you can cover it when you style your hair."

"Is her memory loss a problem?" Adam asked.

"No. Retrograde amnesia is common after a concussion. Hers seems to involve a short time span, and that's good. Sometimes the memory comes back, but even if it doesn't, it's probably no major loss. Otherwise, Carrie's neurologically intact."

Carrie turned her head a bit more, ignoring the pain now. She looked at both men—she wanted to see their faces when she got her answer. "Do the police know who did it?"

"No," Adam said. "I told them we were sitting in the parking lot talking when someone took a shot at the car."

Phil spread his hands. "Why would someone do that?"

"I have no idea, Phil," Carrie said. She wasn't about to blow Adam's cover at this point. If the incident strengthened Phil's suspicions that she was involved in something bad, so be it. Meanwhile, she moved to the question that was most important to her right now. "So when can I get out of here? When can I go back to work?"

"We want to watch you for another day to make sure there's no late intracranial bleeding," Phil said. "Then you should take a couple of days off to recover from the shock of all this."

"I don't need a couple of days off," Carrie said. She leaned forward as if she were about to get up. "And I want to leave now. I'm a doctor. I know what to watch for. Can I talk with my neurosurgeon?"

"You don't have one. I took charge of the case myself."

Carrie frowned. "I guess I owe you my thanks—but why you? Why not get Dickerman or Neece to look in on me?"

Phil had the grace to blush. "I was headed for the ER when you were brought in. My first reaction, of course, was to take charge. By the time we knew you were stable, I saw no need to call in a neurosurgeon. I'm not totally incompetent, you know."

"No, Phil. I trust you." Carrie relaxed back onto the pillow as wooziness threatened to overcome her. "And I think I was a bit premature in saying I want to go home. Maybe I'd better rest." She managed a smile. "Thanks, both of you."

Adam said, "You're welcome. And don't forget the guy who helped me get you from the car to the ER. He said he was a paramedic. His name was . . ." He paused, apparently searching his memory. Then his face brightened. "Rob Cole."

The rattle of cart wheels and the clatter of dishes roused Adam. He stretched, feeling as though someone had put every bone in his body into a vise before twisting the handle as far as it would go. He opened his eyes, squinted, then looked at his watch. Six a.m.

Carrie had finally dropped off to sleep less than three hours ago. Adam mounted guard from a chair in her room, rousing with every noise. He intended to keep Carrie safe, no matter what it took. He didn't think the potential killer was still in the hospital, but there was no way to know. Unconsciously his hand reached to his ankle, where, through the cloth of his pants, he felt the comforting presence of his pistol.

A light tap at the door preceded the entrance of an older woman. She wore dark blue hospital scrubs, partially covered by a red-and-blue print jacket. "Good morning, Dr. Markham."

Carrie came awake slowly. "I guess I'd forgotten that patients are awakened this early."

The nurse's smile never wavered. "Some of us have been up all night. But I'm glad you got some rest."

The woman, whose nameplate read "Grace," went through a routine Adam had heard Carrie call "vital signs." She helped her patient slide toward the top of the bed, pushed a button that raised her to a sitting position, and said, "Ready for some breakfast? Dr. Rushton said you could have a general diet if you wanted it."

Carrie started to nod, stopped abruptly, and flinched. She said in a soft voice, "Yes, please. Especially coffee."

"Coming right up," Grace said over her shoulder.

Adam looked into Carrie's eyes. They were bloodshot, with dark circles beneath them, and he thought he'd never seen any that were more beautiful. He shuddered as he realized how close she'd come to death last night.

"Have you been here all night?" Carrie asked.

Adam nodded, but didn't speak.

"You don't have to sit here and guard me."

"I'm not about to leave," he said.

"This wasn't your fault," Carrie said.

"I still think—"

"Don't think. Neither of us could have prevented this. The shooter missed, and I'm going to be okay, except for a scar on my scalp."

The conversation paused while a dietary worker served Carrie's breakfast tray. When she'd gone, Carrie said, "I'm not sure how much of this I'm going to eat, but I don't want to feed you leftovers. Why don't you go down to the cafeteria and get a hot breakfast?"

Adam was already shaking his head. "I'd rather stay here."

"Do you think he might make a try for me while I'm here in the hospital?"

Adam didn't have to ask who she meant. "I don't think so," he said, "but I'd rather not take any chances."

"Well, at least go to the nurse's station and let them get you a cup of coffee."

Adam finally agreed, and in five minutes he was back in Carrie's room, Styrofoam cup in hand.

He raised his cup in a toast. "To better days."

She nodded and took a sip from her cup.

"I'm so sorry," he said. "I wish the bullet had hit me instead. I'd give anything to spare you."

"I love you for saying that." She swallowed a bite of toast and washed it down with coffee. "But I'll say it again: this is not your fault. Besides, we don't really know who the bullets were intended for."

"True, they could have been meant for either of us . . . but they almost killed you."

Carrie settled her coffee cup onto the tray and pushed away the wheeled table that held her food. "I don't think I'm hungry anymore."

Adam lowered the head of Carrie's bed to a more comfortable position. "Do you want me to go?"

Carrie hesitated so long Adam thought his heart would stop. Then, in a tiny voice, she said, "Stay. Please."

Adam felt his heart start beating. He could breathe again. "I was hoping you'd say that. And I hope I can bring this thing to a close soon. I want us to begin living our lives again without looking over our shoulders."

Carrie tried to hitch herself upward on the bed. Adam was

on his feet in an instant, tenderly helping her. As she leaned back on her pillow, she said, "What did the police say when you talked with them last night?"

"When the policeman taking my statement found out my name—and I couldn't think of a way to lie myself out of it—he ran it through his computer. When it spit out the information that I reported shots through my windshield not long ago, followed by having a Molotov cocktail thrown through the window of the building I was in, he got a lot more serious with his questions. I kept insisting that both episodes were probably just malicious mischief. Finally, after he'd pretty well pumped me dry, I followed him around as he checked the shooting scene."

"Did they dig out the bullets like they did from your car?"

Adam shook his head. "Nope. The bullets went all the way through both the driver's side and passenger side windows. They're somewhere out in the field that borders the parking lot, and good luck finding them."

Carrie lapsed into silence. Adam saw her eyes close, and he used the opportunity to slip out of the room and get another cup of coffee. When he came back, she was snoring gently. He eased into his chair, leaned back, and tried to recreate the shooting scene, focusing on where the shooter was.

The Prius was in the farthest corner of the lot, with probably a dozen empty parking spaces to the left, the direction from which the shot was fired. The shooter probably hid behind the nearest vehicle, a Hummer. Call it a hundred feet.

Adam was no expert on handguns, but he figured their effective accurate range was nowhere near a hundred feet. So this was more likely a long gun, a rifle of some kind.

That led him to two conclusions. The first was that it made

no difference whether the police compared the bullets fired at him in front of the theater to those fired in the hospital parking lot. Two different weapons were used. In the first attack someone drove slowly by and fired a handgun out an open passenger window. Adam had seen it. The second attack came from farther away, and he was willing to bet the shooter used a rifle.

The second conclusion opened up a whole new train of thought. If the shots came from behind the Hummer, how did the attacker get away? There'd been no squeal of tires, no headlights moving in the parking lot.

Where was the rifle? Surely the police would have found it, but they'd said nothing to that effect. Maybe the shooter stowed the rifle in the trunk of his vehicle, then escaped into the hospital. Or perhaps the person ducked into his car and simply waited until Adam was inside the building before driving away.

Adam's focus had been on Carrie, not suspicious persons in the area. The shooter could have been anyone he'd encountered last night, or someone he hadn't even seen.

Carrie stirred, and Adam eased to her bedside. She opened her eyes and blinked a few times. "I'm here," he said. "Nothing to worry about. I'm here."

As Adam stepped off the elevator, the smell of food from the cafeteria reminded him that his last meal had been almost eighteen hours ago. The coffee this morning helped, but why not have a quick lunch? No, he didn't want to take the time. The charge nurse promised to keep an eye on Carrie's room while he was gone, but Adam still hated to be away for very long. He had things to do, and he needed to hurry.

Adam checked his watch and decided he'd better call the office first. He stepped outside to use his cell phone. Brittany answered and put him right through to Janice Evans. He explained what had happened and told her that although he planned to stay at the hospital with Carrie today, he'd be at work the next morning. She told him to call if things changed.

While he was outside the hospital, Adam decided to look at the scene of last night's shooting. Carrie's Prius was where he'd left it, surrounded now by other cars. The policeman told Adam last night that he could remove the yellow crime scene tape and move the car this morning. He would have done so except that when he retrieved Carrie's purse, he'd locked the car and dropped the key into it. The purse—and key—were in a closet in her room. So the Prius would stay there for a bit longer.

The driver's side window was partially shattered, and glass fragments dotted the front seat. The passenger side window showed damage as well. The grassy area beyond the car was quiet now. He pictured figures there last night or early this morning, combing the area with metal detectors to look for the expended slugs, occasionally stooping to pick up something, then discarding bottle caps, coins, and other objects that made the instruments whine. Good luck finding that particular needle in this haystack.

He was certain the police had already searched for ejected shell casings as well, but Adam wouldn't be satisfied until he carried out a search of his own. He turned and made his way back toward the ER doors. The Hummer was still there—at least, he thought it was the same one. It was in what seemed to be the right place, and the windshield and back window were covered with dew from overnight. He stood behind the left rear fender of the vehicle, the position from which he figured the shots were fired.

Adam looked around but saw nothing but a few bits of trash. He dropped into a push-up position and peered beneath the Hummer. No, nothing under there except a small puddle of grease near the right front wheel—maybe a bad seal on an axle boot. But that wasn't what Adam was hunting.

He wasn't a hunter. Adam had never fired a rifle in his life. But somewhere in the deep recesses of his mind was a picture, probably from a movie or something, showing a hunter firing a rifle, working the bolt, and shells ejecting to the right side. So he was looking in the wrong place.

He returned to his position behind the left rear fender of the Hummer, faced Carrie's car, and scanned the area to his right. Nothing there. He moved across the aisle, got on his hands and knees, and searched the area under the Hyundai sedan parked there. Still nothing. Finally he reached under the car and felt beneath the rear tires. There his patience was rewarded. His fingertips brushed a small object wedged beneath the edge of the right rear tire of the car. He started to pick it up, then thought better of it. If there were fingerprints, he should preserve them. He used a pen to tease out the shell, then pulled his handkerchief from his hip pocket and picked up the tiny brass casing, then twisted the cloth to make a small bundle that he stowed in his pants pocket.

He might have smeared any fingerprints on the casing when he picked it up. Even if he hadn't, how could he get it checked? Adam still couldn't wrap his head around asking the police for help. There'd be too much explaining to do. Maybe he'd call Dave.

Adam turned and trudged back toward the hospital. At least he was doing something. And, if the opportunity presented itself, he'd do more. He felt the assuring weight of the pistol in its ankle holster strapped to his right leg. He might have been passive for the past two years, but now he was ready to actively defend himself—and Carrie.

FIFTEEN

CARRIE SENSED, MORE THAN HEARD, MOVEMENT IN THE ROOM. She'd been shuttling in and out of sleep, her dreams and semi-waking thoughts a mishmash of men with guns, shadowy figures whose faces melted into new ones before her eyes, and patients tugging at the hem of her white coat to beg for healing.

Now she heard a noise—soft footfalls on the tile floor. She opened her eyes and saw Phil Rushton standing at her bedside.

"Sorry to wake you," he said. "You need your rest."

"No, no. I was through with those dreams—nightmares, actually. I needed to wake up." She lifted her wrist to look at her watch but found it was gone. "What time is it anyway?"

"About noon," Phil said. "Let's have a look at you."

He took a few moments to examine her, then settled into the chair at her bedside. "You're an extremely lucky woman. An inch lower and that bullet would have cracked your skull, maybe required surgery. Two inches and it would have penetrated into the brain, and you'd be dead or permanently disabled. As it is, you had a concussion. That's all."

Carrie pushed the button to raise the head of her bed. "So am I okay for discharge?"

"You know better than that. I told you yesterday, we need to watch you for a while."

"Phil, I feel fine, except for a headache that would put a mule on its back. I'm a doctor. I know the signs of a problem."

"Knowing the signs is different than being able to recognize them in yourself." Phil shook his head, and his expression told her she wasn't going to win this argument. "I'd like to keep you a few more hours—make sure no late neurologic changes show up. Can we settle on five or six tonight?"

"Not what I'd like, but . . . I never thought I'd say these words. You're the doctor." She shrugged and offered a hint of a smile.

Phil was almost to the door when Carrie called after him. "Phil, how did you happen to be there to take care of me last night?"

He shrugged. "Had to come back to the ER anyway. Heard the commotion, saw you on the gurney. After that it was all reflex."

As Phil went out the door, Adam came in. The two men did a clumsy do-si-do through the doorway before turning to face each other.

"Doctor." Adam reached out his hand. "Thanks for what you've done."

"Glad I could help." He shook the proffered hand, then turned back to Carrie. "I'd wanted to meet this fabled Adam of yours, but not under these circumstances."

"I'll bet you're beat," Adam said. "Are you going to get some rest today?"

"No, but fortunately I only have office hours. No surgery, unless an emergency comes in." He turned to face Carrie. "Let the nurse know if you have any increase in headache, any double vision, any nausea—"

"I know all the signs, Phil. Thanks."

The surgeon grinned and left.

Adam moved to Carrie's bedside. "What did the doctor tell you?"

"I can go home late this afternoon if there's no change." Carrie lowered the head of her bed slightly. "What have you been up to?"

"I stopped in the cafeteria for a quick cup. I'll have to say, the coffee down there is absolutely terrible."

"One of the first things I learned in med school," Carrie said. "Bad hospital coffee is better than no coffee at all. But I'm glad you ate. Maybe by tonight I'll feel like eating."

Adam reached into his pocket and pulled out a crumpled handkerchief. He unfolded it, careful not to touch what it held. "I found this in the parking lot."

Carrie reached out, but Adam pulled it away. "Don't touch it. I'm going to see if my brother, Dave, can check the fingerprints on it."

"Why not the police?" Carrie asked.

"Because I trust Dave. And I don't have to explain things to him."

Carrie decided not to start that argument again. She stared at the shell casing for a moment. "Twenty-two long rimfire," she murmured.

"What did you say?"

"My dad had a rifle—called it a 'varmint gun.' We lived in Austin, and he used to take me out in the country and let me shoot it. It fired twenty-two caliber long bullets. And I always had to pick up the ejected cartridges, or 'clean up my brass,' as he called it."

"Think this will help me find out who shot at you?" Adam asked.

"Probably the most common rifle in this part of the country. So don't get your hopes up about using this to trace the shooter."

"Well, we can still check the casing for fingerprints," Adam said.

"You can try . . ."

Adam dropped into the chair. "That's all I can do. I have to keep trying." After a moment he made a "just a second" gesture, rose, and walked out. He returned with a pen and a thin pad of paper. "Got these from the nurse's station. I think it's time to start our list."

Fifteen minutes later Adam dropped the pen and said, "This is ridiculous. The shooter could be anyone who's moved to Jameson within the past six months or so."

"Or someone who was already here, but with a Chicago connection that would let DeLuca's family reach out to them, even after he died."

"Oh, that helps a lot!" Adam said. "Why don't I get the Jameson phone book and stick a pin in a random page?"

"Look at it another way. Let's focus on last night. You didn't see or hear any cars burning rubber out of the parking lot. So either the shooter got away without you seeing them—"

"Which was possible," Adam said. "Remember, I was concentrating on you."

"Or they stayed around. You mentioned that Rob Cole helped carry me in?"

Adam nodded.

"And what was he wearing?"

"A black T-shirt and jeans."

Warning bells were going off in Carrie's mind. "Why would he be there?"

"He told me he was an EMT. I assumed he'd just gotten in off a call."

"No," Carrie said. "If he'd been on duty, he would have had on a medium blue shirt with a logo on the pocket and navy cargo pants."

Adam picked up his pen. "I guess he could have been the shooter. Shot at you from behind the Hummer, dumped the rifle into his vehicle, and emerged to be a Good Samaritan, thinking it would put him above suspicion."

"Or if the target was supposed to be you, when he saw he'd hit me, guilt could have motivated him to help," Carrie said.

"Good point."

"Who else was there when you brought me in?"

"The doctor—Dr. Rushton. He burst through the double glass doors right after I did," Adam said. "He took charge immediately. Seemed like a natural thing."

Carrie frowned. "He told me he had to see a patient, and I assumed he was already in the ER. But if he came from outside, why couldn't he have fired the shot, dumped the gun, and burst in?"

"Do these guys have something against you?"

"I haven't figured out Rob Cole. He's acted . . . strange. And Phil Rushton? About the time I decide he's trying to ease me out of the clinic, he says or does something nice."

"Like save your life," Adam said.

"I doubt whether his care made that much difference, but, yes."

"And these are just the people we know about. The shooter could have been anyone."

"This is bringing back my headache." Carrie turned her head away and closed her eyes. She was certain of only two things. One, her life was in danger. And two, aside from Adam, she couldn't trust anyone.

"Are you sure you want to leave the hospital already?" Phil Rushton asked.

Adam stood in Carrie's hospital room behind the wheelchair in which she sat. He noticed that she hesitated before answering. He couldn't blame her. In here it was safe, or at least, relatively so. Because there were no metal detectors at the door, Adam had been able to ignore the signs and keep his pistol with him inside the hospital. To get a security guard required a simple phone call. But once she went out the hospital doors, out into the world, Carrie would once more be a potential target for the shooter. And whether he was aiming at Adam or at her, if a bullet struck her the end result would be the same.

"Yes," Carrie finally said. "I'm ready."

Rushton raised a cautionary finger. "Remember to—"

"Yes, Phil," Carrie snapped. "I'm a doctor. I know how to

take care of a scalp wound. I know about the complications after a concussion. I know to take it easy for a day or two." She took a deep breath, and when she spoke again, her tone had moderated. "I'm truly grateful for your care. You didn't have to do it. You could have passed me on to the ER doctor or one of the neurosurgeons. Don't think I'm unaware of that. But I'm a grown woman, as well as a physician. I need a measure of independence."

Rushton spread his hands wide. "Okay. But call—"

Adam could tell how much it cost Carrie to keep her voice level. "I'll call you if I need anything. Right now Adam is going to drive me home, where I plan to soak in a warm tub and eat a pint of Blue Bell ice cream. I'll be at work . . . What is today, anyway?"

"Tuesday, late afternoon," Adam chimed in.

"I'll take tomorrow off and be in on Thursday. If you'd let the schedulers and my nurse know, I'd appreciate it."

While an aide wheeled Carrie away, Adam, this time armed with the key, hurried to the parking lot to retrieve her car. The first thing he did was lower what was left of the shattered side windows. It made the car drafty but presented no other problem. Then he swept glass fragments off the front seat. That action brought a sense of déjà vu, as he recalled doing the same thing after the gunshots in front of the theater—gunshots that signaled the start of this nightmare.

Adam pulled the Prius into the circular driveway where discharges were sent on their way. With Carrie belted safely into the passenger seat, he stepped on the brake pedal, pushed the button to start the car, moved the selector lever to Drive, and pulled away from the hospital.

"See, driving a hybrid isn't so difficult, is it?" Carrie asked.

Adam ignored the remark. "Don't you have some flowers to take home?"

"I asked that they be distributed to other patients in the hospital."

"That was generous," Adam said. "When we get to your house, would you like me to stay there with you? At least for—"

"Stop right there!" Carrie turned to face him. "Adam, I love you. I've missed you, but I don't think I'm going to be good company. Once I'm inside, I promise to lock all the doors and windows. If anything suspicious happens, I'll pick up the phone and call 911." She saw the hurt in his eyes. "But you'll be my second call."

Adam nodded. "Would it be okay if I phoned to check on you?"

Carrie looked down at her lap. "Of course. And I'll call you. But I was serious about the long soak and the pint of ice cream."

They were quiet for the rest of the journey. Adam insisted on helping her into the house. He reached down to his right ankle, unsnapped the Velcro fastener securing his pistol, and with the gun in his fist, went through all the rooms. Empty. No evidence that anyone had been there since Carrie left.

Then, with her safely inside the house, Adam pulled Carrie's car into the garage and lowered the door. He found her in the living room, relaxing in an easy chair. He dropped her keys on the front table and pulled out his cell phone. "I'm going to call a taxi to take me back to the restaurant to get my car."

Carrie pushed herself out of the chair. "I'm not sure I've said it, and even if I did, I probably didn't say it enough—thank you."

Adam grasped Carrie's shoulders, kissed her, and pulled her to him. "Believe me, if I could undo all this, I would. But if I did that I wouldn't have you in my life. And right now you're the only thing that gives me hope—you and the knowledge that God's in control. He's got my back in all this."

Carrie looked up at Adam. "Not only yours—mine too. Ours." Tears sparkled in her eyes. "I've kept God at arm's length too long. I'm trying to make Him part of my life now, like you have all along." She buried her head on his shoulder, and Adam felt as though his heart would burst with happiness.

———————————————— ⟋\⟍ ————————————————

True to her promise, Carrie luxuriated in a warm bath until she felt like a prune. During the soak she consumed the remains of a half-gallon of Blue Bell Rocky Road ice cream she found in her freezer. Now she lay under the covers of her bed, wrapped in her ratty but extremely comfortable robe.

She toyed with the idea of sleep, but it was still too early. Besides, she felt as though she'd done nothing but sleep for the past twenty-four hours. TV? Not really. The critic who called that medium a "vast wasteland" had been right when he'd said it, and it was still true. She picked up the book at her bedside, read a few words, then put it down when she found her mind wandering.

Like good doctors in her specialty, she loved a diagnostic puzzle. She enjoyed the challenge of taking clues, putting them together this way and that, until the mystery began to come clear. Now she was involved in a mystery of her own, one that had life or death implications. And since she had time available, Carrie decided to shuffle the pieces of information she had to see if they formed a pattern.

She retrieved the pad and pen from her bedside table, a necessity for doctors receiving phone messages, and headed the page "Possibles." After a moment's thought, she crumpled and discarded the sheet. As Adam had said before, she might as well pick up the Jameson phone book. On the next sheet she drew a vertical line. To the left of it she wrote "Adam," to the right, "Carrie." Then she drew a line under both names, forming a T-chart. Again, the left-hand column offered almost infinite possibilities. The column under her name was more limited—mainly patients and their family members who could be so displeased with her they might try to harm her . . . or harm Adam as a way to get revenge on her.

There was no doubt in her mind. The top name on the list in the right-hand column was Calvin McDonald. Carrie shivered as she recalled her last encounter, when he passed her in the hall of the clinic and glared wordlessly at her. She remembered thinking, *If looks could kill . . .* Carrie wrote a few more names under his, including Mrs. Freemont, but after a moment she went back to the top and underlined McDonald's name . . . twice.

The ringing of her phone interrupted her thoughts. Maybe Adam was calling to check on her. Or maybe Phil. She was surprised to find that it was neither.

"Carrie, how are you doing?"

"Julie. So good to hear your voice."

"I've been waiting for you to call. Finally my curiosity couldn't stand it any longer. What's going on with you and Adam?"

"Wow, where do I begin?" Carrie hesitated only briefly. Surely it was safe to share her information with her best friend.

Besides, Julie was a couple of hundred miles away. And who would she tell?

Carrie brought Julie up-to-date on all that had happened, including the shooting that came within inches of taking her life. "Now I'm at home, wrestling with the possible identity of the person behind this."

"I presume you and Adam are good?"

"We're more than good." She paused and weighed her words. "I think that, despite everything that's happened, we're closer than ever."

"That's great. I'm glad to see that God's working in your life and Adam's right now."

"I guess He is. While Adam was gone, I started reading my Bible. One particular verse really hit me, one about God giving us a new heart. And I think He's doing that for me."

"Wait a sec," Julie said. "I know the one." There was the sound of turning pages. Finally she said, "Here it is. Ezekiel 36:26. 'Moreover, I will give you a new heart and put a new spirit within you.'"

"Well, that's what He's done," Carrie said. "And I'm grateful."

After leaving Carrie's home that evening, Adam thought about asking the taxi to drop him at the office but soon discarded the idea. Better to start fresh in the morning anyway. He gave the driver the address of the restaurant where he'd left his car. He'd stop by the grocery store for provisions before heading home.

He'd been in the Rancho Motel for several nights, then a series of one-night stays on his trip, but now he was ready to go home—his real home. As he steered his car toward his apartment, he ran details through his mind. His complex was primarily filled with young urban professionals, most of them not yet home from work. There were no children playing in the courtyards, no foot traffic to speak of. The possibility of witnesses to an attack was slim. Dusk was approaching. All things considered, Adam decided to redouble his efforts at vigilance.

He drove around the block a couple of times, alert for people sitting in cars or standing in doorways. On the third time, he pulled into the covered parking area provided for tenants but didn't go to his assigned slot. Instead, he chose a vacant spot as close to the back entrance of his apartment as possible. He pulled his pistol from its holster and shoved it into the waistband of his trousers, ready for action. Adam eased out of his car and looked around. Nothing stirred.

He emerged from the car and reached back for two bags of groceries, grabbing one with each hand. Adam decided that if shots were fired, he'd drop the bags, duck for cover, and start shooting. Could he really fire his gun? The picture of Carrie in his arms, blood covering her head, came to his mind. If he needed something to steel his resolve, this was more than enough. He flexed his shoulders to relieve the tension there, then pivoted three hundred sixty degrees. No one was in sight.

From the parking lot, he scurried to his back door, which he suddenly realized he needed to unlock. Adam set the bags on the ground long enough to pull out his keys. He gave another glance around, drew the pistol from his waistband with one hand, opened the door with the other. Holding the pistol at his side to partially conceal it, he picked up one bag and shuttled it inside, repeating the process with the other. He made one last trip outside, locking his door behind him, to move his car to its proper spot. Adam didn't want to start a war with the neighbor whose slot he'd occupied.

The walk to his back door, his arm held along his leg to conceal his gun, seemed to take an hour. Finally he was inside, the doors double locked. When he put the pistol on the kitchen table, he noticed his hand was trembling.

Was this going to be his life from now on? Holding his gun in one hand when he took groceries from his car? Flinching from shadows, jumping at every noise? No! It might be that way until he could get the shooter to reveal himself, but he wasn't going to live like that forever. He recalled a line from his childhood, one he wanted to open the window and shout to the person trying to kill him: "Come out, come out, wherever you are." *And when you do, I'll be ready.*

SIXTEEN

WEDNESDAY MORNING SUNLIGHT STREAMING THROUGH A SMALL opening toward the top of her bedroom's drawn drapes woke Carrie. She'd kept them and all the other drapes and blinds in the house closed since she came home from the hospital. With all the doors locked, she felt relatively safe.

Since the shooting, her sleep had been troubled. This morning she had vague recollections of dreams that made her sweat and her pulse pound, yet the details escaped her.

When she left the hospital, she'd told Phil Rushton she'd be in on Thursday. That was tomorrow, and as she swung her feet off the bed and shoved them into slippers, Carrie was happy she hadn't followed her first inclination and declared she'd work today. Of course, it was possible that Phil, in his sleep-deprived state, might have forgotten to pass the word along to the schedulers. Oh well. She'd check that in a minute.

She followed the smell of freshly brewed coffee, grateful

she remembered to activate the auto-brew feature on her coffee maker last night. A cup in hand, she ambled into the living room and dialed the clinic's back line. Although most of the doctors weren't due in for at least an hour, she was certain Marie would be at her desk, making sure the day's appointment sheets were printed off for distribution to the physicians.

Sure enough, Marie answered on the second ring. "Clinic, this is Marie."

"Marie, this is Dr. Markham."

"Oh, how are you doing? I'm so sorry for your accident."

It wasn't an accident. Someone meant to shoot me. "Thanks. I just wanted to make sure I don't have any patients scheduled for today."

Carrie heard keys clack, then Marie's voice back on the line. "Um, we have you marked out until tomorrow. Was that a mistake?"

"No, it's perfect," Carrie said. "I'll see you Thursday."

She needed today off—not necessarily because of her head wound but because of the stress of the situation. Carrie puttered around in the kitchen, deciding which dish she'd choose for her leisurely breakfast. But in the end she came back to what she had most days—juice, a toasted English muffin, and coffee. She flinched only a bit at the pounding in her head when she bent down to retrieve the newspaper from her porch. A second cup of coffee, a run through the headlines, and Carrie was ready to move on.

She took a long shower, careful to keep her head wound dry, followed by time in front of the mirror styling her blond hair to cover the crease left by the bullet. Makeup supplied the final touch. She slipped on a simple white tee and black slacks, slid her feet into cordovan loafers, and was ready for the day. But what was she going to do? Right now she was the embodiment of the phrase "All dressed up and no place to go."

Carrie brought the remainder of her second cup of coffee to her desk and found the T-chart she'd started last night. She couldn't do much about Adam's side of the list. She had suspicions about a couple of people whose names she knew, but some unknown, unnamed person with a connection to Charlie DeLuca could also be the shooter. But she could whittle hers down pretty quickly. The question was whether she was willing to do it.

Lord, if I do this I'll need more strength and wisdom than I have. And, truth be told, I'm scared.

She shoved the list aside and picked up her Bible off the end table. Carrie thumbed through it randomly, hoping to find direction, but nothing spoke to her. She reached to replace it on the table, when it slipped from her hands and fell, open, onto the floor. When Mrs. Nichols gave it to her, she mentioned highlighting a few passages. "These may be helpful for you," she'd said.

The open page was in the book of Psalms, and a passage marked in yellow caught Carrie's eye. "The Lord will protect you from all evil; He will keep your soul. The Lord will guard your going out and your coming in, from this time forth and forever."

Carrie nodded, as though in answer to an unasked question. She picked up the phone and punched Redial. "Marie, this is Dr. Markham again. Would you give me the home address for Calvin McDonald?"

Adam's first day back at the law offices of Hartley and Evans was actually easier than he feared. He came in early, as was his custom. A desk, bookcase, chairs, computer, and all the contents of his old office had been moved into the new one. The only clue that it had once been a storeroom was a stray legal journal in one corner, left behind by whoever had done the moving.

When Brittany arrived, the coffee was already made. Adam was in his office digging through the files he'd found waiting for him when she stuck her head through his open door. "The coffee smells wonderful. Thanks. Her Ladyship never comes in early enough to brew coffee, much less offer to do it. Guess she thinks she's too good."

Adam didn't want to get into a gossip-fest with the receptionist, so he made some noncommittal remark and returned to his apparent study of the open law book on his desk. In a moment he heard Brittany's voice back at her desk, answering the phone.

Greetings from Janice Evans came next, then Bruce Hartley. Mary Delkus was the last one in. Apparently good looks granted certain privileges. As soon as Adam felt sure that everyone was busy, he called up an Internet search engine on his computer and typed in a name. It was a name he hadn't thought of since his second year in law school. But it was the name of a person who might help him with one of the most important problems he'd ever faced.

Finally he was able to secure an address, which led him, after more digging, to a phone number. He scribbled it on a yellow Post-it and shoved it deep into his briefcase. When he was at lunch, he'd make the call. Meanwhile, he had some catching up to do, if he wanted his current "temporary" position to become permanent.

As soon as Carrie got into her car she realized she'd forgotten one detail: the two front windows were missing. Dealing with that was now her first order of business. Fortunately the dealer from whom she'd purchased her car was not only a patient but also a friend. He took her to his service manager and explained Carrie's situation. "I'd appreciate it if you could help the doctor get underway. She's in sort of a hurry."

After completing the paperwork, the service manager pointed to a silver Prius, identical to Carrie's, just pulling into the service drive. "That's your loan car. I'll call you when we get the new windows installed."

"Thanks so much," Carrie said as she drove away. Thank goodness the vast majority of her patients not only liked her, but some were willing to go the extra mile to help her when she needed it.

The house certainly wasn't what Carrie expected. Every time she'd seen Calvin McDonald, the man was dressed in jeans and a nondescript shirt—sometimes plaid, sometimes denim. The clothes showed evidence of frequent laundering but were always clean. Somehow Carrie's mental picture of McDonald was of a man scratching out a living on one of the black-dirt farms outside of Jameson. But the man's home forced her to revise that image.

The house wasn't outside Jameson's city limits. As a matter of fact, it was in one of the nicer sections of town. Rather than the small white clapboard house with a composition shingle roof Carrie visualized, McDonald lived in a two-story red brick home, set in the middle of a well-maintained yard surrounded by a recently painted white picket fence. A black Buick, its surface unmarred by dirt or dust, sat in the driveway in front of a two-car garage.

Carrie screwed up her courage and gave the button beside the front door a tentative push. She waited, her ears straining to pick up any sound from inside. As she was about to ring the doorbell again, the door opened wide, and she was face-to-face with Calvin McDonald.

He gave her the same squinty-eyed glare she'd come to expect, but although the expression was somewhere between disdain and dislike, the voice was surprisingly soft. "Help you?"

"Mr. McDonald. I'm Dr. Carrie Markham. I'm sorry to intrude like this, but I'd like a few minutes of your time."

McDonald's look of surprise lasted only a second. "Come in." He gestured her inside. Carrie wondered if she'd ever pass back out the door again. After all, this man topped her list of people who'd like to kill her. Of course, even if he did, maybe Adam would be out of danger. *Lord, protect me.* She took a tentative step inside, and McDonald closed the door behind her. Then she heard the click of a lock, and a chill ran down her spine.

Carrie was poised to bolt for the door, hoping she could reach it before McDonald intercepted her, when he spoke. "Would you like to have a seat?" He escorted her to what, in an earlier day, would have been called a parlor. Two easy chairs, a sofa, some tables and lamps, and a couple of throw rugs. There was no TV set. Instead, an upright piano sat against one wall.

Apparently this was the room for "entertaining company," as her grandmother might have said.

As she eased into a chair, Carrie noticed that although the room was neat, a faint patina of dust covered some of the furniture. "I apologize for the dust," McDonald said, as though reading her thoughts. "My wife always kept the place spotless, but since . . . since I lost her, I haven't paid as much attention as I should. I have a woman who comes in and cleans, but I've asked her to leave this room alone. It's . . . it's where Bess and I used to sit and talk."

Carrie decided to plunge right in. "Mr. McDonald, I'm sorry for your loss. I tried to tell you that at the time your wife . . . your wife passed away. And I hope you realize I and the rest of the hospital staff did everything we could to save her."

McDonald sat unmoving. No response.

Carrie took a deep breath and went on. "As soon as I saw your wife in the Emergency Room, I made the diagnosis of a perforated ulcer. That's outside my specialty, so I called in a general surgeon. He rushed her to surgery, and I stood by in the operating room in case I could help. Unfortunately, her heart was too weak to tolerate the procedure. The anesthesiologist and I did everything we could to save her, but we were unsuccessful."

Carrie swallowed, remembering the frustration she felt at losing that patient. "I'm not sure anything could have been done differently, but believe me, we gave it our best effort. I'm sorry it happened." She paused, trying to read his expression. It was the same squint-eyed glare she was used to seeing from him. "Now I'm here to make certain you're not carrying a grudge toward me. And if you are, I want to ask your forgiveness."

There, it was out. She held her breath, waiting to see what came next.

"Grudge toward you?" McDonald's glare softened. He wiped a tear from his eye. "The only person I'm angry with is myself. I tried to get Bess to go to the doctor, but she wouldn't budge. I watched her take antacids and sodium bicarbonate, urged her to get her stomach pains checked, but she refused. And when she finally had so much pain she couldn't stand it, I took her to the Emergency Room. I was afraid it might be too late. I prayed it wasn't—but it was." He pulled a handkerchief from his hip pocket and wiped his eyes. "But I don't blame you, Doctor. I blame myself."

Carrie's next words came out without conscious thought. "Then why do you always glare at me when we pass in the halls?"

McDonald reached into his shirt pocket and pulled out a somewhat worn black clamshell glasses case. He withdrew a pair of wire-framed spectacles, hooked them over his ears, and settled them on his nose. "Bess was always after me to wear these, but I hate them. I'd rather squint. Is that better?"

Actually, it was. What Carrie had interpreted as a scowl was gone. McDonald was no longer someone sending a glare of hate her way. Now Carrie realized he was just a lonely old man, sitting day after day in an empty house, missing his late wife.

Carrie started to get up, but something kept her seated. Should she? Maybe it would help him. Maybe it would even help her. "Mr. McDonald, I know something about survivor guilt, and that's what you're feeling. I've been there. If you keep hanging on to it, you'll never move forward. I know from personal experience. Lots of people suffer from it, and they're almost always wrong to do so. Let me tell you a story."

She took his nod for permission. "It's about two doctors. They'd been married since graduating from medical school. It wasn't always easy to make a marriage between doctors work, but they did . . . and they were happy. She found that she couldn't have children, but they decided God had a child out there for them somewhere, so they'd adopt.

"They barely had begun the process when he started noticing fatigue. He was a general surgeon, and he passed it off as working too hard. But the symptoms worsened. She insisted that he see one of her colleagues for a workup. He put it off and put it off, but finally he relented.

"The workup showed an unusual congenital heart problem—it's called Ebstein's anomaly, but the name isn't important. One danger it poses is a potentially deadly rhythm disturbance of the heart. He developed more problems. Medications weren't working. So a specialist proposed a procedure called transvenous radiofrequency ablation."

She saw McDonald's eyebrows rise, so she hurried to explain. "Call it RFA. In it, a doctor inserts a fine plastic tube through a vein in the leg and runs it all the way up to the heart. A wire inside the catheter delivers current to cauterize the abnormal areas responsible for the rhythm problems. It's an accepted procedure, and it's generally safe."

Carrie paused and tried to clear the lump in her throat, but it wouldn't budge. "The risks of something going bad during such a process are small, but they exist. But in this case the wire got into a coronary artery and opened a tiny hole in it. The only chance to save such a patient is immediate heart surgery to repair the damage. In this case, one of the best cardiothoracic surgeons in the state was in that hospital right then. They took the patient immediately to the operating room . . . but he died."

McDonald continued to sit, silent as a statue. Carrie couldn't tell from his expression if he was following the story. She hoped he was. "Naturally, the wife was devastated. She was a doctor. She should have picked up on the clues to her husband's heart problem sooner. She should have insisted that he seek medical attention earlier. She should have been able to prevent the complication—maybe suggested a different doctor, even a different medical center for the procedure. She should have intervened to get her husband to surgery sooner, although she didn't see how she could. She blamed herself every step of the way. She had the biggest case of survivor guilt in the universe."

"It wasn't her fault," McDonald said quietly. "She did her best."

"And so did you," Carrie said. "I should know. I was that woman doctor. The man who died was my husband."

What McDonald said next removed him from Carrie's list of people who might try to kill her and placed him in a whole different category. "I'm sorry for your loss," he said. "I'll pray for you . . . for both of us."

Carrie brushed away tears. "So will I, Mr. McDonald. So will I."

———————————————⌁———————————————

Adam really didn't want to leave the safety of his office, not even for lunch. But he had to—not only because he was hungry, but also to give him the privacy necessary for an important phone call. Besides, it was unlikely the shooter would come after him in broad daylight, and certainly not within sight of both the municipal courts and the police station.

The offices of Hartley and Evans were within walking distance of both those structures. And where lawyers and policemen gathered, there were sure to be eating places, little sandwich shops and cafés where people could snatch a quick lunch, a cup of coffee, a late-afternoon snack without having to go too far. It was to one of these Adam walked, not hurrying but not dawdling either.

Once inside the sandwich shop, he took comfort from the presence of no fewer than three uniformed patrolmen and a couple of plainclothes detectives. The latter didn't have their badges on display, but they might as well have carried signs saying, "Police." Adam ordered a glass of tea and a roast beef sandwich, then headed for the restroom. Behind a locked door he dialed the number he'd unearthed earlier. *Please pick up. Please be there.*

"This is Cortland."

Adam wasn't sure how three words could convey a Texas accent so well, but they did just that. He pictured "Corky" as he typically saw him in law school: dressed in an open-necked blue button-down shirt, Levis, and soiled New Balance running shoes. Adam hoped Corky had upgraded his attire since he graduated.

According to Adam's online search, E. A. Cortland, Esq., had a law practice in Houston, Texas. Adam was banking on Cortland's tendency to skip his noon meal, hoping Corky would answer the phone himself while his receptionist or secretary or whoever usually manned the phone at his office was at lunch. So far, he'd won the trifecta: this was the right

Cortland, the phone number was the one he wanted, and Corky was the one who picked up the phone.

"Corky, this is Keith Branson." Adam had to guard his tongue to make it say his original name.

"Keith, you old dog. How are you?"

"Look, Corky. I have to keep this short, but I'm hoping you can fill in the blanks for yourself. If you do an Internet search, you'll find that my testimony sent my father-in-law, Charlie DeLuca, to jail. Since then I've been on the run. I'm going to give you a number—it's my cell phone. I'm calling in the favor you owe me for getting you through that course on torts. Will you do some digging and call me back?"

Corky acted as though this was the most natural request in the world. "No problem, Keith, although given what you've already told me I'd bet that's not the name you're using these days."

Adam looked at the phone in his hand and discovered he'd pulled his throwaway phone from the brief case. It was just as well. He gave Corky the number. "What I need is more information than I can get from Google or LexisNexis. I need as much as you can give me."

"Sure," Corky said. "But why?"

"Somebody's out to kill me, probably for testifying against Charlie DeLuca. I need whatever you can dig up on DeLuca, especially his associates and family."

"If we both weren't officers of the court, I'd think you wanted me to hack into some sites and circumvent the law."

"Well—"

"Relax. Given enough time and resources, anyone could get this information quite legally. I'm just shortening the process."

Adam chewed on that for a minute. Legal? Most likely it was a gray area, but one in which Corky had always enjoyed working. "Okay. So you'll do it?"

Keys clicked in the background. "Sure. Sounds like fun." More clicks. "I'm already into some sites you'd never penetrate. That was D-E-L-U-C-A, C-H-A-R-L-E-S? He'd be in his late fifties?"

"And he'll never be any older. He died a few months ago."

"Give me time to dig. Why don't I call you back this evening?"

"Great. I appreciate it."

"Not a problem." A low whistle overrode the background clatter of keys. "Just to be sure, which family of DeLuca's do you want to know about? Or shall I check into both of them?"

SEVENTEEN

ADAM FELT THE TREMOR OF HIS CELL PHONE AGAINST HIS THIGH. His throwaway cell, the one he'd asked Corky to use, was in his briefcase. This was his regular number. He didn't want to ignore a call, since it might be from Carrie or Dave.

He eased the phone out, held it shielded by his desk, and checked the caller ID. It was Carrie. Adam lifted the phone to his face, pressed the button, and whispered, "Yes?"

"Can we meet tonight? I have some things to tell you."

"Hang on." Adam rose from his desk and moved to the far corner of the little room. He turned his back to the door and pretended to be engrossed in the titles on a shelf of law books. "We need to make this quick. I should have some information tonight too, but it may be late."

"Late's fine. Shall I come by the Rancho Motel again?"

"No, I checked out before my trip. But I'd rather keep you away from my apartment." He thought a moment. The logistics were possible. "I'll be at your back door about ten this evening."

"Won't you—"

"I'll do what I did Sunday night when I came to your house. The shooter will never know I'm there. Trust me. Just be ready to open the door for me."

"Are you going to call me on your cell when you arrive?" Carrie said.

"I thought I'd just knock."

"Maybe we should have some sort of code so I don't open the door and find myself staring down the barrel of a gun?"

Adam recalled Carrie's special ring for her cell phone. "Sure. How about the opening rhythm of Beethoven's 'Fifth Symphony'? You know. Dah-dah-dah-dah. Four knocks in rapid succession."

They ended the conversation and Adam hurried back to his desk, arriving just as Mary Delkus tapped on the frame of the open door. She looked like a million dollars today in a form-fitting burgundy dress. "Did I hear you talking with someone?"

"You caught me. I was talking to myself. Sometimes I like to present arguments out loud to see how they sound." He gestured to one of the chairs in front of his desk. "Have a seat. What's up?"

Mary smoothed her skirt over the backs of her thighs and sat. "I need to get better acquainted with you," she said.

"Oh?"

"I feel bad." She gave him a look of apology. "I know that I took your job, and . . . well, I'd like to make it up to you by taking you out to dinner."

Adam didn't know what to say.

"How about tonight?" she said, giving him a glimpse of those perfect white teeth.

Adam hadn't known what to expect from Mary's visit, but it certainly wasn't this. He needed to be free to take Corky's call, he had to be at Carrie's late tonight, and he really didn't know enough about this woman to be comfortable going out with her. Maybe the last factor was pure paranoia, but he was taking no chances. "Mary, that's really very kind," he said, "but I have something on the schedule tonight. Maybe another time."

She smiled. "Sure. Think about it and let me know." Adam's eyes followed her as she strode from the office. He had little difficulty understanding how Bruce Hartley was so taken with her. But looks weren't everything. Beauty could be used in so many ways, some of them good, some bad. As for Mary, the jury was still out, but he was getting an idea of which way he'd vote.

———————— ⟋⟍ ————————

When Carrie left Mr. McDonald, she felt somehow freer. For almost a year she'd carried with her a sense that the man hated her, somehow held her responsible for his wife's death. Carrie couldn't bring Bess McDonald back to life, but maybe she'd been able to give some quality to Calvin's life for the years he had left.

Back in her car, after the call to Adam, she wished she'd taken something that morning for her headache. She knew why Phil hadn't prescribed Vicodin or a similar narcotic for the headaches she was sure to have over the next few days. He wanted to avoid masking late symptoms of a complication following her head injury. Carrie's pain tolerance was pretty high, but right now her skull was throbbing.

She decided to stop for a cup of coffee and use it to wash down a couple of extra-strength Tylenol. Maybe the caffeine plus the pills would help stop the waves of pain bouncing around inside her head.

Jameson offered the usual options to those seeking a caffeine fix. The town even boasted a couple of Starbucks. It wasn't Seattle, but still, Carrie had plenty of opportunities to get a cup of coffee and relax.

Her first thought was a small coffee shop near the hospital. After a moment's consideration, she rejected the idea. The place was a frequent hangout for medical staff, and she didn't want to answer a lot of questions about the shooting in the parking lot.

A banner on a building to her right caught her eye: "Now Open: Kolache Heaven." Growing up in central Texas, she'd quickly become a fan of the doughy pastries with centers filled with fruit, cream cheese, or even a sweetened poppy seed mix. The thought of a kolache, together with a steaming cup of coffee, made her salivate. Besides, maybe hunger was contributing to her headache. She wheeled into the parking lot, then waited patiently in line to place her order.

The man in front of her looked familiar, and when he turned she realized why. It was Rob Cole. "Dr. Markham. Glad to see you're able to be out and about. Come to get your kolache fix?"

"Actually, I didn't know I was hungry until I saw the sign. That's when I decided a kolache would be good."

"And you're right. If you've never tried one—"

"I have," Carrie said. She wasn't interested in a long

conversation, but she couldn't figure out how to get rid of Rob without being downright rude. The register next to them opened, and Carrie stepped up and placed her order.

Rob reached into his pocket. "Please. Let me buy."

"Thanks, Rob, but no. I'll get my own." She paid for her coffee and a raspberry kolache, dropped her change in the tip jar, and started to move away.

"Looks like there's only one empty table," Rob said. "Could we share it?"

Carrie resigned herself to prolonging the encounter. When they both were seated, she took a bite of her pastry and a sip of coffee. Then she reached into her purse and pulled out a small vial, shook two Tylenol tablets into her palm, and washed them down with more coffee.

Rob watched with interest but didn't comment.

Carrie had an urge to eat her pastry in three or four huge bites, then make her getaway to avoid a conversation with Rob. Instead, she nibbled at the kolache, alternating with sips of coffee while wondering what Rob's conversational opener would be. She didn't have to wait long to find out.

"Dr. Markham, do you have any idea why someone took a shot at you in the ER parking lot?"

She wasn't sure whether he was naïve, rude, or truly interested. In any case, it was none of his business. "Rob, I think that's a matter for the police." She reduced the size of her kolache by one more ladylike bite and decided to turn the tables on him. "By the way—I've not had an opportunity to thank you." She smiled warmly. "You and Adam saved my life. What were you doing there anyway? You weren't on duty."

Rob shrugged, his expression devoid of guile. "I hang

around the hospital a lot in my off hours. I don't have a wife or family, and it's not a lot of fun sitting around an empty apartment. I'd just parked and was on my way to get a burger in the cafeteria when I heard the shots and saw Mr. Davidson running across the parking lot carrying you."

Carrie didn't particularly want to make this a long conversation, but her curiosity got the best of her. Besides, there were still a couple of bites of pastry and a little coffee left. "I'm sure it can be lonely, living alone." *I know. I do it too.*

"It is. And I don't plan to be alone forever. I know the type of woman I want in my life. And I intend to go after her."

Carrie looked at Rob and wondered if this was another clumsy attempt on his part to flirt with her. Did Rob actually think she might be interested? Or was there something more behind it?

By the end of the workday, Adam was wrung out from constant tension. He kept trying to work through the pile of material on his desk, but the stack of files seemed to refresh itself every time he whittled it down a bit. Meanwhile, he parried the questions and comments from his coworkers: from Brittany, who thought the behavior of the partners was indefensible; from Bruce Hartley, whose only concern was that briefs were filed on time and paperwork brought up-to-date; from Janice Evans, who sympathized with Adam about the problems that seemed to be hitting him one after another; from Mary Delkus, who repeated her offer to take him to dinner. And in the back of his mind was always the cryptic question of his friend Corky. "Which family of DeLuca's?" Corky had to end the call before he could amplify on that. But by tonight Adam hoped to have some answers.

At about three o'clock, the phone on his desk buzzed. He punched the intercom button. "Yes?"

Brittany's voice was unusually subdued. "There's a man from the U.S. Marshalls Service on line 1. He didn't want to give me his name, but he said it was urgent."

Adam's gut clenched. It could only be Dave, and Dave would only call him at work if he couldn't get through on his cell. Adam eased the instrument out of his pocket and checked the display for missed calls. None.

"It's okay, Brittany," Adam said. "Probably something routine. Thanks."

Adam punched the blinking button. "Adam Davidson."

The voice was vaguely familiar, but it certainly wasn't Dave's. "Adam, this is Sam Westerman. Are you able to talk?"

Adam knew that Sam meant, "Can you talk without being overheard?" His emotions did battle. He wanted to hear what Sam had to say, hear it now, but he had precious little privacy in the office. "Call me back on my cell in five minutes."

"I'll need that number. Dave gave it to me, but I can't find it."

Adam rattled off the number and hung up. He grabbed his coat and briefcase and headed for the door, where he stopped. "Brittany, I have to get some papers to a marshall so he can serve them. I'll be back in half an hour." He closed the door firmly behind him before the receptionist could respond.

Ten steps away from the building, Adam stopped and looked around. Where could he go? And how did he know this wasn't some sort of a trap? Was it really Sam calling? Could

Sam be involved in the shootings? Was Dave—No, that was ridiculous. He had to trust Dave and, by extension, trust Sam.

He'd avoided his assigned spot in the building's parking lot. Instead, his car was in a lot behind the building, which he'd entered via the back door. He headed there now. When he reached the little Subaru, he looked in all directions but saw no one nearby. He beeped the vehicle unlocked, jammed himself behind the wheel, and relocked the doors.

Adam had no time to get settled before his cell phone rang. "This is Adam."

"Sam here. I have some bad news about your brother."

The chill Adam felt would have made his mother say someone was walking over his grave. "What?"

"He was with a group of law officers down around the Texas-Mexico border. There was a shoot-out, and Dave was wounded. He's okay, but he made me promise to call and let you know."

"Where is he? I need to go there."

"That's the other thing he made me promise. He knew that was what you'd say, so I can't tell you where he is. The wound isn't severe—he'll probably be out of the hospital in two or three days—and he said there was no need to come down."

Adam leaned forward and rested his forehead on the steering wheel. Did he *need* to be with Dave right now? No, he *wanted* to be there, but there was nothing he could do if he went. As always, Dave was right. "Okay, I guess. Can you keep me posted on his condition? Please promise me that."

"I'll call you again tomorrow," Sam said.

"And if he gets worse . . ."

"I'll let you know."

When Adam ended the conversation, he felt more alone

than he'd ever felt in his life. His brother had always been there for him. Now Dave was out of the picture, at least for a while. Sam would help—he seemed like a good man—but there was something about the blood bond that made trust automatic.

Now, other than Carrie, was there anyone Adam could really trust?

Carrie knew she must have eaten something for her evening meal, but for the life of her she couldn't recall what it was, how it tasted, or anything else about it. She fiddled with the TV set, channel surfing without ever locking in on anything. She paced, peered through the blinds every few minutes, looked at her watch, and in general acted like a child waiting for Christmas morning. And all because Adam was coming over.

Even though she'd had one earlier in the day when she returned from her visit with Calvin McDonald, Carrie decided she needed another shower to help her relax. She stood under the hot water for a long time, then dressed in a plain skirt, a simple blouse, and low heels. When she found herself deciding on costume jewelry to complete the look, Carrie decided that was enough. *For goodness' sake, stop acting as though you're waiting for your prom date.*

By nine Carrie decided she needed something to help calm her. How about a drink? She didn't have liquor in the house, and wouldn't use it if she did. Tranquilizer? Same answer. She flopped into an easy chair in her living room and shuffled through the magazines on the coffee table. There was nothing there worth reading. She picked up the Bible that lay beside the magazines. *Maybe this is what I need.*

She was still reading more than an hour later when a sharp *rat tat tat tat* at her back door roused her. She looked at her watch. Quarter past ten. Adam was here.

Carrie hurried to the kitchen. The top half of the back door was glass, divided into six rectangles by a latticework of wood and covered by a half curtain. She pulled the curtain aside far enough to see Adam standing on her back porch, scanning all around, his shoulders hunched as though by doing so he could make himself invisible. He wore dark jeans and a green sweatshirt.

She turned the latch and opened the door. "Come on in."

He hurried inside. "Lock the—"

Carrie was already working on it. She double locked the door and slid a security chain into place.

"How did you get here without someone seeing you?"

"Same way I did Sunday night." Adam wiped sweat from his forehead and finger-combed his hair. "I parked two blocks away, then came down alleys. I kept in shadows most of the way. Your fence was easy enough to climb. I'm sure no one followed me."

"Is this what you're reduced to now? Sneaking around through alleys in the dark? I thought you were through hiding."

"I am," Adam said. "I'm ready to face the shooter, but I want to choose where we meet. And it's not going to be anywhere near you."

For the first time, Carrie saw the pistol in Adam's hand. "Is that . . . ?"

"Yes. It's my gun." He knelt and slid the pistol into a holster buckled above his right ankle. "And I'd feel better if you had one too."

Carrie chose to ignore the remark. She didn't want a weapon, and she wasn't too happy that Adam had one. "Let's go into the living room," she said. "Do you want something to drink? Coffee?"

"I'd jump out of my skin if I had coffee," Adam said. "Maybe a glass of ice water."

In a moment they were settled side by side on the sofa in Carrie's living room. "I think we both have news," she said. "Who goes first?"

She wasn't sure of the reason, maybe it was the cumulative stress of the past few days, but Adam seemed more preoccupied than usual. He snapped out of it long enough to say, "Why don't you?"

Carrie described her visit to Calvin McDonald. "I don't think he could be our shooter. And the more I think about it, the less certain I am that the attacks have been aimed at me." She was ashamed that she felt a degree of relief at reaching this conclusion. "I believe we can strike Mr. McDonald and Mrs. Fremont and all the other patients and families who might have a grudge against me."

"Good," Adam said. "You haven't discussed my real identity with anyone. Right?"

Carrie tried to keep her expression neutral. *Just my best friend. But Julie has no reason to tell anyone.* "No . . . Well, yes. I've talked to Julie Yates." She saw Adam's expression change, and her voice rose a bit. "Adam, she's my best friend. I'd trust her with my life. And I had to talk with someone about this. Can you understand?"

Adam chewed on his lower lip. "I asked you not to tell

anyone. Don't you think it's possible that Julie could tell her husband, who might mention it to a colleague, who could be an acquaintance—"

"Stop! Julie promised me she wouldn't even tell her husband. I'm willing to bet my life that she's kept the secret."

"Actually, it's my life we're betting too . . . but, okay. I'll accept that."

"Thank you."

"Let's put that aside. I have a couple of things to share," Adam said. He told her about his brother's shooting. "He's doing okay after surgery, but he'll be out of circulation for several days. He was shot in the shoulder—the right shoulder—so if it comes down to a shoot-out, I won't be able to depend on Dave for a while."

"Was that what you'd planned?" Carrie asked. "Get your brother here, maybe a couple of his buddies, then face down your stalker like the gunfight at the OK Corral?" She knew there was sarcasm in her voice, but maybe it belonged there. Surely Adam wasn't planning something like that.

"No, I don't expect my brother to fight my battles for me. That's not the way we grew up. Besides . . ." He touched his ankle where the pistol rested. "Although I hope it doesn't come down to what you call the gunfight at the OK Corral, if it does I'm ready."

"How else do you think we can resolve this?" Carrie asked.

"I plan to use the pistol to capture the shooter, not shoot him. I never thought I'd even own a gun. But I feel as though I'm backed into a corner, and I'll do anything to defend you . . . to defend us."

She patted his arm. Carrie decided it was time to move on to a topic that wouldn't trigger an argument. "You said you had two things. What's the second?"

Adam paused to think for a moment. "Oh, I called one of my law school classmates. Corky has a brilliant legal mind, but he also can coax all kinds of information out of a computer."

"In other words, he's a hacker."

"He assures me that he could get all this information in a conventional manner. It would just take a lot longer. He describes it as taking a shortcut." He took a deep swallow from his water glass, then set it on the coffee table in front of him. "I asked him to check out Charlie DeLuca for me."

"Why?" Carrie said. "You worked with DeLuca. You were married to his daughter. Don't you know enough about him?"

"I wanted a list of family and close friends, people who might be behind these attacks on me even though Charlie is dead."

"Didn't you meet all those folks at your wedding? Maybe at the rehearsal dinner? The reception?"

Adam grimaced. "Charlie said there was no need for a big fancy wedding. A judge in Chicago, one of Charlie's cronies, married us in his chambers. My brother and the judge's clerk were witnesses."

"What did Bella say? Or Charlie's wife?"

"They did what they'd learned to do—they kept their mouths shut."

Carrie picked up a legal pad and wrote "Charlie DeLuca Family" at the top. "Okay, so what was Charlie's wife's name?"

"Doesn't matter. Corky called me just before I came here. He only had a moment, but he told me Charlie's wife died six months after he went to prison." He picked up his glass, found it empty, and put it down again. "Charlie hadn't been what you'd call a model prisoner. He was in solitary confinement at the time, so he didn't get to go to her funeral."

Carrie shuddered. This was the man responsible for attacks on her life, yet she found herself feeling sorry for him. "So we have 'wife—deceased' and 'daughter.' Do we know anything about Bella's whereabouts?"

Adam described the dead end Corky encountered in that respect. "It's 'like she dropped off the face of the earth' was the way he put it. His best guess was that after the divorce and her father's prison sentence, Bella moved, established a new identity, and we'll never find her."

"But if she showed up here, you'd recognize her."

"Right. I don't think there's a plastic surgeon anywhere who could change her appearance enough that I wouldn't recognize my ex-wife."

Carrie said, "Who else?"

"Charlie apparently had an older brother, but he managed to tiptoe through society without leaving a footprint. No Social Security number, no driver's license—at least, not in his original name. My guess is that he wanted to distance himself from his black sheep brother. Maybe, the same way we suspect Bella did, he wanted to wipe the slate clean. He just did it a lot earlier."

Carrie looked at the almost-blank page in front of her. "What about close friends?"

Adam shook his head. "Nope. Charlie didn't have close friends. He had people who worked for him, people who owed him favors, but any loyalty they had to him probably died when he did, if not before."

Carrie dropped the pad and threw up her hands in surrender. "So I guess that's it. We have no knowledge of anyone connected to Charlie DeLuca who might be trying to get back at you on his behalf."

"I didn't say that," Adam said, raising an eyebrow.

Carrie studied him for a moment. "Okay . . . ," she finally said. "What?"

"Apparently one family wasn't enough for Charlie DeLuca . . . He had two!"

EIGHTEEN

ADAM WATCHED CARRIE'S FACE AS HE DROPPED THE BOMBSHELL on her, and he wasn't disappointed. Her jaw dropped like a fish gasping on dry land. He couldn't recall ever seeing someone so totally surprised. Then again, he'd been just as surprised when Corky mentioned DeLuca's second family.

"I think you'd better explain," Carrie said.

"Most of this is conjecture, but it makes sense. Charlie's wife—Bella's mother—was something of a shrew. Charlie's law practice and shadier activities often took him to Cicero, which is sort of a suburb of Chicago. That's where he met a woman who was clerking for a judge—maybe a judge Charlie or one of his associates had 'bought,' so to speak. They started seeing each other, and he eventually married her."

"Didn't his wife—either wife, for that matter—didn't they suspect anything?"

"Not at all. Charlie split his time pretty evenly, and each wife was told his absences were because of business trips."

Carrie picked up her legal pad again. "So what was his name in Cicero?"

Adam grinned. "Charlie DeLuca."

"You're kidding! I can't believe it. He had a second family, a few miles away from the first, both of them under his real name? The man was either incredibly stupid or incredibly confident."

"My personal opinion? He was both."

Adam watched as Carrie wrote "second family" and drew a line under it. Then he told her what Corky had found. Charlie's double life remained undiscovered until after he was about to go on trial. When the second wife learned the truth and realized the second marriage was invalid, she retook her maiden name, found a job at the courthouse, and closed that chapter of her life.

"So she's not going to want revenge," Carrie said.

"Maybe on Charlie, not on me."

"Did they have any children?"

"She had two from a previous marriage—a son and daughter, both grown."

Under "second family", Carrie wrote "son" and "daughter."

"Before you get too carried away with that list, you'd better hear what we know about the children." Adam leaned forward with his clasped hands between his knees. "As best we can tell, the daughter was terribly disturbed by what happened. So disturbed, as a matter of fact, that she entered the novitiate for the Franciscan Sisters. She's currently at Our Lady of Victory Convent in Lemont, not far from Chicago."

Carrie pursed her lips and drew a line through "daughter."

"So what about the son."

"He disappeared."

"Don't tell me he followed his sister's example and went into a monastery."

Adam shook his head. "I don't think so. He was working in a hospital in Cicero and going to night school, getting his certification as an Emergency Medical Technician. After he finished his training, he went to work driving an ambulance there. Then, about a week after the bigamy came to light, he simply didn't show up for work. There's no trace of him since then, at least not by his real name."

"So at least we have one possible out of that list," Carrie said. "What was his name?"

"The name he was born with is Robert Kohler. But we have no idea what he goes by now."

Adam expected Carrie to write down the name. Instead, she gripped the pen so tightly her knuckles turned white. Then she looked up at him and said, "I may know."

Carrie wondered if she was jumping to conclusions. Then again, the pieces seemed to fit together. Adam came to Jameson about eight months ago. Within a few weeks Rob Cole showed up, working as an EMT. About the time it was evident that Adam and Carrie had become an item, Rob started showing more interest in Carrie. She'd thought at first it was infatuation on his part. Now she wondered if it was an attempt to get close to her in order to keep tabs on Adam.

"You're going to think this is crazy," she said.

"No crazier than someone shooting at me—at us. Let's hear it."

Carrie laid out her theory about Rob, watching Adam's face carefully. To his credit, he neither interrupted nor argued. Instead, he listened thoughtfully until he was sure she'd finished.

"Let's look at it objectively." Adam picked up Carrie's pad and pen and wrote "Rob Cole" toward the middle of the page. "There are three things the law looks for in the commission of a crime: motive, means, opportunity. Let's take them in reverse order." Under Rob's name, he scribbled the words *movie, office, hospital 1, hospital 2.* "Let's look at opportunity for each of these episodes."

"I'm with you," Carrie said.

Adam poised his pen over the first line in the list. "So could Rob have shot at us in front of the theater?"

"I don't see why not. Actually, I suppose anyone could."

Adam made a check mark. "Could he have lobbed that Molotov cocktail through the front window of the law offices?"

"Same answer."

Another check mark. "Now we begin to narrow the field. Could he have sent the text that lured me to the hospital parking lot?"

Carrie thought about that for a moment. "Yes. Rob's in and out of the ER all the time. He'd know about the locker where my phone was. And he'd be familiar with the property, including where you'd park if you came to the ER."

A third check mark. "And the shooting in the hospital parking lot?"

"Of course." She waited while Adam made the final check. "You said he was in dark clothes that night, but not in uniform.

We have only his word that he likes to hang around the ER when he's off duty. He could have followed us from the restaurant, shot at me—"

"We've also said that could have been a mistake," Adam said. "Maybe he thought he was shooting at me."

"And when you emerged from the darkness carrying me, he saw what he'd done. So he ran to help you."

Adam ran his finger down the check marks. "All right, we know he had the opportunity. The means presents no real problem here. That leaves motive."

"If he's Charlie DeLuca's stepson from that second marriage . . . We don't know that he is, but if that's true we should be able to connect the dots."

"We need to find out if Rob Cole was originally Rob Kohler," Adam said.

Carrie nodded. She knew two things: that it would be up to her to get that information from Rob, and that she dreaded the encounter.

It was well after midnight before they agreed that their brains were no longer functional. Adam paused by Carrie's kitchen door and wondered if she'd ever forgive him for getting her into this. His doubts were erased by the hug and kiss she delivered, followed by the whispered admonition, "Be careful."

"I will," he assured her.

"And call me when you're safely home."

"I'll make it short. If our friend, the stalker, has some sort of way to track me via my cell phone, that would at least make it less likely he'll know that I'm in my apartment."

Adam slid out the door and ran in a crouch toward the six-foot-high wood fence that separated Carrie's backyard from the alley. The slats were fastened to two horizontal rails. Adam put his toe on the lower of the two boards, grasped the top of the fence, and pulled himself to the top. He rolled over and landed on the narrow strip of grass that separated the fence from the paved alley.

He took a minute to catch his breath, then worked his way slowly through the alleys toward where he'd left his car. The neighborhood was dark. Although there were street lamps in the area, there were none in the alleys. Adam was sure some homes had motion-triggered lights in the backyards, but the fences shielded his movements, so he remained in darkness. The occasional bark of a dog signaled his passing, but he kept moving.

He emerged from the last alley and scanned the area where his vehicle was parked. Other cars sat silent nearby, but all of them were empty—or if there were occupants, they were hidden. Adam gave it a few minutes. He heard no sound, saw no movement. No telltale embers of cigarettes glowed anywhere. The last thought made Adam smile, as he visualized a man clothed in black, lurking in the darkness, smoking a cigarette, occasionally fingering the gun tucked into his belt. *You've seen too many late-night movies on TV.*

He hurried to his car and unlocked it with his key to avoid the beep and flashing lights of the security system. He eased into the driver's seat, glad he'd remembered to remove the bulb from the interior light. He pulled the door closed gently and relocked it. He didn't turn on his headlights until he was half a block away. Then he went through a series of turns to make certain no one was following him. The drivers of the few cars he encountered seemed more interested in getting to their destination than pursuing Adam.

As he pulled into the parking lot behind his apartment, he killed the headlights and scanned the area. He'd made an effort to memorize as many as possible of the cars normally parked there, and he saw nothing out of the ordinary. Rather than taking his numbered slot, he chose a visitor's space toward the end of the row. He recalled his brother's warning about the dangers of predictability. If unpredictability meant being exposed for a longer walk to his back door, so be it.

Before he opened the car door, he pulled up his right pants leg and slid the pistol from its holster. If he was going to need it, now would be the time. Much like a coach giving a pep talk, he reminded himself that although he wasn't a killer, he was the target of one. And if he had to shoot to defend himself, he would.

He eased out of the car and locked it with the key. Adam looked around once more. Nothing moved.

He strode purposefully toward the back door of his apartment and was halfway there when gunfire from behind a Dumpster to his left made him drop to the ground. Two shots in rapid succession were followed by the scream of a car alarm. Adam stood up, pointed his pistol at the area where he'd seen the muzzle flashes, and pulled the trigger twice.

He heard the whine of a car engine revving, the screech of tires on pavement. He got a fleeting glimpse of a bulky vehicle, probably a light-colored SUV, exiting the parking lot. Adam took that as his cue. Already lights were popping on in the apartment building. Witnesses would emerge in a moment, and the police wouldn't be far behind. He sprinted for his apartment, opened the back door, and tumbled inside in one motion. Adam moved toward the center of the apartment, but not before he engaged both the door's lock and deadbolt. Then he duck-walked to an interior wall and eased down against it, trying to catch his breath.

Returning fire had been a reflex, and now Adam wondered at the wisdom of his action. He realized he could have injured, even killed an innocent bystander. Moreover, now the assailant knew Adam was armed. Would that make him even more dangerous?

Should he clear out again, move to another motel? If he stayed, was he endangering his neighbors? He decided that the shooter was unlikely to return that night, so it was probably safe to stay here for the time being. Tomorrow . . . well, he'd decide that after the sun came up.

Adam leaned against the wall, his gun almost forgotten in his hand, and wondered how many more close calls there would be . . . and how many he could survive.

———— ⌁ ————

Carrie wished she could call the clinic and tell whoever answered that she wouldn't be in today. Her head was still sore, but more than that, her brain felt like a house after a tornado struck, her thoughts scattered like pieces of furniture, some fragmented, all out of order. And long periods of staring wide-eyed at the ceiling interspersed with occasional troubling dreams had done nothing to refresh her during the night.

But Thursday was Thad Avery's afternoon off, and she didn't want to ask him to cover for her. No, she'd bite the bullet and go to work. She'd done it before, in medical school, in residency training, in practice. If she could care for patients right after the death of her husband, she could certainly power through headache and fatigue.

In the shower, Carrie tried to avoid getting her scalp wound wet but eventually decided she couldn't stand dirty hair one more day. She carefully washed her blond hair, then dried it gently and used a few light brush strokes to style it to hide the scab left by the bullet. She dressed in a white blouse and black slacks and put on a minimum of makeup. It wouldn't hurt if people thought she was pale—maybe they'd take it easy on her.

Her breakfast was a cup of coffee and two extra-strength Tylenol. Carrie wasn't particularly hungry now. If that changed, she'd grab a donut from the break room mid-morning, by which time a pharmaceutical rep would no doubt have left a couple of boxes of them, along with information on the latest drug from his company.

In her car, she pulled her cell phone from her purse, paused with her thumb over a speed-dial button, then changed her mind. She and Adam had agreed to keep communication to a minimum, not so much to avoid electronic eavesdropping as to allow each of them to carry out the tasks they'd set for themselves. Before he left last night—this morning, actually— they agreed to meet again tonight about ten p.m. at her house. She hated the maneuvers he had to go through to get there, but he insisted that was the best way to keep from leading the shooter directly to Carrie.

Either by design or coincidence, the list of patients Lila placed on Carrie's desk was short. She scanned the names and the diagnosis or reason for each visit and felt herself relax a bit.

She should be able to handle these, as well any emergencies that cropped up. She also found a note from the receptionist on her desk: "See Dr. Rushton." No explanation. Not a request. A command. She wondered if those had been the exact words Phil had used.

In any case she'd see Phil, but first she wanted to check on her hospitalized patients, review the reports and lab work on her desk.

Hospital rounds were easier than Carrie anticipated. In her absence, Thad Avery, the other internist in the group, had seen both her hospitalized patients, found them to be much improved, and sent them home. Maybe she'd misjudged Thad. Perhaps he really was a nice guy. She'd always figured he had a hand in patients switching from her care to his, but she could be wrong. Maybe it was all Phil's work.

Bolstered by her second and third cups of coffee of the morning, Carrie walked down the hall to Phil Rushton's office. There was never any problem finding Phil. From before sunup to after sundown, Phil was either in his office, in surgery, or making hospital rounds. She hadn't seen him at the hospital and his name wasn't listed on the surgery schedule in the doctor's lounge. Therefore, Carrie figured he'd be in his office.

She looked through the open door. Phil was seated at his desk, paging through a journal, occasionally using a yellow highlighter to mark a passage. She tapped on the door frame. He didn't raise his head, didn't acknowledge her in any way. She tapped again, and in a voice that conveyed neither irritation nor pleasure, Phil muttered, "Come."

Carrie entered and took one of the two chairs on the

opposite side of the desk from Phil. He held up one finger in a "give me a minute" gesture. Carrie marveled at the man's ability to focus so completely on the task at hand. She recalled what a colleague had once said about Phil. "His focus is so complete he could burn a hole in a telephone directory with it."

While Phil's head was down, Carrie looked once more at the diplomas and certificates on his office wall. His training had been impressive: Northwestern, Pritzker, Rush. Then, when the puzzle pieces fell together in her mind, her throat tightened and the hairs on the back of her neck prickled.

Doctors as a group might not have a firm grasp of geography, but most of them knew the locations of first-rate medical schools and hospitals. And she knew where all these were: Chicago—the same city that had been home to Charlie DeLuca . . . and his family and friends.

Phil closed the journal and looked up. "Carrie, thank you for coming by. How are you feeling?"

"Fine. Some headaches, some scalp tenderness—nothing that Tylenol doesn't handle."

Phil twirled the highlighter between his fingers. "You know, you seem to be something of a magnet for trouble nowadays. You were in the lawyer's office when the firebomb was thrown. Somebody took a shot at you in the hospital parking lot and barely missed doing grave damage . . . maybe killing you." He looked at Carrie as though he could read the deepest secrets in her eyes. "Is there something going on in your life I should know about?"

Here we go, Carrie thought. *He's building a case to get rid of me on the basis of "improper conduct." Well, I'm not going to let that happen.* "Phil, I'm offended that you'd ask that. My private life isn't the issue here. When I joined this clinic, I signed a contract with all the standard clauses, including the one that lets you terminate me because of improper conduct. But I don't think that gives you permission to delve repeatedly into what I do on my own time." She took a deep breath. "If you're unhappy with my work as a doctor, say so and we can talk about the group buying me out. If not, I'd rather not go into what I do outside the office and hospital."

Phil's response came quickly. "Carrie, I have to ask these questions. If there's something going on that might affect the clinic, I need to know. That's all." He leaned across the desk, radiating sincerity from every pore. "You know I like you—like you a lot. I'm just offering to help."

Carrie marveled at how quickly Phil's manner changed. It was as if he'd flipped a switch, and a caring colleague replaced the all-business administrator. Then again, she didn't totally buy this nice-guy act. "Sorry. I guess my fuse is sort of short these days. Getting shot will do that to you." She shook her head. "Let me assure you that recent events have nothing to do with the clinic or my work here. And on a personal level, I'm fine, and I don't need any help. But thanks for asking."

Phil apparently wasn't through though. "Your ex-fiance— Adam Davidson. You've been seeing a lot of him lately again, haven't you?"

"Yes, but I can't see where that could possibly affect the group."

"I was just wondering. He only turned up here in Jameson a few months ago, right? Do you know much about his past? Is there something there that might be at the root of these attacks?"

Carrie's antenna was tingling. She needed to head this off, and quickly. "I know what I need to about Adam, but I don't see that it's necessary to discuss it with you. Again, that's my private life, and it has no bearing on my professional activities." She looked at her watch, rose, and said, "If that's all, I really need to get started with my morning clinic."

As she walked down the hall, Carrie tried to replay her recent encounters with Phil, now viewing each of them in a whole new light. She felt as though she were trapped in a maze where a new surprise, each one unpleasant, waited around every corner. *They'd need to add Phil's name to the list. How many more suspects? How much longer?*

NINETEEN

ADAM HAD NEVER FELT LESS LIKE ROLLING OUT OF BED TO START A new day. He squinted at the face of his watch and made out "Th." Thursday. The few days he'd been back in town had provided at least a month's worth of excitement. If he could make it through today and tomorrow, maybe he could use the weekend to rest and organize his thoughts. Right now he felt as though he was trying to unravel a tangled ball of yarn, one with multiple loose ends.

The attack last night had left him shaken. He knew he should call Carrie sometime today and give her that news, and he dreaded the conversation. Adam could almost hear her saying, "How much longer?" He'd spent most of the night searching desperately for a way to track down the shooter, but so far he'd come up empty.

After some coffee and a shower, the world looked marginally better. In his bedroom he repacked his briefcase for the day.

He tossed in his cell, then remembered to add the throwaway phone as well, since that was the number he'd given Corky. After that call maybe he could discard this one entirely.

Adam's eye lit on the balled-up handkerchief on the top of his dresser—the cartridge shell he'd picked up in the hospital parking lot. It had seemed like a good idea at the time, but now he wondered if there was any way it would yield usable information. He sealed the brass casing in a plastic sandwich bag from the kitchen and dropped it into his briefcase. Maybe he could check into it later today.

The shell made him think of Dave. He'd planned to ask his brother if he could have it checked for fingerprints, maybe even run the prints through some kind of database. Surely a marshal would have contacts for something like that. But now Dave was out of circulation for a while, in a hospital bed hundreds of miles away.

Adam lifted the semiautomatic from his bedside table, where it had given him a measure of confidence as he tumbled about in fitful sleep. The odor of gunpowder assaulted his nostrils, and he remembered what Colonel Johnson told him during their quick introductory session on the pistol: if you fire it, do two things immediately: clean and oil it, so the barrel isn't pitted by the products of the explosion, and reload it, because you never know how many shots you'll need next time.

Adam ejected the magazine, then racked the slide to clear the bullet that was in the chamber. When he was certain the gun was safe to handle, he set about cleaning it, using the kit sold to him by the clerk at the same store where he bought his holster. He shoved two fresh bullets into the magazine, reassembled the pistol, and set the safety. When he was certain the weapon was ready for action, he strapped it securely into his ankle holster.

Somehow, feeling the weight of the pistol resting against his calf wasn't as comforting to Adam as he thought it would be. In his braver daydreams, the stalker pulled out a gun but Adam's lightning-fast draw allowed him to put a bullet into the assailant's shoulder before the man could fire the first shot. In other, less pleasant fantasies, the gun in Adam's hand was useless while the shooter fired from point-blank range. That vision ended with a black haze descending like a curtain to signal Adam's death.

———————————————⎍⎍———————————————

By ten o'clock Carrie was not only caught up, but a few minutes ahead. "I'm going to get some coffee and a donut," she told Lila.

"Out of luck," Lila said. "The Merck rep was supposed to be here today, but he had to cancel." She grinned. "But if you're hungry, I hid a couple of pastries from yesterday in the fridge. They may be a little stale, but I'll share."

"Sounds good," Carrie said.

Lila microwaved the two cherry Danish, and she and Carrie eased into chairs in the corner of the break room, fresh coffee in hand. "Thanks so much," Carrie said.

"Consider it payback for giving up your Sunday afternoon to come to the ER and take care of my mother."

"How's she doing?"

Lila looked at the clock on the wall. "You can see for yourself. She has an appointment with you just before lunch." She took another bite of Danish, chewed, and swallowed. "But I think she's doing fine."

Carrie reflected on the way she'd solved the diagnostic puzzle presented by Mrs. James, Lila's mother, and her hypertension. Diagnostic puzzles and grateful patients would always be an important part of the practice of medicine for her. They were what kept her going, even when it was hard. And the more she thought about it, the more grateful Carrie was that God allowed her to do something that brought her so much pleasure. *Thank You, Lord.*

Adam worked hard to follow his usual routine at work: he came in early, made the coffee, buried his nose in the tasks left for him, and spoke only when spoken to. He hoped if he did that, no one would notice his bloodshot eyes, the frequent yawns, the two tiny pieces of tissue stuck over the cuts he'd inflicted on himself while shaving.

If he were a drinker, the picture could be passed off as the aftereffects of a hard night on the town. But Adam, in sharp contrast with Bruce Hartley, was a teetotaler, and the staff knew it. So if anyone noticed his state this morning, questions were sure to follow.

Other than a brief conversation with Brittany, who was more interested in relating her own experiences of the prior evening than asking Adam about his, he managed to pass the morning with a minimum of interaction with others in the office. That changed at about eleven, when Mary Delkus tapped on the frame of his open office door.

"May I come in?" The question was apparently rhetorical, because before Adam could respond she was settling herself in one of the chairs across from him.

He composed his features into what he hoped passed for a pleasant grin. "What's up, Mary?"

"I'm still wondering if I could take you to lunch. If we're going to be working together, I think it would be nice if we got to know each other better."

Wheels were spinning in Adam's head before Mary finished speaking. Did she want to know about him so she could undermine his chances of getting his permanent job back? Was she setting him up as a fallback if her relationship with Bruce Hartley fizzled? Or—and Adam sort of regretted the cynicism that put this so far down the line of possibilities— was she truly a nice lady who just wanted to get to know a coworker better? Whatever the cause of the invitation, he needed to wriggle out of it. It had always been important for him to maintain the anonymity that prevented anyone from digging too deeply into his cover story. Right now that was more imperative than ever.

Mary raised her eyebrows in a silent follow-up to her invitation.

Adam tried to deepen his grin. "Believe me, Mary, I'd like nothing better. But I have a luncheon appointment that I can't change, so I'll have to take a rain check."

The raised eyebrows turned into a frown. "Adam, that's twice you've turned down my invitation to lunch. If I didn't know better, I'd swear you were trying to avoid going out with me. It's just a lunch. Nothing more."

Adam spread his hands. "I know, and I wish I could take you up on it. But I've been gone, and I'm trying to catch up." He pulled out his cell phone and opened the calendar function. "How about next week? Maybe Tuesday?"

Mary reached into the coat pocket of her stylish navy suit and pulled out the latest iPhone. She touched the screen a couple of times, then smiled. "I'm putting you down for lunch on Tuesday." The smile stayed on her lips, but her blue eyes conveyed a different message altogether. They said, *No more excuses, mister.*

As Mary left, Adam made a note on his own calendar. This gave him four days before he had to face Mary's questions. And he was sure that there would be questions. The woman might be only a paralegal, but he'd already figured that she'd be great on cross-examination of a witness.

His next step was a phone call. He'd need to be out of the office to make it, which was yet another reason not to accept Mary's invitation. Adam reached into his in-box and pulled out the top sheet. To a casual passerby he'd seem deep in thought. Actually, he was, but not about Jason Whitley's will. He was putting together a cover story to explain his lunch appointment, in case anyone asked. And the way his luck was running, someone would.

———————————————— ⋀ ————————————————

Carrie was pleased to find that, as Lila had said, her mother was indeed doing well. Having been sufficiently frightened by the effects of the weight-loss product from the health food store, she'd decided to substitute willpower for herbs and had lost a pound since her last visit. Her blood pressure was behaving. Carrie assured Mrs. James that if she could drop another eight or nine pounds, she should be able to come off her blood pressure medicine entirely.

"You're welcome to join Mom and me for lunch," Lila said as she escorted her mother down the hall.

"Thanks, but I'll just grab a sandwich at the hospital," Carrie said. She left mother and daughter at the checkout desk.

Fifteen minutes later she was flipping a mental coin between the tuna salad and smoked turkey sandwiches. Finally, her choice made, she took her tray to the most remote corner of the food court and slid into a chair at the last open table for two.

When her husband was alive, he and Carrie unashamedly said grace in public, holding hands, taking turns praying. But after his death, she dropped the practice. Although she was back on speaking terms with God, bowing her head to pray in a crowded environment was still beyond her. She decided to compromise. Without bowing her head, she breathed a silent prayer. She knew God wasn't picky about whether the prayer was voiced or simply formed in her mind.

She had a potato chip halfway to her mouth when a familiar voice caused her to stop. "May I share your table?"

Carrie looked up and put aside any idea of a quiet lunch to refresh her mind and calm her soul. The voice belonged to Rob Cole.

———————————⌁———————————

"Going to lunch," Adam said to Brittany as he hurried by her desk and out the door.

Although his assailant had never targeted him in broad daylight, Adam continued the practice of parking in a space other than his assigned one in front of his office building. He hurried to his car, half expecting to hear a shot at any moment, maybe even feel a bullet sink deep into his flesh. Once in the Forester, he let out a breath he hadn't realized he was holding.

He pulled away, one eye on the rearview mirror, and began a series of turns that by now were second nature to him. Eventually he backtracked toward his office and pulled to a stop near one of the small cafés that was a gathering place at noon for lawyers with business in the courthouse nearby. He made casual conversation with a few of the men as he waited to be seated. If anyone at his office asked about his lunch appointment, he was ready to say he met with someone from another law office, exploring the idea of a position there if his return to Hartley and Evans didn't work out. Beyond that he'd be tight-lipped.

Adam settled in at a booth in the back of the café. He ordered a sandwich and waited until it was served. Then he unfolded the newspaper he'd brought with him. Behind it Adam pulled out his cell phone and punched in a number. He hoped his brother was feeling up to answering—wasn't there some rule against cell phones in hospitals? Maybe they'd make an exception for a lawman. Did Dave even have his cell phone with him?

The call rang for the fifth time, and Adam figured it was about to roll over to voice mail. Then there was a click, a pause, followed by a voice, weak but familiar. "Branson."

Adam felt himself grinning. "Dave, it's me. Adam. Can you talk?"

"Let me see. I have the president and the attorney general here in my hospital room, but I guess I can tell them they'll have to wait." This was followed by what started as a chuckle but ended in a barking cough. "Sorry. Still coughing some. They say it's due to the anesthetic."

"Are you okay to talk?"

"Sure. Other than getting tortured by the sadist in physical therapy twice a day, I just lie here and channel surf. I've watched so much daytime TV my brain is starting to rot."

"What do the doctors tell you?"

"They say I got shot in the shoulder."

"You know what I mean."

Dave's voice took on a more somber note. "The initial surgery was done to stop the bleeding and clean up the wound. I'd lost too much blood for them to do more than that right then. I'm getting built back up, but we have to decide soon what to do next if I want my arm to be fully functional again."

Adam couldn't imagine a marshall with an impaired right arm. Did this mean his brother was going to lose his badge? Did they have to pass some sort of proficiency test? Never mind. Those were questions for another time. "Listen, I need to ask you a question."

"Ask away."

"We . . . uh. That is, someone shot at Carrie and me the other night. Grazed her scalp, but we're fine."

Dave wanted all the details, and Adam spent five minutes pouring them out. He finished with, "Now I have a question for you."

"Okay."

"I went back to the parking lot and found an empty shell casing the police must have overlooked. I'm pretty sure it's one the rifle ejected. Do you think it will tell us anything?"

"Sure. Someone who knows a thing or two about guns could tell you the caliber of the weapon."

"Can it be matched with the gun?"

"I've heard they're working on something like that, but at

present you can't identify a rifle by the ejected shell casing. You have to compare an actual bullet with one that was test-fired from the gun. Do you have the slug?"

Adam thought about police combing the field with metal detectors. "No, and we're not likely to find one." He decided to ask the other question, although the more he thought about it, the more he realized he already knew the answer. "Do you think the shell might have fingerprints on it?"

"Possibly, but if so, they'd most likely be partials. If that's the case, they might not be enough to provide an identity. Sorry."

Adam felt the wind leave his sails. "So it's not worth running them?"

"Let me talk with a friend. Hang on to the casing, and I'll let you know."

They talked for a few more minutes before ending the conversation with Dave warning his brother to be careful and Adam promising to call again the next day. He folded the newspaper and dropped it on the table for the next customer. Then he rose and walked slowly out of the café, leaving his partially eaten sandwich behind.

Carrie knew what she had to do, but she crammed a full-fledged argument with herself into the few seconds that followed Rob's request. Part of her longed for a quiet half hour to recharge her emotional and physical batteries before she returned to the clinic for the afternoon. On the other hand, Carrie recognized this encounter as a tailor-made opportunity to embark on the task she'd set for herself last night: find out more about Rob Cole.

She gestured to the empty chair. "Sure, Rob. Have a seat."

Rob unloaded his food and looked around for somewhere to put his empty tray. Finally he shrugged and shoved it under his chair.

What if Rob was the shooter? Would this encounter put her in danger? No, the tables around her were filled with potential witnesses. Oh, if this were a spy story, Rob might try to touch her with the poisoned tip of an umbrella, but it wasn't. This was real life. And the longer she hesitated, the less likely he was to open up to the questions she knew she had to ask.

She was surprised when Rob closed his eyes and bowed his head over his food. His lips moved, although he said nothing. The grace probably lasted less than fifteen seconds, but in that short period of time Carrie found herself rethinking her opinion of Rob Cole.

Carrie took the first bite of her sandwich, chewed, and swallowed while she pondered how to work her way into her questions. Before she could put down her fork, Rob gave her the opening she needed.

"I'm sort of glad this seat was available," he said around a bite of burger. "I've wanted the chance to get better acquainted. But I'm afraid I've put you off, the way I've gone about it."

This was certainly a different Rob from the brash, almost intrusive EMT she'd seen before. "You have to admit, Rob, that all our interactions have seemed more like flirting than getting to know each other."

"I know. Sometimes I come off that way, but I don't mean to. My therapist says it's a defense mechanism."

"Why don't we start fresh?" Carrie said. "Get to know each other."

"I understand you used to be married. What happened?"

Well, he certainly didn't lob her an easy question to start. Carrie felt the hairs on the back of her neck prickle. She'd kept most of this locked up for the better part of two years. Could she share it now? With a man who might be trying to kill her? Her gut tightened when she realized the only way to find out about him was to make the trade.

Carrie closed her eyes for a moment as the memories came flooding back. "John was a general surgeon, in the same group where I practice." She told him of the fatigue, the struggle to get her husband to see a doctor, the eventual diagnosis of Ebstein's anomaly.

Rob raised his eyebrows. "I don't think I've ever heard of that."

It had been hard for Carrie to share the story with Mr. McDonald. It was pure torture to tell it to Rob. "What John had—what was causing his spells of fatigue—were runs of tachycardia. The runs were so brief I never picked up on the rapid heart rate. Then they changed to ventricular tachycardia."

Rob gave a low whistle. "People can die from V tach. What happened?"

Carrie laid out the events in a flat voice: unsuccessful attempts to control the problem with medications, the failure of cardioversion with an electrical current, and eventually the transvenous radiofrequency ablation—the procedure to destroy the focus of heart muscle that threatened John's life.

Finally she bowed her head and squeezed her eyes shut. She wouldn't cry in front of Rob. She wouldn't. In a moment she looked up and blinked hard before saying, "The catheter punctured one of John's coronary arteries. It's a one-in-a-million thing—but it happened to my husband. They rushed him to surgery to repair it, but it was too late. He died."

"I'm sorry." Rob's simple response seemed sincere.

"Thank you," she said. "I'm trying to move on." She forced a smile. "How about you? Where are you from? What brought you to Jameson?"

Rob took his time swallowing a bite of sandwich and washed it down with water. He sighed. "I grew up in a small suburb of Chicago. Small family—mother, dad, one sister. My dad died the day I was supposed to graduate high school. That turned my world upside down. Instead of college, I started work at a local hospital. Then I found out I could take a night class and become an EMT. It took awhile, but I got through it and even got certified as a paramedic."

"And I'm glad you did," Carrie said. "You're an excellent one."

"Thanks." Rob acknowledged the compliment with a small nod. "My mom remarried, and things were going better. Then—" He shook his head, emptied his water glass, looked away. It took him a minute to regain his composure. "Then my stepdad . . . he did something awful."

Carrie looked at him expectantly. She raised her eyebrows but didn't speak. *Let him get it out. Don't force it.*

Rob pursed his lips and ducked his head. He was silent for a moment. When he looked up again, tears glistened in the corners of his eyes. "He did something so awful that I changed my name and left town."

Carrie felt as though she'd just entered a minefield, where careful steps were necessary, and one misstep would spell disaster. Rob had given her the opening she needed, but she had the feeling that if she asked the wrong question, took him in the wrong direction, he'd clam up and she might never get the answers she needed. She needed to come at it slowly. "How did you end up in Jameson?"

Rob kept his head down. "There are some online sites that list EMT jobs. This one looked good. I always wanted to see Texas. And Jameson was a long way from where I'd been living."

She bought time with a swallow of iced tea, then centered the glass on the napkin beneath it. "Would you like to tell me why you left?"

He shook his head. "This is silly. We started out trying to get to know each other, and now I'm playing true confessions. You don't want to hear this." He shoved back his chair as though ready to spring from it.

Carrie put one hand on his wrist. "Rob, you've said you wanted to get closer to me. Maybe I feel the same way too. But we've never had the time or been in the right situation." For a moment she felt a twinge of guilt for the way she was manipulating him. Then she realized that he might be the same man who'd been trying to kill her and Adam. *Forgive me, John. Forgive me, Adam. You know I don't mean this.* "I've told you about the biggest loss in my life. But what I haven't said is that now I'm trying to go forward, maybe even let someone into my world again. It could be you, but I can't know unless you tell me more about yourself."

Rob's expression was hard to read, and his tone of voice was neutral as well. "What about Adam Davidson?"

She worked to put a frown on her face. "I don't know what kind of trouble Adam's in, but it's almost gotten me killed three times now."

"So there's nothing between you?"

"Let's just say I'm keeping my options open."

Rob eased back into his chair. He placed his hands flat on the tabletop for support as he leaned toward her. "Maybe you're right. It's time to let you know about the real me."

He met Carrie's eyes, but she couldn't read his expression. "What my stepdad did—"

The strident tones of a pager pierced the lunchtime noise of the food court and stopped Rob in mid-sentence. He frowned, pulled the instrument from his belt, and glanced at the display. In one motion he shoved back from the table and stood. "Sorry. Guess lunch is over. Got an emergency call." He grabbed his tray, loaded it with his dirty dishes, and turned to go. Two steps away, he said over his shoulder, "Let's continue this sometime soon. I'll call you."

Carrie's stomach churned, and she struggled not to bring up the few bites of lunch she'd managed to choke down. As she watched him hurry away, Carrie had mixed emotions about her encounter with Rob Cole. She'd been close to finding out what she needed to know about him, but she wasn't sure she wanted to hear it.

TWENTY

AT MID-AFTERNOON ADAM WAS AT HIS DESK, A CUP OF COFFEE AT his elbow, poring over the draft of a new will for Elwood Stroud. Stroud was generally held to be the richest man in Jameson, and according to office gossip, his family could hardly wait for the old man to surrender to the ravages of old age. But Stroud was as tough as the trunk of an old elm tree. He'd already outlived many of his friends and most of his enemies, and he apparently intended to do the same with his three children if that was what it took to keep their hands off the money he'd accumulated in his eighty-eight years on the planet.

"Got a minute?" Janice Evans poked her head in the door. Adam had never seen her look anything but "put together," and today was no exception. "Sure. Just working on this draft of Mr. Stroud's will."

Janice covered her mouth, but not before Adam saw the

ghost of a smile flicker across her lips. "Let me guess. He wants to change two or three of his million-dollar bequests."

"Uh, yeah. That's about it."

"Mr. Stroud, God love him, has enough money to get by on. He'll never be eating dog food, but he doesn't have anything like the money he describes in his will."

"But I thought—"

"He used to be a multimillionaire. Made it in oil and got out before the bubble burst. But he gave away most of it. Anyone who approached him with a hard-luck story got some money. It's common knowledge that he's paid the college expenses of a couple dozen kids from the poorer part of town. And I know for sure that he's bailed out several men who were about to lose their businesses."

"So why do we keep rewriting his will for him?"

She stepped inside and closed the door. "Because this law firm was one of the businesses he bailed out." Evans lowered her voice. "Bruce told me about it when I joined the practice. He'd piled up some gambling debts—big ones—but couldn't stop. Finally, when the man who held his markers sent someone around to *reason* with him, Bruce knew he had to do something. He went to Stroud, and they struck a deal. Stroud would pay off Bruce's debts in return for two things: Bruce would never gamble again, and our firm would handle Stroud's legal affairs without charge."

"I'm presuming Bruce kept his end of the bargain." Adam looked at the thick document on his desk. "So this is . . ."

"Yep. And I have to agree with Mr. Stroud that his kids don't deserve a nickel, considering how much of his money they've already blown through. Every one of the wills does two things: makes a nice bequest to his church and arranges for payment of his final expenses. Beyond that, though, despite what the wills say, there's not a lot of money to spread around." She gestured toward a chair. "Do you mind?"

"Of course. This can wait for a while." Adam shoved the paper aside. "What's up?"

"I think you're owed an explanation for what you walked into when you returned from your visit with your brother."

"I'll have to admit I was surprised to find that Mary had my job."

Evans folded her hands in her lap and looked down at them. "I didn't think what Bruce did was right, but . . . well, he is the senior partner, and he sort of insisted." She raised her head and looked him in the eye. "He was going to let you go, but I did a little foot-stomping of my own. That's why you're still here."

"I appreciate your going to bat for me," Adam said.

"I don't think there's any question that you'll be made permanent in a couple of weeks. But I'm sorry you had to go through this."

She rose and took a step toward the door. "Don't be too harsh on Bruce. I'm sure you're familiar with the legal term 'undue influence.' That's what's at work in his situation right now. You just happen to be the one getting the bad deal as a result of it."

After Evans left, Adam sat staring into space. He hit a key on his computer and the screen saver disappeared. He tapped out a familiar Web address, and in a few seconds the screen lit up with the online site that had largely replaced the familiar bound volume known as Martindale-Hubbell. It was a comprehensive source of information about lawyers in the United

States and around the world, and it could answer the question that had formed in Adam's mind.

He clicked on the search box and entered "Bruce Hartley." When the requested page popped up, he scanned it and realized that his list of suspects wasn't narrowing. It was widening.

Adam needed to call Dave and check on his recovery. It was about time to leave anyway, so he'd do it from his car. He slipped into his suit coat and headed out the door, telling Brittany he'd see her in the morning.

Behind dark glasses Adam's eyes were never still as he walked briskly to his vehicle. He'd purchased a Kevlar vest but decided it was impractical for daily wear. Still, he made sure he varied his routine—the times he came to work and left, the place he parked his car, even the restaurants and cafés where he ate. And, above all, he increased his watchfulness.

After the usual aimless driving, he pulled into a strip shopping center, keeping the engine running to allow the car's air conditioner to function. In a moment he was talking with his brother. "How's the recuperation?"

"Kind of at a fork in the road," Dave said. "The surgeon says I'm stable from my blood loss, but it's time to decide what to do about my shoulder. It works well enough, but if I want full function, the best chance is another operation. I didn't understand it all, but apparently the bullet tore things up, sort of like what a baseball pitcher does to his rotator cuff."

"Is that what has to be done?"

"No, I have choices. If I have the surgery, then go through physical therapy, I stand a really good chance of coming out with a normally functioning shoulder in a few months." Dave paused and Adam heard the sound of swallowing. "Sorry. Don't talk much now, and my throat gets dry when I do. Anyway, my other option is to skip the surgery and just do the rehab. Eventually I'd have adequate function in that arm—but I'd probably never be fit for police work again."

"Sounds like you only have one viable choice," Adam said.

Dave sighed. "Yeah, I guess."

"Shall I come down there?"

"No, he's going to discharge me later today," Dave said. "When I asked the doc for a recommendation, he suggested a Dr. Burkhead in Dallas. Supposed to be a cracker-jack surgeon for this kind of stuff. And I'll be a half-hour's drive from you."

"Great. So I can be there for the operation and help you afterward."

"No, I still think it's best for you to keep your distance."

Adam couldn't understand. Dave, as he'd been able to do all their lives, seemed able to read Adam's mind.

"Your stalker may know who you really are, but he doesn't know about me. Let's keep it that way. I can be your ace in the hole."

Adam figured that a marshall with his right arm in a sling wasn't much of a secret weapon, but he decided not to argue. "After you leave the hospital, would you like to stay here in Jameson with me?"

"Not a good idea. I have a friend in Dallas. I plan to stay with him while I wait to see the surgeon."

Adam wondered what else he'd missed in his brother's life by being on the run these past couple of years. But there was no time for guilty reflection. He was about to ask if Dave had checked on getting fingerprints off the rifle shell when his brother said, "The nurse is here to check my vital signs. Guess I'd better sign off. Be careful . . . Adam."

As he pulled away, Adam wished he could go home to a normal family instead of constantly looking over his shoulder, expecting a bullet to strike him at any moment. Maybe someday. Maybe someday soon.

Carrie's afternoon was busier than her morning, but she was grateful in a way. Dealing with the patients kept her from thinking about her lunch with Rob Cole. The fragment of his story that he'd shared certainly fit with what Adam told her about Charlie DeLuca's second family and the son who changed his name and disappeared. But if that were the case, would Rob have been willing to open up to her so easily?

Had all his flirting simply been an attempt to get closer to her in order to learn more about Adam? Was Rob toying with her now? Could he have triggered his own pager to end their time together, tired of teasing her, with no intention of revealing his real identity? While they were talking, she'd thought she was close to unlocking the identity of Adam's shooter. But now she wasn't sure about that—or much of anything else about the case.

Carrie was deep in thought as she moved to the next exam room, when she heard, "Whoa. Better look up every once in a while."

She did just that and saw Phil Rushton dead ahead. He waved the papers in his hand and said, "Glad we didn't collide. That hard head of yours might give me a concussion."

Carrie wasn't sure whether Phil was joking or referring to her last meeting with him. "I need to talk with you when you've finished with patients. Call my cell phone." And he was off again.

Carrie tapped on the door of the exam room and stepped inside. She tucked Phil's request into a corner of her mind and concentrated on the patient sitting on the edge of the examination table. From the frown on his face it was fairly obvious that the man didn't want to be there. But the presence of his wife gave Carrie her best clue of the dynamics of the situation.

"Mr. Hoover, what sort of problems are you having?"

"I'm not having a problem," Hoover said, almost before Carrie could finish. "But she . . ." A nod toward his wife, who stood beside him with arms folded. "She's afraid I have heart trouble. Just because of this little pain I get sometimes." As if to demonstrate, Hoover held his clenched fist over his mid-chest.

The check-in sheet Lila had handed her showed Hoover's age as fifty-eight, his height as five feet six inches, his weight two hundred ten pounds. Even without the charted blood pressure of one hundred eighty over one hundred, the man's florid complexion alerted her to the likelihood of hypertension.

Carrie asked a series of questions, which were sometimes answered by Hoover, sometimes by his wife. His favorite exercise seemed to be moving between the dinner table and the TV set. Walking a block or less brought on crushing chest pain that sometimes radiated down his left arm and was relieved slowly by rest.

The rest of the exam, and the EKG that followed, confirmed Carrie's suspicion. Hoover had significant coronary artery disease. His tracing suggested that he'd already had one mild myocardial infarction, a "heart attack" that damaged a small amount of the muscle in that organ. It took the combined efforts of Hoover's wife and Carrie to convince him that the best course was imme diate hospitalization. "We'll need to do an angiogram—that's a test where they inject dye into the blood vessels in your heart. That lets us see how much blockage there is. Sometimes a stent can be inserted via the plastic tube that puts the dye into your heart, but sometimes surgery is necessary. We have excellent doctors who do this all the time."

"But my business—"

His wife jumped in at this point. "Arliss, someone else is going to run your business, whether you're in the hospital for a few days or you die and leave it behind. Let's go for the few days' option."

Carrie wrote a note and orders, set up the emergency angiogram, and alerted Phil Rushton's nurse that he might have to do a coronary bypass procedure. She accompanied Hoover to the radiology suite and stood by as he underwent coronary angiography. When she and the interventional radiologist agreed that stent insertion wouldn't be adequate, Carrie pulled out her cell phone to contact Phil Rushton.

Before she could complete the call, Phil walked in. "I was about to call you," Carrie said. "This one is going to require your talents." She summarized the case in a few words. Phil studied the angiogram and nodded.

"I'll talk with them," he said. "Carrie, I presume you have no objection to my taking over at this point?"

Well, at least he's asking. "Just so long as you let me direct his care after you discharge him. He needs weight reduction, control of his blood pressure, a—"

"Sure," Phil said. "I wanted to talk with you, but I guess we can do it tomorrow. Maybe after work, over dinner." And he strode away.

As she watched the surgeon disappear around the corner, Carrie wondered if, despite Phil's assurances, Thad Avery would end up caring for this patient after surgery. She brushed the thought aside. She'd done her best. Mr. Hoover would get good medical care. That was what mattered.

As for the rest of it, she had mixed emotions. She was glad not to have to endure a meeting with Phil, especially if he was going to quiz her about Adam. On the other hand, she was curious to know what he might want. Then she flashed on the information she'd garnered from his certificates—Phil had a connection with Chicago. It wasn't outside the realm of possibility that he had some connection to Charlie DeLuca. Though what kind of connection could it be?

Adam drove carefully, anxious to get home after a trying day but wary that he might be followed. He wasn't sure why he was taking precautions. After all, his stalker knew where he lived—he'd shot at him just the night before—but sometimes logic took a backseat to plain old-fashioned fear. So Adam went through his usual routine: double back, turn without signaling, drive with one eye on the rearview mirror.

He'd spent some time today wondering about whether he should go back to his apartment. Adam had even scanned the yellow pages in search of a motel, but midway through his search he decided that wherever he was made no difference. The stalker would eventually find him. Meanwhile, he could at least enjoy the few comforts left him, including sleeping in his own bed. But his deliberations served to redouble Adam's resolve to unmask the shooter and end this nightmare. He just didn't have the right scheme to do so . . . not yet.

He pulled into the parking lot behind his apartment complex, remembered that he'd parked at the far right end yesterday, so he took a space toward the front and center. He had his hand on his seat belt release when he heard the ring of a cell phone. He pulled his phone from his coat pocket and consulted the display—blank. Then Adam realized what he was hearing wasn't the unique ring he'd purchased for his cell phone, but rather the generic tone of his throwaway phone.

He reached over to the seat beside him, opened his brief case, and pulled out the instrument. The display showed "blocked number." Who was calling? Perhaps it represented a telephone solicitor, robo-dialing numbers. Then again, it might be the stalker, going for a phone call instead of a text this time. *Forget it. Answer it and find out. He can't shoot you through the phone.*

"Hello?"

"Keith? This is Corky."

It took Adam a moment to react to his "old" name. He looked around the deserted parking lot and saw nothing suspicious. Dusk had not fully settled. Maybe he could safely sit here a moment and talk. "Have you found out any more about Charlie DeLuca's family?"

A squeal of tires overrode Corky's voice. ". . . that idiot over there."

"What's happening? Are you driving?"

"Yeah. I'm on the freeway, on my way home, where my wife

is waiting impatiently. Usually I-45 in Houston is the world's longest parking lot. Today, for some reason, most of us are going the posted speed, and some are exceeding that. Those are the ones who've turned into Mario Andretti wannabes." A horn honked, and Adam suspected it was Corky's.

"Do you want to call me back?"

"Nah. This is what I do while I'm in the car. It's my version of multitasking." Another horn. Some muttered curses from Corky. "Idiots! All the drivers today are idiots." He heard Corky take a deep breath. "Anyway, there's someone else who might be trying to avenge Charlie DeLuca. And it's someone you wouldn't suspect. It's—"

Adam suspected the sounds he heard next would keep him awake that night and several more: a long blast from two different car horns, a squeal of brakes, followed by a loud crash, then a deadly silence.

"Corky! Corky!" Adam almost screamed into the phone. But there was no answer.

TWENTY-ONE

AS ADAM EXITED HIS CAR, HE HIT MUTE ON HIS CELL PHONE BUT kept the connection open. Now he sat in his apartment with the door double locked, the security chain in place. The blinds were closed. The drapes were drawn. He hadn't turned on the lights—he still wasn't sure why, but somehow he felt more secure in the gloom. He listened to the sounds issuing from his phone, imagining the carnage at the scene.

At first all he heard were a few muffled thuds. Then voices, all raised, some shouting frantically, added themselves to the mix. Finally sirens provided a wailing counterpoint to the cacophony. He heard the squeal of tortured metal, and someone said, "Let's get him out of there before the gas tank blows." A different voice chimed in, "No, we shouldn't move him. The ambulance is pulling up right now."

Adam closed his eyes and tried to imagine the scene as

the next few moments unfolded. EMTs gently easing his friend from the car. A policeman, or maybe a sheriff's deputy, picking up the phone—maybe removing it from Corky's hand—and consulting the display.

Adam opened his eyes as a deep baritone sounded in his ear. "Is someone still on the line?"

Should he answer? This was his throwaway cell phone. There was no way to identify him through it. And maybe he could add vital information. Was Corky on any medications? Did he have any drug allergies? Then it hit Adam—he didn't know any of those things. He hadn't seen his friend in almost two years. And he'd only called Corky when he needed a favor. Adam cleared his throat. "Yes?"

"Is anyone there?"

"Yes, I'm here."

"Is anyone there?" the voice repeated.

Adam finally realized that he'd muted the phone. He thumbed the button again, and said, "I'm here."

"Who is this?"

"I'm a friend of Corky's—of Mr. Cortland's. I'm in—" Adam hesitated. Caution returned. "I'm not there in Houston. We were talking on the cell phone, and he was complaining about some of the drivers on the freeway. Then I heard a crash. What happened?"

The reply made Adam's blood run cold. "A wrong-way driver hit your friend head-on. A helicopter's on its way to fly him to the nearest trauma center."

Perhaps it was his imagination, perhaps it was real, but Adam thought he heard the *whup-whup* of helicopter blades getting closer. "How is he?"

"That's for the medics to decide, but he looks pretty bad to me."

"Which hospital?"

"Hermann—that's Texas Medical Center. Now who is this? I need to get some information from you."

Adam pushed the button to end the call. There was nothing more he could say to help Corky. He doubted that the police would go so far as to trace the call, but if they did, it would dead end at this cell phone. He'd get rid of it later tonight. He wondered what new information his friend had come up with about DeLuca. Whatever it was, Adam might never know.

Adam's heart cramped as he realized he was thinking of the information Corky had for him as much as about his friend's life. He sank to his knees and spoke in a voice almost too faint to hear, "God, I pray for Corky. I know You can save him. Please do it. Not for me—for him, his family, his loved ones. Please."

———————————⋀——————————

Carrie was about to step into the shower, eager for the hot water to ease soreness in muscles tight for too long, when the ring of the phone stopped her. Her first impulse was to ignore it, but that passed quickly. She was a doctor, and she could never ignore the ringing of a phone or the beeping of a pager. She wrapped herself in a robe and answered, "Dr. Markham."

"Carrie, it's me . . . Julie."

Guilt washed over Carrie. She'd let her promise to keep Julie updated slip her mind. The carousel on which she found herself spun faster and faster, and Carrie had been hanging on for dear life. She owed Julie the courtesy of a call, and instead, her friend had to call her.

Carrie moved to her bed and stretched out. "I'm so sorry I didn't call. It's been—"

"No need to explain," Julie said. "But I've been worried about you since we last talked. What's going on? Are you any closer to knowing who the shooter is?"

"The list keeps getting longer," Carrie said. *And Adam wanted to put you on that list, but I wouldn't let him.* "Someone must've let information slip, but we have no idea who." She told her best friend about what she and Adam had found, ending with Rob Cole's revelation to her just a few hours ago. "So what do I do now?"

"You could direct something at this list of suspects that would make the real shooter declare himself. That is, if you're prepared for a face off."

"That's what Adam wants," Carrie said. "But how do we do that?"

They kicked around ideas. Then Carrie glanced at the clock on her bedside table. "I need to cut this short. Adam's coming by soon, and I really need to clean up."

"No problem," Julie said. "Give me one more minute before you hang up."

"I know," Carrie said. "We need to pray."

"Want me to start?"

"No, I've got this one." Carrie bowed her head, picturing her friend, hundreds of miles away, doing the same.

As she put down the phone and swung her feet off the bed, Carrie flipped on the TV in her bedroom just to have some noise in the house. She looked up as an ad flashed across the screen: "Your kids will love it," the announcer said. Most of the time Carrie ignored such commercials, but this particular one started her thinking. A germ of an idea sprang up, one that might work. Of course, the plan was dangerous. Then again, doing nothing was proving dangerous as well.

Adam stuck to the pre-midnight shadows as he worked his way from his parked car along the alleys to the fence behind Carrie's house. He scanned every driveway, kept his eyes moving, trying to stay concealed while giving the appearance of a man innocently walking to a neighbor's house. The last thing he needed was for someone to call the police.

Since the shooter had already linked Adam with Carrie, maybe these precautions were worthless. Nevertheless, Adam didn't want to lead his would-be assassin directly to her house—not tonight, not any night.

He paused at the fence and looked around to make sure no one was watching, then grabbed the top and pulled himself up. Adam managed to roll over the fence and land in Carrie's backyard without sustaining more injuries than just wounded pride.

He rapped out the code, Carrie opened her kitchen door, and Adam slid through and double locked it.

"This is getting ridiculous," she muttered.

"Not as ridiculous as being killed by a sniper's bullet," Adam said. "And you may recall that almost happened to both of us."

She pointed. "Sit down. I have a fresh pot of coffee brewing."

Once they were at the table sipping from their respective cups, Adam said, "Today I got another call from this law school classmate of mine, Corky."

"The man who was going to hack into sites and get information for you?"

"I told you, he assured me it was just a matter of taking some shortcuts," Adam said. "Anyway, he called me back this afternoon to give me a report." In his mind, he heard again the crash, the sirens, the dire words of the man who'd picked up Corky's cell phone. Adam shook his head as though to dislodge the thoughts. "Unfortunately my friend was in a head-on crash before he could tell me what he'd found."

Carrie frowned and shook her head. "That's terrible," she said. "How is he?"

"I've got to call the hospital later tonight to see. But the man I talked with thought Corky was critical when they airlifted him to a trauma center."

There was a long silence as each sipped coffee, lost in their own thoughts. Then Carrie said, "So what else happened today?"

"Well . . . Mary, the new paralegal, keeps pushing me to have lunch or dinner with her. I've put her off for another few days, but eventually that's going to happen. I don't know what she's up to, but I don't think her aim is to get better acquainted with a coworker."

"You don't think it's possible she's genuinely interested in you?"

"That's flattering, but no. Besides, she's already got her hooks into Bruce Hartley," Adam said. "I suppose I'm being paranoid, but I get a sense that she's trying to uncover my identity."

"Hmm. I don't know which is worse—her trying to make a play for you or her trying to find out who you really are." Carried studied him for a moment. "I guess we can worry about that when it happens."

"What about your day?" Adam asked.

"Pretty interesting. I had lunch with Rob Cole." She went on to tell Adam Rob's story. "I don't know whether he was about to reveal his real name or if he was just toying with me. But I certainly think he's a prime suspect."

"We seem to keep adding names to that list," Adam said. "Anyone else?"

"Actually, yes, but . . . I don't know . . . ," Carrie said.

"What?"

"Well, I was in Phil Rushton's office today and noticed the diplomas on his wall."

Adam's eyebrows went up. "And?"

"All his training was in Chicago."

"That doesn't necessarily tie him to Charlie DeLuca, but it's certainly a potential link," Adam said.

"Not only that, but Phil's been acting sort of funny toward me lately." She paused. "He even asked about you, wanted to know if I knew your background." She shook her head. "I think we have to consider him a suspect."

"I suppose," Adam said. "And I have another name for our list. Janet Evans stopped by my office today—during the course of our conversation she mentioned some gambling debts of Bruce Hartley's that one of our clients paid off. Apparently it saved the firm."

"Really?" Carrie seemed shocked. "What's the significance of that?"

"One of the things Charlie DeLuca was involved in was loan sharking," Adam said. "Anyway, I looked up Bruce in Martindale-Hubbell."

"In what?"

"It's the list of all the attorneys in the United States. When I saw that he went to law school in Wisconsin, I was about to log off. Then I decided to see where he grew up."

"Chicago?"

"Close. Elmwood Park, which is a suburb of Chicago, with one of the largest Italian populations in the area."

"So he could have had contact with the DeLuca family . . . ?"

"Right," Adam said. "So we have Rob Cole, Phil Rushton, and Bruce Hartley, plus no telling how many others as suspects. Now how do I find out which one is shooting at us? And why."

"Are you really determined to confront the shooter?" Carrie asked.

Adam thought about it for a moment. He clenched his jaw so tight it ached, relaxing it only long enough to say, "If that's what it takes."

Carrie took his hand and squeezed it. "I don't like it, but if there's no better option, I have a plan that might help us identify the person stalking you."

Carrie was at her desk the next morning, sipping on a cup of lukewarm coffee and flipping through her phone messages, when Lila popped her head in the door.

"Can you return Tim Gallagher's call as soon as possible? He phoned early this morning and said it was important that he reach you."

That puzzled Carrie. She had encountered Gallagher a time or two at parties but was pretty sure he wasn't a patient. If he had a medical emergency, he probably would have gone to an ER or urgent care center, not call her office. Maybe this was a personal call. He'd seemed like a nice enough guy—middle-aged, good-looking, if you liked the jock type. But wasn't he married? Besides that, if he was calling to ask her on a date, he wouldn't do it this early in the morning, would he? On the other hand . . . *Oh, stop it. Just phone the man.*

Carrie found the proper slip and dialed the number. Gallagher answered before the first ring was complete. "Coach Gallagher."

Coach? She had a vague memory that he was a teacher, and now that she thought about it, he sort of looked like a coach. "This is Dr. Markham. You said it was urgent that I call you back. Do you have a medical problem?"

"I don't think so, but I'm trying to avoid one." A bell sounded in the background—not a gentle tinkle, but a strident sound followed by a crescendo of voices mixed with the shuffling and slamming of metal doors. "Excuse me. School's starting, and I have an eight o'clock class. Can I call you back at nine?"

Carrie hated setting a time to take a call. She much preferred to do the phoning on her own schedule. Besides, she might not be able to turn loose at nine o'clock. But now Gallagher had piqued her curiosity. "Sure. Tell whoever answers that I'm expecting your call. If I can't get free, we'll have to play phone tag, I guess."

"Thanks. I appreciate it." And he was gone.

Carrie turned to her nurse, who was still in the doorway. "Lila, do you have any idea why Coach Gallagher would need to talk to me?"

"None at all," Lila said. "But when he calls back, don't forget to tell me. I'm dying to know."

It was almost nine fifteen before Lila stuck her head in the exam room door. "Can you take that call you were expecting?"

As it turned out, Carrie had just told her patient she'd order some lab work, then see him back in a few days to evaluate how the new medication was working. Lila was dispatched with the patient to schedule the tests while Carrie went into the office and punched the blinking light on her phone. "This is Dr. Markham."

"Tim Gallagher again. Sorry I had to call back like this. I know you're busy."

"No problem. What can I do for you?"

"Do you like baseball?"

The question came out of the blue and left Carrie wondering what was behind it. Was the coach asking for a date? Did he have some tickets he wanted to give away? "Uh, actually, I do. Why?"

"I'm the varsity baseball coach at Jameson High School. We have a game at four this afternoon, and the doctor who usually attends is sick. We don't anticipate any problems—worst we've ever had was a broken wrist when one of my players disregarded my instructions and slid home headfirst—but I kind of like having a doctor in attendance." He paused, apparently decided she wasn't going to respond, so he continued, "Would you consider coming to the game today? Four o'clock. The field next to the high school. I'd really appreciate it. And I can promise you'll see a good game—we're playing last year's district champs."

The invitation brought welcome memories to Carrie. At her high school, girls hadn't been allowed to play "hardball," but they had a killer softball team. She'd pitched and played shortstop, and they'd challenged for the state championship. If she couldn't be on the diamond, she could at least be near it. Why not?

"Let me check my schedule to see if I can get away early," Carrie said.

"Fine. This number's my cell. Send me a text when you know. And thanks."

Fifteen minutes later Carrie sent Gallagher a message. "See you this afternoon at the game." For the rest of the day she found herself humming "Take Me Out to the Ballgame."

Last night Adam had taken the SIM card from his throwaway phone and destroyed it using Carrie's hedge shears. The phone itself went into a dumpster. Today he spent his lunch hour at Radio Shack, purchasing another prepaid cell phone for the project he had in mind. He paid cash, and when the clerk asked for a name, he said Tony Kubek. If this didn't end soon, he'd run out of names of past Yankee players.

Adam would target the three men he and Carrie decided were the most likely candidates to be the shooter: Rob Cole, Bruce Hartley, and Phil Rushton. It had taken some digging, but now he had the phone numbers he needed to carry out the scheme.

Carrie's idea was an attempt to smoke out the shooter. At first what she proposed seemed unnecessarily complex to Adam. Why not make the phone calls from his own phone, using his own name? She reminded him that even if one of these men was guilty, two were not; what would they think if they received such a message from him? No, this way they hoped only the guilty person would be able to decipher the words. Then, if he responded, Adam would be ready for him.

Of course, the scheme carried risk, but it was a risk Adam was anxious to take. She begged him to call his brother for backup, but he reminded her that Dave's right arm was in a sling, and he was just out of the hospital. No, Adam would do this by himself. He had to.

The first step in his scheme demanded some privacy. Both lawyers left the office a bit early, Bruce accompanied by Mary Delkus, so Adam and Brittany were left to close up. "You go ahead," he told her. "I've got a few odds and ends yet to do. I'll lock up." Brittany usually had a date, and apparently today was no exception. She thanked him, and in a moment he heard the door slam.

Adam eased the new cell phone from its charging cradle, checked that the battery and signal levels were good, and thought about the message he was about to deliver. He'd found that both Rushton and Hartley were hardly ever home before eight in the evening. Cole, like most of his generation, had no landline, and he often ignored his cell phone while he was on duty, as he was tonight. Adam's plan was to deliver his message to each man's voice mail from an untraceable phone. Then he would see who responded.

He opened his desk drawer and removed a sack that bore the logo of Toys "R" Us. Adam withdrew a black device that looked like one of the respirator masks worn by painters. He held it close to his mouth and spoke into it, feeling quite foolish. As though the words came from Darth Vader, complete with raspy breathing, he heard himself say, "Testing, testing." Adam couldn't resist adding, "Luke, I am your father." Despite the gravity of what he was about to do, that brought a grin to his face.

Well, here goes. He dialed the first number. If, by chance, they answered, he'd just hang up. But after five rings he got the recorded message. At the beep he—or rather, Darth Vader—said, "I'm tired of this. Let's put an end to it. Meet me tonight at midnight, Ridgewood Cemetery, at the stone angel on the McElroy plot." When he pushed the button to end the call, he was sweating. One down, two to go.

After he ended the last call, Adam leaned back in his chair. It was done. There was no turning back. *God, maybe this is crazy. Maybe it's the only way. In either case, I'm going to need Your help. Please.*

TWENTY-TWO

CARRIE LEANED AGAINST THE WIRE FENCE THAT SEPARATED THE playing field from the bleachers and took in the spectacle before her. Dark green grass, so closely mowed it looked like carpet, contrasted with the rusty tan of the infield dirt. Lines chalked with the precision of a stretched string demarcated the playing field. That was where the action took place— "between the lines."

The home team had the first-base dugout, but right now the bench was empty. Jameson players in white uniforms with the word "Eagles" in blue on the front and numbers on the back were in right field, throwing baseballs, stretching, showing the exuberance typical of high school athletes. A middle-aged man whose uniform bore the number *37* stood near the dugout, hands in his hip pockets.

Carrie called to him. "Coach?"

He turned and flashed a smile. "Dr. Markham. Thanks so much for coming."

"My pleasure." She gestured to the bleachers behind the dugout. "I'll be up here if you need me."

"Hope we don't, but I appreciate having you around."

The game started, and Carrie let the experience carry her back to her high school days. She'd had a major crush on the baseball team's star, the shortstop. She could still see him in her mind's eye: tall, muscular, with wavy blond hair and sparkling eyes. He'd had his choice of girlfriends, so she thought her heart would jump out of her chest when he asked her out. The evening ended quickly, though, when she discovered his main objective was to score—and not by crossing home plate.

Despite Carrie's love of the game, life—in the form of medical school and all that came afterward—intervened. This was the first baseball game she'd seen in at least ten years. She made a promise to herself that it wouldn't be another decade before she saw another.

Carrie snapped out of her reverie and looked at the scoreboard. It was already the top of the second inning. Carrie did a double take as the visiting Wildcat batter stepped to the plate. High school students certainly seemed larger than they were in her day—at least, this one did. The batter was over six feet tall and probably weighed more than two hundred pounds. He looked more like a football player than a first baseman. She wondered if the Eagle pitcher felt the way David felt when he first saw Goliath.

The first pitch was a slow curve that broke tantalizingly just off the plate. The batter took it for ball one. The second pitch was also outside. Two balls, no strikes. Carrie leaned forward in her seat, her clenched fists resting on her thighs. *Walk him. Don't throw him anything he can hit. Be careful.*

The pitcher peered in to the catcher for the sign, shook off a couple, then wound up and delivered a fastball. Undoubtedly he meant for it to be on the outside corner, but instead it headed, belt-high, for the center of home plate. The batter took a short stride with his front foot and swung so hard Carrie thought she felt the breeze.

A loud *ping* from the aluminum bat resonated throughout the park. The ball might have come out of the pitcher's hand at eighty miles per hour, but the line drive going back at him was probably going a hundred. The ball hit the pitcher squarely in the chest, and he dropped like a felled tree.

The baseball spun to rest in the red clay surrounding the pitcher's mound. The batter, now standing on first base, threw up his hands in dismay. The umpire spread his arms and yelled, "Time." And in the stands a stunned silence gave way to a rising murmur.

Carrie was on her feet in an instant. She sprinted toward the gate to the field while yelling at Coach Gallagher, "Get the AED. Have someone call 911."

His teammates stood in a wide semicircle around the fallen player. The umpire and opposing coaches approached but stayed at a respectful distance. Carrie reached the boy, who lay on his side, his legs drawn under him. She rolled him onto his back, ripped open his jersey, pushed his T-shirt upward, and put her ear to his bare chest. No heart sounds. *Commotio cordis*: a blow to the chest, usually in a younger person, hitting at exactly the right time of the cardiac cycle to stop the heart from beating. She had less than three minutes to get it started if the boy was going to live.

Coach Gallagher knelt by her side, holding what looked like a black backpack. "Ready for this?"

"Open it, then make sure everyone stands back."

Carrie pulled a yellow-and-black plastic case from the pack, happy that all athletic events now were required to have one of these at hand. Every model was different, but the principle remained the same: deliver a jolt of electricity to jumpstart the heart.

She made sure the AED—the automatic external defibrillator—was powered. Then Carrie used the tail of the pitcher's tee shirt to dry sweat from his chest. Quickly, she applied the pads, one on the upper right chest, the other the lower left. Did this one have an *analyze* button? Yes. She pushed it and got the expected result. Cardiac arrest.

"Everyone, stand clear. Don't touch him until I say it's safe." She said a silent prayer and hit the button to deliver a shock. No response. She waited for the machine to recharge, then shocked the boy again. Still no heartbeat.

The clock was ticking. How much time did she have left? Maybe a minute, certainly no more. While the machine recharged again, Carrie debated starting external chest compressions. The books said to wait two minutes between shocks. She couldn't wait. If this one didn't do it, she'd carry out external CPR until the emergency medical technicians arrived. After a few more seconds, she said, "Stand clear. Here we go again."

Another prayer. Another shock. This time there was a heartbeat—faint at first, then growing stronger with every beat. The boy took a shallow breath. Then another. Carrie closed her eyes and breathed a prayer. *Thank You, God.*

She checked the heart rhythm, and it appeared normal. A siren in the background signaled the approach of the medics. In the ambulance she could hook him up to an EKG, start an IV to establish a lifeline for delivery of needed drugs. "I'll ride with him to the ER," she told the coach. "Will you notify his parents?"

"Sure," mumbled Coach Gallagher. He heaved the biggest sigh in the world. "I've never seen that happen. Never even heard of it. But I'm sure glad you were in the stands. Thanks."

Carrie nodded once. "No problem," she said. "I guess God wanted me here."

Adam sat in the office for a few minutes after sending his messages, alternately worrying and praying. Finally he stowed the voice changer in his brief case and eased out the door, locking it behind him. By now it was almost dark and every shadow he passed on the way to his car seemed to be the hiding place for someone waiting to kill him.

When he was finally in his car, he didn't bother doing his usual maneuvering to lose a tail. *If you want me, come and get me.* At home he paced the floor, thinking and rethinking his plan. Could he have improved on it? Maybe. Did it really matter if he'd tweaked it? Probably not.

He dressed in the same clothes he'd worn for his last stealthy trip to Carrie's: green sweatshirt, black jeans, dark athletic shoes. He considered smearing his face with camouflage paint but discarded the idea. He'd feel ridiculous.

Adam thought about calling his brother, but what good

would it do? Dave would tell him he was crazy, then offer to drive to Jameson and serve as backup for Adam. And his brother was in no shape to face a gunman. Matter of fact, Adam was probably in no shape, but things had been set in motion, and there was no way to stop them now.

Thoughts of Dave made Adam remember something he needed to do before keeping his rendezvous. He should give Carrie his brother's cell phone number. If tonight's showdown ended badly, Dave would know what to do. Of course, there was no way Adam was going to mention the worst-case scenario to Carrie. He'd just give her the number.

He pulled out his Ruger, ejected the magazine, checked the load. Would he need an extra magazine, more bullets? No, if ten rounds didn't do it, he'd be dead. Adam pushed the thought aside. He slid the pistol into his ankle holster, pulled it out, then repeated the process until he was sure he could draw the gun easily when he needed it.

Adam opened his closet and found the Kevlar vest he'd purchased at the same time he bought the holster. It had resided in his closet to this point, but now was the time to wear it. He'd leave it on the bed until he left though.

Finally he pulled out his cell phone—the regular one—and made one last call. "Carrie, I'm about to leave for the cemetery."

Her voice betrayed her anxiety. "Are you sure you want to do this?"

"I don't *want* to do it. I just don't see any other options."

"Will you call me when it's over? Even if it's late?"

"Sure."

Adam gave her Dave's number. "If anything bad happens..."

"Don't say things like that," Carrie said.

They talked for a few more minutes before Carrie said, "Adam, I love you."

"And I love you, Carrie. When this is all over, I hope you're ready to talk about our life together."

"We can talk now," she said.

"No, I need to get going. I'll call you when it's over."

"Adam?"

"Yes?"

"Please be careful. I don't want to lose you."

"I don't want to lose you either," he said.

They exchanged more "I love you's" before ending the conversation.

Then Adam donned the vest, checked his gun again, and did a final run-through of his mental checklist. Time to go. It was only ten thirty, but he wanted to be in place early.

Adam chose Ridgewood Cemetery as a meeting site for a number of reasons. It was older and full of tall monuments and a few mausoleums, so he could hide easily. Like most cemeteries there was a fence around it, but the gates were never locked. And it was isolated enough that a gunshot wouldn't attract curious neighbors. Of course that gunshot could be from his gun or that of his stalker, but he was willing to take the chance. Anything to bring this nightmare to a close.

Adam had done some scouting, so he knew where he was going. He'd found an open barn for the storage of equipment and material, and that was where he concealed his Subaru, between a tractor with a bucket for digging on the front end and another that pulled a small mower. It took him ten minutes to work his way through the cemetery to the spot he'd picked for his observation post. He was just settling in when he heard a single, faint noise off to his left. It was more than an hour before the appointed time, but Adam expected the shooter to come early. He eased his pistol from its holster and began a slow belly crawl toward the noise.

A form materialized from the shadow of a mausoleum. Adam stayed in his prone position, raised himself on his elbows, and braced his gun in a firing position with both hands. He flicked off the safety and took up the slack on the trigger. Working to keep his voice steady and authoritative, he said, "That's far enough. Put your hands up. If I see a gun, I'll shoot."

"Adam?"

Adam exhaled deeply, and he felt his heart start beating again. He eased his pressure on the trigger. "Carrie? What are you doing here?"

"I couldn't let you do this by yourself. So I came to help."

Adam dropped his voice to a whisper. "Get over here, and get down. We don't want to alert the shooter."

In a moment they were crouched behind the mausoleum Adam had chosen as his hiding place, peering around the low granite building toward the marble angel marking the McElroy plot. Adam thought about scolding Carrie for coming, but in truth, he was glad to see her. He put his mouth next to her ear and whispered, "Did you bring a weapon?"

She reached into the side pocket of her black cargo pants, pulled out a small canister, and held it up. "Mace," she whispered.

The whine of a transmission alerted them to the approach of a vehicle. Bouncing headlights made the shadows dance as a light-colored SUV pulled up and stopped on the road near the McElroy plot. The driver killed the lights and lowered the window. He sat there for what Adam figured was five minutes, then the window buzzed up, the engine started, headlights flared, and the vehicle drove off.

"Could you see inside the SUV?" Adam asked.

"No," Carrie said. "But I recognized the license plate as it drove away."

"What was it?"

"It was a personalized Texas plate: HRT SRGN. It belongs to Phil Rushton."

TWENTY-THREE

CARRIE FIGURED HER ADRENALINE LEVEL WAS SO HIGH SHE'D BE awake the rest of the night. Instead, she was dozing soundly when she felt Adam shaking her shoulder.

"Carrie, it's one a.m.," he whispered. "I don't think anyone else is coming. Let's go home."

She smothered a yawn. "Okay. Can I get a ride with you?"

"Where's your car?"

"I didn't want to leave it here, so I took a taxi."

"A taxi to the cemetery this late at night? Didn't the driver think you were crazy?"

She shrugged, although she knew Adam couldn't see it in the darkness. "I told him this was the anniversary of my husband's death, and I planned to spend the night sitting by his grave."

"Where did you come up with such a story?"

She climbed to her feet, using the edge of the mausoleum

for leverage. "Actually, on the first anniversary of John's death, I did just that—spent the night at the foot of his grave." She pointed. "It's right over there." Her voice broke on the last words.

Adam took her arm. "Do you want a moment alone?"

There was a long moment of silence, then Carrie said in a small voice, "I'd like that."

They walked several yards before she stopped and looked around. She took a few steps to the right and let her hand caress the edge of a simple granite marker. "John," she whispered. Then she bowed her head and was silent for a moment. Adam placed a hand on her shoulder, but said nothing.

Carrie's emotions were in turmoil. She was standing at the grave of her first husband, with the man who might become her second at her side. *John, I did the best I could, but we couldn't save you. Now it's time for me to move on. I hope you understand.*

Finally Carrie lifted her head, wiped her eyes, and said, "I'm ready to go now."

When they reached his car, Adam unlocked it and held the door for Carrie before climbing in himself. He eased the vehicle out of its hiding place, flipped on his headlights, and turned onto the main road that ran through the cemetery.

Carrie turned toward him. "What do you think—"

Another set of headlights appeared on the horizon. Carrie saw them and dropped to the floor of the car at the same time Adam whispered, "Get down."

"You can sit up," he said in a moment. "I thought a car was coming right at us, but it was on the road leading here."

"You know, it seems to me that I've spent more time on the

floor of your car than a floor mat." Carrie laughed. "I'm sort of tired of that."

Adam turned out of the cemetery and set a course for Carrie's house. "That makes two of us. Do you think we're any closer to finding out who's been shooting at us?"

"Maybe. Why would Phil Rushton take a drive into the cemetery tonight?" she said. "So far as I'm concerned, that makes him our number one suspect."

"You've got a point. Do you think you can find out if he has some kind of excuse for coming?"

For a moment, Carrie said nothing. *Another spy job.* Finally she said, "I'll try."

They rode in silence, until Adam said, "I didn't have a chance to ask about your day."

Despite the late hour, Carrie's voice brightened. "Really interesting. Have you ever heard of something called *commotio cordis*?"

———————————————⎍ˏˋ⎍—————————————————

Carrie was no stranger to doing without sleep, but that didn't mean she enjoyed it. The next morning was Saturday, a day when she tried to sleep a bit later if possible. But not today. Today she had to check on the young ballplayer she'd resuscitated the day before.

If his EKG was still normal and his cardiac enzymes showed no evidence of heart muscle damage, she planned to discharge him. He was understandably anxious to go home, so Carrie promised him she'd be by early this morning. Thus the reason she got up at what one of her medical school classmates referred to as "chicken thirty."

When the alarm went off, she forced herself out of bed and padded to the kitchen, only to find she hadn't prepared the coffee maker the night before. She fumbled her way through the process until the coffee started brewing. Then she stood over it until there was at least a cup's worth in the carafe. By the time she'd showered, dressed, and chased a piece of buttered toast with two more cups of coffee, Carrie thought she might make it through the day.

At the hospital, she was moving down the hall toward the ballplayer's room when a familiar voice stopped her. "Carrie, hold up a second." Phil, a cardboard cup of coffee in one hand, a stack of papers in the other, was coming toward her full tilt.

Carrie turned and waited. Phil stopped so close to her that she smelled the fumes issuing from the Starbucks cup. She would have killed for some of that coffee but didn't think Phil would share. Come to think of it, he wasn't the kind to share anything. She put what she hoped was a neutral expression on her face and waited for him to speak.

"Your patient, Mr. . . . The man you referred, the one with the heart attack . . ."

"Mr. Hoover. A. J. Hoover," she said. "What about him?"

"He came through the surgery very well. He's in the SICU if you want to drop by. I'll let you know when I'm ready to discharge him, but feel free to write any orders you think he might need."

"Thanks," Carrie said. "I'll go by the surgical ICU and see him before I leave." What was going on? It wasn't like Phil to be this considerate. She expected that by now he'd have Thad Avery standing by to take over Hoover's post-op care. She frowned, wondering when the other shoe would drop. Surely Phil wanted something.

"We never had a chance to talk about dinner. How about tonight?"

There it was—the shift from rigid taskmaster and senior partner to caring colleague who wanted to get closer to her. She still wasn't comfortable going out with Phil, but she really wanted to follow up on his appearance in the cemetery last night.

"Phil, I think I'd better get some rest tonight. I was up really late." She covered a yawn, a real one, although it did add plausibility to her story.

"Probably just as well to put off our dinner." He yawned as well. "After I finished Mr. Hoover's surgery, I had to take care of a patient with a gunshot wound to the chest. It was almost midnight by the time I left the hospital."

Carrie waited. *Go on. I've given you an opening.* She raised her eyebrows in an invitation to tell her more.

"After the case I called home to check my messages. I usually don't have any—the answering service calls me on my cell—but there was a strange one on my landline last night. It was from someone inviting me to a meeting at the cemetery at midnight. Well, curiosity got the best of me, so I swung by on the way home—stopped at the appointed place, but there was no one there." He shrugged, then took a deep draught of coffee. "They must have called my phone by mistake."

"That's curious." Carrie did her best to keep her expression neutral. "Do you have any idea who could've called?"

"Not really," he said. But there was something behind his eyes Carrie couldn't read. Was he lying? She couldn't tell.

Carrie shrugged. "Well, that's certainly weird. Anything else?"

Phil looked around. They were standing near the nurse's station, and people were coming and going in a steady stream. "No, it can wait. Maybe I'll see you later. If not, why don't you drop by my office first thing Monday morning? We can talk about scheduling that dinner too. Right now I'm going home to take a nap." He finished the coffee, tossed the empty cup into a wastebasket, and plodded off down the hall.

Carrie ended her rounds with a stop in the cafeteria. After inhaling the fumes from Phil's coffee, she considered getting an espresso from the food court but decided to make the trade-off for plain coffee from a container that wasn't cardboard, consumed at a real table in a relatively quiet setting. After a quick trip through the cafeteria line, she was at a table, holding a mug of coffee in both hands, smelling the aroma and feeling the caffeine energize her tired body. She closed her eyes, leaned back in her chair, and tried to analyze what she and Adam knew.

As she recalled, Phil Rushton once said he grew up in a poor part of Chicago. Like most medical students she was sure he either borrowed money or someone financed his medical education and specialty training. Could it have been DeLuca? Was Phil now repaying the debt by trying to kill Adam?

And Bruce Hartley, the senior lawyer in the partnership where Adam worked, had been in trouble for gambling. Could DeLuca have been the one to whom Hartley owed the debt? It seemed unlikely that he'd torch his own office, though what better way to direct suspicion away from himself? Adam said that if Hartley wanted someone shot, he'd hire it done. Still, so far as Carrie was concerned, he was a suspect.

To complicate things further, Charlie DeLuca had another family—a bigamous relationship with a woman living in a Chicago suburb. When the truth about Charlie came out, the wife had the marriage declared void and her daughter became a cloistered nun. The stepson, trained as an EMT, disappeared. Could he have surfaced in Jameson as Rob Cole? Was Rob Cole really Robert Kohler?

Carrie was halfway through her coffee when she realized someone was easing into the chair next to hers.

Rob Cole, looking like someone who had just finished pulling an all-nighter, smiled across the table and raised his cup in a salute. "Mind if I join you?"

"Tough night?" Carrie asked.

"Yes and no. I ended up working a double shift. One of the other paramedics was sick. But it turned out to be a good night. Took a mother in labor to the hospital just in time for the baby to be born somewhere besides the back of an MICU. And probably saved the life of a guy who got shot in the chest."

"Dr. Rushton said he did surgery on a patient like that," Carrie said. "So I guess your night wasn't a total waste."

Rob looked at the ceiling as though trying to decide. "No, it was okay. I had some other plans, fairly important ones, but I guess there'll be another time."

He started to push back his chair, but Carrie stopped him with a hand on his arm. "Rob, you got called away while we were still talking yesterday. Why don't we finish that conversation?"

Rob eased back into his chair. "Honestly, I can't remember what we were talking about."

Carrie paused to gather her thoughts. She had to approach

this carefully. "You were telling me about the reason you changed your name and moved away."

"Oh yeah." He rubbed the back of his neck. "I guess it was the total disappointment after I found out my stepfather really wasn't my stepfather. I'd really taken to him. My sister and I were so happy to have a dad again. When we found out he had another family, that the whole marriage to my mom was a sham, my sister just cracked up. She decided she had to get away, so she cut all ties with us. She . . ." He shook his head. "I can't talk about it."

Carrie plastered a shocked look on her face. "That's tough, Rob." She took a deep breath. "I understand your need to get away for a fresh start, but why did you have to change your name?"

"Sis and I were proud of our new family. Mom's husband said he wanted to be more than a stepfather. He wanted to be our father. Then we found out these terrible things about him. I . . . I ran away. I changed my name because it reminded me of what we had, what he made us lose."

Carrie took a big swallow of coffee. Here it comes. "And what was your stepfather's name?"

Rob hesitated so long she thought he was going to evade the question. Finally he spoke. "Du . . . Lu . . . It was Luciano."

Carrie looked into Rob Cole's eyes, hoping to find a clue there. Had he started to say "DeLuca," then changed his mind? Or was the subject painful enough that he stuttered over his stepfather's name. Was he toying with her? Was this simply a part of the game for him, a game that would end with a bullet for Adam . . . or her . . . or both?

Carrie decided to take a chance and attack the problem

head-on. "Rob, I don't think your stepfather was named Luciano. I think his name was DeLuca. Charlie DeLuca."

Rob reached out for his coffee cup, but instead of grasping the handle, he encircled the thick mug with his hand. He didn't lift it—just squeezed. Carrie watched his hands tremble and his knuckles turn white. She was afraid the mug would shatter, and she shoved her chair back a few inches to avoid the splatter of hot liquid. When she looked up from the cup into Rob's eyes, they were burning into hers. For a moment she thought he might hit her, or throw the cup at her, or lunge across the table and grab her by the throat.

Carrie was on the verge of calling out for help, when, like a balloon deflating, Rob relaxed back into his chair. He leaned forward so that their faces were just inches apart. "I don't think I want to talk about this anymore. And I've changed my mind. I don't want to get to know you better after all."

TWENTY-FOUR

ADAM HAD THE OFFICE TO HIMSELF ON SATURDAY MORNING. After he set the coffee brewing, he used his computer to get the phone number for Hermann Hospital in Houston. It turned out that the facility's official name was Memorial Hermann-Texas Medical Center, but he finally found what he needed. He picked up the phone on his desk, then replaced it and dialed the number on his cell phone. The firm would probably have no problem with a long-distance call, but he didn't want to leave any record. He couldn't give a reason for his caution, but he'd learned to trust his instincts. And his instincts always told him to leave as few footprints as possible.

He started with patient information, then was transferred to the ICU, where he was put on hold for what seemed an interminable length of time as the ward clerk found a nurse who'd talk with him.

"Who's this?" she asked in a voice that was a study in neutrality.

"This is Ad—Sorry. This is Keith Branson. I'm a friend of Mr. Cortland's. I was talking with him yesterday when the wreck happened."

"Which Mr. Cortland would that be?"

"All I've ever called him was Corky. Give me a sec." He searched his memory. What was Corky's listing in Martindale-Hubbel? That was it. Edgar A. He relayed this information to the nurse.

"Are you a colleague?" she said. "A lawyer?"

"Yes. Corky and I were in law school together."

"Then you're familiar with HIPAA."

It was a statement, not a question, and Adam knew what was coming next. He had come up against a wall—a wall called "patient privacy." Although he knew that the intent of the Health Insurance Portability and Accountability Act of 1996, known as HIPAA, was good, he longed for the old days when a friend could find out someone's condition without the patient having to include his name on a list of those cleared to receive that information.

The argument didn't last long, mainly because Adam knew the nurse was acting properly. He thanked her and hung up. But he still wanted to find out about Corky. This meant more work with the computer, and using Switchboard.com he soon determined that E. A. Cortland lived in a rather nice suburb of Houston and had a listed number for his residence.

Before he dialed, Adam tried to recall something. He was pretty sure Corky hadn't been married when they were in law school. Had Corky mentioned his wife's name on the phone?

No, he had not. So Adam was calling blind. But he'd done that before.

The phone was answered on the fourth ring by a man's soft voice. "Cortland residence."

"This is a law school classmate of Corky's. I understand he was in a bad accident yesterday, and—"

"Let me stop you. This is his father-in-law, and I guess you're calling to get the details. Well, the service is day after tomorrow at the—"

It was like a punch in the gut. The man was still talking as Adam disconnected the call. He laid his phone on the desk and put his head in his hands. He felt sorrow about the loss of a friend as well as guilt at having let that friendship lie dormant for so long. But along with all that, Adam felt despair as he watched his hope of learning the hidden secret about Charlie DeLuca's family disappear into the coffin with Corky.

"Is someone in here?"

A familiar voice interrupted Adam's thoughts. The office door was locked, so he'd assumed he'd be alone this morning. But it was Mary's voice that had startled him, and Mary had a key.

He was trapped. There was no way to avoid an encounter with her. "Back here," he called.

"Be right there."

In a moment Mary appeared in the doorway, holding two cups. "The coffee pot was still full, so I figured you hadn't had yours yet. I poured an extra cup for you. Black okay?"

"Sure. Thanks." Adam took a sip and put the cup on his desk.

"What are you doing?" she asked.

Apparently Mary had no hesitancy in asking questions.

He drank a bit more coffee, hoping the caffeine would keep his brain sharp. "Just finishing a little extra work. What brings you in today?"

"Actually I was driving by and saw your car here, so I thought I'd stop and see if you were free for lunch."

"Uh, that would be nice, but I've got to get home to meet a repairman. The cable's acting funny, and with the weekend coming up, I want to watch the games. I think the Rangers are playing the Yankees on Sunday." Adam thought he was right. He wasn't really much of a sports fan, but he was hoping Mary wasn't either.

She frowned, almost as though the rebuff was expected, and took in half her coffee with a couple of gulps. "Well, I'd hoped we could do it earlier, but I still have you down for lunch on Tuesday. Right?"

Adam was tired of putting off what seemed inevitable. "Sure. Let's set the details when we see each other Monday morning."

He addressed himself to the computer, attacking the keys furiously as though writing a document that had to be completed by sundown or the world would end. In actuality he'd opened a blank Word document and was typing gibberish, but she couldn't see the screen from her vantage point across the desk.

The ruse must have worked, because Mary took the hint. She put her cup down on a side table near Adam's door. "I won't keep you from your work. Have a good weekend."

Adam heard the door open, then Mary called, "See you Monday." The door closed, and in a moment he heard a car drive off. He waited another couple of minutes, then sneaked to the front of the office and peered out the window. The parking lot was empty. Once more he'd avoided giving Mary a chance to probe too deeply into his background. And maybe the identity he'd created would hold up under her questioning anyway, so he had nothing to worry about.

He hoped so. He had enough worries on his plate as it was. There was no need for another.

Carrie was halfway through her front door, her arms laden with groceries, when her cell phone rang. She hurried into the kitchen to deposit the sacks on the kitchen table, then pulled her phone from the pocket of her slacks and checked the display. Adam. She could feel the smile spread across her face.

"What's up?" she asked.

"Have you caught up on your sleep after our late night?"

"Not really. I had to see some patients this morning. But I ran into Rob Cole at the hospital. Adam, I think he's really Charlie DeLuca's stepson."

"Why do you say that?"

After she finished describing her encounter, Carrie said, "I don't think there's any doubt that he's the son of Charlie DeLuca's second wife. And he's very angry right now—I don't know if it's at you, or at his stepfather, or at me for confronting him with it. And I have to wonder why he showed up in Jameson. I mean, coincidences happen, but this is a big one."

"Well, I've been busy too," Adam said. "I think we need to get together to share information and plan our next move."

Carrie dropped into a kitchen chair and brushed a strand of hair from her forehead. "Do you want to come by again tonight?"

"No!" The force behind Adam's retort startled her. "I'm tired of sneaking around in the dark. This is no way to live. I want to bring this thing to a close, and in the meantime, I want us to be able to be out in the daylight. I'm beginning to feel like a vampire."

Carrie grinned at the image. "What do you suggest?"

"It's Saturday, and I think we should celebrate the weekend. Let's have a picnic. It's a beautiful spring day, too pretty to be inside."

"Where? How?"

Adam was picking up steam now. "I know a place. I'll pick up the supplies, then swing by your house to get you." There was a pause, apparently for him to check the time. "It's eleven now. I'll see you at twelve. Okay?"

It was closer to twelve thirty when Adam pulled up in front of her house, but Carrie had filled the time with her own preparations. When she saw Adam's car, she hurried out the front door, locking it behind her, and climbed into his little SUV.

"What's in the bag?" he asked.

Carrie held up a shoulder bag, about the size of a briefcase. "Stuff we may need. Now let's see where you're going to take me."

The drive took about half an hour, but it was through lesser highways lined with the spring wildflowers of Texas—bluebonnets, paintbrush, a few early Gaillardias—and they both enjoyed the scenery. Adam kept an eye on the mailboxes along the road, and at one he turned onto a one-lane gravel road lined on both sides by fields of corn. He followed the curved roadway to a small farmhouse, pulled into the yard, and shut off the motor.

"Here we are. There's a table on the front porch with a couple of chairs. We can set up our picnic there and enjoy the isolation."

Carrie stepped up onto the porch and looked back. The cornfield was better than a privacy fence. There wasn't a sound around them—no cars, no humans, not even any farm animals. It was the perfect spot for a getaway. "What is this place? Doesn't someone own it?"

"A farmer lived here alone after his wife died. Then he passed away. His only child, a son, lives in Kansas City. Our law firm is handling the estate. We're supposed to sell the property, furnishings and all, and send him the money. Meanwhile, it sits here idle." He reached into his pocket and pulled out two keys on a metal wire loop. "Water comes from a well. Electricity is still on. There's no phone, but that's a plus."

Carrie gave a happy sigh. "Let's stay here forever," she said.

"Or at least until we get tired of it." Adam uncovered the top of a wicker basket he'd carried from the car and spread the cloth on the porch table. "But let's eat first. I'm starved."

Adam unloaded bread, deli meats, cheese, and a couple of soft drinks, the bottles still wet with condensation. From her bag, Carrie added two apples, chips, and napkins. Adam pulled utensils and more napkins from the basket.

In a moment they sat down to a perfect picnic meal. They looked at each other, and without a word, they joined hands across the table and bowed their heads. "Shall I?" Adam said.

Carrie surprised herself by saying, "No, let me." She took his silence for assent, and said, "Dear God, I've shut You out of my life too long. All I can say is, I'm sorry. But You already know that. I'm grateful You've brought Adam into my life. However this situation ends, we know that You're in control. We leave it in Your hands, and thank You for bringing us this far. We pray that You will bless the food and our time together. Amen."

They ate in silence for a moment, both lost in thought. Finally Adam said, "What about our other suspect? Did you find out why Phil Rushton was at the cemetery last night?"

"He gave a reasonable explanation for his presence there, and it's sort of a stretch to find a motive for him, even if he does have Chicago connections."

Adam rubbed his chin. "And I don't think Bruce Hartley's the guy. He's got Chicago roots too, but frankly I don't think Bruce has the guts to do something like this."

Carrie leaned back in her chair and pushed her plate away. "So how do we approach Rob? Do you have enough to go to the police? Can your brother help us?"

Adam shook his head. "Not really. I guess my next move is to confront Rob. Maybe if I make him mad enough, he'll show me he's the shooter. And if that happens, I'm ready." He reached down and patted the gun in its ankle holster.

"You're not going to shoot him in cold blood, are you? We're not even sure he's the one who's been trying to kill you. All we have is suspicion."

Adam shook his head. "I'm not a murderer, even if I'm backed into a corner. But I'm certainly prepared to protect myself if it comes to that. And if he pulls a weapon . . ."

Adam didn't complete the sentence, but Carrie knew what was coming next. He had a gun. She shivered, despite the sunny day.

Adam didn't want the day to end. Maybe he could buy the farm and they could live here in peaceful serenity. *Get real.* Yeah, that wasn't going to happen. It wasn't even practical to consider it. But they'd had a great afternoon together, a needed respite, offering them both a chance to recharge their batteries. Now it was time to get back to the real world.

It was late afternoon when he pulled up to Carrie's door. "Give me your keys," he said. "Let me check inside first."

He could see her hesitate, her sense of independence doing battle with the reality that danger could lurk around any corner.

"Pull into the driveway," she said. "We'll go in together, and you can look around inside to make sure everything's okay. After that I promise I won't open the door for anyone . . . except you, of course." She punctuated the last sentence with a peck on the cheek. "Thanks for a wonderful day."

"What about church tomorrow? Can I pick you up?"

She seemed to consider it. "Call me later tonight. We'll talk about it then."

He made a thorough inspection of the house, even checking under beds and looking behind clothes in all the closets. When he put his pistol back into its holster, he said, "All clear."

"Thanks. And thanks again for a wonderful afternoon." The kiss she gave him wasn't on the cheek, and it lasted quite awhile.

Adam stepped back. "Tell me there'll be more of those."

Carrie smiled. "As many as you want."

"Does that mean . . . ?"

"Not yet," Carrie said. "Let's get everything settled first."

As Adam drove to his apartment, he realized the potential danger he'd faced today. If his stalker had followed him, he could have wiped out both Adam and Carrie in the isolation of the farm. Maybe there had been a sudden decision on the part of the stalker to stop trying to take Adam's life. Maybe shooters took the weekend off—or not. Maybe Adam had just been lucky.

As he neared home, he watched the rearview mirror carefully. He went through the usual maneuvers to check for a tail. And in the parking lot, he chose a different space to leave his car. Once inside he double locked his door. The first thing he did after that was to remove the Ruger from its holster and put it on the kitchen table.

He'd no sooner put his feet up and turned on a baseball game—the Rangers were indeed playing the Yankees and the score was tied—when his cell phone rang. Caller ID was no help, labeling the call "private." He shrugged. Might as well answer.

"Hello?"

"Adam? Adam Davidson?" It sounded like Bruce Hartley, but the voice was somehow different.

"Yes."

"It's Bruce."

Why was Bruce Hartley calling on Saturday afternoon? Was he about to fire Adam, doing it by phone? Did he want to talk about something at the office? Adam wracked his brain and came up empty. "What's up?"

"Sorry to bother you on a weekend. Our firm is the executor for the Caraway estate, and we finally have a buyer for the house. I'm meeting him and the Realtor there in half an hour."

Bruce paused, and Adam heard him take a couple of deep breaths. "Aren't you a notary?"

"Yes. You insisted I become one when I went to work for the firm."

"Well, I need you to meet us and notarize some documents." The words seemed to gush out, as though Bruce couldn't wait to say them. "I know it's Saturday afternoon, but this is the only time the buyer can do this, and we need to get it wrapped up."

Adam searched his memory and came up blank. "I don't think I know where the Caraway place is."

Hartley gave him directions to a house on the outskirts of town. "Can you make it in half an hour? If we don't get this done, I'm afraid the buyer will change his mind."

"I'll have to go by the office to get my notary stamp first," Adam said.

"Just hurry."

This was unusual, but if the Caraway property had been vacant for some time, he could understand why Bruce might want to get the buyer's signature before he changed his mind. It seemed to explain why he was in such a hurry.

As Adam drove to the office, he thought about calling Carrie but decided not to disturb her. She'd had a late night, and most likely was taking a nap—which was what he'd like to be doing. He yawned at the thought. Oh well. One of the downsides of the legal profession was getting calls at night or on weekends, although he thought he'd left that behind when he shifted into his new identity as a paralegal. This would be a good story to share with Carrie when he talked with her later that night.

Carrie browsed in her refrigerator and finally assembled what might pass for an evening meal. She'd much rather be eating with Adam, but they'd settled on a phone call tonight. Besides, she'd be with him at church tomorrow—she'd already decided they would go there together, despite the risk.

She settled into a comfortable chair in front of the TV, her food on a tray in front of her, and flipped through the channels until she came to an old movie, one she'd seen years ago but wouldn't mind seeing again.

When the phone rang, she turned off the TV, expecting it to be Adam. He was a bit early, but that was okay with her. She missed him already.

"Hello?"

"Dr. Markham?" It was a man's voice, unfamiliar to Carrie. And it carried a tone of stress that she couldn't categorize.

"Yes, who is this?"

"Never mind. If you want to see Adam Davidson alive again, come to the old Caraway place right now. Come alone. Don't make any calls—no police. We mean business." The words were unaccented, almost mechanical, as though the speaker were reading them.

"What's going on? Who is this?"

"Here are the directions you'll need. Write them down. If you're not here in forty-five minutes, Davidson dies."

Carrie grabbed a pen and paper and scribbled the directions. "Wait—"

A click in her ear signaled the end of the call.

TWENTY-FIVE

CARRIE WONDERED IF MAYBE THIS WAS ALL A GIGANTIC HOAX, someone wanting money. She'd get to the rendezvous, only to find a note sending her somewhere else, and eventually she'd be told to leave some huge amount in unmarked bills at a desolate location. Maybe someone had learned of the attempts on Adam's life and decided to use the situation to get some money from her, while Adam dozed at home in front of his TV set.

She had to be sure. Carrie phoned both Adam's cell phone and landline, but there was no answer. She tried again, and once more her call rolled over to voice mail. She thought about going by his apartment, but that might make her miss the deadline the anonymous voice gave her.

She made what preparations she could, then jumped into her car and headed out. The roads were blessedly empty, and she edged her speed up to about ten miles an hour over the speed limit. What would she do if a policeman stopped her?

Would she ask him to hurry and give her a ticket? Would she tell him everything and beg for help? Her instructions had been "no police," and she didn't want to risk violating that admonition.

Forty-two minutes after she hung up from the threatening call, Carrie wheeled her Prius to a stop outside a house on the outskirts of Jameson. Adam's car was parked beside a white SUV. Light was visible from behind curtains in the front window. Aside from her and whoever was in the house, there didn't appear to be another soul anywhere around.

She breathed a silent prayer. *Help me deal with whatever's in there.* Carrie unzipped her shoulder bag and let her fingers roam among the contents until she found the canister of Mace. It wasn't much, but it was the only weapon she had. She wished she'd followed Adam's lead and armed herself with a pistol. Now it was too late.

She exited the car and hurried up the steps onto the porch. Should she knock or just go in? The front door was locked, which answered her question. It had two inserts of leaded glass, allowing her to see movement on the other side but no details. She rapped sharply on the door and saw a figure in black walking toward her. Carrie took an involuntary step backward as the door swung inward and she found herself facing Mary Delkus.

"Right on time," Mary said. Her shoulder-length black hair framed a beautiful face, one that Carrie had only seen once before, but which was hard to forget. Mary wore a loose-fitting black sweater, tight black jeans, and dark running shoes. The color of the clothes matched the boxy-looking pistol she held. "Come on in."

Once Carrie was inside, Mary reached back with her foot

and kicked the door closed. An incandescent bulb with a frosted shade hung from the room's ceiling. With one exception, there was no furniture. That exception immediately caught Carrie's eye. In the corner, a middle-aged man with a receding hairline and a frightened expression was secured to a straight chair by multiple layers of duct tape that encircled his body like a silvery cocoon. Another strip of tape covered his mouth.

"That's Bruce Hartley, senior partner in the law firm where Adam—or should I say, Keith—works," Mary explained. "He made the phone call to you, and it only took the slightest bit of prodding."

Carrie noticed for the first time that Hartley's feet were bare, and there was blood on them as well as the hardwood floor beneath. She couldn't be certain, but it appeared that the nails were gone from some of his toes.

Mary gestured with her gun. "I believe the person you came to see is in here." She herded Carrie through a door into the kitchen.

Adam sat in a straight chair in the middle of the room. He was bound with duct tape, his hands secured behind him, his legs taped to the chair legs. Adam's mouth was sealed with another strip of tape. When he saw Carrie, his eyes widened, then a look of apology swept over his features.

Mary glared at Adam. "I know. You want to talk with her. Maybe I'll untape your mouth just before you die, so you can say your last good-byes."

Carrie's mind was swimming, but she thought she'd put things together. She turned full-face to the woman, trying to ignore the gun in her hand, and said, "You're the shooter."

The woman looked directly at Adam, and Carrie detected a gleam of madness in her eyes. "Bright girl you have here, Adam. I think I'm going to continue to call you Adam. That's the name under which I located you. And that's the name that will be on your tombstone."

"Why?" Carrie said. "Why are you doing this?"

Mary shrugged. "Simple. After a little persuading, Adam told me how he dug into the family tree of Charlie DeLuca. Unfortunately he didn't look hard enough to find out more about Charlie's brother, who was a silent partner in almost everything. When it became obvious that the DA was after Uncle Charlie, my dad rolled up everything he could—gambling, prostitution, protection—and moved it to Kansas City. He changed his name to Delkus, greased a few palms to have Gino DeLuca and his family disappear from public records, and started over again."

"So you're Charlie DeLuca's niece," Carrie said. "Did Charlie ask you to avenge him? Is that why you're doing this?"

Mary grinned. "Did he ask? No. He didn't have to. We're Italian. The code of *vendetta* originated centuries ago in Sicily, and we still believe in revenge. My Uncle Charlie didn't die in prison—he died the day his freedom was taken from him." She glared at Adam. "Now the man responsible for that is going to die. And you're going to do it."

"But—"

"Enough!" She turned her gaze and the gun back on Carrie. "I intended to kill him, but then I decided it would be even better if you did it." She pointed to a black backpack on the kitchen table next to Adam. "I was in the stands when you used one of these to restart that boy's heart. It seems to me that an electrical shock should be able to stop a heart as well as start it. So that's what you're going to do."

Carrie's response was a loud "No!"

Mary's eyes hardened even more. "If you don't, then I'll simply shoot you and take care of him myself. But my way will be slower . . . and a lot more painful."

The germ of an idea tickled at the back of Carrie's mind. It was risky, but it might work. Besides, it could buy some time, and every second was precious. She delayed her answer as long as possible. Just as she saw Mary's lips start to move, Carrie said, "You win."

She moved to the table and pulled the defibrillator from its pack. This one was different from the unit she'd used at the ball field. "I need to figure this out," she said. "Why don't I just make him hurt a little first?"

The gun in Mary's hand was still pointed at Carrie. "So long as you finish him off."

"First, I have to put on the electrodes. One goes on the chest." She unbuttoned Adam's shirt and pulled it open to expose his chest. "And one goes on the leg." She reached down to push up his right pants leg. Her hand touched an empty holster.

"Looking for this?" Mary reached beneath her sweater and pulled Adam's pistol from the waistband of her jeans. "Good try. By the way, I was watching you at the ballpark. I know how this works. Both electrodes go on the chest. Do it right." She emphasized her words with a gesture from her gun.

Carrie searched desperately for words to calm this woman. "I don't . . . I mean—"

"If you don't stop stalling," Mary said, "I'll work on Adam the way I worked on poor Bruce. I understand that having toenails pulled out isn't pleasant." She tucked the Ruger back in her waistband, but kept her own pistol trained on Carrie.

"No, please." Carrie blinked to clear her eyes of tears. She needed to delay, but she was almost out of options. She fumbled as much as she dared, but in a moment the electrodes were in place on Adam's chest, held there by the adhesive on the pads.

"Now set the machine and push the button," Mary said.

"I have to figure this one out." Carrie had to keep Mary talking. "How did you find Adam?"

"His trail wasn't hard to follow. And once I found him, it was a delicious coincidence that he was working in a law office. My training is as a paralegal, so I decided to get a job in the same office."

"Just like that? How could you be so confident you'd get the job?"

Mary laughed, but it was full of evil, not mirth. "Once I met Bruce Hartley, I knew I could have the job, Bruce's car, or anything else I wanted. I wasn't sure where Adam had gone, but I figured he'd be back, and I was right."

"So all your efforts to get to know him—"

"That's enough! Stop delaying. Find out which button to push to stop his heart. If I have to do it with a bullet, I will, but first I'll make him suffer."

Carrie's fingers roamed across the keyboard, then hovered over a button. She looked at Adam. "I'm so sorry." She pushed. The display showed "normal rhythm."

Mary peered at the unit. "You pushed the diagnostic button. You're not going to do this, are you? Well, I'll have to do it the old-fashioned way. Maybe I should shoot you first though." She raised her gun until it was pointed directly at Carrie.

"That's enough. Drop the gun, turn around, and freeze!"

The voice was one that Carrie had heard only once before. She'd heard it on the phone when she called before leaving for this meeting. Dave Branson was taller than his brother, slightly stockier, and the facial resemblance was striking. He was dressed in jeans, boots, and a flannel shirt. There was a badge of some kind affixed to his belt on the left side. His right arm, from elbow to fingertips, was contained in a navy blue sling.

Mary didn't turn. Instead, she kept the gun trained on Carrie. "I don't think so. And who might you be?"

Dave's voice betrayed no trace of tension. "U.S. Marshall David Branson. And you're under arrest for kidnapping, attempted murder, and probably several other charges that I'll leave to the authorities. Now I'm warning you. Drop the gun and turn around with your hands up."

An evil smirk lightened Mary's face. "Another family member. Good. The history of *vendetta* includes a number of instances of wiping out the entire family of the murderer. I was going to be satisfied with her." She nodded toward Carrie. "But you're just a bonus."

"Last warning. Drop the gun."

"Not on your life," Mary said. Suddenly she whirled to level her pistol at Dave.

Carrie was watching Mary's gun hand, and almost missed the tiny puff of smoke that issued from the end of Dave's sling. The report wasn't as loud as she expected a gunshot to be. But there apparently was enough firepower behind it to do the job. Mary took a step backward and collapsed onto the floor. Her gun skidded into a corner. Blood gushed from her chest, and frothy pink bubbles formed at the corner of her mouth.

Dave rushed over to Carrie. "Are you okay?"

"Yes. Cut Adam loose, will you? I'll see about Mary."

Carrie knelt beside the woman and put one finger on her neck to feel for a carotid pulse. It was feeble and irregular. Blood continued to gush from a wound high in Mary's chest. With every labored breath Carrie could hear the sucking sound of air rushing into the chest cavity, robbing Mary's lungs of the ability to take in precious oxygen.

Sucking chest wound. Got to seal it. Carrie grabbed the roll of duct tape from the kitchen table. In one quick motion she pulled Mary's sweater up to expose the gunshot wound. The bleeding was slowing already. Not good. She tore off several pieces of the waterproof tape and applied them over the bullet hole. The sucking sound diminished in intensity, but Mary's breathing was shallower, slower, more labored.

"Mary, open your eyes. Look at me."

The woman looked up, blinked rapidly, then moved her gaze from Carrie's face to the ceiling, as though she could see something written there. She took one deep, ragged breath and let it out slowly through pursed lips.

"Dave, call 911!" Carrie shouted.

"Already did it. How can I help here?"

The blood pulsating from the wound was darker now and had slowed to a trickle. As Carrie watched, the flow stopped. The bullet must have caught a major blood vessel, maybe the aortic arch. Carrie placed two fingers on Mary's neck. The feeble carotid pulse beat she'd felt earlier was now gone. Full cardiac arrest.

Carrie's first reflex was to pump Mary's chest, but if there was no blood to circulate, cardiac compressions wouldn't help.

She looked helplessly at the defibrillator on the kitchen table, the leads hanging loose where Dave had ripped them from Adam's chest.

"Can I do something?" Dave asked again.

"There's nothing you can do—nothing anyone can do now."

Carrie had the knowledge. She had some of the equipment. But she couldn't save the patient. The woman who'd tried multiple times to murder her and Adam lay dead before her. And strangely enough, she felt no triumph—only frustration. Maybe that was what being a physician was about. Carrie tried to save them all, even her enemies. Some she could. Some she couldn't.

The verse ran through Carrie's head again: "I will give you a new heart." The words weren't meant to describe a beating, pumping organ, although certainly Mary could use one of those now. Instead they referred to a spiritual awakening. Surely this scenario would have played out differently if Mary had claimed that promise. But now it was too late.

TWENTY-SIX

MARY'S BODY LAY WHERE SHE FELL WHILE INVESTIGATORS TOOK
their pictures and memorialized the scene. Adam didn't need
any of that though. He'd remember every detail for the rest of
his life.

Bruce Hartley sat in the chair from which he'd been cut
free, trying to drink from the glass Adam handed him. His
hands shook, and most of the water dribbled down his chin,
but he didn't seem to notice. He took a few sips before looking
up with eyes as sad as a spaniel's. "Adam, I swear, I had no idea
what she was trying to do."

"I know, Bruce. She took advantage of you." No need to
berate the man. Anything Adam wanted to tell Bruce, the
lawyer was probably already telling himself. And if he hadn't
yet, he would. "I know she forced you to make that phone call
to Carrie. And it's apparent that you held out as long as you
could."

A tear rolled down Hartley's cheek. "She . . . she took pliers and pulled out my toenails. I couldn't stand it any longer."

An EMT put his hand on Hartley's shoulder. "Sir, we're ready to take you to the Emergency Room. Do you want to walk to the ambulance?" Then he saw the lawyer's bloody feet. "Never mind. I'll get the gurney."

A sheriff's deputy approached Adam, with Dave and Carrie right behind him. "Mr. Davidson, let's hear your story one more time."

Adam began slowly at first, not eager to relive the harrowing moments, yet knowing he must. "When I walked in, Mary was here with a gun. Hartley was already secured to a chair. After she restrained me, she held a script in front of him and forced him to read it to Carrie."

"And how did she force him to do that?"

Adam pointed to a bloody pair of pliers still under the chair where Hartley had been. "Eventually he made the call. Then Mary silenced him with tape over his mouth and sat down to wait for Carrie."

The deputy scribbled a few notes. "Why did she do all this?"

It took Adam the better part of an hour to give the deputy what he needed, with Carrie and Dave adding information where it was needed.

Dave surrendered his off-duty gun, the one he'd concealed in his sling. Ballistic tests would confirm that a bullet from his Taurus .38 Special killed Mary, but he'd given her every chance to surrender. Instead, she chose to turn and aim her gun at him. Her last words—"Not on your life"—had been prophetic.

The deputy was putting his notebook in his pocket when a stocky, older man with a badge pinned to his golf shirt approached the group. Dave stuck out his hand. "Len, sorry to get you out tonight."

The man smiled. "Sorry you had a spot of trouble, Dave." He turned to the deputy. "Got what you need?"

"Yes, sir," the deputy said.

By now Adam had figured that this was the county sheriff. The man said, "You folks can go. I need you to stop by my office on Monday so we can get formal statements." He shook hands all around, and when he came to Carrie, he said, "Ma'am, I think it was pretty gutsy, the way you tried to save the life of a woman who'd been trying to murder you."

Carrie shook her head. "I did what any physician would do. I only wish I could have done more."

Even as she spoke, Carrie wondered at the truth of her words. What would she have done if the wound hadn't been mortal, beyond her ability to treat in the circumstances? What if, for some reason, use of the defibrillator could have saved Mary's life? Would Carrie have applied it, or would she have stood back and watched her enemy die? Although she hoped she would have done the right thing, Carrie was glad the decision had been made for her.

———— ⅃⌐ ————

Carrie fought to keep her eyes open as she drove back to town. Adam was right behind her in his car. When she'd told him she had one more stop to make before going home, he insisted on being with her.

She wheeled into the Emergency Room parking lot and

felt reassured when she saw Adam bring his car to a stop beside hers. They exited and walked together toward the ER entrance.

"I guess there's no need to feel like I'm in someone's cross-hairs anymore," he said.

"It's going to take some time for it to soak in," Carrie said, "but I think you're right."

"Are you sure you want to do this?"

"Yes. This is the last piece of the puzzle, and I can't rest until I deal with it."

They moved through the sliding glass doors, and Carrie made her way to the desk where the clerk and triage nurse sat. "Is Rob Cole driving tonight?"

The clerk nodded through the double doors leading into the Emergency Room. "He and his partner just brought in a patient." She looked at the clock on the wall. "They're probably taking a break before their next call. Do you need to see him?"

"I'll find him," Carrie said. "Thanks."

She indicated that Adam should follow her. In the ER she navigated a maze of gurneys, patients, families, staff, equipment, and miscellaneous roadblocks, her eyes moving constantly until she spotted Rob heading for the break room. "There he is. Come on."

They caught Rob at the coffee urn, drawing a cup.

"Rob, we need a moment of your time."

Rob's initial reaction was that of a trapped animal. His eyes shifted back and forth and his body language warned of impending flight, but in a moment his features dissolved into another emotion—shame. "Dr. Markham, I'm sorry I acted that way. It's . . . I can't talk about it."

"I think I can help you," Carrie said. "Let's sit down."

A sofa and two overstuffed chairs, long past their prime, were arranged along two walls of the break room. Rob, Carrie, and Adam found seats and sat for a moment in uncomfortable silence.

Carrie decided to get right to it. "This is about Charlie DeLuca." She noticed the tensing of Rob's muscles at the name, but she plunged on. "You see, someone has been shooting at Adam and at me. We thought it might be you, trying to avenge Charlie's imprisonment."

"But—"

"No, we've discovered it wasn't you. It was Charlie's niece." Carrie shook her head. "She's no longer a threat."

"What happened?"

Carrie took a moment to explain. "But the reason we're here now is that we want to help you. And to do that, we need to know why you blew up at me when I mentioned DeLuca."

"I told you. I don't want to talk about it."

"Rob, we'd like to get you some help."

Rob moved his cup from hand to hand but made no attempt to drink. He looked at the ceiling. He looked at the floor. Finally he looked into Carrie's eyes. "I've been seeing a therapist, but I still . . . struggle. I guess that's why I've acted sort of funny toward you. He says I don't know how to relate to women, at least not appropriately."

Carrie opened her mouth but caught Adam's quick shake of the head, so she waited for Rob to continue.

"When Charlie DeLuca was indicted, there was something else we found out, something that was even worse than bigamy, worse than the crimes that sent him to jail." He tossed his half-full paper cup into the trash. "It was what he'd been doing to my sister. It was so terrible . . . Well, she couldn't forget it. So she left us to become a cloistered nun. Now her name is Sister Rafael. We haven't seen her—can't see her—since this happened. She withdrew from the world because she found out how terrible the world can be."

Carrie leaned forward in her seat and noticed that Adam did the same.

"The night before she left home, my sister told me this, but made me swear not to let our mother know. She was glad Charlie DeLuca wasn't really our stepfather. She was glad he was going to prison. Her words were, 'I hope he rots in hell.' Then she told me about how he'd come into her room every night when he was at our house and . . ." He put his head in his hands and started sobbing.

Carrie let out a breath she'd held for what seemed like an eternity. She could guess the rest. And her heart broke—for Rob, for his sister, for Adam, and for all the others who'd been affected by the sins of one man.

On Monday morning Adam dressed for work, but this time he didn't strap on the ankle holster. His gun was in the sheriff's property room, and that was fine with him. If they chose to check it for fingerprints, they would find his, along with those of Mary Delkus, but he doubted that would ever happen. The case was closed.

Adam parked in his marked spot at the law office and carried his briefcase through the front door without a single glance over his shoulder. He walked by Mary's office, the one that used to be his. He wasn't sure what would happen next, but whatever it was, he'd handle it. As he and Carrie had said to each other again and again yesterday, God was in control. That was enough.

Brittany poked her head in his door. "I've already made coffee. Would you like some?"

"That would be nice. Thanks."

She was back in a moment, holding two cups. She put one on his desk and said, "I've heard what happened over the weekend. I'm sorry for what you've been through."

Adam started to respond when he heard the phone ringing at Brittany's desk. She held up a finger. "Sorry, I've got to get that," she said, then turned and hurried away.

No sooner was Brittany gone than Janice Evans came in. She looked at the chair opposite his desk with raised eyebrows, and Adam said, "Please. Sit down. What's up?"

"I talked with Bruce last night. He told me some of the story. Then I called a friend in the sheriff's department and got the rest of it. You had a busy day."

"How's Bruce doing?"

Janice sipped her coffee and seemed to choose her words carefully. "Bruce was hurting from having his toenails pulled out, but he was also hurting because he'd been so stupid. We all thought he hired Mary and let her lead him around because she was so good-looking. That may have been part of it, but the other part was that Mary's father, Charlie DeLuca's brother, held Bruce's gambling debts years ago."

"Was that when Elwood Stroud bailed him out?"

"Yes. Although Bruce's debts were settled long ago, Mary said if he didn't do what she wanted, she'd see to it that word got around about Bruce's gambling history. Apparently there were some stories from back then that might get him in trouble even now with the ethics committee of the bar association."

"Is he still worried that might happen, now that Mary's dead?"

"He doesn't care. Bruce is ready to get out of the rat race. He told me he wants to sell his share of the partnership to me."

Adam drank some of his coffee, cringing at the bitter taste. He'd better get there early the next day to brew it. Brittany had lots of good qualities, but making coffee wasn't one of them. "Well, sounds like things are ending okay."

Janice leaned toward him. "Bruce heard you tell the police your backstory, and he passed that information on to me when we talked. I'd always thought you were too good as a paralegal, and that explains it." She removed her glasses, and Adam saw only sincerity in her gray eyes. "With Bruce leaving, I'm going to need another lawyer here. Is your license still current?"

"It is in Illinois. Does that state have reciprocity with Texas?"

"I looked it up last night. As it happens, it does. I hate to lose a good paralegal, but good lawyers are scarce too. And I have an idea you're a very good lawyer. Would you consider joining the practice?"

Adam knew he should say, "Let me think about it." He probably should even say, "Let me pray about it." Instead, he said, "I'd be thrilled to."

"Great. We'll start drawing up an agreement later today." She rose, but stopped to ask him, "I suppose your law license is in your real name. Do you want to go back to being Keith Branson?"

Adam had to think about that for a moment. "You know, I've had several names since this all started. It wasn't so bad getting used to them, but I've always regretted giving up my family name." He blinked a couple of times. "My parents are dead, and my brother and I are the last surviving Bransons. David saved my life, and I'm proud to share his last name. I think I'd like to go back to being Keith Branson . . . Dave's brother."

Carrie planned to start her Monday by quietly telling a few people what had happened over the weekend, but apparently the grapevine worked well, even when the staff wasn't together at the clinic. It seemed everyone already had the news.

Lila met her at the door. "How are you doing?"

"I'm fine," Carrie responded. Actually, she was better than she'd been in weeks—better than at anytime since Adam's windshield shattered and gunshots propelled her into the nightmare that just ended. "Is my patient list ready?"

"On your desk," Lila said. "But Dr. Rushton wants to see you first thing. Would you like some coffee?"

"In a few minutes," Carrie said. "I don't think this will take long." She had successfully resisted Phil's repeated requests for the two of them to get together. Now it was time to face the music. She searched her memory for something she might have done that would bring down the wrath of the clinic's managing partner, but nothing came to mind. Oh well. She'd see soon enough.

Carrie tapped at the open door of Phil's office. He rose and walked to her, enfolded her in a hug, and led her to one of the chairs in front of his desk. He took the one beside it and turned it to face Carrie. So far this was a totally different Phil Rushton than the one she'd come to know, respect, and sometimes dislike.

"Are you okay?" he asked. "Would you like some coffee?"

"Nothing, thanks. And I'm fine—thanks for asking." She leaned forward in the chair. Might as well get this out of the way. "Phil, you need to know that strange message you got came from Adam." She went on to explain about the three suspects in the shootings and why Phil was on the list. "Obviously you were innocent, and I want to apologize for suspecting you and for the way it might have influenced our relationship."

Phil shrugged it off. "No problem. I can see why you might think that, with my Chicago connection." He shifted in his chair. "And that brings me to the reason I've been wanting to meet with you."

Carrie frowned. "O-o-okay."

"You already know that I'm from Chicago, did all my training there. I've always wanted to go back, and now I have the chance. I've received an offer to head the division of cardiothoracic surgery at Loyola in Chicago. I'm going to take the job."

Carrie had trouble processing that for a moment. Phil was leaving? Then again, this was a great honor, and he'd be foolish not to grab the opportunity. He deserved it.

"Wonderful. Congratulations."

"That means we'll need another cardiothoracic surgeon here." Phil reached back to his desk and lifted three thin manila folders from it. "Here are three men we need to interview."

Carrie wasn't sure what to say. "What can I do?"

"You'll head the search committee, along with two other clinic members of your choice."

"Why me?"

"Because I'm suggesting that you replace me as managing partner. You've been here as long as any of the other doctors. You're levelheaded. You've demonstrated that you can be cool in stressful situations, and this job has a lot of them."

"I'll need to—"

Phil held up his hand. "I know. I've sprung this on you without warning. Why don't you and Adam talk about it over dinner tonight? I've made a seven o'clock reservation at The Grotto for you to have dinner on me. It's all taken care of."

Back in her office Carrie had the phone in her hand, ready to dial Adam, when it struck her. This was great news, but it was the kind to share face-to-face.

When Adam answered, his first words were, "I was about to call you. I have something I need to tell you."

"Me too. But I'd like to see the look on your face when I share my news."

"Can you spare some time at noon?" he asked.

"Sure," Carrie said. "Come by my office and we'll have lunch together." *And will I have a surprise for you.*

Keith—he'd have to get used to that name again—could hardly contain his excitement. He checked his watch every fifteen minutes, and finally at eleven twenty he couldn't wait any longer. He grabbed his coat and told Brittany, "I have a luncheon meeting. See you in a couple of hours."

Keith had trouble holding his car under the speed limit, he was so anxious to see Carrie, to share his news and hear hers. When he was halfway to her office, he reached a decision that sent him on a detour. Despite the delay, he was waiting in Carrie's office when she walked in at noon.

She kissed him and started to shed her white coat. "Where should we have lunch?" she asked.

"We'll get to that in a minute. But before we do, let's talk about our news."

"Okay, you first," Carrie said.

He told her about the offer from Janice Evans, his opportunity to resume his law practice and take back his real name.

"Wonderful."

"You're sure the name change won't be a problem for you?" he asked.

Carrie didn't hesitate. "This isn't just a chance to reclaim your name. It's the opportunity to reclaim your life." She grinned. "I may call you Adam a couple of times, but I promise that from now on you'll be Keith Branson to me," Carrie said. "And I'll love you, whatever you're called."

Adam beamed. "Now what's your news?" he asked.

Carrie shared what Phil Rushton told her. "All this time I was worried that he wanted me out, but instead I have a chance to become the managing partner of the clinic."

"Sounds like good news all around."

"It amazes me," Carrie said. "There were times when I couldn't see any way out of the predicament we were in. But God brought us through it . . . and brought me back to Him in the bargain."

"So what did you tell Phil?" Keith asked.

"Nothing, yet. He thought you and I could talk it over at dinner tonight," Carrie said. "He made seven o'clock reservations at The Grotto, his treat. Want to pick me up at a quarter to seven?"

"Sure." Keith pointed to the picnic basket on the floor. "And as for lunch, I figured you'd be pressed for time, so I thought we'd eat here. I have deli sandwiches, chips, and soft drinks."

Carrie smiled. "As I recall you put together a mean picnic lunch." She pulled a pile of medical journals off the small table in the corner of her office and dropped them on the floor. "Want to spread it out there?"

"I wish we could go back to that farmhouse and have a real picnic."

"So do I."

Keith arranged the food on the table. Then he brought over one of the chairs from in front of Carrie's desk and gestured to her. "Have a seat."

She did so. "Now join me."

"Just a second. There's one more thing in the basket." Keith reached in and pulled out a paper napkin twisted into a small bundle. "I guess this is sort of corny, but after all we've been through, I wanted to do it right this time." He dropped to one knee in front of Carrie. "There are no secrets anymore. And it's never been a secret that I love you." He unfolded the napkin and held out the engagement ring. "I hope you're ready to accept this now. Dr. Carrie Markham, will you be Mrs. Keith Branson?"

At first, Carrie's eyes glistened. Then tears ran down her face, but the smile that accompanied them told Keith they were tears of happiness.

There was a catch in Carrie's voice when she said, "Yes." Then her kiss told Keith that everything was right with the world once more.

READING GROUP GUIDE

1. What was Carrie's relationship to the Lord at the beginning of the book? Do you think the chasm was justified? Can you put your finger on the factor(s) that brought her back?
2. Contrast where Carrie and Adam were in their Christian walks at the beginning of the book. What do you think was the cause of the difference? Do you think you might have felt the same in their situations?
3. Was there any justification for Adam hiding his past from Carrie? Is there ever a valid reason for a lie or partial truth? Why or why not?
4. What is your mental image of Adam's older brother? What was their relationship? Why?
5. Phil Rushton is a complex character. What was your overall opinion of him? If you didn't know about Phil's marital and family status, what would you guess it was? Why?

6. For a long time, Adam resisted getting a gun. What pushed him over the edge? Do you think he would have used it?

7. What was your takeaway message after finishing the book?

ACKNOWLEDGMENTS

READERS MAY HAVE THE IDEA THAT NOVELS SPRING, FRESHLY formed and complete, from the fertile minds of writers. Far be it from me to disillusion you, but it doesn't happen that way. For instance, here's what it took to put this novel in your hands.

I'm privileged to have a wife who is my first reader, my biggest fan, and my most discerning critic. Kay helped me shape this story from its inception to the final step along the way. Thank you, dear. I truly couldn't do it without you.

My fantastic agent, Rachelle Gardner, has believed in me when others didn't. She presented this concept, and the novel that followed, to my editor, Amanda Bostic, who applied her editorial talent to point me in the right direction. Then Traci DePree exercised her special touch to help me improve the story even further. I appreciate all of these ladies so much. They deserve chocolate . . . or at least a round of applause.

While I was writing, Kristen Vasgaard was designing a

dynamite book cover. After the edits were completed, Becky Monds and the rest of the Thomas Nelson crew shepherded the novel through production. Meanwhile, Katie Bond and Laura Dickerson got the word out so readers would know about the book. My sincere thanks go to every one of these good folks.

My writing journey has been long and, at times, difficult. Along the way I've received encouragement, instruction, and mentoring from lots of people, including (but not limited to): Karen Ball, James Scott Bell, Colleen Coble, Brandilyn Collins, Alton Gansky, Jeff Gerke, Dennis Hensley, Randy Ingermanson, DiAnn Mills, Michael Palmer, Gayle Roper, Barbara Scott, Terry Whalin, and too many more to mention.

And, of course, I've been blessed with the support of my family and friends through it all.

Finally, I'm grateful for my loyal readers and the opportunity to share these words with you. Thanks for coming along for the ride. I hope you enjoyed it.

AN EXCERPT FROM *STRESS TEST*

ONE

DR. MATT NEWMAN KNEW ALL ABOUT THE HIGH. HE'D EXPERIENCED it many times. The high was intoxicating, even when the low inevitably followed. Of course, sometimes there was no high at all, no pleasure, only the sadness, the melancholy. How many times had Matt asked himself if it was worth it?

It began tonight, as it frequently did, with a phone call that rolled Matt out of bed after less than an hour's sleep and sent him speeding to the hospital. A teenager lay bleeding to death from internal injuries, the victim of a car crash that killed the girl riding with him.

Tonight Matt's efforts were rewarded with a high unmatched by anything from a glass, a bottle, or a syringe. Tonight there would be no heartbreak of telling a grieving family his best hadn't been enough to save their loved one. Tonight Matt could savor the high—at least for a little while. This case was a good way to go out, to leave private practice behind.

But already Matt's exhilaration was giving way to fatigue. His eyes burned. His shoulders ached. His mouth was foul with the acid taste of coffee left too long on the hot plate. He was running on fumes.

The pneumatic doors closed behind him with a hiss like an auditory exclamation point. As Matt moved from the brilliance of Metropolitan Hospital's emergency room into the mottled semidarkness of the parking garage, he imagined the weight of responsibility slipping from his shoulders. Tomorrow Tom Wilson would take over his patients and his practice. Tomorrow Matt would assume his new position as assistant professor of surgery at Southwestern Medical Center here in Dallas. He'd teach medical students at Southwestern and instruct residents at Parkland Hospital, always emphasizing not only the science but the art of medicine. Matt knew he had a lot to give. He could hardly wait.

One of the benefits of the new job was supposed to be a more structured life: less on-call time, responsibilities shared with other faculty members, assistance from residents in patient care. Matt was looking forward to the change, not just for himself, but for the way it might benefit his relationship with Jennifer.

Matt couldn't give up medicine entirely—he'd invested too much of his life in it, and it remained a passion with him— but he also felt a passion for Jennifer, perhaps even loved her. She was beautiful, witty, and fun to be around. She might be "the one."

It wasn't hard for Matt to spot his silver Chevy Impala in the darkest corner of the deserted garage. There weren't many cars still there at two a.m., and soon there would be one fewer. He fished his keys from the pocket of his white lab coat and thumbed the unlock button on his remote. His hand was on the door handle when something yanked him backward and cut off his air in mid-breath. Matt dropped the keys and reached up with both hands to pry at the arm that encircled his neck.

In an instant Matt was slammed facedown to the cement floor. He heard a crack and felt the knife-like agony of breaking ribs. The searing pain in his chest made each labored breath more difficult. A weight pinned him to the ground like a butterfly on a specimen board.

Matt struggled, but his assailant held him fast. Fire shot through his shoulders as his arms were yanked together. There was a quick rip of tape, and in seconds his wrists were bound tightly behind him. Rough hands encircled his ankles with more tape, leaving him helpless and immobile. At the same time, someone else grabbed his hair and lifted his head. Matt gave a shrill cry before three quick turns of tape muffled his voice and turned the world black.

He tried to lift his head, but stopped abruptly when something hard and cold pressed against the back of his neck. Matt lowered his face onto the garage floor and went limp. He felt hope escape like air from a punctured tire.

There were murmurs above him, questions in a high-pitched singsong, answers from a harsh rasp like grinding gears. At first the words were indistinguishable. Then they became louder as the exchange heated.

"Why not here?" Was there a faint Hispanic accent to the whining tenor?

"The boss said not at the hospital." The growling bass

flung out the words, and spittle dotted the back of Matt's neck. "I know just the place to get rid of him. Let's get him into the trunk of his car."

In the darkness that now enveloped him, Matt struggled in vain to move, to speak. He strained to hear what was said. He could only make out a few words, but they were enough to drive his heart into his shoes. "Get rid of him."

He angled his head to catch the sounds around him: a jingle of keys, the sharp click of the trunk lock. Hinges squeaked. Matt had a momentary sensation of floating as he was lifted, carried, dropped. His head struck something hard. Splashes of red flashed behind his closed eyelids, then vanished into nothingness.

Matt floated back to consciousness like a swimmer emerging from the depths. How long had he been out? Hours? Minutes? A few seconds? At first he had no idea where he was or what was happening. Little by little, his senses cleared. He tried to open his eyes but there was no light. He tried to speak, but his lips were sealed. He cried out, but the result was only a strained grunt. Finally he heard the faint sound of voices from inside the car, a menacing rumble and a high-pitched whine. The voices brought it all back to him.

He was on the way to his death. And the trunk of his car would be his coffin.

The story continues in Stress Test
by Richard L. Mabry, M.D.

DR. FRASIER COULDN'T SAVE THE
GUNSHOT VICTIM ON HER FRONT LAWN.
NOW SHE'S FIGHTING FOR HER LIFE.

RICHARD L.
MABRY, M.D.

CRITICAL
CONDITION

AVAILABLE APRIL 2014

ABOUT THE AUTHOR

Photo by Jodi Westfall

DR. RICHARD MABRY IS A RETIRED PHYSICIAN. THIS IS HIS SIXTH published novel of medical suspense. His previous works have been finalists for the Carol Award and Romantic Times Reader's Choice Award and have won the Selah Award. He is a past vice president of American Christian Fiction Writers and a member of the International Thriller Writers. He and his wife live in North Texas.

Praise for
SEVEN NIGHTS
TO SURRENDER

"Jeanette Grey has become a must-read voice in romance. SEVEN NIGHTS TO SURRENDER is lyrical, stunningly sexy, and brings swoons for *days*."

—Christina Lauren, *New York Times* bestselling author

"A must read! I couldn't put it down. Jeanette Grey's writing is *so* refreshingly honest. SEVEN NIGHTS TO SURRENDER is intensely emotional and sexy as hell. I need the next book ASAP!"

—Tara Sue Me, *New York Times* bestselling author

"With its sexy setting and sensual story, Jeanette Grey's SEVEN NIGHTS TO SURRENDER sparkles!"

—J. Kenner, *New York Times* and international bestselling author

"Achingly sexy and romantic—I couldn't put it down!"

—Laura Kaye, *New York Times* bestselling author

"Sensual, sultry, and exquisite, SEVEN NIGHTS TO SURRENDER will sweep you away and seduce you on every page! Crackling with tension and steamy with sensuality, it's a feast for the senses you don't want to miss!"

—Katy Evans, *New York Times* bestselling author

"With her unique flair, Jeanette Grey delivers a deliciously sexy and irresistible romance that keeps you turning the pages for more. You'll savor every word so you don't miss a single sizzling moment."

—K. Bromberg, *New York Times* bestselling author

Praise for
WHEN THE STARS ALIGN

"I couldn't put it down! I loved every sentence! The writing is outstanding, the setting entrancing, and the characters stole my heart. Fresh, flawed, and instantly lovable, you'll root for Jo and Adam at every turn."

—S. C. Stephens, #1 *New York Times* bestselling author

"The heat of the island has nothing on the off-the-charts attraction that sizzles between its feisty and fiercely unique heroine and idyllic hero. The journey to being the best you is often equal parts beautiful and tragic, and Grey sets the scene perfectly. A sassy and sexy read full of heart and adventure. This romance is like a breath of fresh air."

—Jay Crownover, *New York Times* bestselling author

seven nights to
SURRENDER

JEANETTE GREY

FOREVER

New York   Boston

Forever
Hachette Book Group
1290 Avenue of the Americas
New York, NY 10104

HachetteBookGroup.com

Printed in the United States of America

RRD-C

First Edition: November 2015
10 9 8 7 6 5 4 3 2 1

Forever is an imprint of Grand Central Publishing.
The Forever name and logo are trademarks of Hachette Book Group, Inc.

The Hachette Speakers Bureau provides a wide range of authors for speaking events. To find out more, go to
www.hachettespeakersbureau.com or call (866) 376-6591.

The publisher is not responsible for websites (or their content) that are not owned by the publisher.

Library of Congress Cataloging-in-Publication Data has been applied for

ISBN 978-1-4555-8979-1

To Scott, for all the journeys we've been on so far, and all the journeys yet to come.

Acknowledgments

I am so incredibly grateful to the people who've helped make this book a reality. My thanks to:

My editor, Megha Parekh, who saw exactly what the story needed to make it shine.

My agent, Mandy Hubbard, who championed me every step of the way.

My critique partners: Brighton Walsh, for holding my hand, sharing my room, fixing my *furthers/farthers*, and dragging me out of my sad little introvert corner time and time again. And Heather McGovern, for being a voice of sanity when the world was squishy, as well as the best enabler a girl could hope for.

The beautiful blogging ladies of *Bad Girlz Write*, for always raising a glass, and the amazing folks at Capital Region Romance Writers of America, for their constant guidance and support.

And my incredible husband, family, and friends, for accepting me and loving me for precisely the ball of crazy that I am.

seven nights to
SURRENDER

chapter ONE

It was ridiculous, how pretty words sounded on Kate's tongue. Right up until the moment she opened her mouth and spoke them aloud.

Worrying the strap of her bag between her forefinger and thumb, she gazed straight ahead at the woman behind the register, repeating the phrase over and over in her head. *Un café au lait, s'il vous plaît.* Coffee with milk, please. No problem. She had this. The person ahead of her in line stepped forward, and Kate nodded to herself, standing up taller. When her turn finally came, she grinned with her most confident smile.

And just about had the wind knocked out of her when someone slammed into her side.

Swearing out loud as she was spun around, she put her arm out to catch herself. A pimply teenager was mumbling what sounded like elaborate apologies, but with her evaporating tenth-grade knowledge of French, he could have been telling *her* off for running into *him*, for all she knew. She was going to choose to believe it was the apologizing thing.

Embarrassed, she waved the kid away, gesturing as best she

could to show that she was fine. As he gave one last attempt at mollifying her, she glanced around. A shockingly attractive guy with dark hair and the kind of jaw that drove women to paint stood behind her, perusing a French-language newspaper with apparent disinterest and a furrow of impatience on his brow. The rest of the people in line wore similar expressions.

She turned from the kid, giving him her best New Yorker cold shoulder. The lady at the register, at least, didn't seem to be in any big rush. Kate managed a quick "Désolé"—*sorry*—as she moved forward to rest her hands on the counter. She could do this. She smiled again, focusing to try to summon the words she'd practiced to her lips. "Un café au lait, s'il vous plaît."

Nope, not nearly as pretty as it had sounded in her head, but as she held her breath, the woman nodded and keyed her order in, calling it out to the girl manning the espresso machine. Then, completely in French, the woman announced Kate's total.

Yes. It was all she could do not to fist-pump the air. She'd been exploring Paris now for two days, and no matter how hard she rehearsed what she was going to say, waiters and waitresses and shopkeepers invariably sniffed her out as an American the instant she opened her mouth. Every one of them had shifted into English to reply.

This woman was probably humoring her, but Kate seized her opportunity, turning the gears in her brain with all her might. She counted in her head the way her high school teacher had taught her to until she'd translated every digit. Three eighty-five. Triumph surged through her as she reached for her purse at her hip.

Only to come up with empty air.

Oh no. With a sense of impending dread, she scrabbled at her shoulder, and her waist, but no. Her bag was gone.

She groaned aloud. How many people had cautioned her about exactly this kind of thing? Paris was full of pickpockets. That was what her mother and Aaron and even the guy at the travel store had told her. An angry laugh bubbled up at the back of her throat, an echo of her father's voice in her mind, yelling at her to be more careful, for God's sake. Pay some damn attention. Crap. It was just— She swore she'd had her purse a second ago. Right before that kid had slammed into her...

Her skin went cold. Of course. The kid who'd slammed into her.

Tears prickled at her eyes. She had no idea how to say all of that in French. Her plans for a quiet afternoon spent sketching in a café evaporated as she patted herself down yet again in the vain hope that somehow, magically, her things would have reappeared.

The thing was, "watch out for pickpockets" wasn't the only advice she'd gotten before she'd left. Everyone she'd told had thought her grand idea of a trip to Paris to find herself and get inspired was insane. It was her first trip abroad, and it was eating up pretty much all of her savings. Worse, she'd insisted on making the journey alone, because how was a girl supposed to reconnect with her own muse unless she spent some good quality time with it? Free from distractions and outside influences. Surrounded by art and history and a beautiful language she barely spoke. It had seemed like a good idea. Like the perfect chance to make some really big decisions.

But maybe they'd all been right.

Not wanting to reveal the security wallet she had strapped around her waist beneath her shirt, she wrote off all her plans for the day. She'd just head back to the hostel. She still had her passport and most of her money. She'd regroup, and she'd be fine.

"Mademoiselle?"

Her vision was blurry as she jerked her gaze up. And up. The gorgeous man—the one with the dark, tousled hair and the glass-cutting jaw from before—was standing right beside her, warm hand gently brushing her elbow. A frisson of electricity hummed through her skin. Had he really been this tall before? Had his shoulders been that broad? It was just a plain black button-down, but her gaze got stuck on the drape of his shirt across his chest, hinting at miles of muscle underneath.

His brow furrowed, two soft lines appearing between brilliant blue eyes.

She shook off her daze and cleared her throat. "Pardon?" she asked, lilting her voice up at the end in her best—still terrible—attempt at a French accent.

He smiled, and her vision almost whited out. In perfect English, with maybe just a hint of New York coloring the edges, he asked, "Are you okay?"

All those times she'd been annoyed when someone spoke English to her. At that moment, she could have kissed him, right on those full, smooth lips. Her face went warmer at the thought. "No. I—" She patted her side again uselessly. "I think that guy ran off with my wallet."

His expression darkened, but he didn't step away or chastise her for being so careless. "I'm sorry."

The woman at the register spoke up, her accent muddy. "You still would like your coffee?"

Kate began to decline, but the man placed a ten-euro note on the counter. In a flurry of French too fast for her to understand, he replied to the woman, who took his money and pressed a half dozen keys. She dropped a couple of coins into his palm, then looked around them toward the next customer in line.

"Um," Kate started.

Shifting his hand from her elbow to the small of her back, the man guided Kate toward the end of the counter and out of the way. It was too intimate a touch. She should have drawn away, but before she could convince herself to, he dropped his arm, turning to face her. Leaving a cold spot where his palm had been.

She worked her jaw a couple of times. "Did you just pay for my coffee?" She might be terrible at French, but she was passable at context clues.

Grinning crookedly, he looked down at her. "You're welcome."

"You really didn't need to."

"Au contraire." His brow arched. "Believe me, when you're having a terrible day, the absolute last thing you should be doing is *not* having coffee."

Well, he did have a point there. "I still have some money. I can pay you back."

"No need."

"No, really." Her earlier reservations gone, she reached for the hem of her shirt to tug it upward, but his hands caught hers before she could get at her money belt.

His eyes were darker now, his fingertips warm. "As much as I hate to stop a beautiful woman from taking off her clothes. It's not necessary."

Was he implying...? No, he couldn't be. She couldn't halt the indignation rising in her throat, though, as she brushed aside his hands and wrestled the hem of her top down. "Stripping is *not* how I was going to pay you."

"Pity. Probably for the best," he added conspiratorially. "The police are much more lenient about that kind of thing here than they are in the States, but still. Risky move."

Two ceramic mugs clinked as they hit the counter, and the barista said something too quickly for Kate to catch.

"Merci," the man said, tucking his paper under his arm and reaching for the cups.

For some reason, Kate had to put in one more little protest before she moved to grab for the one that looked like hers. "You really didn't have to."

"Of course I didn't." Biceps flexing, he pulled both cups in closer to his chest, keeping them out of her reach as she extended her hand. "But it sure did make it easier for me to ask if I could buy you a cup of coffee, didn't it?"

For a second, she boggled.

"Come on, then," he said, heading toward an empty table by the window.

This really, really wasn't what she'd had planned for the day. But as he sat down, his face was cast in profile against the light streaming in from outside. If she hadn't lost her bag, she'd have been tempted to take her sketchbook out right then and there, just to try to map the angles of his cheeks.

As she stood there staring, all her mother's warnings came back to her in a rush. This guy was too smooth. Too practiced and too handsome, and the whole situation had *Bad Idea* written all over it. After the disaster that had been her last attempt at dating, she should know.

But the fact was, she really wanted that cup of coffee. And maybe the chance to make a few more mental studies of his jaw. It wouldn't even be that hard. All she had to do was walk over there and sit down across from him. Except...

Except she didn't *do* this sort of thing.

Which might be exactly why she should.

Fretting, she twisted her fingers in the fabric of her skirt. Then she took a single step forward. She was on vacation, dammit all, and this guy was offering. After everything, she deserved a minute to let go. To maybe actually enjoy herself for once.

Honestly. How much harm could a little conversation with a stranger really do?

Rylan Bellamy had a short, well-tested list of rules for picking up a tourist.

Number one, be trustworthy. Nonthreatening. Tourists were constantly expecting to be taken advantage of.

Number two, be clear about your intentions. No time to mess around when they could fuck off to another country at the drop of the hat.

Number three, make sure they always know they have a choice.

Lifting his cappuccino to his lips, he gazed out the window of the café. It hadn't exactly been the plan to buy the girl in front of him in line a cup of coffee or to pick her up. It *definitely* hadn't been the plan to get so engrossed in the business section of *Le Monde* that he'd managed to completely miss her getting pickpocketed right in front of him. But the whole thing had presented him with quite the set of opportunities.

Trustworthy? Stepping in when she looked about ready to lose it seemed like a good start there. Interceding on her behalf in both English and French were bonuses, too. Paying for her coffee had been a natural after that.

Clear about his intentions? He was still working on that, but he'd been tactile enough. Had gotten into her space and brushed his hands over her skin. Such soft skin, too. Pretty, delicate little hands, stained with ink on the tips.

Just like her pretty, pale face was stained with those big, dark eyes. Those rose-colored lips.

He shifted in his seat, resisting looking over at her for another minute. The third part about making sure this was all her choice was necessary but frustrating. If she didn't come over here of her own free will, she'd never come to his apartment, either, or to his bed. He'd laid down his gauntlet. She could pick it up right now, or she could walk away.

Damn, he hoped she didn't walk away. Giving himself to the count of thirty to keep on playing it cool, he set his cup back down on its saucer. Part of him worried she'd already made a break for it, but no. There was something about her gaze. Hot and penetrating, and he could feel it zoning in on him through the space.

He rather liked that, when he thought about it. Being looked at was nice. As was being appreciated. Sized up. It'd make it all the sweeter once she came to her decision, presuming she chose him.

Bingo.

Things were noisy in the café, but enough of his senses were trained on her that he could make out the sounds of her approach. He paused his counting at thirteen and glanced over at her.

If there'd been any doubts that she was a tourist, they cleared away as he took her in more thoroughly. She wore a pair of purple Converse that all but screamed *American*, and a dark skirt that went to her knees. A plain gray T-shirt and a little canvas jacket. No scarves or belts or any of the other hundred accessories that were so popular among the Parisian ladies this year. Her auburn hair was swept into a twist.

Pretty. American. Repressed. But very, very pretty.

"Your coffee's getting cold," he said as he pushed it across the table toward her and kicked her chair out.

A hundred retorts danced across her lips, but somehow her silence—and her wickedly crooked eyebrow, her considering gaze—said more. She sat down, legs crossed primly, her whole body perched at the very edge of her seat, like she was ready to fly at any moment.

He didn't usually go in for skittish birds. They were too much work, considering how briefly they landed in his nest. He'd already started with this one, though, and there was something about her mouth he liked. Something about her whole aura of innocence and bravery. It was worth the price of a cup of coffee at the very least.

She curled a finger around the handle of her cup and tapped at it with her thumb. Wariness came off her in waves.

"I didn't lace it with anything," he assured her.

"I know. I've been watching you the whole time."

He'd been entirely aware of that, thank you very much. He appreciated the honesty, regardless. "Then what's your hesitation? It's already bought and paid for. If you don't drink it, it's going to go to waste."

She seemed to turn that over in her mind for a moment before reaching for the sugar and adding a more than healthy amount. She gave it a quick stir, then picked it up and took a sip.

"Good?" he asked. He couldn't help the suggestive way his voice dipped. "Sweet enough?"

"Yes." She set the cup down. "Thank you."

"You're welcome."

She closed her mouth and gripped her mug tighter. Reminding himself to be patient, he sat back in his chair and rested his elbow on the arm. He looked her up and down.

Ugh. Forget patience. If he didn't say something soon, they could be sitting here all day. Going with what he knew about her, he gestured in her general vicinity, trying to evoke her total lack of a wallet. "You could report the theft, you know."

Shaking her head, she drummed her finger against the ceramic. "Not worth it. I wasn't a complete idiot. Only had thirty or forty euros in there. And the police won't do much about art supplies and books."

"No, probably not."

The art supplies part fit the profile. Matched the pigment on her hands and the intensity of her eyes.

He let a beat pass, but when she didn't volunteer anything else, he shifted into a more probing stance. Clearly, he'd have to do the conversational heavy lifting here.

Not that he minded. He'd been cooling his heels here in Paris for a year, and he missed speaking English. His French was excellent, but there was something about the language you grew up with. The one you'd left behind. The way it curled around your tongue felt like home.

Home. A sick, bitter pang ran through him at the thought.

He cleared his throat and refocused on his smolder. Eyes on the prize. "So, you're an artist, then?"

"I guess so."

"You guess?"

"I just graduated, actually."

"Congratulations."

She made a little scoffing sound. "Now I just have to figure out what comes next."

Ah. He knew that element of running off to Europe. Intimately. He knew how pointless it all was.

Still. He could spot a cliché when he saw one. "Here to *find yourself*, then?"

"Something like that." A little bit of her reserve chipped away. She darted her gaze up to meet his, and there was something anxious there. Something waiting for approval. "Probably silly, huh?"

"It's a romantic notion." And he'd never been much of a romantic himself. "If it worked, everybody would just run off to Prague and avoid a lifetime of therapy, right? And where would all the headshrinkers be, then?"

She rolled her eyes. "Not everyone can afford a trip to Europe."

Her dismissal wasn't entirely lighthearted. Part of his father's old training kicked in, zeroing in on the tightness around her eyes. This trip was an indulgence for her. Chances were, she'd been saving up for it for years.

Probably best not to mention his own resources, then. Mentally, he shifted their rendezvous from his place to hers. Things would be safer that way.

"True enough," he conceded. "Therapy's not cheap, either, though, and this is a lot more fun."

That finally won him a smile. "I wouldn't know. But I'm guessing so."

"Trust me, it is." He picked up his cappuccino and took another sip. "So, what's the agenda, then? Where have you been so far? What are your must-sees?"

"I only got here a couple days ago. Yesterday, I went out to Monet's gardens."

"Lovely." Lovelier still was the way her whole face softened, just mentioning them.

"I mostly walked around, this morning. Then I was going to sit here and draw for a bit."

Asking if he could see her work some time would be good in terms of making his intentions clear. It was also unbearably trite. He gave a wry smile. "A quintessential Parisian experience."

"And then...I don't know. The Louvre and the Musée d'Orsay, of course." The corner of her mouth twitched downward. "Everything else I had listed in my guidebook."

Ah. "Which I'm imagining just got stolen?"

"Good guess."

Eyeing her up the entire time, he finished the rest of his drink. She still had a little left of hers, but they were closing in on decision time. He didn't have anything else going on today—he never really had anything going on, not since his life had fallen apart. But was he willing to sink an entire afternoon here, offering to show her around?

He tried to be analytical about it. Her body language was still less than open, for all that she'd loosened up a bit. Given her age, probably not a virgin, but he'd bet a lot of money that she wasn't too far off. Not his usual fare. He preferred girls who knew what they were doing—more importantly, ones who knew what *he* was doing. What he was looking for.

This girl...It was going to take some work to get in there.

If it paid off, he had a feeling it'd be worth it, though. When she smiled, her prettiness transcended into beauty.

There was something else there, too. She was romantic and hopeful, and between the story of her lost sketchbook and her delusions about Paris having the power to change her life, she had to be a creative type. Out of nowhere, he wanted to know what kinds of things she made, and what she looked like when she drew.

He kept coming back to her eyes. They hadn't stopped moving the entire time they'd been sitting there, like she was taking absolutely everything in. The sights beyond the window, the faces of the people in the café. Him. It was intriguing. *She* was intriguing, and in a way no other woman had been in so long.

And the idea of going back to the apartment alone made him want to scream.

Decision made, he pushed his chair out and clapped his hands together. "Well, what are we waiting for then?"

"Excuse me?"

"Travel guides are bullshit anyway. Especially when you've got something better." He rose to his feet and extended his hand.

Her expression dripped skepticism. "And what's that?"

He shot her his best, most seductive grin. "Me."

chapter TWO

Kate stayed firmly planted in her seat as he offered to help her up. Trying her best to appear unaffected, she arched one eyebrow. "Does this usually work for you?"

The guy didn't pull his hand back or in any other way appear to alter his strategy, and Kate had to give him points for that. "Yes, actually."

"Interesting."

The sad truth was, his offer was beyond tempting. The attention was nice, especially after her self-esteem had been beaten down the way it had in the past year. Hell, in the past twenty-two. It wouldn't hurt to have someone who spoke fluent French showing her around, either. That he was as attractive as he was just made the deal sweeter.

"Not working so well on you, then?" he asked as she considered him.

"Not so far."

His smile only widened. "Good. I like a girl who's hard to crack." Standing up straighter, he held his palms out at his sides. "Come on, what have you got to lose?"

"I'd say my wallet, but that's already gone."

"See? Low stakes. Listen, you don't trust me." That was an understatement. Was there a man left on earth that she did? "I don't blame you. Devilishly handsome man wanders into a café and buys you a drink without asking? Offers to show you around town? Very suspicious."

"Very."

"So let's make this safe. You said you wanted to see the Louvre? Let's go to the Louvre. I'll show you all my favorites, and then if I haven't murdered you by suppertime, you let me take you someplace special. Someplace no guidebook in the world would ever recommend."

She was really running out of reasons to say no. It was a good plan, this one. They'd be in a public place. She'd have time to feel him out a little more. And if he wasn't too much of a psycho, well, everyone had to eat, didn't they?

Still, she kept up her air of skepticism. She rather liked all his efforts to convince her. "I don't even know your name."

The way his dimples shone when he lifted up one corner of his mouth was completely unfair. Extending his hand again, he offered, "Rylan. Pleased to make your acquaintance."

Rylan. That was unusual. She liked it.

"Kate," she volunteered in return, and with no more real excuse not to, she accepted the handshake, slipping her palm into his. Warm fingers curled around hers, his thumb stroking the side of her hand, and *oh*. The rake. He bent forward as he tugged on her hand, twisting ever so slightly so he could press his lips to the back of her palm.

"Charmed."

"I'll bet you are." But her pulse was racing faster, and the kiss felt like it seared all the way to her spine.

This man was dangerous.

He straightened up but he didn't let go. Sweeping his other arm toward the door, he asked, "So?"

She hummed to herself as she gazed up at him, as if there was any question of what she was going to do. His blue eyes sparkled, like he already knew her answer, too.

"Well." She rose from her seat, feeling taller than usual. More powerful. Maybe it was all the flattery of a guy like this hitting on her. Maybe it was the headiness of making this kind of a decision. Either way, it made her straighten her shoulders and insert a little sway into her hips.

"Well?"

"Lead on," she said.

He didn't let go of her hand. "That's what I was hoping you'd say." With a squeeze of her fingers, he took a step toward the door. "Let's go look at some art."

External pressures aside, she had come to Paris to be inspired by beauty. She could find it on the walls of a famous museum. And she could find it in the lines of this man's shoulders and throat. The latter might not have been what she'd had in mind when she'd set out, but what was a little bit of a diversion?

You couldn't find yourself without taking a couple of side trips, after all.

The girl—Kate—wiggled her hand free as they approached the front of the café. Disappointing, but not really a problem. Rylan reached forward to get the door for her and shepherded her through it with a gentle touch at the small of her back. Following her out onto the sidewalk, he gestured down the street. "It's only a little ways. You up for walking?"

"Sure."

Good. Paris came alive this time of year, with the trees and flowers in full bloom, the sky a brilliant blue. Even the traffic seemed less suffocating now that summer was on the horizon. The influx of tourists made the walkways more congested, but at least the travelers occasionally smiled.

As he led them off in the direction of the museum, she fell into step at his side. He pressed his luck whenever the crush of pedestrians got thick, keeping her close with a hand on her hip, letting his fingertips linger. She fit so well against him, every brush of their bodies sending zips of awareness through him. Making him want to tug her closer in a way he hadn't entirely anticipated.

The whole thing seemed to amuse her, but her efforts to act like she wasn't affected were undercut by the flush on her cheeks. The way she allowed him to keep her near.

Until they paused to wait for a light to change, and she pulled away, turning so she was facing him. "So. Rylan."

A rush of warmth licked up his spine. His name sounded so good rolling off her tongue. Far better than Theodore Rylan Bellamy III ever had. He'd rid himself of the rest of his father's burdens only recently, but he'd shed the man's name years ago. And yet it still made him smile whenever someone accepted the middle name he'd taken as his own. Didn't question it the way his family always had.

Ignoring the ruffle of irritation that thought shot through him, he met her gaze and matched her tone. "Kate."

She looked him up and down. "What's your deal?"

Right. Because this wasn't all just flirtatious touches. He'd asked her to a museum for God's sake, not back to his bed. She wanted conversation. To get to know him.

Just the idea of it made him feel hollow.

He put his hands in his pockets and shifted his weight, glancing between her eyes and the traffic going by. "Not much to tell." Liar. "Jaded expat skulking around Paris for a while. Ruthlessly showing lonely tourists around the city in exchange for the pleasure of their company."

"What makes you think I'm lonely?"

Shrugging, he put his hand to the base of her spine again as the light switched to green, feeling the warmth of her through her jacket as they crossed the street. "You have that look."

"For all you know, I could be here with a whole troop of friends, or my family. My"—her breath caught—"boyfriend."

And there was a story there, a faint, raw note. Temptation gnawed at him to press, to dig to the bottom of it.

But if he went digging into her pain, that gave her the right to do the same.

He hesitated for a moment, then went for casual. "Ah. But then you'd be with one of them, and instead you're here with me."

She didn't contest the point, moving to put a few inches between them as they stepped up onto the opposite curb. Changing tacks, she asked, "How long have you been—what was it? Skulking around Paris?"

"About a year. I wander elsewhere from time to time when I get too bored, but a man can do a lot worse than Paris."

"And what do you *do*?"

Nothing. Not anymore. "I pick up odd jobs from time to time," he hedged. The things he had to do to get at his money felt like a job, sometimes. "But I don't have a lot of expenses.

Buying intriguing women coffee doesn't put too much of a dent in the wallet."

"Hmm." One corner of her mouth tilted downward.

"You don't like that answer?"

"I'm sure there's more to it than that."

Perceptive. "Sorry to disappoint."

"So, what, are you staying in a hostel or something?"

There he hesitated. "Something like that." After all, the bed was the only thing in the place that felt like his. "Is that where you're staying? A hostel?" It would be the most logical choice, if she were worried about money.

"Yes."

"Which one?"

She actually rolled her eyes. "Like I'm telling you that."

"Fine. I'll just wait to find out when I walk you home."

"Is that a threat?"

"An offer. One I hope you'll accept." He leaned in closer and caught a whiff of her hair. Vanilla and rose. Sweet and warm. It drew him in, awakening something in his blood. "Because I would love to"—his lips brushed her ear—"see you home tonight."

She gave a full-body shiver. Flexed her hands at her sides so her knuckles brushed his thigh. Inside, he crowed.

Then she crossed her arms over her chest and took half a step to the side. A twitch of disappointment squeezed at him. But he wasn't fooled.

He laughed as he let her have her space. Resistant though she might be, she was warming up to the idea. He didn't have any worries.

He bumped his shoulder against hers. "And what about you? What's your 'deal'?"

"Not much to tell." It was a clear imitation of his own response, and she narrowed her eyes for a second before shrugging. "I'm from Ohio, but I went to school in New York. My mom sends me paranoid emails, asking me if I've gotten mugged yet once a week."

He winced. "At least you'll have something to say to her this week, then?"

"Yeah." She frowned, patting her side as if to touch the purse that wasn't there. "Four years living in this sketchy part of Brooklyn, and I come to Paris to get robbed." She dropped her gaze away from his. "Mom warned me about it, too, you know. Told me Paris was full of thieves."

Her expression was growing more and more unhappy. God. She really didn't know how to guard her emotions at all, did she? Nothing like the people he'd once surrounded himself with. The ones who would've looked at such naïveté with contempt. Here and now, it sparked a tenderness inside him that was new. He wanted to wipe the frown from her lips—or better, kiss it off. He wanted to know what had put it there in the first place. Neither reaction made sense.

So instead of touching or pressing, he steered the conversation onto safer ground. "Is it just you and your mom?"

"Pretty much. My dad's...out of the picture." And oh, but there was a minefield under there, based on the tone of her voice. She crossed her arms over her chest. "How about you?"

Speaking of minefields...

Before he could try to find a way around talking about the train wreck that was his family, they rounded a corner, and he let out a breath in relief. He craned his neck and pointed. "Look. Those banners up ahead?"

Kate followed his gaze, rising up onto tiptoes. Easily distracted, thank God. "Yeah?"

He reached out to grab hold of her hand and nearly got lost in the softness of her skin. He licked his lips and swallowed. "Come on. We're nearly there."

The crowds of tourists were more overwhelming right around the museum, though not as bad as they would be once July hit. Letting him interlace their fingers, she quickened her pace, falling into step as they weaved their way along the sidewalk. The great walls of the place finally gave, and he dragged her along through the archway.

"Don't we have to go in through the Pyramid?" she asked, sounding breathless, evoking the famous entrance to the museum.

He twisted to look at her and winked. "Would I lead you any other way?"

They emerged out into the stone courtyard. He let go of her hand to throw his arms out wide. *Ta-da.* "Your Pyramid, madame."

Pei's Pyramid. It was a glass and metal structure, located at the center of the courtyard, housing the main entrance of the museum. His mother had always hated it, but he'd never really minded the thing. Besides, it was in all the guidebooks, and in high school French textbooks. Tourists typically wanted to see it.

She stood there staring at the monument for a long moment before scrunching her face up. "That is both so much cooler and so much less impressive than I expected."

Well, at least she was honest. He threw his head back and laughed. "Welcome to international travel, my dear." He dug in his pocket for his phone. "You want a picture?"

"Actually, kinda. Yeah."

"Stand over there." He motioned her to stand where he had a good view of her and the Pyramid. The sky was a bright, perfect blue, and it brought out the red in her hair. Her photo smile wasn't as arresting as her real one, but he'd take it anyway. "Say 'fromage.'"

He snapped the shot, then held it out so she could see. He expected the requisite look of embarrassment all girls gave him when he showed them images of themselves, but instead she simply nodded. "Nice composition."

It made him pause. She had been planning to spend her day sketching, had been swayed by his offer to take her here of all places, so the comment shouldn't have surprised him. But his estimation of her rose. When she looked at something, she looked deeper. Saw more.

The idea of wandering around a museum with her suddenly took on a whole new kind of charm.

He glanced at the picture again before flicking back to the camera app. "Easy when there's a pretty lady in the frame."

She cast her gaze skyward and was just starting to move away when he caught her arm.

"What?"

"One more."

"The one is plenty," she argued.

"One more for *me*." With that, he reeled her in, wrapping his arm around her shoulder. It was a cheap ploy, but he couldn't resist the chance to get her close. Her scent wafted over him again. He took a second to breathe her in, to really feel her against his side before he held his arm out for the selfie, shooting his own best ladykiller grin at the lens.

Her laughter sounded more indulgent than charmed, but

he could work with that. "Does *this* move usually work for you?" she asked.

He pressed the button on the screen to take the shot. "Better than the tour guide offer, even." He snapped his teeth playfully near her ear. "Because this one gives me an excuse to *touch* you."

Making a show of mock-growling at her, he gave her one rough squeeze and let her go. She took only a half step away, but the loss of her left his ribs cold. He mentally shook his head at himself.

Before he could give in to the urge to tug her back in, and without a pretext this time, he turned his attention to the screen. A pang fired off inside him. They looked good together. Like a real, happy couple—the kind he'd been taught didn't exist. Her eyes positively danced, her smile as wide as her face.

And so was his. Not a thing about his expression was forced or fake. The contrast alone made his throat tighten. This wasn't one of the usual selfies he took with girls. Not one of the awful pictures snapped on the courthouse steps. Or the others. The ones from before.

His hands curled into fists, and he had to forcibly relax them.

Shutting that line of thought right down, he turned off the screen of his phone. "You'll have to tell me where to send them later."

Oblivious to where his mind had gone, she raised a brow. "Ah, now I see your game. You want my email address."

"Yes," he said dryly. "It's all been a clever little ploy so I could subscribe you to all sorts of mailing lists for natural male enhancement."

She arched a brow. "Am I going to need that?"

Nicely played. "Not if you take *me* home tonight." He threaded his arm through hers. "Come on. The masterpieces await."

"Are you sure we're still even in the museum?" Kate spun in a circle, looking around in awe. "How can this place be so huge?"

The vaulted archways seemed to soar above her, and the ceilings were almost as gorgeous as the paintings. The whole place smelled of *art* somehow, even though the works were all hundreds of years old, the oils dry and the varnishes cracking. The figures within the canvases glowed with how masterfully they'd been rendered, and something inside of her felt like it was glowing as well.

She'd thought the Met had been amazing, the first time she'd been there. But she'd had no idea. No clue.

She finished her slow circle, coming around again to face the center of the room. To face Rylan. He stood there, arms crossed over the expanse of his chest, gaze hot and heavy on hers, and a tremor coursed its way down her spine.

Then again, she'd also never wandered around the Met with a man like him by her side.

To think, she'd been worried when she agreed to let him take her here. She hated being rushed through museums, and she'd been resolved to take her time. But Rylan had stood by patiently as she looked her fill, had been waiting to take her hand at the end of each set of paintings. Big, strong fingers curled firmly around her palm, and the warm, male scent of him mingled with the wood and polish of the gallery to make her head spin.

Swallowing hard, she checked herself. He was practically a stranger—it shouldn't be so easy to fall into step with him like this. And yet she felt more comfortable with him than she had doing this with any of her other friends. Definitely more comfortable than she ever had with Aaron. Maybe *because* he was a stranger. There was no point pretending to be anything she wasn't. She never had to see him again if she didn't want to. So she had nothing to lose.

Catching her eye, he tilted his head toward the next room, a silent invitation, asking her if she was ready to continue. She nodded, moving into his space again. The heat of his hand seeped into the base of her spine, but she didn't flinch. Ridiculous, how quickly she was getting used to all these little touches. What had it been? A couple of hours?

A couple of *amazing* hours.

They'd seen a bunch of the highlights already. The sweeping statuary of *Winged Victory*, which had been so much bigger and more imposing than she'd expected. Tiny, lovely *Venus de Milo*. And much to Rylan's frustration, they'd even stood in line to see the *Mona Lisa* nice and close. She'd shoved him when he'd asked with that odd mixture of amusement and derision if she was satisfied. She'd known going into it that that particular piece had a tendency to underwhelm, but she hadn't cared. She'd seen it. In real life.

In her head, she was rearranging all her plans for the week she had left in Paris. She *had* to come back and spend a whole day here alone with her sketchbook and her pencils and pastels.

"You are having a total art-geek-gasm, aren't you?" he asked, releasing her so she could get closer to one of the paintings.

At this point, they were in one of the more remote galleries, one he'd insisted they make the time to visit, full of big, classic pieces done up in vivid colors, depicting scenes from legends and myths. None of it was what she'd really come here to see, but she found herself getting lost in them all the same.

She was about to tell him as much when she glanced over at him, and he had that expression on his face again. It made her pause.

She didn't have any illusions that he was here for any reason other than to humor her. He was going above and beyond as far as the amount of time and energy she expected any guy to put into a pickup, but it was still a pickup.

Only, he kept looking at her like this. Like somehow, despite his worst intentions, he was seeing more than just her breasts.

She let a grin curl her lips as she turned her attention back to the walls. "It's amazing."

"It gets even better."

Hard to believe, but how could she resist?

"So the thing that really gets me," he said over his shoulder as he meandered forward into the next gallery, "about European museums is the *scale*."

She followed, craning her neck as she passed through the archway and—wow. He wasn't kidding. The whole room was full of paintings that stretched from floor to ceiling. The canvases must have been twenty feet tall, some of them maybe double that in width.

"Holy crap." In awe, she turned, trying to take in everything. She pointed to a painting at the end of the room. "That one is bigger than my apartment back in New York."

It might have been a tiny studio apartment, but still.

"Don't see this kind of thing in museums in the States, huh?" he asked.

He was standing behind her now, his breath warm against her ear. It felt...nice. But not nice enough to distract her from trying to memorize the images surrounding her.

"I've never seen anything like it, anywhere."

She stepped forward, away from his heat and toward the painting on the opposite wall. He let her go, walking backward to perch on the bench in the center of the room. He sat with his knees spread, his elbows on his thighs. She turned her back to him, but she couldn't help but be aware of him—his presence that felt so unreasonably large in such an enormous room.

"That used to be one of my favorites," he said, gesturing at the canvas she'd been drawn to.

"Oh?" It was arresting, the composition and the arrangement of the figures drawing the eye in. Bringing her hand to her mouth, she read the placard beside it. *"Zeus and Hera?"* She took a step back and tilted her head.

The two figures were seated in a garden, staring into each other's eyes. A smile colored the edge of Zeus's lips.

"They look happy." His shrug came through in his voice.

Really? The king and queen of the Greek gods weren't exactly known for their perfect marriage. How many people had died on account of their fits of jealousy and pique? She furrowed her brow. "Not exactly how I usually think of them."

From behind her, he chuckled. "No. Not usually." He paused, then added, "I think maybe that's why I liked it so much."

She hummed, asking him to elaborate.

"It was just a reminder. No matter how awful things were between them most of the time, they still had their moments. Their good times."

A sour taste rose in her throat. "Doesn't change the fact that he'd knocked up half the pantheon."

If her mother hadn't fallen for all the good times with her father...If the good times with Aaron hadn't blinded Kate...

"And the better part of the mortal realm, too," Rylan agreed, a wry twist to his tone. "But still. I always used to like to imagine that at one point they were like this."

"Used to?"

He chuckled wryly. "We all have to grow up sometime."

They were silent for a minute as she tried to take the whole thing in.

When he spoke again, it echoed in the space. "The first time I ever came here, I was...maybe eight? Nine?" A shade of memory colored his voice. "A few years before my parents got divorced." He cleared the roughness from his throat. "My mother brought me to this room, and I remember finding this picture and not being able to look away from it." He gave a little rueful laugh. "My sister gave me so much shit for ignoring all the giant battle scenes to look at two people who weren't even naked or anything."

Kate glanced over her shoulder at him. That was...kind of a lot of information, actually, considering how evasive he'd been while they'd been trading histories earlier. Turning back to the painting, she cast about for something to ask him more about. Not the divorce—not with the way that topic always brought her own hurts to the surface—though she tucked that away for later. After a moment's indecision, she landed on, "You came to Paris when you were a kid?"

"The whole family did. My dad's work had us doing a bunch of travel."

"What did he do?"

"Finance stuff. Very boring. And a very, very long time ago."

She frowned. "It can't have been that long ago. How old are you?"

"Twenty-seven. Don't try to tell me nineteen years isn't a long time."

He made it sound like a lifetime. For her it nearly was.

"Believe me, it's a long time. I'm only twenty-two."

"That's not so young."

She considered for a moment. "It's old enough."

"Old enough for what?" Suggestion rolled off his tongue.

His flirtation made her bold. "For knowing better than to be taken in by men like you?"

"Men like me?" His tone dripped with mock offense. "Men who take you to beautiful museums." He was off the bench and at her side again, pushing her hair from her face. "Men who want nothing more than to show you their big, huge—"

She made a noise of half laughter, half disgust and shoved him off.

"Paintings! I was going to say paintings."

"I'll bet you were."

"I was." He held his arms out to indicate the whole of the room. "Do you like them?"

And she couldn't lie, not even a bit. She spun around another time, nice and slow, taking in everything. As she twisted back toward him, something inside of her softened. All the innuendo and playfulness had fallen from his lips, and he was simply standing there, waiting for her opinion.

Looking for all the world like he actually cared what it would be.

Impulsiveness took her close to him. "I do." And this was stupid. But she did it anyway—leaned in and pressed the quickest, lightest kiss to his cheek. "I love it. Thank you."

He grinned as she danced away before he could reel her the rest of the way in. "Does that mean you're ready to agree for me to walk you home?"

A little thrill shot through her. How nice would that be? He'd been trying so hard, and she'd enjoyed every minute of it. After months of being on her guard, nursing her bitterness, it was tempting to just let go. To say yes for once. He was funny and smart, charming and gorgeous. She could do a lot worse. But she wasn't entirely sure she couldn't do better.

And besides. She'd never known it could be so much fun to watch a guy work for it.

She started toward the exit from the gallery, a little bounce in her step. "Let's start with you walking me to dinner." Glancing back at him, she smiled at the look of smug satisfaction on his face. "No promises for after."

"I would never dare to assume."

"And it had better be something good." She slowed down so he could catch up, and she didn't bother to stop him when he moved to interlace their fingers. She'd already let enough of her inhibitions go, lulled by the ease of his smile and his touch. Why not accept this, too? Especially when it felt so good. "Off the beaten path. Nothing I could find in a tour guide."

"Don't you worry." A sly grin made his eyes sparkle, and his hand squeezed hers. "I have just the thing in mind."

chapter THREE

"I have to admit," Kate said, licking at her thumb.

It was distracting, watching that little pink tongue. "Hmm?"

"This is not what I expected."

"What can I say? I'm full of surprises."

And he'd had a feeling she would enjoy being surprised like this. Instead of going to whatever cozy, intimate bistro she'd probably imagined her Lothario would take her to, they'd stood in line for almost an hour at the best little crepe stand in Paris and ordered galettes from a man who'd made them right in front of them. Eggs and onions and mushrooms and spinach, all wrapped up in a buttery crepe for her. Ham and cheese for him, and a final one with Nutella and banana clutched in his free hand for dessert. He was still holding out hope she'd let him lick it off her, but it was starting to matter less to him.

He was having too much fun. Ambling around the Latin Quarter. Eating crepes with a pretty girl. He took a big bite and swallowed it down.

"So what *did* you expect?" he asked, nudging her with his shoulder.

"I don't know. You talk such a big game. I was thinking candles, wine. Maybe a table, at least."

"Ooh, big spender."

She gave him a sideways glance.

Sloppy. He'd been giving off all kinds of mixed signals when it came to his finances, and she was too smart by half. He was going to have to be a bit more careful about that if he wanted her to buy into the idea that he was working with a budget.

And he...did. It wasn't a game he'd played before—not with any real sense of dedication. A Black Amex was such a shortcut to seduction, and he'd been leaning on it more heavily than usual this year. Throw a little cash around, and women tended to throw themselves right back at you in return. It was easy, uncomplicated.

But with *this* woman...He'd made the split-second decision to do it differently, and now he was in so deep. Opening up to her, showing her that painting as if she gave a damn about the faint hope he'd clung to as a boy that his parents didn't hate each other quite as much as they always seemed to. And she had. She'd glanced back at him with those soulful eyes that saw so fucking deep, and asked him questions about his life. She'd acted like she cared.

It warmed something in him that had gotten so cold.

Dropping her gaze back down to her crepe, she tugged at the paper it was wrapped in, and a smile teased the edges of her lips. "Just as well." She waved a hand vaguely. "Skipping the whole fancy dinner thing."

"Yeah? You like this better?"

"I do." She took a careful bite and chewed. "But I think you knew I would."

"I had a hunch."

She was the kind of girl more interested in the experience than the cliché. The food over the ambiance. The romance of open air and a warm Parisian night.

"Good hunch."

By the time they'd finished up their entrees, they'd wandered into a busier part of the neighborhood. Colored lights from restaurants and storefronts made the darkness glow, and the pavement seemed to shine, the air buzzing with sounds of life that didn't quite manage to pierce their bubble.

He tossed the wrappers from their crepes in the trash, then took her hand and led her over to a low stone wall that separated a patch of grass from the sidewalk. She'd grown increasingly accustomed to him touching her as the day had rolled on. At this point he was damn near addicted, craving more and more. Releasing her fingers, he trailed the backs of his knuckles over her thigh through her skirt, over the smooth, bare skin at her knee. It sent fire licking down his spine, but he forced himself to pull away. He breathed hard against the simmer of arousal in his blood, but his voice pitched lower all the same.

"Have you had a Nutella crepe before?" He unfolded the paper protecting it. The contents had cooled, but they were still warm enough.

"No, but I've never met a Nutella anything I didn't like."

"You're not about to be disappointed. The funny thing is that they should be the same anywhere. The filling comes from a jar, and the crepe is just flour and milk and eggs. But their griddles must be magic, because"—he tore off the gooey corner of the crepe, the edge crisp, and brought it up toward her lips—"these, my friend, are the best dessert crepes in the city."

"Those are some pretty high expectations you're setting."

"And yet you're still going to be blown away."

Her expression was skeptical, even more so when he tsked her attempt to take the bite from him with her hands, insisting on feeding it to her directly. She rolled her eyes but opened that soft, pretty mouth, and his throat went dry. This was cliché, was so close to the kinds of seductions he'd carried out without thought before, but never with this kind of anticipation. Never with this level of focus on how close they were, this dedication to savoring every sight, every sound. Maybe because he'd had to work so hard for every one of them.

He placed the morsel on her tongue with care, barely grazing the edge of her lip with his fingertips, tempted to press his thumb inside and feel the warmth of her closing her mouth around him. But no. Not yet. He let his hand fall away while his body thrummed.

Gazing straight at him, she rolled the flavor around in her mouth, taking her time about it. Once she was done, she smiled, eyes sparkling. "Okay"—her voice trembled, her only tell that the low intimacy of his feeding her was affecting her as much as him—"that's pretty amazing."

"Didn't I tell you?" He tore off a piece for himself and then another for her.

"You don't have to do that," she said when he offered it to her again. Embarrassment colored her cheeks, and they couldn't have that.

"Of course I don't." He made as if to pull the crepe away. "I don't *have* to share my dessert with you at all."

Except he did. The desire to slip that sweetness between her lips had risen to the point of need.

She narrowed her eyes at him. "Ha-ha."

"I'm not joking. I'll take this and walk away."

She paused for just a second. "No. You won't."

It wasn't said as a challenge but as a statement of fact. Something in his chest gave a little twist. It bothered him, that she was right, but it was offset by a deeper understanding of what they were saying. His throat went rough. "And you're not going to, either." He swallowed hard. "Open up."

A long moment passed as they gazed at each other. She tilted her chin upward before softening her jaw, lips parting gently. He didn't move his hand, but she bowed her neck, keeping her gaze steady as she dipped to take the bit of crepe from him. He watched the way she moved, the bob of her throat, the pink of her tongue as she swiped it across her bottom lip.

And he wanted to tell her a line, something about how Paris wasn't as pretty as she was, or about how he adored her mouth. All the words that came to him were true enough—as true or truer than when he'd said them in the past. But for one time in his life, the delivery felt false.

So he held his tongue as he fed her and fed himself. When they were done, she had a dab of chocolate at the corner of her lips. He brushed it away with his thumb, and her cheeks pinked. She shifted her gaze and shifted her body, looking off to the side as if something had caught her attention, but if there was anything to see there, it'd slipped right past him.

At the moment, all he was seeing was her.

"Was it good?" he asked, leaning in close. He liked the smell of her hair, the soft sheen to her skin. "Was it everything I promised?"

He would promise her a lot of things, if there was any chance she'd believe them. Things about how he could make her feel good. About what he could do with his tongue.

She nodded stiffly. Her shoulders had gotten tense. She looked at him, though, and her eyes held an invitation. He just had to strip a layer of fear from her. Distrust. Whatever was holding her back.

Slipping his hand over the breadth of the stone between them, he placed his palm atop her knee. Edged in close so his breath washed hot across her cheek. "Open up," he said quietly.

His lips brushed the corner of her mouth, and she was sweet and warm, letting him kiss her for just a moment. Just a heartbeat. Then she was turning away, a little stutter to her breath.

The warmth of the space surrounding them shivered, but he closed his eyes and pressed his face against her hair. Pressed another soft kiss to her cheek. "What are you afraid of?"

A huff of a laugh escaped her throat. "I don't know what kind of game you're playing with me."

"No game." He'd played games all his life. Had thought he was starting one with her when he had picked her up, but it didn't feel like one now. He let his voice deepen. "I just *want* you."

She looked away, off into a distance. "And that's the thing." Turning her gaze back to him, she said. "That's the part that I don't understand."

Kate held herself together tightly as those words hung in the air. She could hardly believe she'd said them.

For God's sake. She wasn't a demurring flower or anything.

She knew her weaknesses and her strengths: pretty enough but not a knockout, talented but not so talented she didn't have to work hard. The idea that a guy wanted her wasn't entirely the norm, but it was hardly an alien concept.

Men were good at telling a woman what they wanted to hear. And then turning into something else entirely the second you let your guard down. Her father had done it to her mother—had played with Kate's head, too. Until she'd tried to push herself into a shape that was all wrong, just to please him, leaving her with phantom aches to this very day from twisting herself so hard.

He wasn't the only one. Aaron had done it. And the guy at the bar that once...

Rylan pulled away, brows uneven as he stared at her. He hesitated for a moment, and she was ready for him to turn the charm on even higher. Spout some too-rehearsed poetry, or worse, start quoting One Direction lyrics. But then, instead, he tilted his head to the side and asked, "Who was it?"

Excuse me? "Who was who?"

"The person who made you think every man you came across would use you."

Her breath caught in her throat as memories swamped her. But before she could go too far down that road, she pushed those thoughts from her mind. Laughed him off. "And who made you think you could spend an entire day trying to work your way into a stranger's pants and then ask that kind of question?"

"Touché." He grabbed her hand and held it to his chest. "But you're deflecting. Which means I'm onto something. So who was it?"

Seriously? Was there anyone out there who *didn't* teach a

woman that? "Um. My mom? The US Senate? *Law and Order: SVU?*"

"No." He shook his head. "What was his name?"

That made her pause. When he phrased it like that, she couldn't help it. She'd been burned enough times now, but there were those still-lingering bruises, throbbing hotly in the center of her chest. She dropped her gaze and tried to tug her hand free. "It doesn't matter."

She didn't want to think about her dad. Or about Aaron. About how she'd nearly made her mother's mistakes all over again. She'd been such an idiot. Such a fool.

"Of course it does." He let their hands fall from his chest, but he didn't let go, wrapping his fingers around her palm. Rubbing his thumb into the tender spot in its center where the muscles always cramped from drawing. "Because I'm not him." When she made another move to pull back, he held on even tighter. The heat in his tone abated, a forced casualness taking over. "I mean, sure. You're not from around here. You're only in town for, what? A few days? A week? It's a fling. But a fling can be fun for both of us. I didn't decide to spend the whole afternoon in an art museum or invest the absurd sum of nearly five euros on your dinner just because you were the first girl I happened to lay eyes on."

That made her crack a smile. He ducked his chin, and brought his other hand up to touch the side of her face.

"See?" he said. "That right there. That goofy smile when you like one of my crappy jokes and don't entirely want to admit it? That's why I'm still here."

"Just my smile?"

His gaze darted upward. "And your eyes. I like how they seem to watch everything." He trailed his fingers down the line of her neck. "I like how you give me shit and don't let me get away with anything."

"You like a challenge?"

"A conversation. They're hard to come by with the kind of life I lead."

It hit someplace resonant inside of her. She'd come on this trip all on her own without really thinking about the solitude. How many times had she spent all-nighters in the studio, or locked herself in her tiny apartment for days to paint? Conversation wasn't something she needed. But not being able to have it, being surrounded by a language she didn't understand, even on the radio and the television... it was lonely. And Rylan made her feel anything but.

She faltered for a second. "And if you didn't like any of those things?" She made her tone flippant, to try to hide how much his answer mattered. "You wouldn't still be here, trying to get laid?"

"I might be." His smile was lopsided. Soft and kissable. "But I wouldn't care as much about whether or not it worked." With that, he leaned down and pressed his lips to her hand. He lingered just a little too long, breath warm on her skin. Then he pulled away and rose, tugging gently to help her up. "Come on. Let me walk you to the Metro station."

Her head was spinning as she stood. He'd just basically said he was invested now, but if he was offering to walk her to her train, did that mean he was giving up? For all her resistance, the idea of it made a little bubble of disappointment lodge in her throat.

Maybe she should kiss him. Make some kind of statement that no matter how uncertain she was about this, she wasn't entirely ready for it to end.

Or maybe it was all for the best.

Mind working overtime, trying to sort out the possibil-ities, she followed him down the street. They walked side by side, hands entwined. When the entrance to the subway loomed, he slowed, stopping to lean up against a lamppost.

Her heart thundered behind her ribs. All her worries about him giving up had been premature, because the way he was looking at her now didn't even begin to speak of resignation. Leaning in close, he cupped her face with his palm, fingers weaving themselves through her hair.

He nosed at her temple, and his breath was warm against her ear. "Invite me back to your hotel."

God, she was tempted. Her bones felt watery, and there was a heat coiling up in her abdomen, flames fanned by the scent of him. By the subtle press of his body to hers. Her chin tilted back, spine arching ever so slightly.

But then her breath caught in her throat. "I can't."

"Why not?" He danced his fingertips up her arm and pressed his lips to the column of her throat.

"I—" She couldn't even remember why. Except— Oh, right. "Can't. Actually can't." Why was her voice so breathy, her skin so sensitive? "Cheap hostel, remember? Roommates."

"All those friends you said you were traveling with?"

"Worse. Strangers."

"Strangers you don't want to know what you sound like when you come?"

Jesus. Part of her wanted to grab him by the collar and pull him down into that subway, just for the heat of that promise.

A promise no man had ever bothered to make to her before. A promise no man had ever managed to fulfill.

His words and kisses were all persuasiveness, like he could

feel her wavering on the point of indecision. "Because," he continued, "this may be a fling." He pulled his lips from her skin, shifting until his face was right in front of her. His eyes burned hot and dark. "But I promise. You will get exactly as much out of it as I will. More, if you're willing to show me what you like."

And god*dammit*. Men broke their promises—they did it all the time, but she wanted to believe this one. She'd had sex only once since she and Aaron had broken up, and it had been awful. Worse than it had been with Aaron even, and after everything...didn't she deserve something good?

Before she could overthink it any more, she reached up. Grabbed him by the hair and pulled him down, taking the kiss she'd been so afraid of a few minutes before.

And it was *worth* it. He tasted like chocolate and sin, the rasp of stubble a delicious burn against her chin. He was still against her for all of a second before he pulled her close, surrounding her with his warmth and pressing forward with his tongue. Scraping his teeth over her bottom lip and accepting everything she offered.

But giving back to her, too. With every push forward, he let her in a little more, until her skin hummed and her breath was coming too fast, heat and need pooling deep inside her abdomen.

This was insane. It was how she'd landed herself in trouble last time. She should disengage, get her breath back, calm the racing of her heart.

But it was also *nothing* like the last time. This man had coaxed her along, patient through every step, his kiss and his million casual touches promising she wouldn't regret letting him in. They'd talked, shared stories. She'd glimpsed more than simple lust in his eyes.

She could do this. This one time, maybe she could have this.

Before she could talk herself out of it, she tore away with a gasp, fingers curled tightly in the fabric of his shirt, breasts pressed to the solid muscle of his chest. "Your place?"

His laugh was pure frustration as he tucked her head against his shoulder, rocking them side to side. "Not a good idea, either, sadly."

Dammit. "Roommates?"

"Something like that." He dipped his head again and kissed her, softer this time but with no less warmth or intent. With one last sweep of his lips over hers, he retreated to rest his brow against her temple. "This isn't going to happen tonight, is it?"

"Doesn't seem that way." She shouldn't feel so conflicted about that. Reason said it was better to wait, but her body said she only had so many days here. She could be laid out on a bed right now, being taken apart the way she'd always imagined the right man could.

Putting his hands on her shoulders, he took a step back, looking at her square on, and there was an intensity to his gaze. One that went straight to the very center of her. "Meet me tomorrow."

"I—" The tick of hesitation caught her by surprise. She had so many things she wanted to see and do and experience in this city. While he was swiftly moving up that list of things, she wasn't ready to ignore the rest of them. "When?"

"When are you free?"

If she took the morning and maybe the early afternoon for herself, she could hit a few sights. Spend some time with a pad of paper and her charcoals trying to capture the light.

Think some more about what the hell she was going to do with her life.

With this man.

"Maybe four?" she suggested, then hedged. "Five o'clock?"

"Four thirty it is." He didn't sound disappointed about it being so late. "You know the Tuileries Garden, right? Back near the Louvre?"

"Of course."

"Meet me there. By our statue."

"*Our* statue?"

He smirked and nodded. "Our statue."

"We've never been there before."

"Nope. But we're going tomorrow." He leaned in and kissed her once more, lightly, on the mouth. "And you'll know it when you see it."

She remembered looking at the garden on her map, before it had been stolen from her. The place was huge, its sculpture legendary. She could spend half the day trying to figure out which piece he happened to be thinking of.

"And you'll know I didn't when I'm two hours late."

"Not going to happen. And anyway, as we're proving tonight"—he tweaked her chin—"I can be a very patient man."

"Ha."

He dropped his arm and turned, but then he paused. "You'll meet me, then?"

She knew the answer in her toes. Her lungs fluttered as she filled them with breath.

This might be insanity. Might be folly of the highest order, and a distraction she couldn't afford. Her smile wavered. Still, she nodded. "It's a date."

chapter FOUR

It didn't seem to matter how long he'd been living like this, or how late he'd been up the night before. Barring the worst kind of jet lag, Rylan snapped awake at seven every morning, alert and blinking and ready for somebody to start barking at him.

Sighing, he forced himself to relax and sagged against the headboard, scrubbing a hand through the mess of his hair. He looked around at his surroundings, at the pale light streaming in through the curtains. The four gray walls and the bookshelves and the sheer quantity of *stuff* he'd managed to accumulate over the course of the past year. There were noises out on the street, but in here it was blissfully quiet. It was just him in the apartment, same as every morning.

Well, most mornings. He chuckled to himself as he slid his palm down his face. The few occasions he did bring someone back with him—the even rarer ones when they spent the night—they usually weren't *barking* at him. Not his scene, thank you very much.

No, his scene was pretty art students, apparently. Pretty art students he could have had in his bed right now, if only he'd been willing to give up the pretense of what kind of life he was leading here in Paris.

Roommates. She'd wondered if he had *roommates*.

He groaned and shook his head at himself. He probably should have just been upfront about things with her. There hadn't seemed to be much reason to, though. She hadn't even told him how long she was going to be in town, but it wouldn't be more than a week. Two at the most. Why rock the boat? She wanted her charming bohemian adventure, replete with shitty hostels and smelly, backpacking roommates? He wouldn't spoil it for her.

He wouldn't spoil it for himself. She hadn't known what he had to offer, and she'd kissed him anyway. She'd chosen normal, ordinary him. No one else had ever done that before— he'd never given them the chance to.

Besides. He really didn't want to see the look in her eyes once she knew. He typified everything charming bohemian types abhorred. Shallow, rich, lazy. Hollow.

To distract himself from that whole train of thought, he grabbed his phone from his bedside table. Sure enough, there were a handful of alerts. He scrolled through them with disinterest. A couple of things from his broker, and one from his father's crony. McConnell. He deleted that one without even looking. The one from his sister he gave a cursory glance, but really, he shouldn't have bothered. She had only one thing on her mind these days, and it was nothing he wanted any part in.

He wasn't going home, no matter how many guilt-tripping emails and phone calls they all laid at his feet. Not now. Not after . . . everything.

Maybe never.

With a sigh, he turned off the screen and set his phone aside. He threw off the covers, rolling over to the edge of the bed and levering himself up to sit. He had until late afternoon to get his shit together, and he basically had nothing to do. Still, it wasn't as if he was going to be able to get back to sleep. Resigned, he arched his spine and stretched his arms up overhead, then gave his bare chest a scratch. Flicked his thumb against the ring that hung from the chain around his neck. Finally, with a yawn, he rose and headed over to the wardrobe in the corner, where he plucked out a T-shirt and tugged it on. Between that and his boxers, he was decent enough.

It was somehow even quieter out in the main rooms of the apartment, and not the good kind of quiet. More the kind that had him out in cafés and museums and, well, anywhere else, most days. Ignoring it all the best he could, he made a beeline for the coffee machine and got some espresso going.

While the thing was grinding, he wandered over to the window and looked down at the world below. He liked the look of Paris in that post-dawn glow. The first commuters were already out, grabbing their croissants and heading to the Metro, but the tourists were still asleep, and the air smelled of bread instead of exhaust. It was peaceful.

This apartment was supposed to be peaceful. His mother had explicitly told the designer that. He turned around, though, and forced himself to really see it, and it made his teeth grate. It set his bones on edge.

Japanese screens and modern art and artisanal vases filled with single fake buds had nothing to do with peace. They had to do with showing off.

With creating a nice little space to drag the douchebags you were fucking back to, while your husband was home in the States robbing the company blind.

Shit. Shit, shit, *shit*.

Rylan stormed his way back over to the espresso machine before he could put a hole through something useless and priceless. He poured the coffee into one of the dainty little china cups the place was outfitted with and slugged it down. It was bitter and it burned in his throat and he didn't care.

He needed to get out of there, and not just for the afternoon. For a few days, at least. Maybe for good. He set the cup in the sink for someone else to deal with later and braced both hands on the counter, breathing in deep.

When it struck him—a solution so obvious, so perfect—he couldn't believe it hadn't occurred to him earlier.

Without bothering with anything else, he stalked back to his room for his clothes and his phone.

He had planning to do.

The glare from the sun was almost blinding as Kate spilled out of the cathedral, blinking hard against the sudden on-slaught of light. She fumbled at her side for the new bag she'd picked up at a random stall that morning and kept tucked close against her body all day. Winding her way through the crowd milling around the exit, she managed to lay her hands on the cheap plastic sunglasses she'd bought from the same vendor and slid them up her nose. Vision thus shielded, she cast a glance up and back.

Notre Dame Cathedral, real and in the flesh. Well, stone. It was another sight to cross off her list of must-sees, and she was glad she'd made the time to check it out. The stained glass had been as beautiful as promised. The arching ceilings and tile.

It hadn't been as much fun as the Louvre, though. None of the places she'd visited on her own had been.

Frowning to herself, she slipped her way between the clusters of people milling about the square, scanning until she spied an open bench. She made for it and plunked herself down, resting her purse in her lap and looking around. There were so many things to see, so many people to look at, languages to hear. Rylan would probably have had an interesting comment about them all.

Rylan. She'd see him in a couple of hours, provided he showed—and that she could follow his cryptic directions to their meeting spot. Part of her wished she'd gotten his number, that she could ask him to meet up with her sooner. But no. It was better this way. He was good company, sure, but nothing worth getting attached to. Even if he wasn't just after a one-night stand, everything about him screamed *casual*.

It also screamed *confident in bed*. And didn't that send a shiver of anticipation up her spine?

A lonely night in a room with a bunch of other people who'd shared none of her compunctions about having intimate relations around strangers had made her rethink her prudishness from the night before. No, she wasn't usually the type to sleep with people she didn't know, but she was on vacation, and he was gorgeous, and she just *knew*. He'd know his way around a woman's body. He'd live up to the promises he'd whispered in her ear and pressed against her lips.

Later.

For now, she had come to Paris with a purpose, and this

was it. Opening up the main compartment of her bag, she drew out the sketchbook and pencils she'd brought with her for the day. She was still pissed about having lost a brand-new book the day before, but she was grateful, too. Fresh pages could be replaced, if for a small fortune. Near-full books? They were priceless, for the story that they told.

She flipped through the one in front of her for a moment, watching as faces and scenes and still-life illustrations flew by. She'd been slowly filling it over the last couple of years, and she'd been proud of it—proud of all the things she'd made in her final semesters of school.

And yet, looking at it now, all she could hear were the words her mentor, Professor Lin, had said in their last critique session.

"Mastery of every style, Kate. It's an impressive thing." Lin had tapped her fingertip against the frames of her glasses. "But unless you make a style your own...it's all just imitation."

A sour pit opened in the bottom of Kate's stomach. She'd played with so many different styles in this book. There were faithful renderings, near-perfect photorealism. Fauvist color studies and gestures intended to capture movement. Impressionistic smudges decorated a few, and she'd even ventured into abstraction. By and large, they were good, she'd concede. But they could have been done by anyone. They could have been done by fifteen *different* someones.

You had to have a voice in art. A vision.

And that was the quiet secret of this trip, the one she hadn't dared reveal to anybody before she'd gone.

It was her last-ditch hope that she could find a vision of her own. One she could take to graduate school with her.

She had to stop herself from crumpling the page in her grasp. If she couldn't find it, she'd have to settle down. Take the corporate job she'd been so, so lucky to land, and go sit in a cubicle for the rest of her goddamn life, surrounded by gray, fabric-covered walls. She shuddered. Soullessness and stagnation and the only thing her father had ever let her believe she'd be good enough for.

She'd spent her whole life trying to prove him wrong. But deep down inside, sometimes, she believed him.

Not today, though. Not here.

Squaring her shoulders, she skipped past the rest of her completed sketches, turning to one of a handful of bare white pages and lifting her gaze to the city around her. Paris had something so vital to it, an energy and a romance. The city felt like she wanted her paintings to look, and if she could only capture that...

Maybe she'd have something worth fighting for.

Kate's first sign that time had started flying on her was the angle the sun made with the horizon. She sketched it in behind the cathedral's tower, then frowned to herself. Absently, she flipped to her first study, and yup. The sun had been a lot higher then. She went instinctively for her crappy little flip phone, but the thing had kept resetting itself to New York time, and she didn't trust it.

Crap. How the hell did she ask a stranger for the time?

Frowning to herself, she turned to the person sitting on the other end of the bench. "Pardon?" she asked.

The man turned around, giving her a quick up and down before smiling and rattling something off in French.

She'd known this phrase, back a half dozen years ago. "Quelle..." *What...* Shit, what was the word for time again? In frustration, she tapped her empty wrist.

The man laughed. "Trois heures et demie. Three thirty."

"Thank you." She corrected herself. "Merci."

He said something else, but she was too busy stuffing her things into her bag, a little pang of regret beating inside her chest. She'd needed just another fifteen minutes or so to play with that last sketch she'd been working on. Three times, she'd drawn the same basic view of Notre Dame, the first with an eye for accuracy, and the second with a quicker hand. That last one, though, she'd felt certain she was onto something. There'd been a different quality to her line work, a life to the planes of stone. It had felt better than the other drawings. Better than any of her work had felt since she'd graduated.

But she'd have to sort it out another time.

The Tuileries Gardens were only a handful of blocks away, but her sense of direction had never been good, and worse, Rylan hadn't exactly given her a cross street. She might need the whole hour she had left to figure out where she was going and find the statue he'd told her to look for. What the hell had he even meant by that? *Our* statue?

She snagged a Wet-Nap from her purse and took a quick swipe at getting the charcoal dust off her fingers before she stood. With a little nod of her head toward the guy who'd given her the time and a wistful glance back at the cityscape, she slung her bag over her shoulder and headed off in the direction she was pretty sure she was supposed to go.

To her surprise, she even turned out to be right.

Feeling a little more confident, she slowed her pace as she entered the garden. She was smart enough to keep her eyes peeled and her bag clutched to her chest as she combed the pathways, but the bulk of her attention was on any hunk of granite or marble or bronze she happened to cast her sight on. They were all gorgeous, all epic in their scale and in their subject matter, but not a one of them screamed *me and Rylan* at her.

As she searched, despair coiled up tightly behind her sternum. Rylan had seemed so genuine, but if he'd really wanted to see her again, he could have given her something more specific than some twenty square blocks to scour. Or maybe a phone number. An email address. A last name. Anything that might help her out right now.

If he didn't show, or if she couldn't find him...well, it wouldn't be the first time she'd been disappointed by a guy. Not even close. But that didn't prevent it from stinging.

In the distance, the obelisk that marked the western end of the gardens loomed, and she slowed her pace. It had to be four thirty by now. How long would he wait? Was it even worth doubling back and looking for anything she might have missed? Dropping her arms in resignation by her sides, she turned in a circle, looking for anything that might give a clue.

When she spied something even better. Much better.

A single, choked peal of laughter caught in her throat as she spied him, all messy dark hair and clear blue eyes, dressed in a black leather jacket and jeans that fit him to a T. And held loosely in one hand, a rose the color of a garnet.

Rylan.

And behind him was a bronze. A Rodin—it had to be. A bigger-than-life-sized statue of a man and a woman in a passionate embrace.

It was cheesy. Tacky. Swiftly approaching tawdry, even. But as her feet drifted forward, leading her toward him, all the doubt squeezed out of her heart. He'd made her smile so many times in the day and a half since they'd met. He'd made her body come alive, and worse, he'd seduced her with *art*. If that wasn't worth a shot . . . then she didn't know what was.

chapter FIVE

According to Rylan's usual game plan, his expression should have been a sultry smirk. But as Kate approached, a real smile stole over him instead, one that made his lips stretch and his cheeks tight.

Who the hell did he think he was fooling? If he'd been following his typical playbook, he would have taken the girl home last night, and there wouldn't have been a second encounter. A second—oh, Christ, this was a date. Apparently, the rules had all gone out the window the second Kate had been completely underwhelmed by his charm.

She wandered toward him with her hands folded in front of her and a flush to her cheeks that said she'd been running to try to find him. She was a couple of minutes late, and he had to admit he'd been starting to worry. All that concern was evaporating now, though. Her hair was loose today, the long waves of it framing her face and shining in the sun. She still wore tennis shoes, but she'd paired them with jeans that hugged her hips, and a shirt that dipped low in the neckline and that...was smeared with charcoal?

She stopped short a couple of feet away from him, raising a brow and pointing. "Is that for me?"

He'd nearly forgotten the flower he'd bought on his way to the park.

"What, this?" He twirled it back and forth between his fingers. "Nah. Random homeless person gave it to me while I was waiting. Think he thought I was getting stood up and wanted to soften the blow."

"Sorry. I lost track of time." She narrowed her eyes. "Though it didn't help that *somebody* didn't exactly give me the clearest of instructions."

"*Somebody* miscalculates from time to time." With that, he held out the rose and drew her in, tugging at her hand to pull her close. And hell, but he hadn't been playing this up in his head. She felt as good against him as she had the day before—better, maybe.

Today, she hadn't just gone along with his cajoling. Today, she'd decided to come to him. To seek him out.

Swallowing down the fierce, sudden burst of pride within his chest, he darted his gaze across her face. Raised his hand to her cheek and rubbed away a sooty smudge. He found it unaccountably endearing. "Let me guess. Busy day drawing?"

"Yeah. I got a lot done."

"Good." Did she even know how amazing that was? All his wasted days, and she spent her vacation making things. And then she had stopped—had probably run here if her breathing was anything to go by, because he'd asked her to. His heart gave a squeeze behind his ribs, and he cupped her jaw, taking pains not to grip it too firmly. "I'm glad you came."

"Me, too." But she averted her gaze as she said it, like she was embarrassed to admit it.

Dipping down, he brushed his nose against hers, leaving their lips just a whisper's breath apart. She smelled sweeter than the flower he'd brought her, and her skin was softer than its petals. And nearly as red. Her embarrassment grated at something inside him. Here he was, reveling in her choice to meet him again. He didn't like the idea that she was any less pleased by it. Or that she was having second thoughts.

Whatever doubts she might be having, he resolved to cast them off.

Pressing his brow to hers, he grazed his lips against the corner of her mouth. His chest swelled as she let him kiss her. "You look beautiful today."

She relaxed a fraction in his arms, laughing as she curled her hand around his neck. "You're one to talk."

Pride surged within him again. "You like?"

"Yeah," she said, voice uneven and dipping darker. She smoothed her hand down his chest, lighting fires beneath his skin. "I like a lot."

"Good." His looks weren't worth much more than his bank account, but if they'd won him this chance, at least they were something he'd worked for. Something he'd chosen to invest his time in. Without another word, he captured her mouth with his, parting his lips and darting forward with his tongue. Her curves came flush against him as he reeled her in, perfect and soft and lush. *Willing.*

And that was the sweetest part of all. None of her hesitance from the night before clung to her today, and the way she pushed up into the kiss shot like lightning through his veins. Forget the rule book—the long game was worth playing sometimes, even with a tourist.

Surrounding her with his arms, he kissed her hot and hard

enough to put the statue behind them to shame. Just when it hit the point of testing his control, he pulled away enough to free his lips. Stayed close enough to still share air as he let a growl creep into his voice. "I'm really, *really* glad you came."

She looked a little glazed, her red lips full and wet. "Me, too."

And it was so tempting to try to hurry his plan along, but no. Not this time, and not with this girl.

Yesterday, their trip to the museum had started out a ploy to make her trust him enough to invite him to her bed. But somehow, it had turned into the best day he'd had in this long and pointless year. It had been connection and seeing art through this beautiful woman's searching eyes. Seeing himself through her eyes, too. Not the man who'd had all his choices stripped from him, only to be shown the ugly underbelly of the life he'd been told he had to lead. The man who had seen it, and then turned around and run.

He was just a guy to her. One she liked the look of. One she'd invited to take her home last night. One who could make her disheveled and glazed just from a kiss.

His pulse roared. He wanted her like this, naked and laid out for him, all right. But he wanted the rest of it, too. He wanted *more*.

It took an exercise of will, but he managed to take a step back. His breath was still coming too fast, and he had to will his body to calm down as he forced some distance between them. Dinner. They were going to have dinner. And then they could have the rest.

"Come on." Entwining their hands, he reached down to grab his pack off the ground.

"What's that?" she asked.

Condoms and a fresh change of clothes, mostly.

"Nothing." He slung the bag over his shoulder and tipped his head toward the exit of the park. Changed the subject before he could talk himself out of his own plan to not rush this along. "How do you feel about Ethiopian food?"

"It's not French." Her voice quirked upward with uncertainty at the end.

"Astute. But do you like it?"

"Never tried it."

Perfect. "Feeling adventurous?"

She chuckled and squeezed his hand, letting herself be dragged along as he maneuvered them down the path. "I think that's pretty obvious."

And he liked that—the idea that this was an adventure. One that he was leading her into, but that she was taking him along on, too. In a year of conquests, he hadn't tried it this way, not with dates and dinners and kisses in a park. Not even once.

Had he ever, really? With all the fucked-up examples of relationships he'd had to look to, with the games the people in his life liked to play...

Here, with this girl who didn't know who he was, though, who would be on this continent for only so long. It somehow seemed worth a chance.

The restaurant, when they got there, wasn't quite as shabby chic as grabbing food to go from a literal hole in the wall, but it wasn't precisely fine dining, either. Tucked into an alcove on a little side road, the place was below street level, the lighting dim but the colors loud, all the walls painted in orange and red and gold. Keeping Kate close, Rylan glanced around the space, past all the woven baskets on the tables and the tapestries on the walls. He frowned. Lucille always worked on Saturdays.

Ah, there she was, slipping out from behind the beaded curtain near the kitchen. They made eye contact across the room, and she smiled as she took him in. She raised an eyebrow as she sashayed her way to the front, dark skin gleaming in the lamplight. "Deux?" *Two?*

It was unusual, he could concede. He typically showed up alone.

"Deux," he confirmed, guiding Kate over to a cozy table near the wall. As he pulled out a chair for her, he checked, "This okay?"

"Sure?" She didn't sound so certain about that, so he leaned down, cupping her shoulders in his hands and kissing her cheek.

"It'll be fine. Trust me."

She made a little humming noise as she settled her purse in her lap. She was pretty protective of the thing today. Maybe to the point of verging on paranoia, but he couldn't exactly blame her, considering.

Projecting confidence, he sat down opposite her and swung his own bag over the back of an empty seat. Turning to face the table again, he caught Kate eyeing the pack with as much curiosity as she'd had before.

Good. Let her keep thinking about it.

Lucille dropped a couple of menus on the table in front of them. "You need a minute to look?"

It was odd. He'd never heard her speak English before. "Yes, please."

She nodded and slinked away, but not without running her fingertips over the back of his neck. Troublemaker. He shot her a restrained glare, partly in warning and partly to show Kate he wasn't amused.

As for Kate, she didn't seem to know what to think of any of it. She gestured vaguely at Lucille's retreating figure. "You're a regular, I presume?"

"You could say that."

He liked to find little eateries with their own flavors—ones with owners who doubled as waitstaff, and where everyone was family. Walking in a world of strangers, it was nice, having places like that. Places where they knew only one of his names.

Like Kate did.

"So." He flipped open his menu. "Anything you don't eat?"

"Not really." When she reached for the other menu, he put his hand over hers to stop her.

From the look on her face, that might have been a douche move. He shifted, curling his fingers around her palm instead of preventing her from doing her own perusing. "You can take a look if you want, of course. But . . . if it's not too scary, maybe let me?"

"I'm not scared." She could have fooled him.

He shook his head, trying to allay whatever concerns she might have. "The idea here is you order a few different things. They all come out on a big tray lined with bread. Everybody tries a little bit of everything."

"Uh-huh."

Letting his lips slant upward, he rubbed her knuckles with his thumb. "I don't pretend to know your mind, but I have a few favorites I'd like you to try. What do you say?"

And there was that look again, like she was peering straight through him. It should have felt invasive, but it never did. Instead, it left him wondering what on earth it was she saw.

Whatever it was, it must have met with her satisfaction. As if just to check, she asked, "Nothing too spicy?"

"I can do mild."

"All right, then." She nodded decisively. "I'm game."

Good. He squeezed her hand and turned around to catch Lucille's eye. Once she'd made her way back over, he paged through the menu, picking out a variety of flavors for Kate to sample, mixing up the choices of featured vegetables and meats.

"Will that be all?" Lucille asked when he was done.

"Yeah. Thanks." He passed the menus over to her, never letting go of Kate as he did.

Apparently, his message was received. While Lucille smiled at him fondly, she didn't try to touch him this time.

He'd have to thank her for that later. For now, he had more pressing things to think about.

"So tell me," he said, focusing all of his attention on the woman before him. He picked up her hand in his, spinning it around and uncurling her fingers from her palm. Rubbing at the hints of pigment ground into her skin, he grinned. "Whatever have you been up to today that's gotten you so filthy?"

It probably shouldn't have been quite so appealing, the way Rylan could make something sound seductive and serious and ridiculous all at once. Kate laughed, letting him turn over her hand and inspect her fingernails. The warmth of his touch felt nice, and he was just the right combination of delicate and firm.

And no matter what she felt, she refused to flinch or yank her hand away. How many times had she been nervous about the condition of her hands? Wouldn't a guy prefer the girls with the smooth, soft skin and perfect manicures over the one covered in little cuts and ink and glue? If he cared, he didn't give any sign of it. He loosely grasped her knuckles and tugged at her arm, getting her close enough that he could press his lips to the back of her palm.

"So?" he asked, returning their hands to the table.

"N-nothing all that interesting." Her voice came out raspy in a way she hadn't expected, for all that it matched the jumpy, keyed-up feeling in her chest. The tingling in her breasts. "Just some sketching."

His face lit up at that. "Can I see?"

"It's nothing fancy." The temptation to pull her hand from his grew, but for entirely different reasons.

She didn't like showing anyone her stuff—not if it wasn't finished. Hell, she was kind of squirrelly about it even when a piece was done. It wasn't just insecurity, either. She knew she was reasonably good at this.

But letting someone see your work was like showing them a whole other part of you. And when you didn't even know what your drawings stood for, it was worse. It was showing the other person an unfinished version of yourself. Fragmented and dissolute. The messy insides that hadn't quite formed themselves into the shape of a person yet.

"Come on," he pressed. "I mean, if you don't want to, I understand, but I bet they're great." He tilted his head, looking at her through dark lashes with the most beautiful, clear blue eyes.

"They're not."

"I won't judge."

And he seemed so *interested*. As she wavered, considering letting him have this glimpse inside her head, his eyes shone.

She'd been made to feel self-conscious about what she did so many times and by so many people—her dad, Aaron. Hell, even her mom, sometimes, though she tried to be supportive.

Kate was probably a sucker for letting his eagerness get to her, but it did.

And besides, it was like she'd told herself the day before when she'd given into his entreaties. She didn't know this man from Adam, and he didn't know her. So why not?

Oh, hell. "Fine." Her heart rose up in her throat, her nerves making her fingers twitch. But as she slipped her hand from his, she opened her purse.

She flipped past the vast majority of the pages, not ready to show him quite that much yet. When she got to her first sketch of the day, she frowned. It didn't look any better now than it had while she'd been working on it. But Rylan was peering at her with such keen interest, like he really cared about what she was about to show him, and it was too late to withdraw the offer now.

Fighting for composure, even as her face went warm and the back of her neck cold, she folded the book in half and passed it over.

His gaze dropped to the page immediately as he took it from her. "Notre Dame?"

A little of her unease slipped away. "At least it's recognizable." With its iconic windows, she'd figured it would be. But it was nice to hear all the same.

"Easily." He didn't make any other comment on the quality of the work, and it wasn't until that lack of praise that she realized how much she'd been waiting for some kind of affirmation. Even just the normal, polite sort of approval your average stranger felt obligated to confer. He started to turn the page, then paused. "May I?"

They'd already gotten this far. She nodded, holding her breath.

He examined the next drawing with a look of concentration on his face. "Same basic scene."

"Yeah. I—" Was it worth describing her process to him, when she scarcely understood it herself these days? "It takes a couple looks to figure out where I want to go with it."

Another glance at her for assent before he flipped to the third and final piece. She sucked in a breath as he held the page out at arm's length and pulled it back in, gaze moving over it.

When her resolve cracked, she forced an exhalation and wet her lips with her tongue. "I didn't quite get to finish that one." With weak humor, she explained, "Had to go and meet someone."

His only response was a twitching at the corner of his mouth. Finally, after what felt like forever, his eyes darted up. "I like it."

"You do?"

"Very much." He checked the surface of the table before setting the sketchpad down with the drawing facing up. He tapped the corner of the paper. "This one especially."

And just like that, she was glad he hadn't jumped to say he liked them right away—that he had taken his time and considered each one. It made the compliment more meaningful, made it seem like he actually meant it as opposed to saying so just to be polite.

"Yeah." She let out a sigh, the shaky anticipation of opening herself up to him melting away. Her tongue, tied up in knots this entire time, suddenly loosened, and she leaned across the table, angling herself closer to him. "I felt like I was kind of getting somewhere with that one. Wish I'd had a little more time to finish it."

"You'll go back."

"If I have a chance."

"You'll go back," he insisted. He thumbed the corner of the page. "You know what sets this one apart?"

She wanted to laugh. "That it doesn't suck?"

"No. The others aren't bad. Only there's not as much...*there* there. You were drawing what you saw. But in this one, you were drawing it the way you wanted us to see it. Through your eyes. It's subtle." He slid the sketchbook over to her. "But it makes a difference."

Humming to herself, she turned the page around so she could see it right-side up, and he had a point. It wasn't just a famous church staring back at her as if from a postcard. The big, round window at the center connected to the pointed arches and the tops of the towers, which connected to the sky and to the ground, coming together to give a sense of warmth. Of wholeness. She'd been starting to interpret. To pull it all together and make an image you could *feel*.

Notre Dame. Our lady. A woman standing free and on an island all her own.

Rylan smiled and pointed at the picture. "It's paying off. You can't love what you don't know, and you can't draw like that unless you love."

He wasn't wrong, but she'd never heard it put that way.

How would it be to draw him? She'd never been the best at portraiture, but she could imagine it now. Spreading him out and having him pose for her. Naked, perhaps. He'd be beautiful, and with enough sketches... It would be dangerous.

It was the road to falling in love.

She closed the cover of the book and returned it to her bag. "How do you know so much about art?"

A shadow crossed his eyes, but it was there and gone in an instant. "I've always appreciated it. Never was much good at it myself, though."

Before she could inquire any further about that, the woman who had taken their orders appeared beside the table again. Kate refused to shrink at her presence, opting instead to look up at her and smile. But she couldn't help glancing at Rylan when the lady put her hand on his shoulder as she set a basket on the table in front of them. "Your food is almost ready."

"Merci," Rylan said, not reacting to the proximity.

So Kate wouldn't react to it, either. She'd known what kind of person she was getting involved with. His easy intimacy with beautiful waitresses wasn't anything she shouldn't have expected. It was a good reminder, even.

The nervous patter of her pulse settled down into a low simmer as the woman walked away, leaving them alone again. Looking only at Kate, he lifted the top of the basket, releasing a thin cloud of steam and revealing tightly rolled rows of little towels. He picked one up, tossing it from hand to hand as he cleaned himself up. Setting it aside, he reached for another and looked to her. "May I?"

Oh. "Okay." She held her hands out, only for him to take one gingerly into his palm. The cloth was damp and hot as he swiped it across her fingers with practiced ease.

She swallowed hard. She'd known what kind of man he was, and yes, it came with flirty waitresses. But it also came with this—a relaxed air and a skill with his hands. Deep in her belly, a coiling heat burned and flared.

He'd know what he was doing with her body, if she let him have his way with her. And maybe that was worth the insecurity and the casualness of the encounter. The whole idea was frightening and exciting and new.

And it struck her. If he pressed—and he would—she *could* take him to the hostel with her. There was nothing stopping her but her own inhibitions. The reservations she'd earned over the past couple of years about sex and intimacy and love. Who cared about her roommates, with their quiet groans and creaking bedsprings? Or about how sex had always gone for her before.

Who cared if you could trust a man when you were only going to sleep with him once?

A partner like him—it was something she'd never had, never been sure she even wanted. But maybe it was something she deserved the chance to try.

At that very moment, he looked up at her, and it was like the room shifted. He had no idea that her whole conception of how things might progress between them had changed. He must have sensed that something was different, though. His lips parted and he gave her a lopsided smile. "What?"

"Nothing."

Shaking his head, he rubbed the cloth over the creases of her knuckles one more time before balling it up and putting it aside. "There we go. All clean."

"They weren't all that dirty before."

"But now they're cleaner." He kissed the back of her hand before letting her go.

And just in time. Their waitress cleared the towels and the basket from their table, exchanging them for a circular platter big enough to hold a pizza. As promised, it was lined with some sort of bread, with more rolls of the stuff laid out along the edges. Topping it were servings of things she couldn't begin to identify. They were colorful and different, and filled the air around their table with a hundred scents she'd never encountered in her life.

A dark hand appeared above the tray, pointing at each little area in turn. "Chicken, beef, potatoes, vegetables, lentils, greens." The waitress looked between them for approval.

Rylan nodded, grinning at her, and said something too quickly in French. Her reply was equally incomprehensible, and he laughed, shaking his head.

As the waitress walked away, Kate looked at him with curiosity. "What were you two talking about?"

He unrolled a napkin and placed it over his lap. "I told her it looked wonderful, and she told me to let her know if you chickened out and wanted a sandwich."

"Hmm." Kate grabbed her own napkin, then glanced toward the waitress. "She forgot our silverware."

"No, she didn't." He chose a piece of bread and tore a section off, using it to pick up some of what looked to be the chicken. "See?"

Oh. Suddenly, cleaning their hands made a lot more sense.

It was awkward, but she ripped a bit of the bread and tried to follow his example. It wasn't as messy as it looked, but it wasn't particularly neat, either. "You know," she said, "my mother always told me never to order French onion soup on a date because you'd make too much of a mess. Turn the guy off."

Rylan looked as dapper licking lentils from his fingers as he ever could have in a fancy restaurant sipping champagne from crystal. He laughed. "Well, you officially have my permission to order whatever kind of soup you want to in the future. No need to impress me." He popped his handful into his mouth, then swabbed the corner of his lips with his napkin. Shrugging, he said, "I like a girl who has an appetite. I like things that taste good. I don't think enjoying things is a turn-off. Much the opposite."

He looked at her expectantly. The whole time he'd been talking, she'd still been sitting there, gripping her sauce-soaked bread between her fingers and her thumb. Oh, well. Nothing for it. She took a bite and widened her eyes. The bread was spongy and just a little bit sour, the meat tender and flavorful. It was like nothing she'd ever had before, rich and sweet and delicately spiced.

"So?"

"It's good," she said, and it shouldn't have been such a surprise.

"Here." His smile had deepened into something unaffected as he tore off more bread and scooped up some of the vegetables. He brought it up to her mouth in offering. "Try this."

It was so like what he'd done with the crepe the night before. Except instead of in the open air of the city, they were in a cozy little restaurant, no prying eyes but for the other patrons and the waitress, and Kate had nothing to hide. Not from any of them. She dipped her head and took the morsel from his hand. His eyes flashed dark, and a little thrill ran through her as he let his fingertips linger, stroking a slow curve along the bottom of her lip.

She swallowed, holding his gaze.

"I like that, too." The way he touched her and looked at her and gave her exotic, foreign delicacies to taste.

His throat bobbed as she licked her lips. "Aren't you glad you trusted me?"

And wasn't that the question of the evening? Of the trip, even?

She hesitated. But she couldn't deny the truth. "Yeah. I am."

"Well, then." He prepared another bite for her and brought it to her mouth. "Here's to trying something new."

chapter SIX

It was such a cliché—the ennui that settled in on a person when there wasn't anything he wanted. Rylan had resigned himself to being a certain number of clichés. The jaded expat, the casual skirt-chaser. The lone wolf, hiding from the people who reminded him of who he'd been and what he'd walked away from.

Apparently, it was time to add another to the list.

How long had it been since he had wanted something—someone—so badly? Women fell into his bed. They amused him and pleasured him, and he made them feel good in return. But they left the next morning, if not the moment they were done. They didn't get into his head. Not like this.

As he and Kate spilled out onto the alley, though, her hair hung loose around her shoulders, and her eyes were bright, the long, pale column of her throat so smooth. He didn't know if he'd ever seen her look so beautiful, and he *wanted* her. Desired her with a power that hadn't possessed him in this long and lonely year—and that was what got him. His time in Paris had never struck him as lonely before. He'd never felt bored. But here, with this woman, on this night, all his diversions seemed to crumble beneath his feet.

And he couldn't help himself. Before they could turn the corner onto the main street, he grabbed her shoulder, feeling high on good food and good company and the warmth of a beautiful girl. Emboldened, he turned her and pressed her up against the stonework of the outside of the restaurant. His heart surged behind his ribs as he closed his hand around her shoulder and crowded her up against the wall, chest to chest and mouth to mouth. It'd be so easy to sweep in and claim her the way he'd been longing to—

Alarms went off inside his head, and he stopped himself cold. This was too much, was the complete opposite of how he'd been working so carefully to coax her along. He darted his gaze up to her face, prepared for fear.

But no.

She put her hands on his chest, and her eyes were big and dark. She skimmed her tongue between her lips as her fingers latched on to his shirt. Ready for it.

Relief flooded him, washing away the final traces of his restraint. He tipped forward, pulse thundering as she opened to his kiss. *Fuck.* She tasted of sex and spice, and he wanted to taste her all over—the ripe swells of her breasts and the slickness between her legs.

He dared to let his hand drift up her rib cage, right to the point where his thumb brushed the outer curve of her breast. When she pulled away to gasp for air, he kissed his way across her cheek, burying his face against the sweet scent of her hair. He fairly growled, "You're not going back to that hostel alone tonight."

Laughing, she dropped her head against the stone, lifting one of her hands to run her fingers through his hair. "My roommates had sex last night."

"Yeah?"

"Yeah." She pulled him to her lips and kissed him even more deeply.

It made him burn hotter, imagining her there, alone in a narrow, rented bad, listening to the noises other people made as they came. He edged his hand up higher on her ribs, asking between kisses, "Did it turn you on?"

She squirmed, but her hand on the back of his neck didn't relax its grip at all. "It was embarrassing."

"Not answering my question."

"Maybe. A little."

All his plans receded in his mind, making way for a whole new set of dirty fantasies. He pulled back enough to see her face. "Did you want to put on a show? While we watch them put on theirs? Is someone a little bit of a voyeur?"

"No." But her cheeks were flushing. "No, but I'm not afraid to. If they don't care, then I—I won't care, either."

And he could read it in her eyes and in her breath. She was simply waiting for him to ask.

The words were on his tongue, right on the cusp of spilling out. If he kissed her throat and sucked her ear. If he pressed his hardness against her hip and told her to take him home, she would. He could lay her out on those borrowed sheets in the dark and take her apart. In muffled moans and whispered instructions, he'd touch her and find out how she arched and what she'd shout. Press inside and take what he wanted, no matter who was listening, lying in their own beds on the other side of the room.

It would be so. Fucking. Hot.

But after, they'd be sleeping on a single bed, and the shame of it all would stay at bay only so long. She'd squirm, or maybe outright ask him to go, and no. He'd just awoken from his haze. This thing was temporary, but he wouldn't doom it to a single night.

No. His plan was better.

He gripped the hem of her shirt in his fist and squeezed his eyes closed against the arousal that was growing too sharp, making it almost hard to think. "What if I had a better idea?"

"Hmm?"

She was lost in it, too, and he had to separate them. It took too much of his will to pull a half step back and put some air between their bodies. He did it, though. He put his hands on her shoulders and looked her in the eye.

"Neither of us likes where we're staying, right?"

"No." Her brows furrowed. "But—"

"So what if we pooled our resources?"

"I don't understand."

And he had to be careful how he worded this. "Money for two bunks at hostels. Add it together, and it pays for a real hotel." He slid his hand lower to stroke the hollow of her throat with his thumb. "A private room. Private bath." He dipped in closer so he was speaking in her ear. "I'd make love to you on a big fluffy bed, and then in the shower. Put my face between your legs against the counter. And you could scream as loud as you wanted to. No one to hear. No one to see how many times I make you come."

The moan that poured out of her at that sent sparks skittering down his spine.

She was shaking her head, but her eyes were glazed, and

she parted her thighs to let him slide a knee between them. "Already paid for tonight."

"So this first one's on me." He drew a line up her cheek with his nose. "If you don't have the best night of your life, you can go back to your tiny bed and your roommates tomorrow. But you won't." Nipping at her jaw, he let his voice go rumbly and dark. "I'm very, very patient. I don't let up until everyone is . . . *satisfied*."

Her resolve was faltering. "You have a place picked out?"

"Reserved and everything. Five stops on the Metro." A perfect place on a quiet street, nice enough for his tastes but not so fancy as to make her uncomfortable or put the lie to all his not-quite truths. "Clean white sheets and a little balcony and a bakery down the street. I'll buy you a chocolate croissant in the morning and eat it off your hip."

Her laugh was like bells, her hands gripping him in a way that told him she wouldn't let go. "Well, if there's chocolate involved . . ."

"Anything you want." And God, he really meant that.

She shifted, nudging him back so she could look him in the eye. "And if I do have the best night of my life?"

"Then I'll give you more of them." He swallowed hard, surprised by the fervency in his own voice. By how much he wanted this. "As many as you can stay for. They're all yours."

For what felt like centuries, indecision colored her features, bright white teeth flashing as they dug into the corner of her lip. It was all spread out before him—her hesitation and her need. Her body was coiled so tightly, and he wanted nothing more than to give it what it clearly craved.

Say yes, he chanted in his mind. *I'll be so good to you.*

But there was so much uncertainty there, too. Inhibitions

he'd do his best to peel away, but it would take time. Time and a leap of faith.

He held his breath.

Finally, *finally*, she pushed off the wall and lifted up onto her toes, dragging him down for a softer, briefer kiss. His heart did the strangest things inside his chest; he had no idea how much he'd been counting on her to say yes. This kiss didn't taste like yes. He didn't know what it tasted like, and the uncertainty set him on edge. People didn't say no to him, not about things like this.

She dropped down and released his lips, but before his worry could take over, before he could pull her back in and state his case more ardently, she threaded her hand through his.

"All right," she said.

The clouds parted in his mind. That was it. What he'd been waiting for.

Kate wasn't sure what she'd been expecting when Rylan had told her he'd gotten them a room for the night. Really, nothing would have surprised her, and as long as they hadn't been sharing with any patchouli-scented backpackers, she would have been content.

She was more than content.

The room wasn't overdone, but it was nice. Tasteful. Crisp, clean white sheets, just like he had promised, and red draperies framing the doorway that opened out onto a tiny little balcony. Cream-colored walls decorated with a big mirror and classic-looking paintings. A little desk with a chair and a rose-colored settee.

Rylan had excused himself to the restroom, so she was left standing there alone, taking it all in. Trying to calm her nerves. She ran her hand over the headboard, and then the corner of the nightstand. What looked like an intercom was set into the wall to one side of the bed, and she stooped to examine it more closely. When she pressed one of the buttons in the center of it, static crackled, followed by faint strains of music. Édith Piaf. A radio. A radio with five stations, and she moved through them, smiling as the old chanteuse gave way to quiet jazz, then an American power ballad from the eighties. And then a... polka? Shaking her head, she turned the thing off and faced the room again.

But all she kept coming back to was the bed.

She shivered, crossing her arms over her chest and working to force her anxiety down. Neither of them had made any pretense about why they were here. When he was with her, though—when he was kissing her mouth or smoothing his hands down her hips, it all made sense. When she was alone, all she could think was that she had no idea what she was doing. The entire venture was a terrible mistake.

The air in the room suddenly felt too warm, and she crossed to the opposite wall. It took a little bit of fiddling, but she got the doors out onto the balcony to open. Fresh air poured across her face, bringing with it the sounds of the city below, and she closed her eyes as she stepped out onto the landing. She set her hands on the railing and bowed her head.

She was going to do this. She wasn't going to freeze up, the way Aaron always accused her of doing. It was going to be fine.

She opened her eyes, and they stung. Why had Rylan left her alone with nothing to do but *think* for so long?

The sound of running water from within had her fighting for her composure, but she hadn't quite found it yet by the time Rylan's footsteps announced his presence. She stiffened without meaning to, unable to stop the way she flinched at a warm hand on her arm.

Rylan was silent for a moment, and it gave her time to breathe. Without crowding her, he stepped out onto the balcony, his chest not quite touching her back, his palm shifting to settle at her waist.

"Nice view," he said, lips close to her ear.

"Yeah." She hadn't really taken it in yet, too busy letting her nervousness get the best of her. Eager for the distraction, she refocused her gaze on the world beyond their little room.

Sure enough, it was pretty. Much prettier than what she'd been able to glimpse through the tiny alley-facing window in her room at the hostel. They were only a few stories up, but that was high enough in a city like this. She looked out over the quiet street, at the shop fronts and stones and pavement, and then higher, toward the skyline in the distance, twinkling with lights against the gathering dusk.

He chuckled softly, sweeping her hair to the side. Pressing a kiss to the quivering skin of her throat. "I didn't mean the city."

And somehow, it was so like their first conversation in the coffee shop. Part of her was still adrift as her mind raced ahead to what would come next, but a different part sighed in relief as she got a little of her footing back. Relaxing her grip on the railing, she tipped her head to the side. "That line work on most girls?"

"It's not a line."

"Uh-huh."

She could hear and feel his smile. He sidled up a little closer to her, moving slowly, as if to give her time to tell him no. When his body made contact with hers, something in her melted by a fraction, and then another, and then all at once she remembered why this had felt so easy before. With warm lips and just the barest hint of teeth, he took a nip at the lobe of her ear.

"It's not a line if it's true."

How many times had she fallen for a man insisting he was telling the truth?

Taking a chance, she released her hold on the railing, and he wrapped her up in his arms. Kissing down to where her neck met her shoulder, he let his hips meet her backside. A whole other kind of tremor made its way through her body, a heat so intense it seared. He was hard. On instinct, she shifted her hips away, but he didn't let her go.

As if he could sense the root of her anxiety, he murmured, "We don't do anything you don't want to do."

She laughed and curled her hand around his forearm where it draped beneath her breasts. "It's not a matter of want."

"You want me to touch you?" His fingertips played with the hem of her top, and there was so much *promise* there.

Her breath stuttered. "Yes." She squeezed her eyes shut tight again. "Only—"

His fingers and lips both paused. "Hmm?"

"I just—I don't do this much."

Slowly, he pressed another kiss to the side of her throat. "What? Have sex?" His lips drifted higher. "Or let yourself be seduced by a man you just met in the most romantic city in the world? Because if it's the latter, I can't say I'm shocked."

Her laughter this time was easier and sadder, all at once. "I've gone all the way with exactly two people, and one of them was a pickup, and..." She didn't really want to think about it. "...and that wasn't much fun."

She'd been into it enough, but they'd both been drinking, and it had all started moving too fast. When he'd gotten her onto all fours, she hadn't been ready, and it hadn't been horrible. But that was the best she could say.

The way Rylan held her shifted. It was still loose enough that she could get away at any second if she wanted to—she didn't doubt that. But there was a possessiveness there. "If I *ever* make you feel like this 'isn't fun'—" He cut himself off and took a slow, deep breath before restarting. "I will never take anything from you that you don't want, or before you're ready to give it. There is nothing I want to do tonight but give you pleasure."

She couldn't help the twinge of doubt. "Nothing?"

"Nothing." He swallowed. "It'll be torture, but I'll walk away right now if you tell me you're not interested." At some point, he'd pulled his hips back, but now the long line of him pressed against her rear again, not insistent or demanding at all. Just there. "Make no mistake about it. I want you. Badly. But that's all secondary to what you want. If you never touch me but still let me make you come..." Trailing off, he ran her hand down her side. "I promise I'll be satisfied."

She opened her eyes. What was this man doing to her?

Even with Aaron, sex had never been *fun.* He'd had a good enough time, but she'd never managed to get him to understand what she needed him to do. He'd never asked.

And now Rylan was offering her all these things... And she wanted them. So much.

"I want to touch you." Her voice came out whispery and low. "Only—can we . . . can we take it slow?"

"As slowly as you want. I have just one request."

Her stomach sank. "Oh?"

Taking a partial step back, he turned her around until they were standing before each other, eye to eye and face to face, and his gaze was burning. "Please. Kate."

"Yes?"

"Please tell me you'll at least let me taste you."

chapter SEVEN

Kate's breath caught in her throat. It wasn't that she'd never had a man do that before. Aaron had tried a few times. It had been warm and wet, and mortifying. Mostly mortifying, though.

She'd never been so close to giving in and faking it already as she had been, lying there, waiting for him to get bored.

Heat rising in her cheeks, she played with a button on his shirt for something to look at. "You don't have to."

"I don't have to do anything." He ducked, giving her no choice but to meet his gaze. "And neither do you. But I want to."

She shrugged. "It's just never done much for me."

"Then whoever was doing it wasn't doing it right."

"And you think you'll do better?"

"I know I will." With that, he took her by the hand and made to lead her off the balcony. "Come on."

As she followed him into the room, he paused to close the door, drawing a pair of sheers over the glass but leaving the heavier draperies open. Squirming inside and uncertain what else to do, she faced the bed and took a deep breath.

He came up behind her, encircling her waist with his arms, just like he had out on the balcony. "Is this all right?"

"Yeah."

Apparently, he was starting everything on established ground. "And this?" He smoothed her hair out of the way before kissing a longer, wetter line down the side of her neck. The soft scrape of teeth against delicate flesh made it all the better, and some of the stiffness left her limbs.

"Yes."

He moved so slowly, sliding his lips across her skin. With one arm holding her flush against his chest, he brought his other one up. Warm fingertips dragged across her throat and along her collarbones, lingering there before drifting lower. He swept them down the valley of her breasts. At her navel, he turned his hand over and retraced the circuit, again and again, until the thrumming in her abdomen felt like a smoldering glow. She relaxed her arms. Let her head fall back against his shoulder.

"See?" His voice was a low rasp. "Isn't that nice? Don't you like it when I touch you?"

She did, and the pit of heat flared, something clenching deep inside. "Yes." And she should be touching him, too, shouldn't she? She reached to wrap her palm around his thigh.

But he *shh*ed her, brushing her overture aside. "Later, if you want. For now, just let me."

It wasn't easy, but an instinct she'd thought had been burned out of her wanted to do precisely that. To give over and give in. She dropped her arm back to her side and took him at his word.

His hand drifted to her hip. Her breath hitched. On the

way back up, he barely skimmed the apex of her thighs through her jeans, and a sound passed her lips.

Two minutes ago, she'd been so nervous about him coming anywhere near her, and now she was losing her mind, all but whimpering at a teasing glance across her sex.

Murmuring words she couldn't hear against her neck, he skated his hands up and down her body, flirting with but never quite making contact with the places that were slowly starting to strain for it. When another, breathier sound of desire escaped her, he groaned, pressing himself tighter against her spine. Letting the line of him sear its way into her, until she was liquid, yearning for his touch.

He didn't have to ask a question. She closed her eyes and answered it. "Yes."

"Good girl."

It should have been cold water on her flame, but somehow it was anything but. She wanted that praise again, wanted that soft, gravelly voice telling her she was exactly what he wanted her to be.

Sucking the lobe of her ear between his lips, he rubbed the hem of her shirt between his fingertips, transcribing what he was going to do and giving her room to tell him no. Her breath went shallow as he rucked the fabric upward, skimming warm fingertips over her abdomen. He didn't push it all the way up, though. Pausing with her breasts still covered, he ran the corners of his knuckles around the outer curve.

"Can I?"

She nodded minutely, arching forward and holding her breath.

He didn't grab or squeeze at her as he finally let his hand traverse the center of her chest. She exhaled shakily with the relief of his gentle touch, pleasure simmering with the graze of his thumb across her nipple, the pressure of a broad palm encompassing the full swell of her breast.

He nudged at the hem of her top again, and she lifted her arms. He stripped her out of it and let the material fall to the floor before molding himself to her spine again, running his hands more freely over bare skin. Electricity seemed to trail behind every touch, winding her up higher and higher until he dipped into the cup of her bra, brushing the hard, naked nub at her peak, sending crisp and white sparks branching. Panting, she turned her face into his neck, and he held her, even as he was cupping her more firmly, sliding his hand in deeper beneath the satin.

"No one ever took their time with you, did they? Never got you screaming for it before they tried to get theirs, huh?"

She'd thought she'd gone slow before, but it had never been like this. She wanted to twist all the way around inside his grasp. Open her legs and wrap them tight around his hips. She felt so empty and hot and *soaking* with how much she wanted this.

"Gonna take my time with you," he promised, gravelly against her cheek. "Gonna take you apart all night, until you're shaking."

"Please."

Her little begging gasp echoed in the room so loudly. Before she could even muster up the presence of mind to be ashamed of it, he was picking her up. Her eyes flew open, a scream forming in her throat as she scrabbled to keep from falling, but then her spine hit the soft surface of the mattress. She looked up, and he hovered over her, on his knees between her spread legs, staring at her like she was something to eat.

No. Like she was something to treasure.

Her breathing sounded deafening to her own ears as he stared down at her, blue eyes pinning her, the sharp point of his jaw and the lines of his cheekbones glowing gold. Without looking away, he undid the buttons of his shirt and shrugged it off his shoulders, then reached over his head to grab the neckline of his undershirt. His face was obscured for a moment as he tugged it off, and she took the chance to glance downward.

A fine trail of dark hair led into the waistband of his jeans, and above that was the smooth plane of his abdomen, lightly defined musculature glinting in the lamplight. His chest was just as sculpted, widening out into the broad cut of his shoulders before drawing the eye inward to the dip of his collarbones and the hollow of his throat.

And there, dangling from his neck, a plain silver chain.

She didn't have a chance to see what was hanging from it as he dropped the ball of cotton to the side. Leaning over her, he grinned, clearly having caught her ogling, but the smirk receded into an expression that was quieter and more intense. Her chest heaved as he perched on his haunches over her, the muscles in his biceps flexing as he laid his palms on her knees. Slowly, looking up at her through thick lashes, he dipped his head. Placed one kiss and then another on the inside of her thigh, trailing upward, and she could hardly breathe. She clenched her hands as his nose nudged the crease of her hip through her jeans.

Oh God, he'd said he wanted to taste her, but would he? Like this?

He lifted up a fraction of an inch to look at her squarely, and her heart was beating overtime, all her nerves firing off

at once, every inch of her body concentrated on the space between her legs. He hadn't even really touched her yet, and
already she was gasping for breath.

Her whole chest felt like it was caving in when he lowered
his head again, and Christ, God, he pressed his lips right to
the center of her jeans, right over her clit. She could feel the
warm rush of his breath even through the fabric, the weight
of that touch pushing her to the point where she thought she
would explode just from this.

Light-headed, her belly and her sex alive with heat, she
arched her spine. She'd never had a man make her come
before, but the feeling was already gathering, an ache that
bloomed and spread, familiar and foreign all at the same
time.

He pressed a little harder, sending a wave of heat through
her, and she tightened her muscles, unable to believe this was
really happening. But then he lifted his mouth to look up at
her, and he was smirking. All at once, the tension that had
been building within her dropped away, and she clenched,
restless around nothing. As she groaned in frustration, soft
lips pressed to her abdomen, then an inch above her navel,
then higher and higher. He kissed the tops of both breasts,
dragging his torso through the valley of her legs.

"So," he said, hovering above her, face to face. He held
himself up with both hands planted beside her head, his knees
between her calves, hips a firm presence against her pelvis,
warm and vital and *there* if not yet grinding in. He kissed the
corner of her mouth and then the other, sliding the tip of his
nose against her cheek. "Is that a yes to letting me taste you?"

And she couldn't stop herself. She laughed, sliding her
hands into his hair and letting the thick strands twist be-

tween her fingers. He'd gotten her so *close*. She'd probably say yes to anything. "It's definitely not a no."

"I can work with that."

Shaking her head, she tugged more insistently at his scalp, drawing him up her body. Half-naked like this, he was all warm skin and the scent of amber and lust. He lowered onto her, fitting hips to hips, and *oh*, there was that pressure again, right where she wanted it. Letting out a noise of pleasure of his own, he thrust against the cradle of her thighs, and she felt like she was melting as their lips met. The kissing and the weight of him overwhelmed her, making the air too thick and her lungs tight.

He dragged his lips along her jaw to her ear. "Do you think you're wet for me?"

She wasn't sure she'd ever been slicker. But the words, so easy for him, wouldn't come to her mouth. With a sound that was half whine and half hum, she put her hands on his back, running them over hot, smooth flesh, then lower, to the waistband of his jeans, trying to urge him on.

It was encouragement enough. He kissed the shell of her ear before sucking at it. "Bet you'll be so sweet." Encompassing her hip with his palm, he ground into her harder. "Think you're ready for me to find out?"

She was ready for anything. If he wanted—if he really wanted, she'd let him have it all, misgivings or no. He'd taken such good care of her body so far. Who was she not to trust him with it now?

He lifted his hips and pressed his brow to the pillow beside her head, breathing fast and shallow against her hair. Everything inside her tensed as he shifted his hand, sliding it along the top of her thigh.

When the heel of his hand connected with where she was desperate and aching, she nearly screamed with the relief of it.

"That's right," he murmured. "God, I bet you're soaked. You're burning up, aren't you? Just waiting for me to take you over."

"Please." She was shocked to hear the plea fall from her lips. "No one's ever— I'm—" *Close. Scared.* It was hot and vulnerable, shaking apart like this inside a man's arms, letting him see all these pieces of her as they broke, their hidden facets exposed.

"Shh." He made his way to her mouth again, kissing her softly but with no less heat. "I've got you."

But his reassurances didn't soothe anything at all. Her legs were stiff with how long she'd been tensing, waiting to fall, but all his rubbing at her through her jeans only made her need coil tighter without any of that sweet unfurling of release. If she could just get her own hands on herself...

For one hysterical second, she thought about faking it, the way she'd been so tempted to in the past.

But then he was kissing down her body, undoing the fasteners of her jeans.

"What are you—" she started, but it was a stupid question.

"Tell me you don't want this." He had the side of his face mashed up against her stomach, his long fingers parting her zipper. Brushing against the fabric underneath.

She didn't want to pretend to come. She didn't want to lie.

He turned, burying his mouth and his eyes against her skin. "You're aching for it. I can *feel* it. God, let me do this for you."

What was left for her to do but nod?

As if he'd been dying to do it, he tore her pants down her

legs, cursing in frustration when he got to her shoes. Somehow he got them shoved off, and they bounced across the carpet to the other side of the room, followed by her pants, and then he was hooking fingers into the lace at the hem of her panties.

Shooting one last glance up at her, he peeled them down.

Naked but for her bra, she felt even more uncomfortable and vulnerable. Weird and cold, and her breath was shaking as she tried to close her legs. He wasn't having any of that, though.

More tenderly than she would have imagined, he parted her thighs. Put his palm to the place where her leg met her torso.

The first swipe of his thumb over the length of her slit was a bright burst of pleasure, almost like pain, it was so sharp. Her leg jerked, and she reached to try to still his hand, but then he shifted, getting his fingers into the mix. They were softer as they spread her open, and she forced herself to breathe. To relax.

And then he moved in with his tongue.

"Oh *God*." It was warm and wet, like she remembered, but instead of just spelling out his English homework, this man moved around. He touched and licked, across the less sensitive side of her clit and then at the point where everything was too intense.

Then he found the right spot, and her whole abdomen went molten.

"Rylan—"

Without shifting from her sex, he reached up for her hands. Put one in his hair and grasped the other one tightly, and it gave her something to hold on to. A way to be grounded when words had left her, everything had left her. Everything but the sweet pulsing and the building wave.

Over and over, he lapped at her, through each false start, when she was so close she swore she could taste it, only to have it slip away and leave her panting and frustrated. She whined and clutched him tight, probably pulling too hard at his scalp, but he hummed and dove in more hungrily, nuzzling and kissing, licking and sucking.

Tensing hard, she pushed into his touch, into the eager heat of his mouth, and it was there—*right there*. Warm fingers pressed against her opening, then just inside.

Her eyes snapped open, and her whole body arched, and she reached—reached—

"Rylan—"

God, it wasn't a wave. It was a tsunami and relief and this crashing, incredible, pulsing oblivion. She shattered, over and over again, swearing out loud and groaning his name, and just wanting him to keep her right there. Against his tongue and his kiss and this trust. This promise.

That he had fulfilled.

When the fire and blackness and flesh-ripe taste of fruit inside her mouth collapsed, she opened her eyes, twitching at the few last laps he took across her clit. She drew her hand from his hair and, too sensitive, nudged at his head to try to get him to stop. Pressing upward with his fingers, he placed one more kiss to her sex before pulling away. Another aftershock rocked through her, only to be followed by a dull emptiness when he withdrew.

Rising up onto his knees, he was a vision, all bare skin to his waist, lips and fingers slick from what he'd given her. He dragged the back of his wrist over his mouth, and she whimpered. For a second, he closed his eyes, tilting his head upward as if he were appealing to a deity. When he looked to her again, his gaze was burning, a hunger so intense it sent a lick of misgiving curling up her spine. She moved to close her legs but he was still between them.

"You have no idea how sexy that was," he said. He ran his hand down his torso, skimming it over the bulge in his jeans, and something inside of her clenched down again.

She'd do something for him. He'd probably want to be inside of her, and she could do that. If he insisted. It was only fair.

But as he looked down at her, he seemed to recognize the uncertainty tugging at her heart. He hung his head a little, shifting forward, moving to put one knee to the outside of her hip while the other one stayed planted firmly between her thighs. His thumb and forefinger played at the button of his pants. "I want to come so bad."

"Yeah. We can—" She reached forward to help him.

He shook his head. "Not until you're ready, beautiful."

Still, he pulled at the fastener and lowered the zip. She watched, frozen, in a bizarre kind of fascination as he slipped his hand inside, groaning loudly as his wrist disappeared beneath the waistband.

And he was going to— Oh God, he was. Through the fabric, his hand moved, and she shook her head.

"Want to see."

She'd never witnessed a man touching himself before, and the idea made her tingle, even as sated as she was.

He didn't ask if she was sure. Everything about him was glazed with arousal, and he was looking straight at her as he pushed his pants and underwear down around his hips. Pulled himself out.

And it shouldn't have been so *hot*, but there he was, muscles standing out in stark relief, gaze black with lust, and his cock— She sucked a breath and pulled her lip into her mouth. He was flushed, long and thick, glistening at the tip with fluid.

"See how hard that made me?" he asked, voice husky and dark. "Eating you out. You taste so good, and the noises you make—" He cut himself off with a moan as he took a long stroke down his length with his palm. The foreskin retracted back, revealing more of the head. He took his other hand, still wet with her, and slipped it around the shining skin at the end, leaving it slicker. "*Fuck.*"

In a punishing rhythm, he thrust his hips into his fist. She lay there, frozen in a sort of fascinated awe. Groaning long and deep, he threw his head back, squeezing out more liquid from his slit.

And it looked *good*. His pleasure looked amazing, sexy and gorgeous in a way she'd never fully understood before.

Hardly thinking, she extended her hand, slipping her fingertips over the head of his cock. The flesh was hot and achingly hard. "Let me—"

Before she could finish the offer, he gasped out a sound like he'd been punched, his body a tight bow, mouth open. "Kate, Kate, I—"

His come flowed over her hand, spattering down onto her hip in white streaks that felt like possession. She never would've expected it, but in that instant, being marked that way made a dark flare of satisfaction awake beneath her skin.

"God*damn*," he groaned, taking a couple of last, slow pulls at himself before sliding free of his own grip. His damp fingers entwined with hers, and he squeezed. "Sorry. Didn't mean to get you all messy."

"It's okay."

Something in her chest turned over. Because it was. She didn't mind.

She hadn't been a virgin when she'd met him. They hadn't had sex. But as she lay there, his body between her legs, her flesh wet with him...it felt like she had done something for the very first time.

Like she would never be quite the same as she had before.

chapter EIGHT

Rylan was wringing a washcloth out in the sink when he happened to look up. The bathroom was a little cramped, to be honest, but it was clean, the big plate-glass mirror over the vanity smoothly polished.

The man staring back at him from inside of it looked like he'd just had the best fuck of his life.

Balling the washcloth up in his fist, he ran his other hand through his hair, settling it down from where it had been standing up on end. Kate had done a number on him in that respect, tugging hard at his scalp—almost too hard in the moment right before she'd arched and screamed and pulsed against his tongue.

Just thinking about it made him lick his lips. He'd slept with more than his share of women, but he couldn't think of any that had gone to pieces quite like that. He probably had nail marks all up and down his shoulders and his neck.

He'd been the first to make her come. And it had shown. God. She'd been wound up, and toward the end there, even he'd been starting to doubt if it were possible. She hadn't seemed a stranger to the little death—and wasn't that an image? The idea of her getting herself off? But either she'd been psyching herself out or he had lost his edge. Either way, she hadn't asked him to stop, and she'd been so *into* it that he'd had to keep going, drunk on the sound of her moans. She'd clung to the edge for what had felt like forever, and when she'd finally let go...

He hadn't even gotten inside her, and it had been one of the most intense sexual experiences of his life.

So intense, he hadn't wanted to ruin it by pressing for something she'd clearly been uncomfortable with. Sex had been off the table, but he'd been so worked up. He'd thought it would take maybe a dozen strokes of his hand.

In the end, it had taken exactly one of hers.

Spent as he was, his cock gave a little twitch of interest inside his boxers. Which reminded him of what he was here to do.

Making a face, he got himself out and cleaned up the best he could. Not that he'd really made much of a mess of himself. His breath caught short at the image, seared into his mind, of his release on Kate's pale skin. He hadn't taken her, not yet, but that twisted animal hindbrain of his had enjoyed what claim he'd managed to stake.

A claim that had to be getting pretty damn uncomfortable by now.

He set the rag aside and ran a fresh one under the tap, as hot as he could stand, before squeezing it out and folding it up. He turned, stepping forward to face the open door leading onto the main room.

Kate lay there still, all creamy skin and the tumble of her hair against the white of the sheets. She was looking right at him, and for the first time all night, he felt self-conscious.

"You watching me?" he asked, putting on a smirk as he leaned against the doorway.

"You're not the only one who can appreciate a view."

It wasn't ego stroking, and that was what made it hit him so squarely in the chest. He worked hard to look good—it was one of the only things he had to put effort into these days. It was nice to be appreciated. But it was also somehow something more.

The wryness to his smile melted away, leaving a curve to his mouth that felt entirely too genuine, and he'd curse himself later for being such a softie. But there wasn't much to do about it now. Shaking his head, he crossed the room to her, sitting down on the edge of the bed at her side. She was still wearing that pretty blue lace bra, and it cupped her tits so perfectly. Made the soft pillows of the tops of them look all the fuller and more inviting. Resisting their temptation, he bent to nudge the sheet from where she'd draped it across her hip, leaving it high enough to hide her cunt without dragging through the puddle he'd left on her skin.

At the touch of the washcloth to her abdomen, she hummed. "Warm," she said.

"Figured you'd like that."

"Yeah."

Once he'd wiped it all away, he bowed to press his lips to the hollow beside her hip. Planting his hand on the bed, he dropped another kiss on her navel and one on the top of each breast. He bypassed her lips, though, leaving a final one on her forehead.

He rose, pushing off to head to the bathroom.

"Thank you," she said.

He paused. "You're welcome?" It was an odd thing to say, right in that moment.

Apparently, she heard his confusion. "For everything. That, with the washcloth. It was nice. And...before. You were really patient with me."

The insecurity dripping from her voice stopped him in his tracks. Forget the nasty rag in his hand. He rounded back toward the bed, dropped a knee to its edge, and probably with too much fierceness, insisted, "You do *not* need to thank me for that."

What he really wanted to do was ask her what kind of assholes she'd been sleeping with. When you got a girl to be with you, you made damn sure she came, with your mouth or your fingers or your dick, and if she wasn't cool with that, then by her own damn hand. Fuck anything else. And when you got a girl dirty, you sure as hell cleaned her up. Took care of her.

And just like that, he wanted to deck any guy who *hadn't* done any of that for her before. She deserved better. So pretty and smart, so giving.

For a second, he squeezed his eyes shut, forcing himself to calm down. Sure enough, when he looked at her again, she had a wariness to her expression, and no. That wasn't okay.

He cupped her face and leaned down, covering her mouth with his as gently and as sweetly as he could. "It was a pleasure," he promised. "Every single moment of it. A privilege."

He slid his hand down her neck before pulling away.

On his way back to the bathroom, he flexed his fingers at his side, still feeling the warmth of her skin against his palm. More often than not, he went to bed with a woman once, and then he moved on. But he hadn't been lying. She'd been beautiful in her pleasure, and it had been a privilege to give it to her.

A privilege he hoped he'd get to have again. At least once.

The man in the bathroom mirror stared at him, and he didn't know who he'd been fooling. He hoped he could have her a lot more times than that.

As many times as he could before she left.

While the water was running in the other room, Kate took the opportunity to quietly freak the hell out. She'd only ever done the one-night stand thing once before, and that had been completely different. The guy had come to her place, and as soon as he was done, he'd left her there, sore and confused and desperate for a shower.

Nothing about this encounter seemed to be heading in that direction.

Still, sharing a bed with a guy wasn't something she'd done a lot of. Rylan had told her explicitly that he'd gotten the room for the both of them, and they could split the cost for the rest of the time she was in town. It didn't seem likely he was going to duck out, or that he expected her to. But what was she supposed to do now? It wasn't that late, and she was way too jazzed to sleep.

Glancing over at the big hiker's backpack he'd left against the wall, she scowled. He could have given her a heads-up about this whole plan of his. What she wouldn't give for some fresh underwear and a T-shirt to change into now. Chewing on the inside of her lip, she played with the strap of her bra. She'd been wearing it all day, and the underwire was digging into her uncomfortably. She'd like to take it off, but...but then she'd be naked.

She rubbed the heel of her hand into her eye. He'd had his face between her legs, and here she was, worrying about him seeing her boobs.

"You wanna borrow a T-shirt or something?"

Somehow, she'd missed the sound of the tap shutting off. She turned, grateful, to find him standing in the doorway to the bathroom again.

"Yeah, actually. That would be really great." She considered for a second. "I mean, we're—we're in for the night, right?"

"Unless you have something in particular you want to do."

"No." Her legs still felt like they might turn to jelly. Staying in sounded like a good idea.

He rummaged around in his bag for a second before tossing her a plain black undershirt. "You want a pair of boxers or something, too?"

She thought about it for a second before nodding. It would be better than nothing. Way better than the pair of panties she'd just about soaked through.

"They're clean." He passed over a crisp blue cotton pair. "Promise."

"Thanks."

"Do you mind if I—?" He gestured at the jeans he hadn't bothered to refasten, hanging loose around his hips.

She didn't want him to be uncomfortable. And really, it was only fair, wasn't it? He'd seen an awful lot of her. She should get to at least catch a glimpse of his legs. "It's fine."

He sat on the edge of the bed to tug off the shoes and socks she somehow hadn't realized he still had on, followed by his pants. Stripped down to his boxers, he was even more attractive. Maybe because he was so comfortable in his skin. His gorgeous, smooth, golden-colored skin.

He smirked as he looked over at her, and she dropped her gaze from the lightly haired musculature of his calves. The man was a figure painter's dream, an anatomy lesson waiting to happen, and she was dying for the chance to draw him.

"You okay?"

"Yeah." She raised her gaze from the sheets and fiddled with the clothes he'd given her.

"Want some help?" Playfully, he ran a finger under her bra strap, then drifted down to tug at the hooks and eyes. "I'm really good at these."

She bet he was. She shook her head at him and held her hair out of the way. "Sure."

He popped the fasteners in a single deft movement. She twisted away from him as she pushed the straps off her shoulders, exposing her breasts, still bashful even after everything.

God but she wished she could let that go. That she could quiet the voice in the back of her mind that kept whispering all these doubts, about her looks, her talents. About what she deserved. She shivered, flashes of memories crowding in around her, feeling tiny and worthless, and none of it had been fair. It wasn't fair for it to be coming back to her now.

She'd taken this huge chance on this man, and it had paid off in spades. So why couldn't she just relax and enjoy it?

Even as she obsessed, Rylan sat there behind her, solid and present and real. He ran his hand down the line of her spine, a whisper-light touch that chased a little of the chill away.

"Pretty," he said, leaning in, pressing his lips just once, quickly, to the center of her back.

She caught the word and tried to hold on to it. To believe it. "Thanks."

He eased off then, giving her space to pull his shirt on over her head. The fabric smelled like him, clean and warm somehow. Comforting. Without lifting the sheet from her hips, she got his boxers on, too. They were big on her, but not too bad. The man had a lean, trim waistline.

"Better?"

"Yeah," she agreed, pulling her hair free from the collar of his shirt. "Much."

"Good." With that, he flopped himself down on the mattress, head on the pillows and legs straight in front of him, one ankle crossed over the other. He held his arm out in invitation.

One she was only too happy to accept. Pulling the covers halfway up, she curled into him, resting her head on his shoulder and letting her hand fall across his chest. He was so warm, and he smelled so good. What had she been saying a minute ago about it not being late enough to go to sleep?

They lay there in silence for a while, him combing his hand through her hair while she danced her fingertips over the lines of definition across his abdomen and chest. It was strangely comfortable.

Until she ran the edge of her nail along the chain draped around his neck. It was a series of little interlocking links, and there—hanging from the center of it was...a ring? Gold and silver with a row of tiny diamonds down the middle. Large enough that it was probably a man's. His fingers stilled in her hair when she touched it.

"What is it?" she asked.

His hand settled over hers in a firm but gentle grip. She let go of the ring as he guided her to rest her palm against his belly instead.

"Nothing." His throat bobbed.

"Nothing?"

"Just my father's wedding ring."

Oh. A hundred questions raced through her mind, but it was invasive, wasn't it? If Rylan was wearing the ring around his neck, his dad was probably gone. Dead or disappeared, or—

"Is he . . ." She trailed off.

Rylan scoffed, apparently hearing what she wasn't sure if she should say. "He's in prison."

Oh.

Another dry chuckle escaped his lips. "The man spent his whole damn life telling me what to do. Imagine my surprise when I find out what he's been up to all these years." A flicker of pain—of betrayal—creased his brow.

"I'm sorry."

He shook his head. "It doesn't matter. I've made my peace with it."

Like hell he had. Everything about him was bristling.

Letting go of her hand, he trailed his fingers up his chest to tap the edge of the band. "He gave me this a long time ago. Right after the divorce. He took it off the second he got back from the lawyer's office and he . . . he made as if to throw it away."

She hummed in invitation, willing him to go on.

Remembering her own father, and how he had thrown them all away . . .

Ever so slowly, he resumed his stroking of her hair. "I asked if I could have it. And he laughed." Bitterness shadowed his tone. "But he still gave it to me."

She stayed there, quiet, waiting for more, but he didn't speak again.

It was the tiniest glimpse. She could imagine it, a younger, wider-eyed Rylan looking up to this hulking father figure. From the sound of it, only to be let down over and over. An ache pressed at the center of her ribs, a sudden need to know more.

The words were right there, compelling her to ask, but before they could escape, she bit her tongue. She hardly knew this man. They'd shared a couple of nights together, and she liked him. A lot. But he didn't owe her anything. Not his history and not his confidence. Not if he didn't want to offer them up to her.

From the stiff set of his jaw, she had a feeling he'd already given more of each than he usually did.

A different instinct crept over her as she stared at him. Not to push, but instead to give him something in return. She considered for a long, silent moment. Then with forced deliberateness, she relaxed her posture, returned her breathing to normal. Stroked the stretch of skin beneath her fingertips, keeping them far away from the shiny glimmer of that ring.

"I haven't spoken to my dad since I was twelve."

Some of the tension bled out of his shoulders. "That's a long time."

"Yeah. Well. He was ... not a nice man." That wasn't even the half of it. He'd left her with this mess in her head, this tiny piece of herself that always said she wasn't good enough, didn't deserve what she did get, was never going to make anything of herself ... She swallowed hard. "Not to me and not to my mom. He..." *Manipulated us. Made us think we couldn't stand on our own two feet and then...* "He lied to her. For years. Cheated." That was an offense anyone could understand. One she could explain without tearing herself apart. "Not exactly the kind of thing you get over quickly."

Or at all.

Rylan chuckled, rubbing his thumb across the back of her palm. "Fathers, huh? They fuck you up."

She shivered. "You can say that again."

She loved that he had said it. He couldn't possibly understand with how much she'd kept unspoken. But for one shimmering instant, it felt like he did.

They lay there, gently touching and holding each other in the quiet of that space. It was tentative, a shaky intimacy built on half-formed confessions and the barest hints of their histories. But it felt good. Safe.

After a minute or two, he let out a breath and squeezed her shoulder. "So." A brightness crept into his tone, a false levity. Letting go of her hand, he reached over to the nightstand for the remote. "You had a chance to try French television yet?"

The fuzzy closeness of the moment shivered, but it didn't shatter.

She turned her gaze toward the screen as it came to life on the other side of the room. "No. I haven't."

"It's an experience."

As he pressed a button, the sounds of fast-spoken French filled the room, and she frowned.

"Do they have English subtitles?"

"Don't worry." He pressed a kiss to the side of her temple. "I can translate."

He flipped through the channels for a bit before he found

something that must have appealed to him, and he set the remote down at his side, shifting to hold her hand again. True to his word, he murmured his interpretation of the dialogue into her ear, his voice deep and warm. She let it wrap around her the way his arms did.

And if she couldn't keep her gaze from flickering to the bit of gold between his collarbones, well. At least she did her best.

chapter NINE

"So." Rylan tapped his razor against the rim of the sink before dipping it under the stream of water again. "What's on your agenda for the day?" He smirked at himself in the mirror. "Besides checking out of your hostel and grabbing your things, of course."

"Of course." Kate's eye roll was audible in her voice. So was the sound of the sleep in her eyes. The hint of a yawn. Not a morning person, that one.

She'd slept in later than he'd thought she would, while he'd blinked his eyes open at the crack of dawn, same as usual.

Well, not quite the same as usual. Most mornings, restless energy plagued him, only he didn't have an outlet for it anymore. He stalked around the apartment or went to the gym or read the business section of the paper, reminding himself even as he did that it didn't concern him anymore. Today... today, there'd been Kate, face soft with sleep. Somehow, just watching her had been enough to calm him. Tracing the line of her throat with his gaze. Gently brushing his knee against her soft, bare thigh.

From the main room, the sounds of her moving around filtered quietly over the running of the tap. He frowned and gripped the handle of the razor tighter.

It was killing him, knowing she was right around the doorway getting dressed while he was standing here, naked but for a towel and the chain around his neck. Still damp from his shower. Half-hard at the thought of what she might be up to out there.

Scowling, he tipped his chin up and swiped the razor across the tricky spot beneath his jaw. He'd promised to be good and not look. It was the only way she'd let him open the damn door to let some of the steam out so he could see his own face in the mirror well enough to shave.

He ran his finger over the damp patch of new skin, feeling for any stubble he might have missed. "Seriously, though. What do you want to do today?"

"I'm not sure. I picked up a new guidebook."

He scoffed. "Which you obviously don't need since you've got me."

She continued as if he hadn't spoken. "Which I haven't had a chance to look at yet. So I guess I should sit down somewhere and go through it at some point."

"Waste of time," he muttered under his breath. Louder, he said, "But what do you *want* to do today?" He considered for a second. "How long are you staying, anyway?"

"My flight home is on Friday." It was Sunday now. They must have both been doing the math in their heads, because just as he was thinking it, she announced, "So, another five full days, including today."

Plus the two they'd already had. Seven nights in total. He could work with that.

Finishing up, he rinsed his razor and set it aside. "Well, you're not going to get as much done today as you might like. Hazard of traveling in Catholic countries."

"Yeah. But there will still be some places open, right?"

"Sure." He turned the tap to full blast and cupped some water in his hands before splashing it over his face, cleaning away what was left of the foam and hair. He dried off and patted on some aftershave, then tiptoed toward the door to sneak a peek.

Except he'd *promised*. Groaning at the conscience he'd apparently grown overnight, he slapped his hand over his eyes. Pitching his voice, he asked, "Can I come out yet?"

"Um. Yeah."

Finally. Grinning in spite of himself, he stepped around the corner to find her perched on the edge of the bed, fingers worrying the strap of her bag, which was sitting beside her. She was wearing last night's jeans, but she'd stolen another of his shirts. He raked his gaze up and down her form.

There was just something so damn sexy about a woman in a man's shirt. The thing was two sizes too big on her, but the way she'd tied it off, her waist looked tiny, her breasts and hips fuller. Worse, she'd only buttoned it partway up, leaving this swath of skin across her collarbones exposed, this hint of cleavage. His throat went dry, his cock giving a twitch of interest that he didn't even bother to try to hide.

All day long, he'd have to look at her like this. See her draped in his clothes. How the hell was he supposed to stand it?

"What?" she asked, pulling his attention from her chest back up to her face. She arched a brow.

He smirked, unashamed to be called out. The way she acted, she could stand to be the subject of some open ogling.

"You're wearing my shirt," he said.

A flicker of uncertainty passed across her eyes, but she lifted her chin and looked at him head-on. "Is that a problem?"

"Only if you expect me to keep my hands off you today."

She flushed, but it was with a pleased little smile playing on her lips. "I wouldn't expect you to keep them to yourself entirely."

"Good." He stalked over to her and bent to place a hard, fast kiss to her lips, hooking a finger into the gap of the shirt and peeking down it. *Delicious.*

Swatting his hand away, she shook her head. Her smile didn't fade, though. "Go get dressed."

"Well, that's no fun," he muttered, but it was getting late. He made his way over to the corner where he'd dropped his bag, considering for a second as he leaned down to paw through its contents. It was slim pickings for five days, especially with how freely she was borrowing from him, but he'd make do. Plus, she probably wouldn't notice if some more clothes magically showed up. He could sneak off to the apartment at some point if he needed to.

Unself-consciously, he dropped the towel from around his hips and shook out a pair of boxers. He was standing with his back to her, and he delighted in the little sound she made as his ass came into view. When he was pretty sure she'd looked her fill, he stepped into his underwear, then picked out a pair of pants. After pulling on a shirt, he sidestepped to check himself over in the mirror on the wall, running a hand through his still-damp hair to mess it up a little.

"Would you like to hear what I had in mind for our outing today?" he asked.

She hesitated. "You really don't have to spend all this time with me. I wasn't expecting..."

Of course she wasn't. He didn't like the note of insecurity in her disclaimer, though. He half twisted around. "Do you not want me to?"

And that wasn't an immediate no forming on her lips.

Huh. He faced the mirror again. "You can have the day to yourself if you want." Annoying, because he'd thought his plan was pretty good, and he wasn't particularly fond of the idea of spending the day alone. Not when there was someone interesting to spend it with.

"I want to get some more drawing done," she said after another brief pause. "But it doesn't have to be today. What were you going to suggest?"

He'd been starting to think she'd literally never ask.

"Well." He fixed the collar of his shirt, then turned around. "Since you're a tortured artist and everything." With a little spring in his step, he threw himself onto the bed, landing on his stomach with his head by her side, his elbows braced beneath himself. The mattress bounced around as he settled, and he laughed at her yelp of surprise as she was jostled. Sneaking in under her arm, he pushed the hem of her—*his*—shirt up and planted a smacking kiss to her side. "What do you say we head up to Montmartre?"

Tugging the shirt back down, she gave him a playful shove. He let her go and twisted around, clambering to sit beside her on the bed, close enough to catch the echoing sweetness of her scent.

"Montmartre, huh?" She reached up, threading her fingers through his hair.

"Sure. See some of Picasso's old haunts, steep ourselves in

what's left of the whole turn-of-the-century art scene. Drink some absinthe. You know, like artists do."

She smiled, a real, nice, genuine smile. "That's actually a really great idea."

"Of course it is. I came up with it." He nipped his way down her neck, sliding an arm around her waist.

Laughing, she leaned into him, and suddenly it wasn't just silliness anymore. They fit together so nicely like this, and his throat got tight.

"Plus," he said. "It's beautiful. All set up on the hill like that. You can walk to the very top, and there's Sacred Heart Basilica. All these gorgeous stained-glass windows. And the view from up there? You can see all of Paris, spread out at your feet."

"Sounds amazing."

"It is."

He wanted to show it to her. Wanted to show her a lot of things, and as he held her closer, it was a little too easy to imagine they were any ordinary couple, heading off to explore the city together.

Dangerous, entertaining thoughts like that. They were only fucking, after all—and they hadn't even gotten around to doing that yet.

Retreating slightly, he cocked one eyebrow in a leer. "Unless you'd prefer to stay in today."

"Nah. Tempting as you are"—she unwrapped her hand from around his neck, sliding it lower, fingertips lingering for a second at the chain where it crossed his collarbone—"daylight's burning. And there's plenty of time for that later." Her voice wavered, and her thumb stroked lower, drifting closer to his father's ring. "Right?"

Instinct had him grabbing her hand, but his rational mind stopped him from pushing her away from the ring. Instead, he lifted her knuckles to his lips, kissing each one in turn. "Plenty," he agreed.

Five more days, he reminded himself.

The golden band against his breastbone felt like a weight.

Five days was more than enough.

Kate didn't think she would ever get enough of Paris.

Rylan was barely hiding the bemusement on his face as she all but skipped along at his side, her hand wrapped around his elbow. She *loved* Montmartre. How much time had she spent studying all the people who had lived and died and loved and painted here? Pablo Picasso and Henri de Toulouse-Lautrec. Renoir and Degas and Van Gogh.

So much must have changed since their time, but the whole place had this feeling to it, like you could picture someone whipping out an easel and a set of paints at any moment. She and Rylan had had brunch in the kind of dingy café she'd always imagined artists sipping coffee in—not one of the fancy ones near the museums down by the Seine. Ducked into little shops and even taken cheesy selfies in front of the Moulin Rouge, and she was bursting. She just wanted to set up shop and draw hungover people in black clothes, smoking cigarettes and talking, forever.

And always, in the background of every one of those scenes would be Rylan. Rylan with his self-satisfied smirk and his fake frown. He liked to stand aside and watch her have her fun, scowling at it all, but she saw through him. He was having fun in spite of himself.

It was sort of strangely adorable. Like a cat who didn't want to admit he loved being petted.

"Okay," she said, putting down a hat she did *not* need to spend any of her dwindling resources on. She tugged at his arm as they set off down the sidewalk again, nudging him until he took his hand from his pocket so she could intertwine their fingers. "You've indulged me all day."

"Really? I hadn't noticed."

She was ignoring that. "So now what do you want to do?"

Suggestiveness colored his tone. "I can think of a couple of things."

She could think of a couple, too. Montmartre had kept the lion's share of her attention today, but it had taken effort not to slip into daydreams about how patiently he'd touched her the night before. Images of those big hands on her breasts and framing her hips. The warm lapping of his tongue...

Blinking, she squeezed his hand harder. "Things you want to do *in Montmartre*," she clarified.

"You're not narrowing it down much."

"Be serious."

"Well, that's no fun." He eyed her legs, but not in quite so suggestive of a manner. "Your feet too tired yet?"

They were, a little, but considering how much walking she'd been doing, that was basically to be expected. "Not too bad. Why?"

He gestured up the hill, and she squinted against the brightness of the sky. "It's a heck of a climb, but it's worth the effort."

She considered. "That's Sacred Heart up there, right?" A big, old, famous church. That didn't sound like something that would be particularly enthralling for him.

"Yup."

"Why do you want to go there?"

"Isn't it on your list of things to see?"

"Yeah, but I asked what *you* want to do."

"I told you." He wasn't looking at her. "I want to show you around town."

"Which you've done. A lot of. There must be something you'd like to do for you."

His mouth settled into the lines of a frown, and he didn't answer for a solid minute. Finally, just when she'd been about to start needling him, he offered, "It's got the best view in the entire city. If we're this close already..." He shrugged. "I'd like to see it. And I'd like to see *you* see it."

"Oh."

And it wasn't lost on her, that half his entertainment really did seem to amount to watching her taking in the city he'd clearly come to know so well. She couldn't pretend she entirely understood it, but she wasn't going to question it anymore.

"All right," she said, looking to cross the street in the direction of the hill. "Let's go."

He yanked her back, chuckling at her as he led her farther down the way. "Lesson one about navigating any European city. The shortest path between two points is never a straight line."

"No?"

"Nope. Gotta go this way."

She was glad he knew where he was going, because by the time they reached the steep stairs heading up, she was out of breath and completely turned around. He slung an arm around her shoulders, tugging her close as they avoided a couple more aggressive street peddlers, deflecting them with his body language and a short burst of annoyed-sounding French. It made a warmth grow in her chest, to have him looking out for her like this.

Working to keep up with him as they ascended, she asked, "How did you get to be such a good tour guide, anyway?"

"Dunno. Just had a lot of time to learn my way around the city. Figured out what my favorite places were and decided to share them." His voice trailed off before he could mention how many people he had shared them with.

And it was funny—she didn't have any illusions that she was the first one he'd given this tour to. He'd taken her to places that had seemed tailored to her tastes, but he was clearly pretty practiced at this whole thing. Hell, he'd basically admitted that his shtick had served him well with women in the past.

Still. Her gaze drifted to the center of his chest, where the drape of his shirt concealed the ring he wore around his neck. Maybe the hitch to his voice as he'd told her about his father had been a part of the act, but she didn't think so. This time they were spending together was only temporary, and she was far from unique. But she had *some* claim on him. Something that set her at least a little bit apart from the rest.

That thought made her bold.

"You know." Glancing at him out of the corner of her eye, she tested the waters. "You never did tell me what brought you here."

He hummed, frowning, and subconsciously or not, picked up the pace at which he climbed. She quickened her own gait, hooking her hand into his belt for something to hold on to.

"What brings anyone to Paris?" he asked after a moment, shrugging and dropping his arm. "Great city, good art, better food. I already knew the language, so I figured why not?"

"Those are all good arguments for Paris," she agreed. She could have let it go there, but she couldn't help pushing. "But you're not from here."

"Nope."

God, this was like pulling teeth. Why the freedom with his story last night and this brush-off today? "So where are you from?"

"New York, originally. The city."

"Is that where your family still lives?"

He shot her a look she couldn't quite decipher. "You know full well my dad's not *living there* anymore."

Yeah, she did know that. Not exactly the most sensitive way she could have phrased it. "Right." She cleared her throat. Tentatively, she prompted, "And your mom...?"

He let out a short bark of a laugh that sounded pained. "Who knows? Could be in New York. Could be in Argentina or Shanghai, for all I know."

Casting a glance over his shoulder, he sped his pace even more as they passed a clump of slow-moving tourists, and dammit all. This hill was *steep*, and his legs were a hell of a lot longer than hers. The bastard didn't even seem out of breath.

"Jesus," she finally said, giving up. She let her hand slip from his waist as they hit another set of stairs, not even caring that the family they'd just passed would now have to get around them. Her thighs burned, and she grabbed her chest, winded. "What the hell are you running from?"

All at once, he froze. And she almost missed it. The way

his eyes widened and his mask of casual flirtatiousness evaporated, leaving this wretched, surprised expression. Betrayal and hurt, and...she didn't even know what. As fast as it had appeared, it retreated, and he blinked a couple of times, brows furrowing. "Excuse me?" he asked.

What the hell? She just wanted to know why he was walking so damn fast, and...

And then it struck her all at once. She'd been needling him and needling him, and without even meaning to, she'd tripped right over the truth.

He was here, in Paris, thousands of miles from home, avoiding her questions about his life *because he was running away*. From what, she couldn't guess, but from something. Something big.

She swallowed hard, and her voice cracked. "Literally. I meant, literally."

"Oh."

The grin she'd been waiting for made a valiant attempt at surfacing on his face but ultimately couldn't quite seem to manage it. Looking away from him, she put her hands on her knees, hunching over to take a few good deep breaths. Silence hung over them, low and sticky like the air felt after their uphill jog. When she dared glance up at him again, he was leaning against a railing, arms crossed in front of him.

And clearly determined to ignore everything he'd unwittingly revealed in the last few minutes.

"You good?" he asked. And he didn't sound distant, precisely. Just guarded in a way he hadn't been. It felt more like the show he'd been putting on that first day, picking her up and buying her coffee and trying to be so debonair.

Trying and succeeding.

She nodded, standing up straight again. "Yeah. I'm fine. So long as you don't do your Road Runner thing and take off on me again."

"I'll try to restrain myself."

Ignoring the group of people currently passing them, he held out his arm to her, and she slipped her hand into the crook of his elbow. He felt warm and solid and dependable.

It was deceiving. How many times had her mother told her—you could never really trust a man. Especially not one that could do better than you. She swallowed hard. It didn't matter how open Rylan seemed sometimes. This was a man who wasn't telling her everything.

Arm in arm, and at a much more reasonable pace this time, they set off up the hill again. They talked idly about the things they passed and how far it still looked to the top, but it was superficial, allowing a wide berth around whatever they'd nearly stumbled into a few moments before.

She kind of hated it.

Finally, after what felt like forever, the stairs gave way, and he steered her to the right.

And suddenly her feet didn't hurt and her lungs didn't burn. "Wow," she murmured absently.

"Told you."

He hadn't been lying. The basilica itself stood off to the side, but it barely fazed her, because they were on the top of the world, the sky was blue, and all of Paris lay beneath their feet.

"Come on."

Taking her hand, he wandered through the crowd, somehow managing to find a clear place against the railing to look out over it all. Urging her to stand flush against the fence, he stepped in behind her, hooking his chin over her shoulder, his chest warm against her spine.

"Do you have a camera?" she asked. If she'd known this was going to be so spectacular, she would have insisted on going to her hostel first so she could grab hers.

"Don't worry about it." He shook his head and held her closer. "We'll worry about it later. For now, just enjoy it."

Her breath caught in her throat. She wanted some images to remember this moment by, but also to use as references for paintings she might do someday. But what was the point of remembering a moment she was too busy recording to be a part of?

She needed to soak this in.

Fact was, she had a lot of things to worry about. Between the progress she'd been hoping to make with her art and the decisions facing her as soon as she got home and all these twisty-turny feelings Rylan was awakening in her . . . her head and heart were more than full with troubles.

But then something happened. He rubbed her hand and stroked his fingers up and down her side, the steady rhythm of his breathing making the noise of her thoughts and the rest of the world die down. Just a little bit. Just enough for a warmth to replace them. For her to give in to being surrounded by so much beauty.

They stood there together a long, quiet time before he squeezed her close and pressed his lips to her temple.

"There are a lot of reasons why I'm here, in Paris." His voice was gruff, but it was honest. "Not all of them are the best reasons. But what matters—what I prefer to think about—is that I am here. In this moment, in this spot." He bent to place a soft, more lingering kiss against her cheek, then whispered beside her ear, "With you."

Just like that, the wariness she'd donned like armor mere minutes ago faded away, his words worming their way past her defenses. She didn't even care that it was a line. It didn't sound rehearsed. It sounded true.

And in that instant, that was all that mattered to her, too.

chapter TEN

Rylan was a bastard. First, for misleading Kate about where he came from in the first place. Second, for being so damn evasive all afternoon—for keeping his cards so close to his chest every time she asked him about his past. He'd given enough away already, but the details she seemed so eager to ferret out of him were getting too real. This had become a vacation for him, too, a respite from the tedium he'd settled into. A chance to not have to think about all the things he'd left behind.

Third and finally, he was a kinky motherfucker of a bastard for what he was about to do right now.

"Come on," he said, guiding her with a hand at the small of her back. They'd reversed their trip up to the top of Sacre Coeur and were down in Montmartre proper again, which she had loved. But she hadn't seen all of it yet.

"Where are we going?" She laughed, a high, warm sound that he was glad to hear again after everything had gotten so serious there for a bit. She'd better still be laughing when she saw where they were going next.

"You'll see."

It was a subtle transition, the way all the kitschy shops and little cafés gave way to the area's red-light district. The first couple of places they passed with dildos in the window, she didn't even seem to notice.

But then her steps slowed and her eyes narrowed.

"Rylan," she said, all warning.

Damn, he was a bastard. And this was going to be way too much fun.

"You know what brought Toulouse-Lautrec to Montmartre, right?"

"This isn't funny."

"Whores, dancing girls. It's part of the experience."

"Rylan!"

"What do you think the Moulin Rouge was? A nursery school?"

"That's not why I wanted to come here."

"I know it's not." He pulled out the trump card he'd been saving. "But you did ask me—repeatedly, if I might add—what I was getting out of this trip."

"I'm not going into a—a *brothel*."

He put on an expression of mock offense. "Of course you're not." They'd started moving forward again in spite of her misgivings, and—perfect. He stopped and put his arm out, gesturing to just the place he'd been planning to bring her. "You're going into a sex shop. Totally different."

"I don't want to—"

"But I do." He leaned in close, and she might be angry, but she didn't flinch away. "I want to buy you a present, and then tonight I want to show you how to use it." He let his arousal at the thought seep into his voice. "I want to find out how many times you can go before you beg me to stop."

She drew back, and her face bloomed tomato red. But she put her hands on her hips, a defiant set to the angle of her chin. She looked around. Made sure they were alone before she choked out, "I know how to use a—a—" She lowered voice comically. "A *vibrator*."

Well, color him surprised. "You do?"

"Of course I do." She glanced over her shoulder again, looking uncomfortable but in a different way. She leaned closer, still keeping her voice down. "I *told* you. No guy has ever managed to. You know."

"Make you come?"

God, he could feel the heat coming off her face from here. But her silence was her agreement. "So..."

"So?"

"*So* a girl has needs."

"Never doubted it." He'd been pretty sure she knew what an orgasm felt like, considering the way she'd arched into his touch and bucked against his tongue. Just the idea of her reaching between her legs and sating that ache had him hardening. The image of her doing it with a little mechanical assistance had him ready to pull her into an alley right here and now.

But he had patience. Not much of it, but enough.

He raised an eyebrow in challenge. "What I doubt is that you have any idea how to tell a man what those needs are. Which is why"—he stepped to the side and opened the door to the shop—"we are going to practice."

She looked from the open door to him and back again, but her feet seemed glued to the ground. After what felt like an eternity of indecision, her flush deepened to the point where he was actually starting to worry she might blow. But just when he was half expecting her to go running for the Metro without him, she crossed her arms over her chest. "Fine."

With that, she stormed into the store, and damn. He liked it when she got all fired up. Chuckling to himself and shaking his head, he followed in after her and let the door fall closed behind them.

Inside, the place was well lit. There were some racy images on the walls, and all the shelves were lined with books and DVDs and toys, but it wasn't the typical place people imagined perverts in trench coats sneaking into to find material for jerking off. Only a handful of people were browsing, but more of them were women than men. Hopefully, that would set Kate at ease.

He picked up a basket and nodded at the girl behind the counter before wandering over to where Kate was standing, eyeing a display of glass dildos.

"Pretty, aren't they?" He picked up a bulbous one with red swirls and put his lips close to her ear. "Wonder what this one would feel like inside of you?"

She squirmed. "Sounds cold."

"It would be." He set it down. "But that's half the fun." Grabbing one still in its packaging, he placed it in his basket.

She put her hand on his arm. He opened his mouth, ready to argue for why this was a good idea, why he'd love to rub this up and down her slit and watch it slip inside. But in the end, all she did was lift it out and replace it with a slimmer, purple one.

He practically swallowed his tongue. "Good choice."

She hummed, walking past him to keep looking around.

While she was doing her own perusing, he grabbed a bullet that looked interesting and considered picking up some lube, but that seemed a little presumptuous. Maybe next time.

When he caught up with her again, she had the package for a mini-wand-type thing in her hands.

"Find something good?"

She startled but didn't lose it on him again. She added it to their purchases with a shrug. "Travel-sized version of one I know I like."

"Smart thinking." He gestured at the rest of the store. "Anything else that gets your motor running?" Speaking of which, they had to stop for some batteries, too. "Handcuffs? Whips? Porn?"

"No, thank you."

Fine by him.

Up at the front counter, he paid for everything in cash, keeping his open wallet out of her view. He waved her off when she tried to contribute. "It was my idea," he insisted.

"Fine. But I'm getting dinner tonight."

He rearranged his mental list of places he'd been thinking about suggesting for the evening. "Fair enough." He twirled the box for the wand she'd picked in his hand. "And then, after, *dessert* is on me."

Kate stood before the mirror in the hotel room. *Their* hotel room. She swallowed hard, watching the way her throat moved in the foggy glass.

Except for a towel, she was naked.

After they'd gone into that store of his, they'd had a simple dinner, then swung by her hostel to check her out and grab her things. They'd been banal enough activities, but static had crackled in their air between them with every step, anticipation a hot, heavy thing in the hollow of her abdomen.

The previous night, she'd had a sense of where things might be going, but tonight, the whole way back, she'd *known*. He would strip her clothes off and put his mouth to her skin. Run those warm, careful fingers of his along the swells of her breasts and hips, dip them into the secret places she rarely showed to anyone. Her whole spine tingled, lit up with an equal mix of nerves and thrill.

He'd probably expect to have sex tonight. After he'd been so patient with her yesterday, how could he not? She still wasn't so sure how she felt about letting him do that to her, but had been psyching herself up for it as they'd walked through the door.

Before he could start turning her to mush with little kisses up and down her neck, though, she'd broken away, insisting on a shower. Alone. If he was planning to be putting his mouth on her again—especially *there*, she wanted to be clean for him. And besides, she'd needed time to get her head on straight.

She'd stayed under the spray for as long as she'd dared. It still hadn't been enough.

Picking up her brush, she focused her attention on the tangles in her hair. Her chest and face were flushed from the steam, and little beads of water still clung to her throat and the tops of her breasts. Setting the brush aside, she pushed the damp strands of her hair behind her shoulder. Grazed the tips of her fingers over her clavicle, letting her own touch linger.

Her anxiety was high, but she couldn't deny it. She'd never felt so *sexual* before. She wanted this. And she just had to trust: If she were in Rylan's hands...somehow, she'd be all right.

Before she could change her mind, she opened the door to the bathroom and walked out.

Rylan sat on the bed, elbows braced on his knees. He'd stripped off his jacket and his button-down, leaving him in an undershirt and jeans. Behind him, the covers had been turned back and a handful of pillows had been arranged as a cushion against the headboard.

His head snapped up as she emerged from behind the doorframe, and his gaze raked up and down her body. He licked his lips. "Feel better?"

"Yeah. Much." She fought to keep her hands at her side. Not to reach up and fidget with her towel or hold it more securely across her breasts.

"Good." He rose and strode forward to meet her, stopping shy of pulling her into an embrace. With one hand, he traced the edge of her face, then down over her shoulder, to the place where the towel gapped over the center of her chest. He didn't pull at it, though. Didn't move to reveal her any further. "You look edible."

A full-body shudder moved through her. "You look good, too." He always did.

And there was that smirk. "Go." He gestured to the bed. "Lie down."

He stroked her cheek again, then moved toward the chair near the entryway to pick up the bag from the sex store. Her face heated, but she didn't comment. As he took their purchases with him to the bathroom, she turned to face the bed, ignoring that he was washing them up and probably filling them with batteries.

She still wasn't exactly sure what he planned to do with those things. She hadn't been lying when she'd said she had some experience with them. Her roommate her junior year of college had spoken about her vibrators rhapsodically and had been shocked when Kate had confessed to not knowing anything about them. At the time, she'd been involved with Aaron, so she hadn't really thought much of it. He hadn't ever succeeded in getting her off, but they only spent the night together a few times a week. She'd been able to find time to...attend to her needs when he hadn't been around. But the idea of actually going so far as to procure sex toys had felt a little too much like admitting defeat.

After he'd fessed up to everything—after she'd walked away—defeat had pretty much been the order of the day.

Her first attempt at ordering a vibrator would probably have been comical if it hadn't been so mortifying. After going back and forth on it a hundred times, though, she'd finally settled on one and clicked "buy" before she could stop herself. The thing had come in a plain brown package a few days later, and when her roommate had been gone, she'd locked the doors and turned on some music. And proceeded to have the best orgasm of her life.

Until last night.

Combining Rylan's unnatural understanding of her body and the power of a couple of double A's very well might kill her. Still, it was with reluctance that she clambered onto the bed. Her small, carefully chosen collection of little mechanical friends wasn't something she talked about, much less shared with anyone else. She kept them hidden in pouches, tucked under pajamas and respectable novels and anything else she could toss into her nightstand drawer to make sure no one would ever find them. Rylan might act like they were no big deal, but to her, they'd always been a shameful secret— like the idea that she ever touched herself at all.

In the other room, the sound of the water running cut off. Showtime. Keeping the towel wrapped around her, she settled herself gingerly on the bed, pulling the sheet up to her waist. Was it too awkward to lie back against the mound of pillows he'd created? Should she have dried her hair?

Before she could obsess too much or work herself up, Rylan reemerged from the bathroom. "Comfy?" he asked, tilting his head to the side.

No. "Yup."

The corner of his mouth crept upward, showing just how little he believed her, but he didn't call her on it. Instead, he crossed the room to her. Pushing the covers down partway, he spread a towel on the mattress beside her, then laid out the things he'd decided they should buy. Everything about his demeanor was practical and casual, as if this were something normal people did every day.

Her breathing sped a hair faster. Maybe this was something *he* did every day.

"Hey."

She looked up at him. Felt the warmth of his touch against her bare arm, and it helped relax her, pulling her down from the edge of neuroticism she'd been in danger of going over. The best she could, she pushed her worries and fears aside. Yes, this kind of stuff made her nervous and embarrassed. Yes, Rylan had a lot more experience than she did. But that was okay. He knew what he was getting into. And through everything they'd done together, he'd never seemed to mind having to take the lead before.

Letting out a long, deep sigh, she put her hand over his and gave him a weak smile. "Sorry. Just nervous."

He leaned in to kiss the point of her shoulder. "Don't be. Only good things are going to happen here."

Right. It was hard to believe after all the ways she'd been beaten down, but Rylan hadn't given her any reason not to trust him yet. "Okay."

"Here." He nudged at her. "Scoot forward a bit."

She rearranged herself at his direction, only realizing as he climbed onto the bed that he was maneuvering to sit behind her.

"Aren't you going to—?" She cut herself off.

"Hmm?"

He had taken off his socks and shoes, but other than that, he was still basically dressed.

"I—" God, why was this all so hard for her to talk about? "I don't want to be the only one who's naked."

He laughed, but not in a mean way. He ran a fingertip along the edge of the towel where it stretched between her shoulder blades. "You're not naked yet."

"I might as well be."

"Fine, fine." He tugged his undershirt off and stood to take off his pants. He still had his boxers on, though, as he settled in behind her again.

"What about—?"

"In a minute." Once he'd gotten himself arranged, he pulled her in against his chest. She sat in the V of his legs, awkwardly reclining with her spine to his front, unsure what she was safe to lean against. He made a little groan when she tried to relax into him, and heat seared through her. There he was—the hard line of him pressed against the small of her back. "See?" he said, rubbing his hands up and down her arms. "If I take everything off, I'm going to be right there." He tilted his hips forward, dropping his voice. "And I don't think either of us is ready for that."

She certainly wasn't, but feeling him there, knowing he was erect and so close—it made a fresh, new wave of heat roll through her body. His chest was broad and firm beneath her, his hands so sure in their strokes. He smelled good and sounded good, and she had him for only so long, but he was here for her. He wanted *her*.

With a quivering breath, she closed her eyes.

"That's right," he said as she relaxed. "That's beautiful."

Drawing his fingertips in expanding circles, over her arms and up her torso, across the naked swaths of skin above the cover of the towel, he leaned in. His mouth was hot and wet against her neck, and he had to know what this was doing to her. As she slowly lost the tension she'd been carrying, a new one settled in its place, but instead of nerves, it was all desire. Her skin felt like it was humming, unnaturally sensitive to every stroke of his hands and lips. Between her legs, a deep ache settled in, liquid flowing, making her feel warm and ripe and glowing.

"That's perfect," he murmured. "Let me make you feel good."

She didn't know how long she lay against him like that, letting him touch and trace. When it started to become too much, she shifted, pressing her thighs together, but it didn't help. He made a sound low in his chest and, pausing for just a second, let his hands drift lower. Through the towel, he caressed her breasts and her sides, then down. Gliding warm hands over her hips and the tops of her thighs, but bypassing the needy center of her. After a few passes, her attention all seemed to be focusing there, the one place he refused to touch, and a worry flickered deep in her belly.

Would he make her say it out loud? Make her ask, or worse, beg?

A gasp of a whine escaped her lips, and it made him press harder, cupping her with more eager hands.

All at once, it struck her—he wasn't the only one who could move here.

As if her arms had suddenly come unfrozen, she reached one up, tangling her fingers in his hair. She craned her head to the side as she pulled him down, and when their lips met, it was with a crush of heat and need. He parted for her, pressing forward with his tongue and letting hers in beside it. He tasted like sex, and he made her *feel* like sex, heady and powerful and reeling.

Breathless, she pulled away for air, but it was only to have her lungs seize in her chest. His index finger played over the stretch of skin right above where her towel was tucked, teasing at the terry cloth.

"Can I?"

He sounded as lost in this as she was, as turned on and wanting. She tilted her head up, stretching her neck to sip from his lips one more time. Her heart thundering against her rib cage, she released the kiss and moved so she could look into his eyes.

Her voice seemed to echo in the room. "Yes."

chapter ELEVEN

It was all Rylan could do to keep his movements even and slow, building up the anticipation as he unwrapped Kate like a gift. She'd been so squirrelly about letting him see her really naked the night before, and those hints of uncertainty still lingered in the way she braced herself.

Fear had no place in his bed. He was going to have to teach her that. Again.

Leaving one hand on her cheek to keep her angled toward his mouth, he worked the other one under the fabric of her towel. The cloth gave way with the slightest nudge, going loose across her breasts, and he closed his eyes as he nipped at her lips. He was hard as diamond against her spine, and he needed to pace himself if he was going to make this good.

It was the work of a moment to get himself back under control. Gently, carefully, he peeled one side of the towel away, and then the other. Her breathing picked up as he revealed her. With the lightest touch, he traced his fingertips through the valley of her breasts. Her skin was so smooth, water-warm from her shower, a delight against his palm as he let it graze across her nipple. A high-pitched little noise leaked from her lips at the touch. He left her wanting, though, drifting lower, down the soft planes of her abdomen.

Just before he reached her cunt, he paused. She'd been so wet last night, so sweet against his tongue, and he wanted to feel that again. But he had a game plan for tonight.

He let his other hand slide from her face, teasing the line of her throat before grazing lower. Overlooking the way she tensed, he parted his lips from hers, opening his eyes and shifting to look down the length of her body where it was splayed out before them.

The sheet lay across her thighs, barely obscuring the sweet, dark triangle of her pussy from his view, but the rest of her was entirely on display. And what a sight it was.

Her breasts weren't large, but they were soft and round, her nipples a dusky rose, hard and pointed where they peaked. He drew his hands back up her body to cup the fullness of those curves.

"Do you like that?" he asked as she shivered.

She nodded, but was squirming. Uncomfortable, and he had to remind himself that he was trying to show her something here.

"Has anyone ever done this before? Given this much attention to just touching you?"

"No."

"Idiots." There were treasures here—pleasures so much greater than a quick come in a warm hole. But here was the real question. "Did you ever ask them to?"

She laughed, and it was a sad thing that made his frustration boil even hotter.

"You've been sleeping with idiots," he repeated. He kissed the shell of her ear, wet and slow. "Here's the trick. You can get a man to do all kinds of things. But you have to tell him what you want."

Uncertain silence met him at that. It was no surprise, but it still bothered him.

"Come on," he said, more taunting. "You never miss a chance to give me a hard time. What's holding you back now? You can tell me you want me to suck on your tits." He said it as crudely as he could think to, and the way her throat moved, the way her spine pressed against where he was still so damn hard for her confirmed that it had been the right move. "Or touch your cunt."

Her hips tilted forward at that, and she shifted, like she was trying to cross her legs, and no. There wasn't going to be any of that. In a deft maneuver, he hooked his ankles over hers, holding her open.

"Don't close up for me now," he murmured. With a last stroke of his thumbs across her nipples, he dropped his hands to her thighs, running them up and down the smooth flesh, nudging the sheet lower with every pass until he could see everything. He edged higher, slipped his fingers along the creases where torso met leg, so close to where she wanted him—so close to where he wanted to be.

"Why are you so afraid of this?" he asked.

"Not afraid." She could have fooled him. Her voice shook with it.

"No? You could barely even admit to me that you'd gotten yourself off before. Still can't tell me what you want me to do to you." And he was getting into dangerous territory here, he knew. "Those other men. The ones who never made you come. Could you tell them what to do?"

She shook her head, but there was something anguished about it. "This isn't as easy for everybody else as it is for you. Girls, we—" She cut herself off.

"What?" He gave her a second to finish her thought, but when she didn't he could guess where she was going with it. "What? You don't want to seem easy? Or like you know what you're doing? Well, let me assure you." He dragged his hands all the way up her body again, over her breasts and then down to hover once again above her cunt. "There is nothing sexier than a woman who knows what she wants. *Nothing.*"

"But—" The words sounded choked. "I can't."

Couldn't what? Talk about it?

And then it occurred to him—the most brilliant idea he'd ever had. His cock throbbed at the thought of it. He moved his right hand to put it on top of hers. Lifted them both and brought them to her thigh.

His throat bobbed. "Can you show me?"

Kate felt all the blood drain from her face.

She was so tangled up—on a knife's edge of arousal, confused and mortified, and he was challenging her in all these different ways. In her head, she knew she should be fine with this. A woman should stand up for herself, should stick up for herself in bed and anywhere else.

And deep down below that, she was a writhing mass of insecurities and shame. She didn't want to have to ask for things. Asking meant opening yourself up to being told no, to being told you weren't good enough, didn't deserve it.

God, there was that voice in her head again. The one that had haunted her all her life.

Only Rylan spoke over it, drowning it out. He pressed her hand closer to the center of her need. "I want you to show me what you like."

He chased away one kind of doubt, leaving her with just the one.

She didn't know how to let him see her like this.

"But—" She curled her fingers into her palm, resisting. "You know how to—" *How to make me come.*

He'd done it last night. Why was he putting her through this?

"Yeah, I do. And I could do it right now, but I'd rather do this."

"Why?"

"Why?" He skated his other hand down her thigh. "Because it turns me on. Because I still have things to learn for the next time I eat your pussy out." He exhaled, breath hot against her ear. "Because I want you to be able to do this for the next man you meet who wouldn't know his way to a woman's clit if he had a map."

Of course. She was only here for a handful of days, and then she'd never see him again. She'd known that from the very start, had actually seen it as a positive. As an excuse to let go. And yet to hear him put it so plainly took her breath away, a sharp sudden pang.

She pushed the thought away, but it wouldn't loosen its hold. No matter how little time they had together, right now he was here. With her.

And she wanted nothing more than to be closer.

"Can we..." She twisted, craning her neck to look at him. He gripped her hip, as if trying to stop her—as if he thought she were trying to escape. "The towel," she said. Trying to explain.

If she could feel the heat of his skin, maybe it would ground her. Keep her in the moment, this tiny pocket of time when it was just him and her.

"Of course."

She gulped. "And your boxers?"

"You sure?" he asked after a brief pause.

She considered it. Yeah, she was certain. "Yes."

"All right."

She sat up and away from his body long enough for them to get the towel out of the way, and for him to tug his underwear off. When he pulled her back against him, into the cradle of his thighs, all she could feel was warm, firm flesh beneath her, and it made her pulse hotter. The wiry hair of his legs and chest tickled her. And the smooth, silky line of him, bare and damp against her spine lit her up from the inside.

"Fuck," he said, a low breath against her ear as she settled against him. "Someday..."

Her breath caught. "Someday what?"

"Someday," he continued, grasping her wrist, curling her fingers and bringing them, this time, unerringly to her sex. "When you're ready..."

The first brush of her own hand against her folds was electric. God, she was soaked, and it was such a relief to finally get some pressure there, where she was slick and hot and aching.

Still, something deep inside of her told her this was wrong. She tried to pull her hand away, but he gripped her palm, and when she didn't delve any deeper into her pleasure, he took the initiative. Fingertips covering hers, he slid them around in the liquid, sending a low, rolling wave of pleasure up her spine.

With his other hand, he cupped her breast, teasing at the peak, and she gasped. She'd never known her nipples were so sensitive, but he'd spent so much time working them up before. There was a rawness to the sensation now as he twisted and squeezed. The scrape of a nail across the tip had her shifting her own hand against her sex, needing something, anything to push against her clit.

"That's right, beautiful." His voice dropped a level as he praised her, and that made a whole fresh wave of need surge through her.

God. What was she doing?

Unable to take it anymore, she let out a sound that was half a sob as she started touching herself in earnest. It felt good—it felt amazing.

And then he was *talking*. "Someday," he resumed, still caging her hand against her sex, still pulling sparks of desire from her breast, "when you're ready, I'm going to strip you down, just like this. Open you up and put your legs over my shoulders. I'm going to lick you out for *hours*."

Damn. Oh, damn. She rubbed harder at her clit, losing herself in it.

"But I'm not gonna give you my fingers. Not gonna give you anything to fill that ache inside. Leave you all empty and coming around nothing until you're dying for it. Do you want that? Do you feel how bad you want to be filled up?"

She *did*. It was a hollow deep inside, and she didn't want to come like this, no matter how close she was.

"Yeah," she groaned.

"Don't you want something in that pretty little pussy while I lick you?"

"*Yes.*" So badly. She pressed harder, fingers working furiously against herself even as she shied away from the abyss that was yawning at her feet.

His hand dropped from her breast, and all she could hear was the slick sounds of her body, embarrassing, horrible, but it felt too good. She couldn't stop.

Not even when he took her other hand in his. Wrapped it around something long and cool and smooth.

"What—" She snapped her eyes open to see the glass toy they'd purchased there inside her grasp.

Another new level of mortification rose up, choking her, but it didn't matter. She wanted it. Wanted him to make her feel like this.

"Come on," he urged. "It's gonna feel so good. It's gonna *look* so good. Don't you know how pretty this is going to be inside of you?" At her shaky exhale, his voice deepened further. "Can't you feel how hard I am, just thinking about filling you up?"

Her focus shifted in an instant, forgetting the toy and the thrumming need in her own sex, because, God, yes, he was. His cock pressed into her back, unyielding in its desire. Long and thick, and she could have that. Inside her. All she had to do was ask him for it.

She bit off a curse, not even resisting when he curled his fingers more firmly around hers, solidifying her grip on the glass. Bringing it down to that sweltering need between her legs. And he was the one to press it just between her lips.

Making her. He was making her do this, even though she was willing, and that idea lit a match of need so hot it burned.

Fingers twitching, she helped him aim it, getting it directed into place.

"Do you want me to fill you, sweetheart?"

She clenched her eyes shut tight. "Yes."

The glass felt even colder as it pressed inside, and her body opened, welcoming it, and she moaned aloud. The emptiness was gone, even though it wasn't what she really wanted. Cold and fake, and she longed for hot flesh. For his weight on top of her, pushing her into the mattress. Making her take it.

His voice was liquid sin against her ear. "Someday. Before you go. Before I have to give you up." She whined, that sharp edge of a pang cutting into her again at the thought. But he kept her close, his own breath catching as if it pained him as much as her. He clutched her tight. "After I've made you come a hundred times with my tongue, I'm going to lay you out. And I'm going to be so hard for you. Just *aching* for this sweet little cunt."

He flexed his hips against her backside, sliding roughly against her skin, and letting out a shaking groan of his own.

"Just the way you're fucking yourself with this," he said, thrusting the toy inside. "I'm going to fuck you. I'm going to get so deep inside you."

"Please—"

He pressed something else into her other hand, and she was so far gone it took her a second to recognize the vibrator they'd bought. Breathing hard, she curled her fingers around the handle. With a flick of his wrist he turned it on, helping her to get it right against her clit.

Everything in her leapt to life. It was perfect, hard and rumbly and turning the sweet pulses of pleasure into something overwhelming in their intensity. Together, they bore down, to the point where she wasn't sure who was doing what, only that she was so close and needed to get there. Needed—

He thrust the toy into her harder. His voice needy and rough, "I can't wait to come inside you."

She held her breath. Tensed every muscle and pressed her face into his neck. Pushed down harder with the toy, and—

Her climax tore through her, dark and vibrant all at once, sweeping her along into a cocoon of ecstasy she'd never imagined before. Her throat hurt, and there was screaming, his name and God's, and her whole body sang as she arched, head dropping back. Wave after wave, and he held her through it all.

After what felt like eternity, the pulses started to dim. She fumbled, trying to turn the toy off, and eventually she managed. His hands had shifted, one still keeping the glass held deep within her, while with the other he grasped her hip, and— Oh.

His breath was still coming in harsh rasps as he pulled her more tightly against him. His hot length slipped and skidded over her skin, and her belly dipped. Maybe he'd take her like this someday, her on his lap. He'd be buried deep inside of her, helping her ride him, touching her clit and her breasts, and she *wanted* that.

She reached a hand back, grabbing his hair as she twisted, pulling him down into a fiery kiss.

"I'm going to—" he panted.

Against her mouth, he groaned, and everything went slick against her spine. Deep within, she throbbed, aftershocks trembling their way through her as he came on her skin, painting it with his release.

For a long moment, he stayed there, trembling and tense, pulsing weakly as he clutched her close. Finally, he sighed, lips going slack. He pulled away, kissed her temple and eased the body-warm glass from her sex.

It left her feeling empty, but not unpleasantly so. How could it, after what he had given her?

After what he had shown her how to do?

And yet, as he held her, wrapping both arms around her chest, he was the one to murmur, "Thank you."

Shaking, she curled her hands around his forearms. Wonder pounded through her, the way arousal had moments before.

"No," she said, the words choked. "Thank you."

chapter TWELVE

Another day, another museum.

Rylan gazed at the painting in front of him, trying to come up with something insightful to say about it. His mother had given him some of the language to talk about art, but he was drawing a blank now. Of course. If only he'd known back when he was a kid that he was actually going to need that kind of stuff someday.

He snuck a glance to the side. After more than a little cajoling, Kate had consented to spend the day with him again. It burned him that he'd had to dangle a visit to the Musée d'Orsay in front of her to get her to agree. He was pretty sure he'd paid for the pleasure of her company in orgasms the night before, but apparently, that wasn't valuable enough of currency for her. What she really wanted was Monet and Van Gogh.

He didn't mind, exactly, but there was still something petty niggling at the edges of his thoughts. Like he was torn between loving how she got so *into* all this modern art stuff and being annoyed that she was scarcely paying attention to him. He frowned. Even more annoying was that her preoccupation bothered him at all.

She was staring at a different piece, her head tilted to the side, and he could just about *see* all the art history knowledge running through her head. She took a small step back and into a beam of light streaming in from the window. It made her hair glow, and God. He really *really* wished he had something intelligent to say.

He straightened his shoulders, shaking off the plaintive, insufferable tone to his own internal monologue. Ridiculous. His mother wasn't the only one who'd taught him anything, and there was more than one way to get a conversation going. His father had instilled in him that much.

People loved to talk about the subjects that interested them—whether or not the people they were talking at knew a goddamn thing.

Biting the bullet, he sidled over to stand beside her, and nudged her with his elbow. "So. Teach me about art."

Tearing her gaze from the painting she'd been staring at, she raised an eyebrow at him.

Right. Because she always saw through him.

Speaking slowly, voice colored by both distraction and skepticism, she asked, "What do you want to know?"

He shrugged. He had to do better if he wanted her to actually talk to him. "Everything. Teach me about..." He squinted at the placard on the wall. "Eugène Boudin."

The thing that killed him was, he did actually want to know. Maybe not about Eugène Boudin in particular, but about why she looked at the picture the way she did. What drew her in about all this Impressionism and Cubism and Fauvism?

"Funny." Her tone was desert dry. "The man who paraded me around the Louvre showing off his favorite painting is looking for an art lesson now?"

"I'm serious." More serious than he'd realized a couple of minutes ago. And besides... "I may know the Louvre pretty well, but—" The next words took him by surprise. He cleared his throat to hide his pause. "Mother never really cared all that much for this place."

If she caught his hesitation, she ignored it in favor of her incredulity. She flung her arm out as if to encompass the museum as a whole. "Who doesn't care for *this*?"

She had a point. The building was gorgeous, with warm light pouring in from all the windows, and the statuary and paintings were undeniably masterpieces.

He shrugged, sorry he'd brought it up. "It was still the 'new museum' when I was a child. Mother was more interested in showing us the classics."

She'd appreciated modern art as much as any cultured woman of her social status should. Hell, she'd let that interior designer fill her apartment with the stuff. But it was the work of the old masters that made her seem alive.

Made her eyes light up, the way her husband and children so rarely seemed to manage to.

Of course, what Kate latched onto after all of that was "'Us'?"

"Me and my brother and sister." The Bellamy children. Something in the back of his throat tasted sour.

She pursed her lips. "I didn't know you had siblings."

"We're all scattered. Doing our own things." He'd scarcely spoken to either of them since the trial.

"Let me guess. You're the oldest?"

"Guilty as charged."

"You were probably super bossy, too."

That made him grin. "There I plead the fifth."

"Uh-huh." She leaned in closer to inspect a corner of the painting, and he half thought she'd decided to drop it. But then she turned to him, arms crossed over her chest. "You never volunteer anything, do you?"

He frowned. "Excuse me?"

"Every time it's your turn to talk about yourself, you answer questions. Barely. But you never offer anything."

Her accusation took him off guard.

He'd volunteered plenty, their first couple of days. He'd shown her that painting and told her about his childhood visits to the Louvre. About his father's ring.

He'd volunteered things he'd never volunteered before.

And besides. "This all started with *me* asking *you* to tell me more about what we were looking at."

It had started with a question he hadn't even cared about until it had come out of his mouth.

"But it evolved into us talking about your family. Or at least me trying to."

She wasn't wrong, but nothing about it seemed fair. "So you can be evasive and I can't?"

"I wasn't being evasive. I was just trying to figure out what you wanted."

"To get to know you." He spat it. "Is that such a crime?" He heard what he'd said—heard the hypocrisy in it about a second after it was out in the air. He tried to backtrack, spinning wildly. "That's not the same thing at all. Stories about dead artists versus my whole..." *Clusterfuck of a family.* He was practically pleading now. "It's not the same."

"If you can't tell me anything about who you are, then what are we even—" She cut herself off, eyes shuttering. He'd never seen her so pissed off before, and a ball of dread formed in his stomach when she waved a hand at him and turned, heading toward a sculpture on the other side of the room.

It left him alone, standing there beside a fucking Eugène Boudin, watching her walk away from him. An instinct surged up, telling him *fine*. If she wanted to be like that, what did he care? It was only a matter of time until she walked away in any case. If not now, in the middle of a museum, it would be in a matter of days, disappearing behind airport security, never to be heard from again.

But...but...

Fuck.

Forgetting the people surrounding them, he jogged across the gallery. Came up behind her and took her shoulders in his hands, spinning her around until they were face to face. She gazed at him expectantly, like everything that would happen after this point revolved around what he said now.

Maybe he should cut his losses and go. There were a hundred other women just like her, tourists on their own in a beautiful city, waiting to be shown a good time.

Only none of them were her. None of them would see through all his lines or make him work so hard for it. None would come to him so innocent and yet so fiery. She was the one he wanted to give up his empty days to walk around museums with, and take to quirky restaurants, and kiss and touch. The one he wanted to spread out naked on his bed.

"My name is Rylan Bellamy," he said, and it was the truth.

But like everything he'd told her this week, it was only a partial truth, and the part he didn't say burned. He'd been going by his middle name since college—had settled on changing it the day his father sent in his acceptance letter for him. As if choosing his name were any kind of substitute for choosing his fate. He hadn't offered the rest of it to anyone in years.

But now it rose up in his throat, that monstrosity he'd been saddled with at birth. That weight that had been placed on his shoulders, that had determined his path for his entire life.

Theodore Rylan Bellamy III.

Somehow, withholding it from her felt like a lie.

He darted his gaze up to her face, searching for any sign she'd caught him in it. But her mouth was a flat line, her eyes impassive and impatient. She was still waiting. He needed to give her more.

Right. She'd been asking him about his family.

He took a deep breath. "I'm the oldest of three children. My sister, Lexie, is three years younger than me. She's finishing business school, and she's going to take over the goddamn world someday." She really was. Lexie, the spitfire. If she'd only been a son...Instead, his father had gotten him. Him and... "My brother, Evan, is the youngest. He's a junior in college, and no one knows what he's going to do with his life, but he—" He cut himself off at the pang in his chest. Because Evan was the real disappointment of the family, and yet... "He's like you. And my mother. He loves art, and beautiful things."

And that's why Rylan had always fought so hard to protect him. To keep him from being stuffed into the same airless box that Rylan had.

He'd made sure his brother had a choice.

Kate's mouth had dropped open, like she hadn't been expecting any of that. It hadn't hurt to give it to her, though. All at once he wanted to take back the myriad half truths he'd told her and start anew.

But the idea of it had him reeling, suspended on a tightrope and ready to fall. She'd walk away for real if he did.

That didn't just hurt. It ached, and in ways he wasn't prepared for it to.

Something inside of him lurched, reversing wildly to pull him from the precipice. All the lessons he'd had drummed into him about holding his cards close to his chest, not showing people the tools they could use to ruin you—they crowded in around him. Keeping him safe.

He let her go, drawing his hands to his sides to hook them in his belt. He took a single step back. Squaring his jaw and lifting his chin, he said, "And that's more than I've volunteered to anyone. In years."

Hell, when was the last time he'd given away his last name?

There was danger in all of this, but he stood there beneath the weight of her scrutiny. She'd effectively asked him to let her get to know him. If what he'd offered hadn't been enough, that wasn't his fault. Not now.

After what felt like an hour, she closed her mouth, and her posture softened. She reached out a hand, crossing the space he'd put between them, and the air seemed to shiver as the distance shattered and fell.

Her hand on his was cool and small and soft, but it was a relief. The one she placed against his heart even more so.

Gazing up at him, she smiled, real and tentative. "Thank you."

His throat refused to work, so all he could do was nod.

"Come on," she said after a moment. She nodded her head toward the hall. "I don't have a lot I can tell you about Eugène Boudin. But I hear they have an incredible collection of Cézannes?"

It terrified him, just how good that invitation sounded. Twisting his wrist, he moved to intertwine their fingers, swallowing past the tightness in his lungs. "Lead the way."

The strangest mixture of excitement and nerves bubbled up behind Kate's ribs. Rylan's palm was warm against hers, and he followed her so willingly.

She'd challenged him. Called him out for the evasiveness that had been making her feel more and more disposable with every aborted conversation. And he'd chased her down and told her things. Not much, but enough.

And now he wanted to listen to her talk about art.

She was falling into something entirely too deep with this man, giving him more and more of her trust, despite the way her head screamed at her not to. But as they wound their way through the galleries, dodging other patrons and nodding at security guards as they passed them by, she gave in to it. She felt incredible and in control and *alive*. Consequences were things she could worry about later.

Finally, they reached the part of the museum she'd been thinking of. She skidded to a stop in the center of the room and looked around. Landscapes and still lifes and even a portrait or two lined the walls, all created from thick, short brushstrokes on canvas. All portraying *something* she'd been trying to figure out but had never quite managed to pull off.

She turned her head to look at Rylan and found him eyeing

her expectantly. A moment's doubt rocked her, making her come up short before she could really launch into anything.

"You sure you want to hear me talk about this stuff?"

"I asked, didn't I?"

He had, but she couldn't quite believe he really meant it.

"Just, I get carried away."

"If you do, I think I can manage to get a word in edgewise."

Now that was something she did believe. Gathering up her confidence, she nodded to herself, then gestured around at the paintings on the walls. "How much do you know about any of this?"

He tipped his head side to side. "As much as anyone whose mother took them to the Louvre when they were a kid?" At the look she gave him for that, he shrugged. "A little. No formal education, but I know who Cézanne was." His mouth pulled to the side. "Sort of."

She chewed on her lip, considering. He really didn't need a full-on history lesson here, but he had asked... "So, there were always schools of art, right?"

"That's what I've been told."

She ignored that. "But for ages and ages, it was all basically realism. Lots of variation inside that, and different styles, but for the most part, people used art to capture what the world looked like. There weren't cameras, so you needed some way to make your castle look pretty. Or to document things."

"Makes sense."

And wow, but it was a good thing he hadn't asked for that full-on history lesson, because she was taking some serious liberties here.

"But then things changed," she said. She glanced around

at the rest of the room. None of this was based on her own formal education, which, truth be told, was a little lacking in the art history department. But she'd sat through enough lectures, looked at enough slides. Drawn enough studies of other people's works. "It's not really formally linked to the camera, but I like to imagine it was. When you don't need these painstakingly done renderings just to remember some-one lived or that something happened, why have them at all? Why make art?"

Rylan's smile was low and wry. "To express the inner work-ings of your poor, tortured soul?"

She laughed, a little breathless with it. "Yeah. Basically. That's what it finally became, when it wasn't needed anymore just for documentation." She lifted one shoulder up before setting it back down. "It didn't make sense to pay a painter to take three months to do what a photographer could do in a day." She connected her gaze with his again. "And it didn't make sense to replicate something a lens could do, when as a person you were so much more."

There was a warmth to the way he looked at her then, and she squeezed his hand before glancing away. "So people started mixing it up. Making it personal. Impressionism brought in all these crazy colors and left in all the brush-strokes the old masters would have blended in. They let you see the artist in the art."

And that had always been the place where she'd struggled so much. She'd never known what to let people see.

She still had her father's voice in her ear, telling her there wasn't anything in her *worth* seeing.

Beside her, Rylan nodded. "So it's more about the interpre-tation instead of just about what they saw."

He'd said something similar before, hadn't he? That one time she'd showed him her sketchbook?

"Yeah," she said.

They stood there for a minute before he raised their joined hands and gestured at the images surrounding them. "What made you want me to look at these pieces in particular?"

It was hard to put her finger on. "I don't know. This is technically Postimpressionism, and it's just...it's my favorite, I guess. Things started getting all blocky, and he was playing with..." She stumbled, looking for the right words to describe what it felt like Cézanne had been trying to do. "With the shapes of things. Deconstructing the forms. But it was all still real, you know? That's clearly a rooftop"—she pointed at one picture and then another—"and that's a man."

"A funny-looking man."

"But a more *real* man for all that he's impossible." The idea suddenly gripped her, fervent in a way she couldn't quite explain. "You're seeing what he looked like and getting this idea of who he was, or who the artist thought he was." The thick strokes of paint split the man's face into planes, hinting at where Cubism was heading without quite getting there. They broke him up. Disassembled him, and put him back together, more whole than he could have been if he'd been rendered any other way.

"I don't know," Rylan mused. "I see Cézanne's style more than I see a personality. Am I seeing who the subject was or am I seeing who the man behind the easel wanted him to be?"

"Hard to tell, isn't it?"

He let go of her hand, but it was only to shift to the side, moving to stand behind her and wrap his arms around her waist. With his lips beside her temple, he asked, "What do you want me to see?"

And she didn't know if he meant as a tour guide, showing him the works that had moved her in the past. As an artist in her own right, or as a—whatever she was to him, sharing his days and his bed in this finite slice of time they had.

Something shaky fluttered inside of her, but she pushed it down, folding her hand over his. "I guess I'm still working on that."

chapter THIRTEEN

Rylan set the key to their hotel room on the table beside the door with a heavy hand. The quiet slap of plastic on wood echoed more loudly than it had any right to. Kate had entered ahead of him, and she stood with her back to him, gazing out the window as she lifted her bag over her head, sending the loose tumble of her hair falling across her shoulders. His mouth went dry.

In the past wasted year, and in all the time before, he'd chosen his conquests for a variety of reasons. Most he'd liked the look of. Drawn to full breasts or sultry lips or legs that went on for miles, he'd introduced himself. Turned on the charm and flashed his credit card around.

And then there was this woman. She was beautiful enough, but she was smart and funny and she saw the world in a whole different way than he ever had—talking about art like it could save the world. She was trying to *do* something with her life, and if they'd met on another continent, in another universe, he would have run screaming from the way she made him feel.

Love was a weapon. People used it against you to get you to do things you didn't want to do, to steal from you. They took it and they threw it away.

But this wasn't love. This was a few days of connection. This was lust, for her mind as well as her body, but lust all the same.

He wanted her so much it hurt to breathe.

"Come here."

She turned at the sound of his voice, and the low roughness of it took even him aback.

"Come here," he repeated.

She quirked one eyebrow up, but as she twisted her hair between her fingers, she did as he'd asked, advancing on him. She'd taken off her shoes, and God, even her feet were dainty and lovely, and the lines of her legs from under that skirt made him even harder.

As soon as she was within reach, he struck, reeling her in and pulling her tight against his body. He'd been so patient with her the past two nights, and part of him was aching to take what he really wanted. He could bend her over the mattress the way he had so many girls before, and shove her skirt up and—

"Rylan?"

Torn from the fantasy, he looked down at her. She pressed a hand against his chest, not quite pushing him away but not far from it, either, and while there was arousal in her gaze, there was something else, too.

Fear.

The same fear he'd cursed other men for daring to put on her face.

He closed his eyes and filled his lungs, once, twice, then

made his mouth and his hands both soft, holding her instead of gripping her. "Sorry. Just—" The emotion he'd felt, standing in the middle of a museum, listening to her as she described why an image of a man reading a book had moved her so deeply swept over him. A helpless smile stole over his lips. "You look so beautiful when you talk about the things you love."

Her cheeks bloomed, and she glanced away, but he wasn't having any of that.

Taking hold of her chin, he tilted her head up, all gentleness in his motions. He darted his gaze between her eyes. "You are," he insisted. "The whole time you were talking, I wanted to..."

He'd wanted to stay there, listening to her forever. She was the exact opposite of him, full where he was hollow, caring so deeply while every choice he'd had stripped from him had fed a growing, gnawing apathy. Her vibrancy was shaking his soul to life.

But he couldn't say that. Without the words to describe how she was confusing everything, he showed her the best he could, dipping down to capture her mouth. He'd wanted to do that, too, in the museum. Wanted to kiss Monet and Degas and Picasso from her lips, until they were nothing but brushstrokes and canvas and air.

Deconstructed, precisely the way she'd said. And reassembled by an artist's knowing hands.

Feeling like he was the one being taken apart, he gripped her more tightly, with none of the possession of a few moments before but with an intensity that he couldn't quite explain. She held him right back, though, curling her hand around his nape and threading her fingers through his hair.

He took control of the kiss, trying to push all these thoughts she'd been awakening inside of him into the possession of his mouth.

She made him *feel* things, dammit, in places that had been so cold and empty for so long. Made him want to be *better*.

He swallowed down the lonely throb that thought evoked in him—the undeniable knowledge of all the ways he was lacking, especially now.

He'd left all of his responsibilities behind, had discarded the life he'd been forced into after his father's bullshit had been exposed. He'd been directionless ever since. But here, with her, he had a purpose. Clutching at her hips, he crushed her closer to his chest, bending his will to the warm pleasure of contact. The needy thread of desire pulsing just beneath his skin.

She moaned and opened wide to him, letting him lick into her mouth. The scratch of nails against his scalp set the low burning inside of him thrumming hotter, and everything came into a sharp kind of focus. He wanted inside—wanted to fuck and touch, and be touched, but more than that he wanted to *give* her something.

With his heart hammering and his own need a dull, dense ache, he walked her backward toward the bed. He pressed on her shoulder until she sat, and then he dropped to his knees. Her legs fell apart with the barest of prompting. Dragging both palms up the curves of her calves, he licked his lips. Looked up at her for permission as he skimmed his hands up her thighs, rucking her skirt up higher. When he slipped his fingertip along the elastic of her underwear, her breath stuttered in her chest. The fabric was damp and hot, the perfume of her cunt a soft presence in the air, one that made him even harder.

He slid his thumb along the center panel of her panties as

he stared into her eyes. "This. The whole time you were talking about art. I wanted to do this."

"What?" She'd dug one hand into the hem of her skirt,
clenching it in a fist so tight her knuckles paled. "Get between my legs?"

But it had been more than that. He shook his head and
leaned down, kissed one knee. Then higher, on the inside of
her thigh. With his lips still pressed to her flesh, he curled his
fingers into the waistband of her underwear. Cast his gaze up
the length of her body. "To thank you." For so many things
he wasn't ready to say aloud. So instead he lifted his chin and
smirked. "For teaching me about art."

"Oh, really?" Her words and tone were all skepticism, but
she lifted up when he prompted, letting him tug her panties
down. He eased them over her feet and spread her legs again,
holding them wide with his hands on her thighs.

"Really."

He'd wanted to thank her for letting him see what she was
seeing when she looked at ancient paintings, for helping him
understand what she was trying to do in her own battered
sketchbook.

For giving him this week and all of its diversions, and
making him talk about himself, if only a little.

"Well." It came out like a sigh. She was uncomfortable.
Twitchy and nervous, and her thighs kept pressing against his
hands as if she were trying subtly to close them. None of it
was as bad as that first night, but he still wanted to shake
her—to remind her that only good things were going to happen here. Her throat bobbed. "You're welcome?"

"You can't say 'you're welcome' until I've finished with my
thank you."

"You weren't done?"

He raised his brows. "Believe me. You'll know it when I'm finished with you."

He hadn't even started yet.

With that promise in the air—with the scent of her driving him mad and with his ribs ready to burst, he slipped his fingers along the soft, pink folds of her. He held them open and ducked his head, transcribing his actions, looking up into her eyes before taking a first gentle lick.

Just like the first time, she was all sweetness and musk and the salt-sweat taste of sex against his tongue. She wasn't as desperate—he hadn't worked her up as hard, but he was cresting on his own desire, and he dug in, unreserved and unabashed. He worked teasing circles over her clit and then dipped down to lick inside. Her fingers wound themselves into his hair, finally letting go of the hem of her skirt, and he shifted the fabric higher. There was still something so illicit to it, though, even if he'd lost all sense of shame so many years ago. He knelt there, completely dressed, with his head up a girl's skirt, eating her out on the edge of a bed. It was juvenile, and it was beneath him. And it was *fantastic.*

The noise she made when he pressed his fingers inside had his hand digging into the tender flesh of her thigh, his eyes closing as he sucked her clit between his lips. She'd shown him how and where to touch the night before, had taken the buzzing end of that vibrator and pressed it just—

Her knee jerked up, a sharp shock of impact against his shoulder, and her moan was the most uninhibited he'd heard. He caught her leg before she could do more damage, throwing it over his shoulder and swiping harder with his tongue, curling his fingers, trying to match the way she'd angled the glass as she'd thrust it home.

She jerked hard at his hair, and fuck, it hurt, but in the best way. She tried to let go, starting to stutter out some kind of apology, but he grabbed her hand and put it exactly where it had been.

He parted from her flesh just long enough to glare up at her. "Don't you dare hold back."

Not after all the progress they'd made, not when she was finally starting to give him exactly what he'd wanted.

Even if it wasn't anything like what he thought he'd been looking for when they'd first begun.

It didn't take long after that. As if a spell of her own inhibitions and all that ingrained doubt had suddenly melted away, she gave in to it, pressing her hips forward. He gave her another finger beside the first two, filling her up the way that someday—God, he hoped, someday—he was going to do for real. Kissed her clit wet and sloppy, lapping up the slick taste of her, and when she finally tensed, he locked in. Didn't change a thing, kept pressing and pressing, circling right where—

"Fuck!"

Her walls clamped down around his fingers, thick waves of pulses squeezing him tight as she arched backward, the hand in his hair yanking hard, sending a shock of pain and need straight down to the roots.

And he was dying for it. Was desperate to rise up over her and get himself right up in all that slick, shove himself home and take what he wanted.

Except before he could even ask—before she could give him that *look* again, the one that turned all thoughts of his own pleasure to ash and dust, she was urging him upward.

He parted from her sex, tugging his fingers free, and then she was kissing the wetness from his lips.

"You're welcome," she said. It was breathless and harsh, needy in a way he'd yet to hear from her.

And practically before the syllables were out, she was shoving him over. Getting him onto his back on the bed, and straddling his hips, and he was so ready he could scarcely think to slow things down.

But he didn't have to.

Before doubt could creep in, she put his hand where he was aching for her and cupped him oh so perfectly through his jeans. Her face was flushed and mottled, her hair a mess, and she was beautiful.

She rose up over him and said, "Now it's my turn to thank you."

Kate's body was still pulsing with aftershocks and she was kneeling there, bare beneath her skirt with her hand on a man's cock. He'd made her come, and it had been so *easy*. In these few short days he'd stripped her of her inhibitions, and without them, she'd had nothing left to do but spread her legs and hold on to his hair and let him.

And she was so grateful it hurt.

She didn't have any condoms—she hadn't come to Paris planning for any of this—but she bet he did. Ignoring the taste that lingered there, she kissed his mouth and closed her eyes. She planted one hand beside his head while with the other she worked at his fly. These past few times, she'd scarcely touched him, and he'd seemed fine with that, but it was time.

Fear closed the back of her throat, but she pushed it down. God*dammi*t all.

She was sick and tired of her own hang-ups, of letting the past taint the present the way she always did, in her life and in this bed. This time, sex would work. It had to work.

A little of the fog of orgasm cleared as she got her hand into his boxers, curling it around hard flesh. He was big, but she was as ready as she'd ever be. It probably wouldn't hurt. And she'd be glad she had, later. When she was back in New York alone, remembering the only man who'd ever made her feel like this, and he was here, doing whatever he'd done before he'd decided to do it with her.

A noise of distress fought its way past her throat.

"Hey. Hey."

A warm hand cupped her jaw, edging her away. She sat back, and he grasped her wrist, stilling it against his flesh. His eyes were dark with need, and he was hard in her grasp. She gazed down at him, confused. "What?"

He shook his head. "You seemed a little..." He trailed off, but she could hear the words, and her skin felt hot. *Frigid, scared, stiff.* He stroked his thumb against her cheek, and his voice went softer. "I want you. So much. But we only do what you want to do, and if you're not ready..." He shrugged, but he let go of her wrist, sliding his hand up her arm to her shoulder.

God, this was so frustrating. She wanted to be ready. He'd made her feel so good, and if she was ever going to love sex, it would be with him.

Except, in the end, a voice in the back of her mind whispered *no*.

Forget the fear of physical pain.

Her heart clenched just looking at him. The sharp corners of the jaw that had drawn her in in the first place, and then the things she'd come to love about him since then. The wavy, dark strands of his hair and how they stood up on end once she'd had her hands in them. The subtle cleft of his chin.

The depths behind the piercing blue of his eyes.

He was beautiful and wounded, kind and gentle and so guarded that when he let her see even a fraction of himself, it took her breath away. Already, she felt too much. If she let him inside of her, if he made it as good as he had promised to . . .

Her ribs squeezed so tightly it ached.

If she let this happen between them, how would she ever stop herself from loving him?

The answer pulsed its way through her chest: She couldn't.

She couldn't go through with this.

He must have seen her decision slide across her face, because the questions around his eyes smoothed away. He pulled her down for another kiss. "It's fine." The words washed warm against her lips. He grinned. "I may die a little, but it's fine."

And she couldn't help it. She laughed. "I wouldn't want that."

"A little death never hurt anybody."

She chuckled at the pun, unsure if it had been intentional or not, but then it didn't matter anymore, because his mouth was warm and soft, the kisses tasting of heat, and of a fire barely banked. His hands traversed her spine and sides, slowly coming to rest on her hips. A shiver moved through her. Her body hummed with satisfaction, but want still pulsed through her veins.

She wanted to give him *something*.

With her eyes closed, she parted from his mouth to kiss down the line of his throat, rasping her teeth against the stubble on his jaw. It was rough, his skin salty and male, and the little spot of boldness in her grew.

"Kate..." He threaded his fingers through her hair, neither pushing her up nor down so much as holding on.

There was something more than want or need or even boldness going on here. Something like power.

Her reservations slid away as she undid one button of his shirt and then the next. There was still the cotton layer of his undershirt beneath it, but she kissed her way along the center of his chest regardless. When she reached the bottom of his rib cage, she shoved the fabric up. His abdomen was firm and smooth. She nosed the lines of muscle, flicked out the tip of her tongue to taste the flesh beside his navel.

With a deep breath, she pushed aside the open denim of his jeans.

His fingers tightened against her scalp. "You don't have to."

She looked up the length of his body, and God, his eyes. The sensation of power in her hands swelled. "Do you want me to?"

He threw his head back, exposing the line of his throat, huffing out a sigh of laughter that sounded pained. "Fuck. More than anything." He looked at her again, lifting his other hand to draw a fingertip along the edges of her lips. "Your mouth would look so good around my cock."

Her heart felt like it skipped a beat, and even sated as she was, her sex throbbed. She lowered her head, resting her brow against his hip.

Then, before she could stop herself, she tugged the waistband of his boxers down.

She'd seen him before. Touched him and let him come against her, but being so close was another thing entirely. He smelled like sex, and he felt like silk beneath her fingertips, searing hot and wet at the tip. When she skimmed her thumb down the length of him, the foreskin shifted, uncovering more of the dusky flesh beneath.

Sated as she was, a tickle of arousal moved through her, and she was tempted to dive right in. To find out what noises he made when she was the one bringing him to the edge. But he'd been so patient with her, had taken the time to find out exactly what drove her mad.

She barely recognized her own voice, deepened by lust, as she asked, "What about you? What do you like?"

"Your hands on me." His breath cut off when she curled her fingers around his base. "Fuck." As she took a slow stroke up the shaft, his eyes slipped closed, his head tipping back. "Everything you're doing feels good."

He looked amazing like this, the tendons in his neck straining, abdominals tensing.

Heat spread through her. And suddenly she *got* it. Why he looked at her the way he did, why he seemed so desperate to touch her and make her come.

A hot spark of understanding lighting off inside her, she tightened her grip, and fluid beaded up at his tip.

"Everything you're doing feels *really* good," he revised, biting back a groan.

Triumph echoed behind her ribs, but it wasn't enough. She wanted more.

She let him go, drifting a hand over his thigh. She felt too hot all over, while at the same time prickles of cold dotted her skin.

She dropped off the bed and sank to her knees between his legs.

His moan was loud this time as she took him in the circle of her fist. "Whatever you want to do," he said, sounding earnest, and like it was killing him not to tug her down and guide himself between her lips.

So she turned it on him. "What do you want me to do?"

He cursed aloud, fisting his hands into the bedspread beneath him. "I wanna fuck your mouth."

Lightning blazed through her abdomen and up her ribs. How would that feel? Part of her remembered exactly how it felt to be used that way, but this was different. Rylan was different.

Rylan would make sure it was good.

Still, she shook her head. "What do you want *me* to do?"

"Lick it." There was no hesitation. "Right at the head— yeah." A noise punched from his lungs when she did just that. "Fuck, that's perfect. Get your tongue all over me. Nice and wet."

He tasted like salt, marred by a hint of bitterness, but the warm feeling in her sex and in her chest more than made up for it. He put one hand on her shoulder, light and stabilizing. Just heavy enough to ground her to the earth.

His thumb stroked over her collarbone. "Now open up. Let it slide inside. That's it. *Oh.*"

She knew this part. But it had never felt so good to her before. The way his hips flexed and the noises he made all fed the fire deep inside. Taking a deep breath, she wrapped her lips around the solid flesh, taking him in.

"Jesus. Looks better than I thought it would." His other hand came up, fingertips soft against her lips where they were stretched around him. He stuttered out a long breath as she took him farther. "Fuck *looking* good. You feel...oh shit...wet and warm..."

She remembered this—the weird shame of his praise and how it turned her on in spite of herself. She squirmed, pressing her thighs together.

"You like sucking me?" he asked.

Desire burned through her as she popped off long enough to nod.

His fingers tightened on her shoulder. "So good..."

He trailed off, letting silence fill in around them, pierced only by the soft, slick sounds of her mouth on his flesh. By his breathing and by how much she liked this. How much she loved it.

"Move your hand," he urged.

And she loved that even more. The motion was easy, a wet glide as she followed her mouth with the tight curl of her hand, up and down. His hips rocked up into it, not enough to choke her. She followed his pace, and she was lost in it. Wanted so much for him to—

"Baby—" he started. The muscles of his legs were coiled, his abdomen tight, and the way he sounded..."I'm gonna—" His fingers threaded through her hair, a light tug of warning as his voice cut off, the desperation in it making her burn.

She stayed right on him. Let the first hot pulses coat her tongue, swallowing what she could. When he twitched and pushed her off, she swiped her wrist across her mouth and he *growled*.

"Holy hell, Kate." He hauled her up bodily, sitting up as he got her on his lap. He kissed his own release from her mouth, practically devouring her as he slid his hand back under her skirt.

No easing in this time, thank God. His thumb pulsed over her clit, and she was too sensitive—he'd just made her come with his mouth, but when his fingers pushed inside, she all but sobbed against his lips.

"Beautiful." He broke their kiss to stare right into her eyes, his lips parted, gaze fiery as he worked her faster, pressed deeper.

Her climax shocked her with how suddenly it came over her. Hot liquid boiled inside, and when it burst, she dug her nails into his skin. Buried her face in his neck and screamed.

All she could think, as he held her, was that she'd never known.

Twenty-two years old, and two partners under her belt, and how, how, how had she never known?

chapter FOURTEEN

Sunlight filtered through the gauzy curtains over their window. They must've forgotten to pull the heavier shades the night before.

Just as well.

Rubbing the sleep from his eyes, Rylan turned over in the bed. Kate was still asleep, her hair mussed. She'd insisted on wearing a tank top and some pretty, lacy panties to bed, but the way the sheets were tangled around her, he could almost imagine she was naked.

God, her skin was so smooth and soft. His morning arousal gave a little twitch, and he reached down to adjust himself inside the boxers he'd resigned himself to keeping on for her. All she'd had to do was give him that *look* as he'd been undressing.

All she ever seemed to have to do was give him a look, and he was doing a whole host of things he normally never would.

That should probably be bothering him more.

She made a little sound in her sleep, snuffling and burrowing her face against the pillow. She was resting on her side, twisted away from him, the sheets tucked under her arm and rucked up across the middle of her thigh, leaving her long, bare calf exposed.

He didn't want to wake her, but he couldn't resist. Propping himself up on one elbow, he reached his other hand out, skimming it along her shoulder and pushing her hair aside. A huff of a sigh escaped her lips, but she barely stirred, so he shifted closer.

His chest fit to her spine like they'd been made to lock together that way, and he set his lips to the side of her throat. Trailing a line of soft, sucking kisses along that sleep-warm skin, he let his erection graze her rear and swallowed the groan the contact pulled from him. If they were fucking already, he could pull the panel of her panties to the side. Be buried in all that nice, slick warmth. Take her nice and slow, rocking them to a sweet morning peak.

If they were fucking.

He breathed his want into her skin and grazed the backs of his knuckles down her arm. She hummed, finally showing signs of life as she let him entwine their hands.

"What time is it?" she asked.

"Early." He had no idea, honestly. All he knew was that she was beautiful, and she felt so good against him. He could stay there all day, kissing her and trailing his hands across her skin.

But Kate had other things in mind. Lifting her head, she glanced around. "Ugh, it's after eight," she said, flopping back down and covering her eyes with her arm.

That had him looking for the clock, too. He never slept so late. Sure enough, though, the bright red numbers read 8:17.

Huh.

He shrugged, then resituated himself on his stomach, his hard-on pressing into the mattress as he held himself over her, dipping to kiss her cheek and her ear and her chin. "Day's a-wasting?" He peeled her hand away from her eyes.

But what waited for him wasn't the easy flirtiness he'd been hoping for. Instead, there was actual anxiety. "Yeah, actually. It kind of is."

"Nothing opens until nine anyway. So we grab croissants to go. No harm done." He leaned in to kiss her mouth.

She let him, for a minute, but all too soon she was pulling back. "We should get up."

"I like getting down better."

"Ugh, do you ever stop?"

"Not if I can help it."

She was a mess of mixed signals, body melting beneath his kisses even as she was pushing him back. She half sat up. "Do you want first shower or should I?"

"We could share."

He'd love that. She was always putting her damn clothes back on. Even when she let him get her naked, it was never for long. In the shower, he could touch her all over. Wash her back. Maybe warm her up enough to let him get his hand or his mouth between her thighs.

Or maybe not, considering the look she was giving him.

"What?" he asked. "I hate to waste water, is all."

"You hate to waste an opportunity to get me undressed."

"Waste is a sin in all its forms."

Rolling her eyes, she put her hand right in his face and shoved him away. Apparently, she really meant it this time. She got her legs under her and clambered off the bed, heading toward the bathroom.

"Kate—"

She closed the door behind herself before he could say anything further.

Well, great.

He lay down again on his back, staring up at the ceiling. The light on his phone was blinking, but he didn't want to deal with any of the shit that could be waiting for him. The people from his father's company. McConnell, with his casual updates that fulfilled his duties while making it perfectly clear he'd be happy if Rylan stayed away. Or Thomas with his even worse entreaties to return and set things right. His sister. God, Lexie was the worst. He missed her fiercely, but the only thing she could talk about these days was how much he was letting her down.

He was letting them all down, but they could rot. He'd given them enough. Someday maybe they'd understand that. Until then, they could all wait another goddamn day—or another year. He stretched an arm out to flip the screen over so he wouldn't have to look at the alert.

In the other room, the water for the shower turned on, and he clunked his fist against the headboard. His morning wood had subsided a little, but it wouldn't take much to get it going again. Just thinking about Kate standing underneath the spray, soap bubbles clinging to her curves...

"You coming?"

He startled, sitting up all at once. Somehow, he'd missed the door opening again. And there she stood, leaning against it, invitation written all over her face.

"Hopefully I'm about to be," he mumbled under his breath.

He tossed the sheets off and launched himself out of bed. A handful of strides, and he was on her, picking her up and spinning her around. When he set her down, it was with one hand coming to cup the back of her neck, pulling her into a long, filthy kiss. She didn't fight him this time, so he reached for the hem of her top and pushed it up.

"What's your hurry?" she asked as she let him lift it over her head.

"Told you. Hate to waste water."

"Uh-huh."

Her underwear and his followed quickly enough. His erection pressed against the soft skin of her abdomen and he groaned. "Come on," he said, tugging her toward the shower. "Before I have to eat you out on the countertop."

"Is that supposed to dissuade me?"

He didn't even know.

Somehow or other, they managed to get the shower curtain shoved aside. He climbed in, barely letting go of her as he dragged her in after. Around them, the water threw up little licks of steam as it beat down on their skin, and it was perfect.

It got even better when she reached between them and got a hand around his cock.

"Fuck." He bit down harder on her lip than he'd meant to.

"Okay?" she asked.

"So okay."

He kissed her and kissed her, curling his hands around her tits. All slippery with water, they fit just right in the palms of his hands, and they pebbled up nice and hard when he stroked her nipples with his thumbs. She made the best little noises, too, and what had been starting to look like a letdown of a morning was positively rosy once she got a good rhythm going.

Letting go of one of her breasts, he felt around blindly behind his back until he connected with a bar of soap. He grabbed it and lathered it up, then wrapped his hand around hers. "A little tighter," he urged, and *fuck*, yeah. "That's right."

He rocked his hips, fucking into their fists, and with the soap it was all easy and slick. He clutched her close, mouth open against her temple, urging her faster and faster until—

The feeling came all the way from his toes, drawing his balls tight before exploding forward in a rush. He might have blanked out for a second, and his knees wobbled. He threw a hand out to brace himself against the tile.

She laughed as he twitched. He was shockingly sensitive in her grip as she pumped the last of it out of him. When he couldn't take it anymore, he stilled her wrist, shuddering as she dragged her palm over the head before letting him go. He rubbed his fingers over hers, smoothing the mess away, then caught her face in his hands.

He kissed her, soft and grateful. "What brought that on?"

"You seemed like you needed it."

Kind of an overstatement, but he wasn't objecting.

She turned her face away, looking down and kissing his chest. He wrapped her up in his arms and squeezed her tight.

"Can I return the favor?"

She shook her head. "Maybe tonight."

Disappointing, but not exactly a surprise. Loosening his hold, he pressed his lips to hers. "Definitely tonight." He paused before he let her go; considering what she'd told him about her sex life before this, he wanted to make sure. "You know you didn't have to do that, right? Guys can't *actually* die of blue balls."

"I know." She still wasn't quite looking at him, but there was a sly smile spreading across her face. A new, different one from any he'd seen on her before. "I wanted to."

"Okay." He kissed the top of her head and pulled away.

He set down the bar of soap he'd somehow managed to hold on to through it all and perused the collection of little bottles lining the built-in shelf. When he found one that said shampoo, he picked it up and poured some into his palm.

"Didn't you bring your own?" she asked.

"Yeah. But this isn't for me. Turn around."

She leveled him with a questioning look but did as he'd asked. Her hair was wet enough from the time they'd spent messing around. With gentle hands, he started working the shampoo into it. The slowly forming suds smelled sweet. Not overpowering. Just nice.

"I love your hair," he said quietly.

She shivered.

He took his time, massaging her scalp, giving her the attention she'd given to him sexually, but in a different way. Taking care of her like this . . . it made something in his heart feel raw.

He dropped his hands and shifted to put his back to the tile. "You can have the water."

She gave him another, different look, then snuck past him, tilting her head down into the spray.

The water made the soap cascade along her curves, soft white washes of foam caressing pale skin. His body was still ringing with satisfaction, but looking at her made him want to start things all over again.

To distract himself, he plucked his own shampoo off a different shelf. Working it into his hair with brisk efficiency, he turned his mind to other things.

"So I was thinking," he said.

"Hmm?"

"How do you feel about going to Versailles today?" Girls tended to like all the frilly décor and dresses and things. Not that he took many women there. It was a bit of a trek, after all. But he wouldn't mind a train ride into the country with her.

She twisted around, grabbing a little bottle of conditioner to work into her hair. "I don't know."

He was getting into the idea now, though. He could take her around the castle, then they could grab a nice dinner somewhere outside the city. Get some fresh air. Walk around, hand in hand, like a couple of romantics.

It'd be different. Nice.

"I think you'd like it. It's a weekday, so the crowds won't be too bad."

"I just—" Her tone made him come up short.

Shampoo threatened to drip into his eyes. He wiped it away with his wrist. She sighed, rinsing the conditioner out of her hair before trading places with him again so he could scrub at his own.

His eyes were still closed, and her voice only barely rose over the pounding of the water.

"I was thinking maybe I'd head out and do my own thing today."

Oh. "Oh."

"I mean, I've only got three full days left, and I haven't gotten nearly as much drawing done as I'd planned to. I've still got all these things to figure out before I go home. And I've been having fun with you, but..."

She trailed off, but he could fill in the blanks. He was a diversion. A distraction. She had other things to worry about.

The whole thing made him feel sort of hollow.

Holding his tongue, he took a little longer under the spray

than he really needed. She had limited time here and a lot to do, but he had limited time, too. Limited time with her. Limited time to spend not bored and alone and spinning his wheels.

When he couldn't pretend to have any more soap in his hair, he sighed and turned around. "Fine. No problem."

Her expression was hopeful in a way that just squeezed the emptiness harder. "You sure?"

"Yeah. Whatever you need to do. We can hit Versailles tomorrow." He hesitated, working to sound nonchalant. "If you have time."

"We'll see." She had a mesh pouf in her hand and started working a softly scented lather over her chest.

He flexed his hands at his sides. Then gave up. Keeping his distance was fucking stupid, especially in a five-by-two-foot tub.

"Here. Let me."

He reached out and took the sponge from her, grazing her skin as he did. She consented, flipping her hair out of the way and turning so he could soap her back. He traced the sloping lines of her body with an intensity that surprised even him. Memorizing.

"The thing is—" She cut herself off, and he paused, surprised. "With wanting to go work on some art stuff today."

"Yeah?" He returned to sliding the sponge along her curves.

"Remember how I came here to *find myself*?" Her inflection held the same self-mocking lilt to it as the first time they'd met. When she'd admitted to being an artist and a dreamer, and had begun to wrap him around her finger.

So he echoed it, too, his smile wry. "It's a romantic notion."

"But it's actually true." She turned, and he let his hand drop to his side. She took the sponge from him and bent to soap her legs. When she straightened up again, determination colored her expression. "I got accepted into an MFA program."

His brows rose toward his hairline. A master of fine arts? That was a pretty big deal. "Wow. Congratulations."

Pride warred with demureness in her tone, making her voice pitch higher. "At a really good school, too. At Columbia. In New York, so I can keep my apartment and everything."

"So what's the debate?"

"I didn't want to put all my eggs in one basket. So I applied for a bunch of jobs, too. And I got offered one of them right before I left." She hesitated before adding, "At an ad agency. Entry level, but it would pay the bills."

"Well, that's great, too." Insane that she would even be considering it when she had a chance to pursue what she obviously loved, but great. He guessed.

She pointed toward the water, and he shifted, making room for her to trade places with him. As she stepped beneath the spray, the lather twisted and ran, sliding in foaming sheets along her form, and his throat went dry.

She rinsed herself off in a way that must have been designed to torture him, then hung up her pouf and sluiced the water from her eyes. "I can't do both, is all. I have to decide."

"Is it really that much of a decision?"

"Yeah. Just the biggest one ever." She twisted her knuckles. "So this whole trip—it was supposed to be about finding inspiration, or discovering myself, or whatever. But it's about deciding some things, too."

He couldn't hide his confusion anymore. "But you love art."

She made a snorting sound. "I love eating, too."

"But you *love* art." He wasn't letting that go.

"Love isn't always enough, you know. People don't make a living painting."

It sounded like she was parroting back someone else's words.

He shook his head. "*You* could."

She dropped his gaze, and he reached out, putting a hand on her shoulder and the other on her waist.

"You could," he repeated.

She leaned in and kissed his chest, then rested the side of her face there, inviting him to put his arms around her. "Guess I still have to prove that to myself," she said.

He held her close and bit his tongue.

She had no idea how lucky she was, having the opportunity to decide. Once upon a time, he would've given anything for that chance. Instead, there'd been his father's college and his father's company and his father's entire fucking life laid out in front of him. Even when he hadn't hated what he was doing, he'd had that hemmed-in, caged feeling pushing on him.

And here Kate had all these options. All these dreams.

He wouldn't be the one to stand in the way of her choosing to follow them.

"Okay." He pulled away enough to press his lips against her temple. "I won't pretend I'm not disappointed, but I understand."

"You sure?"

"I'm sure."

He let her go, then reached for his bar of soap. Moving quickly, he lathered it up and spread the suds across his chest.

When she spoke again, it was tentative. "Any idea what you'll do today?"

"Not sure." He hadn't really planned on having a day to kill on his own. "Catch up on some things I suppose." He probably had a lot of emails to delete. That would take at least ten minutes.

"Will you spend it here?"

He slowed the motions of his hands. "Do you want me to?"

She shrugged, then stepped aside so he could get under the spray. "I don't think I'll be gone the entire day. I could meet you when I'm done? Maybe relax a bit before dinner."

He'd like that. "Sure." He ducked his head under the water. Once he'd slicked his hair from his face, he said, "I'll head back here by late afternoon?"

"Okay."

A few hours, cooling his heels by himself. That was practically nothing.

It would feel like nothing, after. When she was gone for good.

He didn't want to think about that now. He finished rinsing off and sluiced the water from his eyes. Despite the curls of steam, she looked cold, standing near the back of the shower. He held out a hand in invitation. "Come here."

She came without resistance. Pulling her flush against his body, he opened his mouth against hers, drinking her in. He closed his eyes. And held on.

chapter FIFTEEN

Kate had let herself get way, way too comfortable with Rylan doing all the work on their adventures together. It gave her an uneasy, restless feeling, realizing how much she'd come to rely on him.

She mentally shook her head at herself. Well, not today. Today, she sat in her seat on the Metro on her own, watching the signs go by. Navigating the system and the language barrier all by herself.

Part of the appeal of foreign travel was finding your way around, after all. Immersing yourself in a whole new place, hearing different words in different tongues. She'd been missing that part of the experience, letting him do all the talking for her.

She'd gained another kind of experience, though. Her cheeks flushed warm as she tried not to think about the things they'd done these past few nights. It had been good. Really good. But that wasn't the point right now. It didn't matter how much she'd been enjoying herself—sex wasn't going to help her figure out her *life*.

And nothing was as easy as Rylan made it out to be.

Her stomach did a twisting set of flips as she recalled his reaction to her grad school dilemma. He'd made it all seem so simple. She loved art, so therefore she should go for it, give it her all. Risk everything. The very idea of it was terrifying.

And thrilling. She'd never gotten that kind of support before. Had someone stand up to her father's voice in her head, telling her that drawing was a waste of time. *She* was a waste of time.

The twisting in her stomach turned into a hard, painful clench.

Rylan's words had made her feel better about considering taking this chance. But they were just a few words, after years and years of being made to feel like she wasn't enough. Sure, Rylan's opinion was the one she wanted to believe. But she still had to prove that she was worth this chance. At least to herself.

Before long, her stop came up, and she rose, clutching her bag close as she made her way off the train and up to the surface.

Of course, that was where she really had to start paying attention.

With her mental map firmly in grasp—and her paper one tucked away so she didn't look like too much of a clueless tourist—she headed north, keeping an eye out for the things that looked familiar. More than once, she half turned to point something out or ask a question. To grab Rylan's hand.

She rolled her eyes at herself as she crossed the street. Stupid. She'd left him behind not only because she needed some time to herself—which she did.

But also because she was embarrassed to admit that she was going back to someplace she'd already been.

Her very first day with him, she'd sworn she'd find some time to go back to the Louvre, but as her time in the city had flown by, it hadn't been the old, grand paintings in the museum that had called to her to visit them again. Instead, it had been the city itself. The version of it that Rylan had shown her. The top of the hill where he'd challenged her to open her eyes.

And she had. And what she'd seen had been beautiful.

Montmartre was just as bustling, the climb to the top of Sacred Heart just as arduous as she remembered. But somehow, when she finally reached the top of it, the view of rooftops and skyscrapers and the swath of city spreading out before her toward the horizon was even more incredible. The feeling of lightness in her chest more expansive.

Winding her way through the thinner weekday morning crowds, she found a spot at the railing near where they had stood together Sunday afternoon. It was earlier in the day, so the angle of the sun was different, but she could work with that. She picked out a place to sit a few feet away and pulled out her tools, planning ahead in her mind. Graphite on paper to start with. Then if she liked where that was going, she had some other options. Colored Conté crayons or charcoal. A cheap little set of watercolors. Concentrating, she decided on a composition and dug in, sweeping her pencil across the page.

Twenty minutes later, she had a fair representation of the scene. She held it out at arm's length and looked at it, frowning. Accurate, but not emotive. It didn't give any sense at all of how it felt to *be* there, looking out across the Paris skyline.

Frustrated, she flipped the page and started again, attacking the scene with more fervor this time, laying down bolder lines and deeper swaths of shading. Trying to pour the light and air and scent of Montmartre into her page.

Her piece of charcoal snapped in half within her grip, and she blinked furiously against the blurring of her vision as she stared down at what she'd done. Her eyes prickled harder, and her breath got short. Shit, this one was even worse.

She wanted to fling the whole damn sketchbook off a cliff. Who did she think she was kidding? This was high school-level work; she'd be laughed out of critique for it. She'd be laughed out of grad school.

And there was that voice again.

The worst part was, her dad had almost never told her to her face that she wasn't good enough. He'd said it with his frowns and his disappointed sighs. His absolute disinterest when she tried to show him something.

He'd said it to her mother. Maybe he'd thought she couldn't hear, or worse, maybe he hadn't cared. She'd been right in the next room. *She's wasting her time on that crap. Like hell I'm paying for lessons. She's gotta grow up sometime...*

Maybe it was time to grow up. To give up.

She dug her nails into her palms, sharp enough to snap her out of it. No. No way in hell she was giving up. She'd spent the last ten years overcoming that kind of thinking, working to banish that doubt. It hadn't been easy, after she and her mother had finally left, but it had been good. There'd been no more tiptoeing around a quiet house, afraid to awaken a sleeping beast. There'd been a tiny apartment full of love, and there'd been her mom, telling her she could do anything. Be anything.

Just like Rylan had this morning. Rylan, who'd taken it for granted that of course she could make it in the New York art scene. Rylan, who barely knew her and who believed in her.

She swiped a clean part of her wrist across her eyes. She was better than this. She could *do* better than this.

Turning the page, she took a deep breath and closed her eyes.

In her mind, she was back there on that Sunday afternoon, on this very hill and on the footsteps of this very church. Rylan stood behind her, his chest broad and solid against her spine, his hands warm on her skin. He'd kissed her neck the way he seemed so fond of doing—the way that made her shiver and turn to mush.

She'd felt something more than just in awe of the city at the time. Tired from the climb, and close to someone who was interesting and beautiful and who treated her like she and her pleasure were precious. She'd felt . . . *connected*. To Paris. To her own life and breath.

To a man with more secrets than she had time.

That wasn't the doubt she needed right now.

If he were here, he'd be sitting right beside her. Quiet and supportive. Reading or playing with his phone, making random comments as they struck him. But he'd be patient. He'd let her see the city the way he knew and loved it. He'd let her make something of what she saw.

She opened her eyes again, and the cityscape in front of her seemed to resolve itself. Without looking, she traded her pencil for a stick of soft, ephemeral vine charcoal and started sweeping out the world in broad strokes.

Once she had the basic shapes sketched in, she eyed the work she'd done. She was calmer now, better able to look at it with an analytical eye. It needed more bulk. More weight. She fumbled for the little tin of powdered charcoal she'd made fun of herself for bringing at the time. It was such a mess, but when she dipped her fingertips into it, the sootiness of it felt *right*. She smeared it onto the page, using the hard pressure of her strokes to show the crevices and depths between buildings. A light blush of it to hint at the wispy expanses of clouds in the sky.

Darker, more permanent compressed charcoal now. Finer lines. Her fingers started adding in other things, too. Spindly intimations of connections between rooftops and streets, anchoring the sky to the earth. Tying her and it and the lover she could almost *feel* behind her back together in one rough portrait of a place. Of a time.

Of herself, from beyond the page.

Finally, she set her stick of charcoal aside. Her shoulders were stiff and her left foot was half-asleep, but in her lap, she had a drawing. She regarded the image for a long, long time. Relief broke over her like the dawn.

When she looked up at the city again, she smiled.

There was something *wrong* with Rylan. His incessant pacing brought him face to face with a wall again, and he groaned before turning around. Putting his back to the plaster, he covered his face with his hands.

Late afternoon. He was supposed to meet Kate back here at the room sometime in the late afternoon, and here it was, barely past two and he was wearing a hole in the carpet waiting for her.

But what else was he supposed to do? He'd gone for a run,

then stopped by the apartment to swap out some of his dirty clothes for clean ones. Had lunch in a café and caught up on the business papers. Deleted emails and voicemails from his inbox.

On a normal day, he'd read a book or watch a movie or maybe cruise for pretty girls beneath the Eiffel Tower, but none of that appealed right now. He just wanted Kate to get home already so he could ask to flip through her sketchbook. Tell her she was amazing, and that she was insane for even considering turning down a chance to pursue her art for real. Take her to dinner and then turn all his charm to getting her naked with him again.

He dug the heels of his hands into his eyes.

What the hell had he been doing with his life before this week?

He'd just about finished another circuit of this stupid, tiny room when his phone buzzed in his pocket. He pulled it out, hoping like hell that it would be some kind of diversion.

His sister's face stared back at him from the screen, and his thumb froze over the button to either accept or ignore the call.

They'd spoken a couple of times in the year he'd been away. It'd been a while, though. The last time, she'd been relentless in her insistence that he come home. He hadn't picked the phone up since.

He surprised himself when he did today.

He stared blankly at the screen as Lexie's voice, distant but there, came across the speaker. "Teddy? You there? . . . Teddy?"

God, he hated that nickname. Forget that he didn't even go by Theodore anymore, that he'd shed his father's name nearly a decade ago. But he brushed it off and raised the phone to his ear. "Yeah." He cleared his throat. "Hey, Lex."

"About time I got a hold of you."

Something about her tone grated his nerves. His hackles rose, and just like that, instead of annoyed and bored, he snapped into annoyed and defensive. "What do you want?"

Her eye roll was almost audible. "Nice to hear your voice, too."

He sighed. Took a deep breath. It wasn't her fault she sounded like their mother and talked like their father—all clipped sentences, all too fast. Even as children, it was like they hadn't spoken the same language sometimes. And somewhere along the way, they'd lost the dictionary.

"Sorry," he said, scrubbing a hand over his face. "How are you?"

"Same as usual. Busy." She was always busy. "You?"

"About the same as usual, too."

She made a huffed sound that got across exactly what she thought about that. "I'm sure bumming around Europe is terribly taxing."

She had no idea. He dropped his hand and rapped his fingers against the wall. "Listen, I don't mean to be a dick, but seriously. We both know this isn't a social call."

"It could be."

"It isn't." It hadn't been. Not since he'd turned his back on the mess their father had left for them, the mess his father had told him was his destiny. Not since he'd walked away.

She hesitated for a second. And then dropped all pretenses. "You still haven't gotten back to Thomas about the new board. He's been trying to get in touch with you for months."

Ugh. "Try a year."

"I don't know what you're running from—"

Yes, she did. She knew all the pressures, all the expectations, because they'd both been forced to deal with them. She'd emerged from the crucible a workaholic, desperately driven to prove their father wrong about her. While Rylan...

He'd worked himself to the bone, rising to the top, just the way their father had demanded. And yet with every floor he rocketed past, the walls had started to close in until he couldn't *breathe*. When the bottom had fallen out...

He'd looked down, only to see nothing but air underneath him, and he hadn't been willing to spend another minute in that fucking box, trying to live up to the expectations of a criminal, of a man who had ruined lives and ruined everything they'd worked for. Even their family name had become a *joke*.

So he'd gotten out, and if his sister couldn't see why he wasn't willing to get back in...

He curled his hand into a fist and worked his jaw. "I'll come back to New York when I'm ready to."

"And when will that be?"

If the pounding in his heart and the cold sweat on the back of his neck were anything to go by, not for a while. "I don't know."

A long couple of seconds passed. "We've only got a few months left before the board becomes permanent. If you don't step up, McConnell stays at the helm, and you know Dad trusted him as far as he could throw him—"

Rylan straightened his spine and widened his eyes, incredulous. "And I'm supposed to care about who *Dad* trusted?"

"Look, I know you're still angry."

"Damn right I am."

"But it's your company now! I'm not old enough to take

over, but you are. If you give a shit about our family, about anything—"

"If Dad had given a shit about our family he wouldn't have fucked it over in the first place. He wouldn't have fucked *us* over, he—" He snapped, shoving the side of his fist into the wall, and fuck. He hadn't let himself get so worked up about this in a year. He forced his fingers to unclench, forced his lungs to expand and contract. Between them, in the space above the center of his ribs, his father's ring hung from its chain, searing like a metal brand against his chest.

Why the hell had he answered the phone in the first place?

When Lexie spoke again, her voice was measured in a way that made the hairs on the back of his neck stand up on end. "You care. You pretend you don't. You fuck off to Europe to avoid all your responsibilities. But. You. Care."

He'd cared too much.

He laughed, and the sound was shaky in his throat. "You always did like to believe the best about everyone."

He tore the phone from his ear, ignoring whatever else Lexie was trying to say, hanging up before he could dig himself in any deeper. When he'd blanked the screen again, he stared at it for a long, aching moment, until his vision flipped and he wasn't seeing the empty screen but instead was staring at his own reflection in the glass.

After all the shit he'd given Lex about her voice. He had his father's face and his mother's eyes. Had their faithlessness and their morals, and every single thing he'd come to resent them for.

He turned his phone over so the dull plastic case was facing him. Then tossed the damned thing on the bed before he could throw it through the window.

chapter SIXTEEN

Kate was practically walking on air as she stepped off the elevator on their floor. She'd filled her sketchbook. Finished it. Images of Montmartre and Sacred Heart and the view from the top of the hill. Little cafés and giant cityscapes, and for the first time, there was this *certainty* buzzing through her veins. The drawings were good. More than that, they were her.

She couldn't wait to tell Rylan how well her day had gone. To see that conviction in his eyes when he told her she could do this after all.

At the door to their room, she rucked her shirt up and reached into the security wallet she still kept strapped around her waist. She grasped the keycard between two fingers and slipped it into the door, pausing long enough for the light to flash green before turning the handle and striding through.

"Hey!" She dropped her bag on the bed and skipped across the carpet. Rylan was at the little desk in the corner, his back to her. She tugged at the chair to spin it around. But when she saw his face, she paused, drawing her hand back. "Are you okay?"

There was something haunted to his eyes—a weariness she'd caught a glimpse of in the past, but not like this. Shadows under his cheekbones and a tightness to his jaw. A coiled anger, an old anger.

For the briefest fraction of a second, he reminded her of her dad.

She blinked and it was gone, but she was already backing away. He reached out, wrapping his hand around her wrist before she could retreat any more. With what looked like effort, he twitched the corners of his mouth upward, but it wasn't a real smile. She knew what those looked like on him now.

"I'm fine," he said. The sharpest edges of his expression bled away, but now that she'd seen them, the signs of his agitation were everywhere, in the corners of his eyes and the set of his lips. His thumb stroked across the bone of her wrist. "Sorry. Was just thinking about some things."

"Things?" She arched her brows, but something inside her was shaking. She fought to push it down. To joke with him the way she normally would. "Like what? Torture?"

He laughed at that, and it made a little of the tension in her shoulders ease. "Close."

Touching his face felt like a risk, like pushing past some kind of boundary. She did it anyway, wary, half expecting him to flinch. He did, a little bit, but allowed the contact. She swallowed to try to slake the sudden dryness in her throat. "Really, though. You okay?"

"Fine."

She almost believed it.

He turned his neck, shifting to press a kiss to her palm,

lips lingering there for a long moment. He closed his eyes. When he opened them again, they seemed clearer. He let go of her wrist to settle both hands on her hips. "How about you? How was your day? Get everything done you wanted to?"

She took a deep breath, the tremor inside of her melting away.

The dark look in his eyes might have echoed an expression she'd seen before, one that had haunted her for years. But it had only been an echo. Her father. Aaron. Any of them. Their bad moods didn't end with them getting a hold of themselves and focusing on how she was doing.

She was safe here.

She slid her palm down past his neck and collarbone to rest against his heart. "It was good. I drew a lot."

"Yeah? Can I see?"

A nervous flutter fired off behind her ribs, but she nodded.

Slipping out of his grasp, she headed over to the bed. She opened her bag and pulled out her book, planning to flip it to the work she'd done today, but before she could, he plucked it from her grasp. He sunk down to sit on the bed and opened to the very first page.

It wasn't just nerves anymore, beating inside her chest. "There's a lot of old crap in there."

Old crap she'd put so much time and energy and dedication into, and letting them be seen like this...It was like letting him see all the unfinished edges of her. A work in progress, and he'd already witnessed her naïveté in other situations. In his bed and with her hands between her legs.

She fought the instinct to rip the book from his grip.

Oblivious to how she was churning up inside, he turned the pages slowly, gazing at each with an appraising set to

his jaw. Her face went another shade warmer with every am-
ateurish imitation of another artist's style, every mistake in
perspective. Every sketch that betrayed exactly what a mess
she was and how little she knew.

"Really." Her voice was rough. "Some of those are ancient."

He lifted up a single finger and shook his head, asking her
to be quiet without saying a word.

She resigned herself to her fate. Picking at her fingernails,
she moved to sit beside him, close but not quite touching.
He'd told her he liked the couple of drawings she'd shown
him before, and he'd expressed such confidence in her ability
to hack it in grad school. But he hadn't really known, then,
had he? He hadn't seen enough to make that kind of statement, and the idea that he might take it back now, after
having seen more, made her stomach clench. It hardened further about halfway through the book, when the quality of
the images changed. That had been about when she'd started
thinking about what she was going to do after college, a hundred futures spinning out in front of her. Grad school and
office jobs. Huge risks and life sentences.

And then the image she'd drawn the day Professor Lin had
pulled her aside. Told her that if she didn't define herself,
she'd never make it as an artist. That she'd never sell.

He paused, hand hovering at the corner of the page.

"You were angry," he said. It was the first comment he had
made.

"Scared," she corrected.

"I can see that."

He flipped past the pictures she had already shown him
from the day she'd sketched outside of Notre Dame, and then
he was looking at the first one she'd done today. His brow fur-

rowed, and he turned his head to look at her. "You went back to Sacred Heart?"

"Yeah?" She didn't mean it to come out like a question, but it did.

The way he was staring at her, it was as if he could see right through her. He didn't look angry or exhausted anymore, not the way he had when she'd come through the door. But he didn't look like the confident, oversexed guy she'd taken a chance on, either.

His gaze held for a moment that felt like it went on and on. Then he lifted a hand, the tip of it stained gray from the charcoal on the edges of her sketchbook. He cupped her cheek and leaned in. The kiss, when it came, was a simple, chaste press of lips on lips, but there was a weight to it. An unspoken moment of connection, of understanding. She'd seen what he'd seen on that hilltop. Had tucked it away and treasured it, and when she'd most needed to recapture some sort of inspiration, some impetus to *make* something with her hands...

That's where she'd gone.

He let her go, drawing back, but the heat of his gaze lingered even as he returned his attention to the page. He flipped to the next and then the next, and she held her breath. This was the one she'd felt so good about, after her first set of false starts. The one she'd done with the memory of his presence flowing from her fingertips, imbuing every stroke and shade with life.

Ghosting his fingers over the dark, black marks, tracing without touching or smudging, he followed the swooping arcs she'd mapped onto the paper. For a long time, he stared at it.

Finally, he started moving through the pages again. She

watched from over his shoulder, her breath coming more easily now. These pictures didn't give her that cringing feeling she got looking at her own work sometimes. She was proud of these. When he reached the last one, he flicked back through them, stopping on the one she'd drawn from the top of the hill.

"These are incredible," he said.

The urge to demur stole over her, even as she flushed with the praise. He'd believed in her before, and he believed in her now. It pushed away the doubt that always plagued her. Made the spark of her inspiration ignite. "I was just playing with something. An idea." She pointed to the web of lines he'd been drawn to before. "Tying everything together."

"It's great. Really." He shifted to look at her. "It's really, really great."

And what could she say to that?

He shook his head, as if he could sense her discomfort at taking a compliment. "I love the way you see things. And these... Not that the rest of your stuff wasn't good, but the stuff you did today. It's something different."

Her lungs felt tight, a warmth and an excitement fit to burst behind her breast. These images had *felt* different. Still, it hadn't just been her and her skill. "It's the city. Paris. It's beautiful."

"No." There was such certainty to his voice. It stopped her cold. "It's you." He shook his head. "I don't know how you can possibly even consider not going to grad school for this. You've got this..."

He trailed off. *Don't say talent, don't say talent.* People always said that, and she hated it. It demeaned all the work that went into what she did.

His mouth curled up into a soft, sad smile, and suddenly he wasn't talking about her future anymore. "It's how you see things, Kate. In these pictures, the ones you made today... It's like I can see through your eyes."

And there was an aching note now. She glanced up to meet his eyes.

All the edges of him were on display again. Not as jagged as before, not as tired. But they were there, and it struck her: She had no idea who this man was. What had happened to him to put those shadows in his eyes. How he felt or where he'd come from.

She wanted to, though. Desperately.

His gaze burned. As if he could hear her thoughts, he closed the book. He grazed a single fingertip along her temple beside her eye.

And then he asked her, "How do you see me?"

The strangest part was, it sounded like he actually wanted to know.

She blinked, once, then twice. With trembling hands, but with a surety she didn't know how to name, she reached for her bag and the supplies that it contained. For the fresh sketchbook she'd picked up on her way back to the hotel.

Because she had wanted this. From the very first time she'd laid eyes on him, she'd been itching for this.

"I don't know." She turned it to the blank first page. "But I'd like to find out."

Rylan glanced between Kate's face and her hands. What she was offering was clear, and it was what he'd asked for, wasn't it?

God, but his mood was twisted right now. He wanted to

be here, enjoying their last couple of days together, but after Lexie's call, all he could think about were his shirked obligations. His mother's face and his father's betrayals and everything he was missing back home. Everything he'd run away from.

All he could see was his own reflection staring back at him, and it was ugly. He didn't even want to look into his own damn eyes.

And there was a part of him, an angry, sullen piece of his soul, that wanted Kate to draw him. He wanted to look at himself through her pretty brown eyes and see the same callousness and apathy he'd been accused of so many times this year. To see it all confirmed would be a relief almost—a sign that his decision to sit here wasting his life alone was as good a choice as any.

He set her sketchbook aside before he could crush the pages with his grip.

He wanted her to draw him. And he wanted her to see something in him worth holding on to.

"Okay," he said finally, mouth dry and palms sweating. He managed a vague half smile. "What should I do?"

"Just get someplace comfortable. Sitting in that chair maybe. Or lying down?"

"Whatever you want."

She looked away, cheeks flushing.

That was interesting.

He ducked to put himself in her line of sight, quirking one eyebrow up. "What do you want?"

"Well, we—" She fidgeted, fussing with the binding of her sketchpad. It seemed to take her actual physical effort to meet his gaze. "We could do a figure drawing."

"Which means?"

"Drawing your"—she gestured vaguely at his torso— "*figure*."

It struck him all at once. "You want to draw me naked?"

She fake-smacked him with the book. "Well, it sounds dirty when you say it that way."

"It sounds dirty if you say it *any* way."

"It's not." A seriousness bled into her tone. She lifted her chin. "You're—you're beautiful. All the muscles, and your jaw and your...you."

Some of the ugliness that had been festering in his heart all afternoon melted away.

She shrugged, looking down again. "You are," she insisted. And she was so brave. He'd never given her enough credit for that. "The first day I met you, part of why I took that cup of coffee was your—your jaw. You were like a statue, and I wanted to get to look at you a little longer." Twisting at her knuckle, she bit her lip. "And then I got to touch you, too, and see you without your clothes, and you're just— I'd like to. If you'll let me."

Finally, she glanced up again, and his breath caught. Gears turned over in his mind, words rising up to the surface, but for once in his life, he couldn't seem to get them to spill forth.

Her face fell. "Or not. If it makes you uncomfortable, or..."

And what could he do? He reached out before she could turn away from him, putting a hand on her face and holding her steady as he leaned in for a kiss. Her lips were so sweet, made all the more so by the foreign warmth inside of him he couldn't seem to tamp down. And why should he?

Pulling back from the kiss, he touched his brow to hers.

"I think that's the nicest thing anyone has ever said to me." When she scoffed, he insisted, "It is."

Sure, he'd gotten compliments before. He'd had people—women—tell him he looked good. But this was something else altogether.

So he tried to treat it with the respect it deserved. "I'd be honored."

It wasn't a line and it wasn't a lie. He pressed his lips to hers once more, then backed away.

"You want to do this now?" he asked.

"Sure. I mean, I've got all my things."

They had a couple of hours before they typically wandered off in search of dinner. He couldn't think of any reasons to delay.

"Okay." He nodded and stood, setting his fingers to the collar of his shirt.

And it was strange, wasn't it? The still-racing beating of his heart and the desert of his throat. He'd gotten naked in front of more women than he cared to count. He wasn't shy about his body. He'd worked hard for it and kept it in the best possible condition. It wasn't as if he'd ever been shy in front of Kate. Hell, just this morning, he'd been wheedling to *try* to get his clothes off in front of her. So why was this giving him pause?

Behind him, she was fussing with something or other. He snuck a glance over his shoulder and spied a neat little row of materials arranged across the desk. Turning around again, he took a deep breath.

Tucking his thumb into the placket of his shirt, he slipped each button through its hole, then shrugged the fabric off. He actually took the time to hang it up, and cursed at himself in his head. Stalling. It was ridiculous—why was he stalling? He tore off his undershirt and dropped it to the ground. Took off shoes and socks, and unfastened his belt. Biting the bullet, he shoved his jeans and his boxers down as one and stepped out of them.

He turned to Kate with as much bravado as he could muster. All he had to do was make a dickhead comment about his—well, his dick, and everything would be fine. Normal.

But he met her gaze, and fuck. There was a warmth to it that was more than simple aesthetic appreciation.

Alarm bells sounded off like klaxons in his mind. He slept with tourists, with women passing through. He'd disappointed enough people, and he didn't have anything to offer a nice girl. It was better to stay unattached. Free.

But in a few short days, this girl had wound herself around him, and there wasn't any point denying it. He'd sunk his teeth in, too.

When it was over, it was going to bleed.

Right now, though, she was still *looking* at him like that. Any pervy joke he would have made died in his throat.

"Where do you want me?" he asked.

"Lie down." She gestured to where she had turned down the bed.

He let her direct him until he was positioned how she wanted him, with a handful of pillows propping him up. One arm extended toward her and the other bent under his head. Legs splayed out across the sheets.

"Perfect," she said after a moment, and she sounded as hoarse as he felt. "Do you think you can hold that for a while?"

He shifted in minute ways, but the discomfort he felt wasn't physical. "Yeah. I think so."

"Let me know when you need a break."

"Sure."

He lay there in silence for a long minute as she arranged herself in the chair, getting her sketchbook settled in her lap and selecting an instrument to draw with. And then, as far as he could tell, she just *stared* at him.

He had to turn his gaze away.

The *skritch-skritch* of pencil on paper told him she'd started working, and he had to fight the instinct to fidget all over again. *Relax. Calm.* He sank into the bed the best he could.

But no matter how deeply he breathed or how hard he focused on letting his mind drift, the simple truth was there.

He'd been naked a thousand times before. But he'd never felt it.

Not like this.

chapter SEVENTEEN

There was a certain kind of focused, aware calm that settled over Kate when she was really in the zone. Staring at the excess of riches laid out in front of her right now, though, she wasn't focused. She wasn't calm.

But she was aware.

Incredibly, brilliantly aware of Rylan's lips and eyes, the tousled mess of his hair and the stubble on his cheeks. He had the most gorgeous shoulders, taut with muscle without being bulky, and his biceps and forearms were sleek and strong. She'd always loved the feeling of his hands on her body, but she'd never truly taken in the shape of them before. Long fingers and blunt nails. The lines of tendons flexing underneath his skin.

And then there was the rest of him. With the subtle twist she'd made of his body, the crest of his hip stood out sharply, shadowing the hollow beneath it, pointing to the dips and curves of his abdominals. Solid thighs and well-formed calves. Hell, even his ankles and his feet were pretty, and she could scarcely catch her breath when she let her vision encompass the whole of him.

He wasn't hard, which was possibly the weirdest thing. She'd seen him in various stages of erectness, even seen him gently deflating in the aftermath of orgasm, but completely soft like this was new. She couldn't help the way her gaze kept being drawn back to it.

She'd touched that part of him. Had him on her tongue and in her hands and pressed up against her spine as he moaned into her ear.

And now it was hers to look at. As much as she wanted to.

With less than steady hands, she adjusted her book in her lap. She'd already done a quick couple of gesture sketches of him, waiting for him to settle. Tension lingered in his limbs, though, and she frowned. He wouldn't be able to stay still for long if he didn't relax.

"Do you want to stretch or anything?" she asked. "Get a drink?"

He blinked a couple of times, chest rising and sinking more rapidly. "Yeah, actually." He sat up in slow increments, rolling his shoulders and flexing his feet.

Just for something to do, she stood and grabbed him a bottle of water.

"Thanks." He took it from her and twisted off the top, lifting it to his mouth and taking a couple of careful, measured sips before setting it aside.

In the time she hadn't been looking, he'd pulled the sheet up to his waist. Part of her wanted to tease. He'd seemed so confident in his own skin before, but now there was a self-consciousness to him.

It was just so...unlike him.

She picked at her thumb, unable to stop staring at the drape of the cloth across his groin. "We don't have to do this, you know."

"I know." He looked down. "I'm fine."

"You sure?"

"Yeah."

"All right." She returned to her chair and picked up her pencil again.

After another minute of twisting and stretching, he shoved the sheet away and settled back against the pillows. The pose wasn't quite the same as the one she'd directed him into earlier, but that was almost better, honestly. What it lacked in drama it made up for in the way he eased into it, some of the stiffness from before bleeding away.

It was even more beautiful, and something in her heart stuttered.

"Is this okay?" he asked.

She looked up to find him gazing straight at her. It took a couple of tries to get the words to form. "It's perfect."

Flawed and perfect. *Just like you.*

She swallowed, forcing herself to relax her grip. She traced all the lines of his body in her mind one last time.

Then she turned the page and began.

It was easier, this time, to quiet his mind. He lay there, splayed out on the sheets, bare but for the chain around his neck.

He should have taken it off, probably. He hadn't thought to at the time, and with the way she was sketching away, at this point it seemed too late. Sometimes, he wondered why he wore it at all.

The scratching of her pencil on the paper settled over him, and he drifted along on it. He didn't want to throw her off by staring into her eyes, so he varied his gaze between her hands and the window and the ceiling above his head. Maybe he should have asked if he could pose with a book, or if they could turn on the television, only...

It didn't seem right, did it? He wanted to know how she saw him. She should see him with his attention undiverted.

And more, there was an energy to it. A humming static to the air surrounding them, moving from her to him and back again. This was intimate.

This was exposure.

Trying to hold still, he sucked the inside of his cheek between his teeth and bit down hard.

Maybe this was how she imagined it would be, letting him inside of her. He'd let it go; every time she'd squirmed or looked uncomfortable at the idea, he'd been quick to back off. But for the first time, now, he thought maybe he understood it. He felt vulnerable, lying there naked for her inspection. It wasn't sexual at all, but that was *why* it was so difficult for him. Sex he was good at. This—being open like this. It was something different, something he didn't quite know how to do.

He unclenched his jaw before he could draw blood. If he told her how uneasy he was, she'd probably say that they could stop again. But he felt like he was on the cusp of a revelation. If he could find a way to work through this, it would mean something. To him and to her.

The person he had been a handful of days ago told him it would get him in her pants at last. But a newer voice said that didn't matter. Whether he got off or not didn't *matter*.

If he made it through this, and if she saw in him something worth seeing...he'd earn her trust.

How much that mattered to him made him tremble.

For a long moment, he closed his eyes, focusing on the sounds of marks being made on paper. Then he shifted his attention. He relaxed his toes and his calves and his glutes. Breathed air into his fingers and his arms. Quieted the beating of his heart.

He looked again to find her staring at him in a way that made him feel not exactly vivisected, but...

Seen.

She smiled at him uncertainly, and he answered with the slightest of shakes of his head.

He let his gaze go soft and aimed it at the gauzy curtains framing the doors out onto their balcony. He gave himself over to it.

And as she kept on drawing, he felt like, somehow, deep in the empty parts of him, he was getting everything he wanted in exchange.

Kate looked down at what she'd drawn and blinked. She tilted her head from side to side and shifted her legs. Rylan had taken two more breaks in the time she'd been working, but she had scarcely moved except to reach for different materials.

Now, it was like coming out of a fog, the haze of creation receding as she examined what she'd wrought.

And it was...good.

Really good, and she didn't say that lightly. She knew better than to let herself get carried away. Ego was an ugly thing on an artist. But this was more than good. It was *right*. Exactly what she'd been going for when she'd set out to capture this man.

Holding the pad at arm's length, she regarded it more critically. She'd gotten the shape of his nose, had left some of the details of his features vague while still suggesting the parts that needed to be seen. She'd captured the pride and the self-assuredness, but between those lines, the rest of him bled through.

Vulnerability. Anger. Hurt.

There was something coiled to the man she had drawn, and the lines she'd penciled in to anchor his form to the sheets only accentuated it. He looked like he was waiting. She didn't know what for—or if he knew, even. But there was anticipation in the cant of his hips and the rigid set to his limbs. His pose spoke of relaxed ease, but it belied a readiness to walk right off the page and out of frame.

She tightened her jaw. She'd gotten that much right at least.

Shifting her gaze back to Rylan, she let the low ache that had been building in her chest all week come to the forefront. She had two full days left in Paris after today. She was the one who was going to leave. And he was going to let her.

"You okay?" His voice surprised her, interrupting the quiet that had descended on them.

"Yeah." She nodded, pulling her thoughts back to the here and now. "I'm fine."

"You sure?"

"Definitely." She tapped the corner of the page with her nail. "You good for a few more minutes?"

"Sure."

Putting the low curl of dread aside, she examined her work one more time. Made a couple of careful marks, darkening shadows and sharpening the appearance of a particular jut of muscle. She swept her gaze over it again, comparing it with the reality of the man in front of her. The drawing was as finished as it was going to be.

But she wasn't *done* yet.

Hoping he wouldn't mind, she turned the page, taking care not to smudge the work she'd just completed. She shifted in her chair to get a slightly different angle as she studied his face.

It wasn't only dread filling her belly now. It wasn't quite affection, either, though there was some of that there, too. It was deeper and warmer, and it hurt inside her chest.

Looking at him *hurt*.

So she channeled it.

With quick strokes, she tried to get down on paper how he made her feel, all twisted up and uncertain—like she was the one on display, exposed, even though he was the one stripped bare for her to see. Roughly intimating the shapes of his features, she focused on his eyes and his mouth, taking them apart into lines and shapes, distilling them into something she could understand.

But the end result didn't help. It was a portrait of the same mystifying, beautiful, inscrutable man, and she wanted to crush the paper in her hands.

A fresh page and another try, and another and another, but none of them put her any closer. Frustration made her blood hot. It wasn't the same angry, self-despairing aggravation that had nearly overtaken her up on Montmartre. It was knowing the solution to a puzzle lay just out of reach, and watching an hourglass about to run out of sand. She only had so much time.

To find herself, sure. But also to get some kind of grasp on what was happening to her, here, with him.

She turned the page once more. On the bed, he was getting restless, either because he'd gone too long without a break, or maybe because he could sense her distress. She had to calm the heck down. Now. Before it was too late and she'd lost her chance.

She took a deep breath and set down her charcoal, trading it out for a hard-leaded pencil. This time, she approached the page with all the quiet she could summon to her mind and her nerves and her hands.

Soft brushes of the graphite across the tooth of the paper. A hint of an outline. And then more line work. More and more, tracing around and across the planes of his face. The eyes she adored and the mouth she had kissed, and the man she . . .

A deep pang made her breath catch.

She didn't know Rylan. She didn't know him at all. But she knew his wit and his secrets and the careful way he'd touched her body. Brought her pleasure. Showed her around *museums* for God's sake. Opened himself up to her like this . . .

She sketched in the curve of his lips, and the last piece of the puzzle slipped into place.

She loved him.

It was written so clearly across the page—couldn't have been more clear if she'd spelled it out. Love shone from the curve of his cheek and the fall of his hair and the tender softness of his earlobe. So many tiny details, and he was going to see.

God, he was going to want to look at this and he was going to know everything.

Beyond her tunnel vision, he stirred, the rustling of sheets a low murmur of a sound, lost beneath the roaring in her ears and of her heart. Warmth on her shoulder, then blunt fingers making a dark contrast against the snowy white of her page as they tipped the book down.

It broke the spell.

She dropped the book, looking up. With the sheet draped around his waist, Rylan stood in front of her, concern twisting his frown. "Kate? You went all"—he waved his hand at her—"pale. You sure you're okay?"

She wanted to laugh.

No. She was the furthest possible thing from okay.

She'd burned her savings on an idiotic trip to Paris. Had gotten her purse stolen and had spent her days ignoring the work she'd come here to do because a *man* was paying attention to her. Was taking care of her and charming her and teaching her all sorts of things she'd never known her body could do.

So like the sad, naïve idiot she was, like her mother's daughter, she'd fallen for him. And she knew it. Without a shred of doubt, she knew.

He was going to break her heart.

She sucked in a breath like she was drowning. If the outcome was a forgone conclusion, what the hell was she doing here? She should grab her things and run back to her nice, safe hostel with its awful roommates and communal baths.

Or she could dig her feet in. There wasn't anything to lose.

If she wanted anything from him, she should go for it. Now. While she still had the chance.

chapter EIGHTEEN

If it hadn't been so scary, it would have been hilarious. Because, seriously, Rylan had driven plenty of ladies out of their minds with his cock.

But he'd never done it quite so literally before.

He stood there, wrapped up in a sheet, trying to pull Kate out of whatever sinkhole she'd fallen into. She stared at him, emotions breaking like waves across her face. Humor and anguish and resignation. One by one, they all ceded until there was only resolve.

"Kate?"

"Do you want to see?" She flipped to the first page of her sketchbook and held it out like an offering. She was still looking at him so strangely, and he wanted to shake her. To make her snap out of whatever had taken hold of her.

But in the end, he just nodded. "Of course." Extending his hand to accept it felt like stepping out onto a ledge somehow. He curled his fingers around the binding and paused, a whole new kind of apprehension taking hold. This entire thing had started when he'd asked her how she saw him. He was about to find out. But did he really want to know?

With a flash of false bravado, he cleared his throat. "You didn't make me ugly or anything, did you?"

"You tell me."

Her tone stopped him cold, because there was dread there. Christ, what the hell had she drawn?

Unable to put it off any longer, he took the book and sat down on the edge of the bed.

The first picture told him very little. It was a series of quick sketches—no detail. Just the outline of his body. He raised an eyebrow at the suggestion of his *anatomy* in one of them. But he really wasn't learning anything here. The second page was much the same, but the third...

His breath stuttered in his chest, and he jerked his head up. She was watching him look at her work, worrying her knuckles and chewing on her lip. The instinct to tell her it was amazing welled up in him. The whole thing—it was incredible. But he knew better than to spit those words out before he'd thought about it. He dipped his head again, studying the image of his own nude body, splayed out across pale sheets.

The likeness alone was remarkable, but there was more to it than that. It didn't just resemble him. It *felt* like him. Like the man he looked at in the mirror every morning, only better. If he'd questioned how she saw him, this was the answer.

She saw him too fondly. In a light he didn't deserve. From the scraps of his messed up, cobbled-together life, she'd made something beautiful.

All that time he'd spent secretly convinced that if you took away the trappings—the money and the clothes and the name—he'd be nothing. He'd taken them all off for her. Since the moment he met her, they'd all been off. And this was what she'd seen.

"It's good," he said at long last. "Like the one from Montmartre." He gazed up into her eyes. "Your perspective is all over it." It made him *feel* things, just looking at it. Things he still wasn't sure he was ready to feel.

Her expression didn't lighten any. "Keep going."

He frowned, peering down again. He wanted to keep studying this one. There were treasures inside of it. All the detail of musculature and fabric and space.

"Keep going," she insisted.

He shook his head, hesitating. If that was what she wanted...

His stomach flipped as he turned the page. She'd gone back to quicker sketches, not quite as vague as the first ones had been, and she'd narrowed in on just his shoulders and his face.

But the images were angry. Frustration bled through the marks. Some of the portraits looked just like him, while others only held the faintest resemblance.

What had she told him about Cézanne the day before? That he played with the shapes of things, making them more real by making them wrong?

It put him off balance. Did she think he was a monster? A puzzle to be figured out?

"One more," she said.

He turned the page, fearing the worst.

Only he shouldn't have.

The drawing staring out at him through the page wasn't like the others. But that didn't put him back on solid ground.

If anything, he listed further in his mind, because this one wasn't angry.

This was unbearably, achingly sad.

"Kate—"

"This is how I see you."

God. It was a web of delicate lines, silvery wisps of pencil marks. The image they created was a perfect likeness, only it evoked the exact opposite response in him as the last one had. It opened a new pit in his stomach. He wasn't so noble or so . . . so unapproachable. He was just a guy. Flawed and scared sometimes. Irresponsible and inconsiderate and so many other things his sister and his father and all the men who ran their company would have called him.

"I don't look like this," he said, quiet and unsteady.

"To me, you do."

He huffed out a wry little ghost of a laugh. "You're too kind to me."

"I'm not. You're just . . . you're gorgeous." She hesitated, as if waiting for him to say something more. When he didn't, she took his hand, lifting the sketchbook from his lap and setting it aside. Her voice was more restrained. "Thank you for letting me do this. You didn't have to, and it meant a lot to me."

"It's no problem."

"No. It was. This was hard for you."

That was an understatement, but the best he could, he shook it off. Still reeling from the vision she had shown him of himself were he a better man, he looked down at their hands. How they intertwined, her dainty, soot-stained fingers against his larger ones. His were stronger, but they were clean. They made nothing, they did nothing.

Except touch her.

When he met her gaze again, her eyes were dark, her full lips parted.

As he watched, she rose up higher on her knees, sliding a hand into his hair and pressing her lips to his. An intensity colored the edges of the kiss, an intent. He tried to give himself over to it, to the warmth and to the taste of her. But in the back of his mind, he was fixated on what she had made of him, and he didn't deserve it.

He didn't deserve the way she lifted her own shirt over her head, baring all that soft, beautiful skin. The way she unbuttoned her jeans.

It struck him all at once what she was doing. His body, already primed by her closeness and his nakedness, went instantly, shockingly hard.

"Kate—"

The look in her eyes as she pulled back left him no doubt. He swallowed, throat working against a tightness that didn't make any sense.

She slid her palm down his chest to rest over his heart. "I want this."

She couldn't possibly want it as much as he did.

And yet, for all his experience, there was something inside of him that trembled. "You don't have to."

"I know I don't." Her fingers splayed out wide across his ribs, and she looked at him with eyes that were so deep. So bold, where before they had always held fear. "Do you want me?"

His mouth went dry. "More than you know."

Gaze steady, cheeks warm, she said, "Then please. Rylan. I'm ready."

* * *

He hadn't seen it.

Even when confronted with the most obvious, incontrovertible evidence of how she felt, Rylan had let it slip right past him. The whole time he'd been staring at the lovesick drawings she'd done, he'd had those ghosts in his eyes again, and her heart had hurt. For her and for him.

There'd only been one other way to let him know. One way to satisfy the emptiness that came with the thought of holding back from him now.

It hadn't been a hardship, beginning to match his nakedness with hers. They'd been together like this enough times by now. It hadn't even taken much to offer him what she knew he'd always wanted. After all: This wasn't that one-night stand she'd had that once. Rylan wasn't drunk, and he'd proven he wasn't selfish. This wouldn't be painful. It would probably feel good.

And she'd get to keep it. Later, after she'd left him and gone back home, she would always have this to look back to.

Rylan's throat bobbed as he covered her hand with his, pressing it harder to his chest. He flicked his gaze from her eyes to her breasts to her hips and back. "Are you sure?"

Just like he had considered her drawings before rendering a verdict, she gave it the thought it deserved. Nothing in her heart wavered or changed.

Then she pulled her hand free of his. Reached back to unhook her bra and let the straps slide down her arms and hoped that was answer enough.

Dropping his gaze to the hollow of her throat, he placed a fingertip there and traced it through the space between her breasts, down to her navel, where he stopped. He looked her in the eyes again. "You change your mind and you tell me. Anything that makes you uncomfortable. If anything I do, if I touch you wrong or..."

She took his hand and brought it to the gap where she'd undone her jeans. He licked his lips and nodded. Together, they pushed the denim off her hips, taking her underwear with it. She grasped the sheet he'd draped across his waist and set it aside.

And then they were naked. Together. She shivered, because it was different this time, with her offering him everything. Knowing how deeply he'd affected her in this handful of days.

Refusing to be frightened, she shifted, edging closer to straddle his hips. It trapped the hard length of him between their bodies as she curled her fingers around his neck and pulled him into a kiss. She opened her mouth, and he slid his tongue inside, letting out a choked sound of desire as he wrapped his arms around her. God. He felt so good like this, so warm and solid and protective. With one broad palm between her shoulder blades, he folded the other around her hip, sliding it down to cup her backside before gliding it along her thigh. Her breasts were pressed against his chest, the ti tingling as they rubbed against firm flesh.

She got lost in it, melting into him, an ache of ing soft and hot and wet within her sex. Wh kisses that went on and on, he kept he she ever doubted that this would be him? Safe. Like nothing could

She shifted her hips ag mouth. He pulled back f across her neck and jaw.

"How do you want this to go?"

"I don't know." She let her head fall to the side, just wanting him to keep doing what he was doing. She gripped his shoulder tighter as he scraped his teeth against her throat. "However you want. Whatever you—"

He *shh*ed her. "I'll take care of you."

God, how had he known that was exactly what she needed him to say? The heat building between her legs bloomed anew as he lifted her, twisting them both until she was falling into the mattress. He shoved aside the mound of pillows he had rested on while she had sketched. She grabbed at him when he moved to pull away.

"Just a second," he promised.

She shivered without his heat, but she didn't reach for the covers. It felt strange to be lying there nude while she waited for him, except—except this had to have been how it had felt for him. For a couple of hours, he had laid himself out for her, entirely exposed.

The least she could do was wait a couple of minutes and not be afraid.

He'd retreated to the foot of the bed, and she furrowed her brows in confusion for a second before he picked up her sketchbook. How could she have forgotten it was there? With absolute care, he closed it and put it on the desk in the corner, turning back to smirk at her. "Wouldn't want it to get messed up."

He padded over to his bag and unzipped one of the pockets on the side. He palmed something, and she tensed until she realized what it had to be.

He set a condom packet on the bedside table before coming to sit at the edge of the mattress beside her. He looked her over, and she tried not to fidget or wilt beneath his gaze. With the softest touch, he ran the backs of his knuckles down the length of her side, tracing the curve of her breast and the dip of her navel. The swell of her hip.

"What I would give to be able to draw right now."

Her lip wobbled, and she couldn't take it anymore. "Come here," she urged, intertwining her fingers with his and tugging him down.

He came willingly enough, rolling to lie beside her, his front flush against her thigh. As he gazed down at her, a warmth overtook her, and for a moment, she could pretend. This wasn't a brief foray into intimacy, and it wasn't just her who had gotten attached.

He let her have her moment. His expression still achingly soft, he shifted forward to kiss her again. It was all the soft motion of his mouth on hers and the heat of his body against her skin.

And then it was more. As he licked into her mouth, he danced his fingertips across her abdomen, lower and lower. Each pass had the restless feeling inside her growing, and she shifted, trying to curve into his touch. She ran her hand up and down his arm, wanting to coax him and not wanting to ask.

When he finally slipped his fingers into the swelter of her sex, she whined, and he smiled, and she wanted to smack him or kiss him or... or more.

She panted against the soft roll of pleasure he wrung from her. "I thought we were going to..."

"We are." He shifted to kiss the corner of her lips, her chin, her jaw. "But not until you're dying for it. Gonna make you wet for it, Kate." His swallow and his breath against her made her pulse. "And then. Only then, when you're scream. When you're slick all down your thighs. That's when I'll know you're ready." He scraped his teeth against her lobe. Pressed the searing flesh of his own desire to her hip, and she shuddered. "Not a moment before that."

She closed her eyes against the feeling.

No wonder no other man had ever succeeded in making her come. None of them had ever approached it like this. Like a privilege and a job, and something they'd achieve if it were the last thing they ever managed to do.

He was good to his word, too. With careful fingers, he took her apart, two of them inside and pressing just exactly where she needed them, his thumb moving in tight circles against her clit. All the while, he kept his lips on her skin, kissing and sucking and *biting*, and when he teased her nipple with his teeth, she twisted hard. Trembling with the electricity shooting between her breasts and her sex and the heat that was rising to a boil, she shifted onto her side, reaching for him, wanting him closer before this feeling consumed her and turned her to ash, but he kept her still.

"You're there, aren't you?" He pulled his fingers free, and she threw her head back, gritting her teeth. "How does that feel? Does it leave you empty and needy and shaking?"

"Yes, God, yes."

Before she knew it, he was on top of her, two hands planted on the pillow beside her head, and the soaring crest of oblivion she had been hovering on fell away, leaving her reeling. The tip of his erection dragged, hot against her hip. She reached down to grasp it, to get that silky flesh in her palm, but he tilted away. Put his face right into her vision, and, God. His eyes were so dark, the intensity of it overwhelming, and perfect, and maybe she wasn't the only one in this.

Maybe it wasn't just her, feeling like everything had changed.

He put his hand on her face. "Tell me," he said, voice rough.

And the words almost slipped out. *I love you. Don't leave. Don't let me go.*

She came to her senses just in time. When he didn't stop her, she curled her hand around his hip. Lifted the other to touch his face.

"I want you." It felt like it took all of her breath, and it might as well have. The force of his kiss stole anything else she had left in her. He dropped down, rocking the hot, thick length of him through the valley of her thighs in an intimation of what he was going to do, so close but not quite there, torment for them both for an instant.

And then he was in motion. He rose up onto his knees and grabbed the condom, tearing it open and getting it rolled on before she could move to try to help. When he held himself over her again, she spread her legs and braced herself.

But all he did then was kiss her. Kiss her long and slow and wet, until she was dizzy with it, until all she knew was his mouth and his embrace and this gaping need inside of her, just waiting to be filled.

This desperate place in her heart, where he had already managed to fit himself, long before she'd invited him in.

When she slid her hand even lower to grasp the solid curve of his rear, he groaned and repositioned his hips. The blunt head of him nudged against her sex, but she didn't tense. He'd promised he'd take care of her.

He looked into her eyes. "You're so beautiful," he said.

The first breaching felt huge, but it didn't hurt. Not even

close. A long, gentle glide inside, and she closed her eyes at the fullness of it. The completeness when his hips met hers.

And then he did something no one else had ever done. He pressed his lips, soft and gentle and chaste to each cheek, even though he was *inside* her.

"You okay?"

She fluttered her eyes open to find him so close, mouth hovering just above hers. "Yeah." Because she was. "More than."

"Good." His lips twitched as he rocked deeper into her, and he stifled a little groan. "Because you feel *incredible*."

"Yeah?"

"Oh, hell, yeah." With that he covered her mouth with his, pulling backward with his hips while surging forward with his tongue, and it felt like a complete circuit. Like she was possessed by this man, and she never wanted to be anywhere else.

With gentle strokes, he pressed into her. She fell into his rhythm like she'd fallen into everything else with him. Each thrust ground him hard against her clit, building that warmth again in her abdomen. She held on tight, clutched him closer and tilted her hips, seeking that pleasure.

"That's right, baby," he murmured. It was less a kiss now and more simply breathing the same air. Being locked up tight inside this tiny bit of space where he was hers and she was his. "Take everything you need."

She closed her eyes and dug her nails into his back, straining, focusing until—

It was just a warmth at first, a soft curl of a promise in the base of her abdomen, but she grabbed on to it. Held on to Rylan and pressed her face to his throat as she whined. Each roll of his hips made the feeling grow. She gripped him harder, moving him against herself, against that hot brightness and pleasure just above where he was filling her. Bucking her hips up into him until it was all searing heat—light and darkness and a rush of nothingness, taking her under and down, and she was afraid she'd shake apart.

But he was there. Holding her together and crushing her close, murmuring in her ear.

It was all she needed to let go.

Her climax crashed down on her in a crescendo of feeling and need. Her voice and her body all shattered as she breathed his name over and over again, and God. To do this with someone who meant so much, to feel the hot breadth of him as he buried himself inside of her.

Only once the fog began to fade did he rear back. She looked up at him, and he was staring right at her, eyes open and cheeks flushed. He took another half dozen long, hard strokes in and out of her, and then he was arching. His mouth dropped open, and the groan that fell from his lungs shook her. His whole body trembled, and her heart twisted.

He was so beautiful in his pleasure. Felt so right inside her body and in her arms.

How was she ever supposed to let him go?

Rylan collapsed over top of Kate, scarcely remembering to catch himself and not force her to take all of his weight. For a minute, all he could do was lie there, breathing into the pillow. Fuck. He was still inside her, still twitching, and he had to squeeze his eyes shut tighter.

Because he'd had sex before. He'd had a *lot* of sex before, but not like that.

And wasn't that just Kate, though? She put him in these situations he thought he knew inside and out, and she made them different. More.

He shuddered and lifted himself up. He didn't need to be thinking things like that. As he got his elbows underneath himself, she stroked a hand up and down his spine, pulling a shiver from someplace deep inside of him. Her face was flushed and glassy, and her legs were folded gently around his hips. A warm rush of tenderness lit the center of his chest. He leaned in closer, stroking his nose against hers and then kissing her mouth, nice and soft. The way a girl should be kissed after letting a guy get that close to her.

She tasted so sweet, and the curl of her thighs around his waist had another round of aftershocks racing through him. He could have stayed like that the whole night.

With a groan and a last little sucking nip at her bottom lip, he pulled himself away. "Back in a sec."

He made his way to the bathroom, feeling less than steady and trying to keep that to himself. Dealing with the condom was the work of a moment, but he dawdled anyway, washing his hands a lot more thoroughly than he usually did, just for something to do while he got himself put together.

Turning off the tap, he dragged one damp hand through his hair, pushing it back from his face. As he did, he caught a glance of himself in the mirror.

Instead of shaking his head and moving on the way he usually did, he straightened his spine and forced himself to really take it all in. Not the sex hair or any of that, but not the shit he usually noticed, either—the too-deep cleft of his chin or the slant to his nose, or the bits that reminded him a little too much of his dad. It wasn't easy, staring at himself that way. No matter what he did, he couldn't conjure up the things Kate had drawn and seen. Was it really any use?

He dropped his gaze and grabbed a towel, drying his hands off as he walked back into the main part of the room. He furrowed his brow when he caught faint strains of music.

And then he stopped, everything in him just kind of going quiet at once.

Kate was sitting on their bed, facing the headboard, a loose sheet tucked under her arms and wrapped around her chest and hips. The crisp white of the cotton against her pale skin made it look all peaches and cream, and he swallowed hard. She was fiddling with a panel on the wall. He'd noticed it before but hadn't really paid it any mind.

The sounds on the air resolved themselves in his mind.

"Édith Piaf?"

She twisted, looking at him over her shoulder, and she was so beautiful he could hardly breathe. The soft curve of her smile cracked his heart. "It's a radio. All it plays is this really random old stuff."

And she looked so charmed.

"Yeah?"

"Yeah." She beckoned him over. "Come here and listen."

His feet didn't seem to want to move. For a second, he could only stand there, staring at her.

If he could draw, he'd paint her in ivory and pink and umber, looking exactly the way she did in that instant. Preserve her forever, to look at when he was old. Just like this.

But he couldn't.

"Rylan?"

"Sorry." He tossed the towel he'd been using in the vague

direction of the bathroom door. Unglued his feet and walked himself over to the bed.

He sat behind her, wrapping his arms around her waist and burying his face against her hair. Vanilla and rose, and layered in with it, the sharpness of his aftershave. The faintest notes of sweat and sex. His throat felt tight, and his heart was pounding too hard.

She put her hand over his. "You okay?"

"Yeah." He breathed her in, memorizing her scent. *Their* scent, all tangled together. "I'm fine."

"You sure?"

Lifting his head, he pressed a kiss to her temple. It was probably too intense, probably lingered too long. When he could, he nodded. "Absolutely. I'm just...happy."

She laughed, a soft, ringing sound. "Good. Me, too."

His heart felt like it was pressing against his ribs, but what could he do? He bit the inside of his cheek and cast his gaze skyward, then gestured at the radio, drawing attention from the way he'd been completely, utterly disarmed. "Does it play anything else?"

She paged through the handful of stations, each stranger than the last. The whole time, he held her, watching her and listening and trading comments about the selection of songs.

And it was another thing he'd heard of in the past—one he'd thought he'd done before. But really. He'd never known what *basking in the afterglow* meant.

Not until now.

chapter NINETEEN

"I can't believe we're doing this."

"What?" Rylan shot her a cheeky smile. "You've never had room service before?"

She tossed her napkin at him. "Not what I meant."

Honestly, she wasn't sure she ever *had* had room service. It was always so expensive. But Rylan had insisted, and at the time, her legs hadn't felt up to working. Even now, an hour after he'd turned her to jelly, her whole body was still thrumming, a warm glow of satisfaction radiating from the very center of her.

Yeah, staying in for dinner had been a good call.

Still. "Eating dinner in bed. Naked." She cocked her brow at him. "This is something you do all the time?"

He was sitting opposite her on the bed with their dinner plates between them. Somehow or other, they'd managed to split the sheet so it draped over his lap with enough left over for her to tuck the other end under her arms. All the important parts were covered, but it still felt illicit. Obscene.

Sexy.

Shrugging, he took a bite of his sandwich and chewed. "It's not exactly a first. But I wouldn't go so far as to say I do it all the time."

That dip was coming in her stomach. The little lurch that happened every time he reminded her that she was one of many.

Only then the corner of his mouth curled upward. "Can't say it's ever been this much fun before, though." He wiped his fingers on his napkin before reaching out to drag the back of a knuckle down the bare length of her arm. "Or that the view has ever been so good."

The anxious dip turned into a flutter. She dropped her gaze to stare at her own sandwich. He did this to her every time. Made her feel like she was special, when really she was just one of the herd.

"Hey." He gave her a second, then hooked his finger under her chin to tilt her head up. "Where did you go there?"

"Nowhere." She tried to smile.

Those piercing blue eyes stared back at her. "You're a terrible liar."

"Don't have a lot of practice, I suppose."

He cupped her face and swiped his thumb across her lip. "Good. I like you like this. All fresh-faced and innocent."

She shook her head. Kissed his thumb before batting his hand away. "Says the man who's been doing everything in his power to corrupt me."

"Not everything." His eyes twinkled. "But a lot of things." His grin receded as he poked at what was left of his pile of fries. "Haven't pushed it too far, I hope."

It didn't quite lilt up as a question, but she heard it as one all the same.

And she could do this. She could talk about the things they'd done. There didn't have to be any shame to it—even if something cold and uncomfortable threatened to unfurl in her lungs. "I—I don't regret anything. If that's what you're asking."

"It's something a guy likes to know." His one shoulder quirked upward and then settled back down.

"I don't regret it." She put more conviction into the words this time, because she didn't. No matter the heartbreak that was bound to come. It had been...amazing. Like nothing she'd ever experienced before. She was glad she'd get to hold on to that. "You were really good to me."

He made a little huffing sound and tore at the bread of his sandwich. "I am never going to stop being angry about the fact that anybody ever *wasn't* good to you. If you—" He cut himself off, fingers clenching into a fist before he relaxed them. "I hope you never let anyone treat you like that. Not ever again."

Right. The little dip in her stomach was back, twisting her insides up. He was talking about the other men she'd sleep with, after she left.

"I won't." It sounded too solemn, but there it was. Out on the air between them.

She'd promised it to herself once before, but it had been an abstract then. Now she knew how good she could've been getting all along. How terrible the bad had been by comparison.

"Besides." Her voice threatened to crack, and was she really going to do this? "There were only a couple of other guys," she blurted. "Before."

Apparently, she was.

Rylan paused. "Yeah?"

She'd told him that much their very first night. He'd prodded her then, clearly wanting her to tell him more about them, but she'd shied away. Now, though... She'd let him inside of her, had given up the one thing she'd been the most afraid to. She could give him just a little bit more.

"One was a hookup," she said, testing the words on her tongue. "I don't think I even got his name."

A month after things between her and Aaron had fallen apart, her friends had decided that enough was enough. They'd told her it was damn well time for her to pick herself up. Get back on the horse. Move on.

So they'd taken her to a club and bought her drinks all night. She'd caught a guy's eye, and she'd been so starved for the attention, she'd let him dance in close behind her. And when he'd asked her if she wanted to get out of there...

"I was...drunk. Not so drunk that I don't remember it or anything, but enough that I was maybe not making the best of decisions." She focused hard on picking at the crust of her bread so she didn't have to meet his gaze. Or show that her hands were trembling. "He was...fine. But he'd been drinking, too. Everything moved way too fast." She shrugged. "And when he was done, that was kind of the end of it."

It'd been the end of her interest in sex. Right up until she'd met Rylan.

"Asshole," he said, quiet but intense. It made her shiver.

But it also made her want to tell him everything else. She wanted him to hear it all, to know it all. She hadn't done anything wrong. But God. What she'd let herself become. How little she'd accepted for so long. It made her gut twist and clench, made her throat ache, even after all this time.

"The guy before that...Aaron." She gave up on her dinner. She'd more or less had enough of it anyway, and just thinking about this made her stomach turn to stone. She pushed her plate away and curled her hands together in her lap. "He was my first. First really long-term relationship, you know? I'd dated here and there in high school, but nothing serious. Definitely not anybody I'd...have sex with."

Rylan made an encouraging noise.

She drew her knees in close to her chest, hugging them tight. "He was smart. A business major. Really practical and driven." Goal-oriented was how he'd put it. The exact opposite of her with all her dreams about galleries and art. "Took me on nice dates and stuff." She paused when Rylan put his sandwich down, something in his gaze darkening. But he didn't try to interrupt her, so she soldiered on. "After a couple of months, he started wanting more, and I did, too." A dark chuckle bubbled up in her throat. "I was a twenty-year-old virgin, you know?"

Part of her had been terrified, as much by the relationship as by the sex. Her parents' marriage had been less of an example and more of a cautionary tale, and she'd carried the metaphorical scars with her for years. Still carried them, really.

Another part of her had just wanted to get it over with.

"He wasn't awful in bed or anything, but when he...did stuff, it never worked. I'd get turned on, and we...had sex. But." Her tongue had gone all twisted up, and her face felt hot, her neck cold. Why couldn't she just *talk* about this stuff? "I couldn't come."

"What?" Rylan looked at her with confusion, a displeased furrow coloring his brow. "He never fingered you or ate you out?"

The heat on her cheeks deepened, flowing down her chest. God. He said it like it wasn't dirty or weird or wrong at all.

Maybe because it wasn't.

"He did," she said. "Sometimes. It just didn't do anything for me."

"And you never took things into your own hands?"

Her laughter choked off with the force of her embarrassment. "Until you made me, I didn't even know that was something I could do in front of a guy." Not without him thinking she was a slut, or a pervert. Or who knew what else.

He'd finished up his sandwich by then, and he leaned over, the sheet sliding off his lap as he twisted to set his plate down on the floor. Sitting up again, he scooted closer to her, letting their bare legs brush beneath the covers. "Kate." He coaxed her to unfurl herself and took her hand in his, the skin warm and vital and strong. "I told you. There is nothing in this world sexier than a woman feeling pleasure."

A lump formed at the back of her throat. Because he really meant that, didn't he? He'd shown her as much with every kiss and every touch, had told her in a dozen silent ways, and this wasn't the first time he'd said it out loud.

"I mean it." His voice grew in its fervency. "You deserve someone who makes you feel amazing."

It was the *deserve* part that hit her like a punch to the chest. She shook her head without even meaning to, this automatic denial.

He squeezed her hand tighter. "You are beautiful and sweet and so fucking talented. You deserve—" He cut off, a flash of bitterness flitting across his face, but it was there and gone in a second. "You deserve someone who can give you every-thing."

Someone like you? The question pressed at her tongue, but she swallowed it whole. Nearly choked on it. Because he had. He'd given her this unreserved support, had shown this faith in her. And here in this bed, he'd taken care of her in a way that no one ever had before.

Because he thought she was worth it.

Her lip wobbled, her breath coming harder as the realization crashed over her, and she tried to tug her hands back, to get herself under control. She'd already accepted that she'd fallen for him, but what he was saying here, this kindness in the face of her sad history—it just made it hurt even worse. Her face crumpled, and his eyes went wide.

"Kate?"

She shook her head, but her voice wouldn't work. "I just—"

An impossible, unbearable warmth wrapped itself around her heart. She closed her eyes against it, but in the next breath, he was shifting across the bed, pulling her bodily into his arms, and the heat inside her went supernova. It burned through her, changing her.

Something that wasn't quite a sob broke past her lips, and he held her tighter. She swabbed at her eyes, but it didn't help. God, this was awful, breaking down on him, and because what? He'd been nice to her?

Muttering quiet assurances into her hair, he rocked her back and forth. "You're okay, baby."

But she wasn't. She was extraordinary.

A new kind of light seeped into her heart.

He treated her this way, gave her his time and his body, opened her up with such patient, tender care, because he thought she deserved it.

"I just—" she tried again. She opened her eyes, and the

world was still upright, the ceiling and the floor still exactly where they were supposed to be. It was her that was floating. The tear that escaped her felt like it glowed. "I didn't realize how badly I needed to hear that."

He practically forced the breath from her, his arms squeezed around her so hard. "I'll tell you every day," he said, and he didn't even bother to correct himself. To put a time limit on it. "You deserve the entire fucking world, Kate."

She didn't have to ask him if he meant it.

And that was it. The whole rest of the story came rushing out.

Burying her face against his chest, she said, "It wasn't just the sex with Aaron." He hadn't been outright abusive or anything. It hadn't ever gotten that far. But... "He started out so nice, but he put me down in all these subtle little ways." The shame of it all crept up on her again, that she'd tolerated it for so long. Had fallen into the same damn trap. "Like these offhanded remarks about how I dressed or the classes I took or what I was going to do after I finished college."

When you're still waiting tables and I'm on Wall Street...

"And it just got worse and worse, until I was believing it." She'd always believed it. "That he was better than I was and I was lucky to have him." That she didn't have any right to expect more of him. More affection or more time. More patience with her body.

Rylan's voice was murderous. "He's lucky I don't know where he lives."

"I could tell you," she said weakly. If it would get Rylan to come to New York, he could beat up as many asshole ex-boyfriends as he pleased.

"Don't tempt me."

She bit her lip. "When I found out he was cheating on me..."

Rylan's huffed-out breath was almost a growl.

And it was that—his fury on her behalf—that gave her the strength to tell him the rest. "There was this part of me that was ready to forgive him, because it was probably my fault." She'd been bad in bed, not attentive enough. Not good enough for him. "Until I remembered, until I realized..."

It was all hitting her again. A dizzying kind of pain and a stab of regret.

Rylan stroked her hair, patient. He was always so patient with her.

"It was the same damn thing that had happened to my mom."

Her crazy, wonderful, amazing mother, who had given up her own dreams to put her husband through school. To raise a daughter who'd come too young, and she'd never complained. Not until...

"My dad did the same thing, only it was so much worse." He was so much worse.

The tiny insults and the idea he'd given them both that they'd be lost without him. Scatterbrained creative types who always messed things up. Who made him so angry sometimes...

But they'd stood strong. He'd gone on to some other woman, and they'd been just fine all on their own.

Kate hadn't learned her lesson, though.

"After I found out about Aaron, I called my mom, crying, and she reminded me how guys just...change sometimes. They start out great and then there's this whole dark ugly other side to them."

It had been like turning on a light. She could suddenly see all the little ways she'd been broken down over the year she and Aaron had spent together. She'd dumped him the very next day, swearing she'd never let the wool be pulled over her eyes again. Her self-esteem might have taken another beating, but she'd promised herself it was the last time she ever accepted so little from a man.

And then Rylan had come along. He'd shown her what she'd been missing.

"My dad did it to my mother, and Aaron did it to me. They started out so nice and then they turned into these assholes, and I..." She could say this out loud. Thanks to Rylan, she could. "I deserve better."

She'd found it. Right here.

But Rylan's throat bobbed, and his hands went still, the little caressing motions he'd been making against her spine suddenly stopping. For a long moment he said nothing, and she sat there.

Bare for him the way that he had been for her that afternoon. And waiting. Waiting...

He sucked in a long breath, then let her go, his gaze burning as he took her face between his hands and kissed her. Her cheeks and her brow and her eyes and finally, finally her mouth. Drawing back he swore, "You do. You deserve the best." He hugged her again, and it was the warmest embrace she'd ever known.

For what felt like forever, she shook in his arms, letting him soak up the old, lingering hurt that had been weighing her down for so long. He murmured vague apologies into her hair, and she let him.

She felt more warm—more *loved*, sitting there, naked and

held by a veritable stranger than she had in her entire time with Aaron. Maybe her entire life.

"You know what?" she said, once she'd gotten her breath back.

"What?"

"I wish it had been you." Christ, she did. "That you'd been my first. That you'd shown me how—how *incredible* it could be."

How differently would things have gone with Aaron, with that random one-night stand, if she had known? Would there even have been anyone else? If she could've had Rylan first? If he'd pushed away all the damage her father had done with careful hands and kind words.

If she could have kept him?

He made a little *shh*ing sound, stroking his hand up and down the bare stretch of her spine.

She buried her face against his neck. "You just—you make me feel really safe, you know?"

Like she could let go. Like she could touch and be touched. Like she was worth it.

"Yeah," he said, clutching her close. "I know."

Aiming the remote at the TV, Rylan clicked the volume down to almost nothing. For the past half hour, he'd been slowly softening his voice as he narrated the romance taking place in French across the screen. But Kate's breaths had finally evened out. As the television went quiet, she snuggled in closer but otherwise didn't stir.

He left the screen on as he lay there with her. The pale blue light washed across her skin, making her face seem to glow. Her head was resting on his shoulder, her hair soft between his fingers. Beneath the sheet, all of her nakedness was pressed to all of this.

And he didn't deserve this. Not the tiniest fraction of it. His heart squeezed, and he had to pull his hand back from her hair, had to cover his mouth with his fist to keep the grunt of distress from falling from his lips.

This whole time, he'd been sitting around, feeling morally superior to the jackasses who had dared to touch her and not make her come. God. When she'd told him the rest of the story, it had felt like the floor was falling out from underneath him.

Like the moment when his father had been subpoenaed. When Rylan's eyes had been opened.

He was just like his father in so many ways. Since birth, people had been telling him that. Every step of the way, he'd been groomed to fill the old man's shoes, and it had chafed. The path that had been laid out for him, each decision he should've gotten to make on his own already predetermined. But it had been worth it. His father was a paragon, a monument, everything a man could hope to be. Everything Rylan was supposed to be.

When Kate had talked about her dad, her ex, those men who had seemed to be so good and who had turned out to be dark and ugly...

That day in his father's office, when the doors had burst open and the agents had filed in.

Dark and ugly. Those words didn't even begin to explain it.

Suddenly, all his father's faults had been laid out. His charm was his philandering, his business sense his greed. Aggression turned to cruelty and callousness, and Rylan had seen them all. He'd seen them in himself.

When Kate saw them in Rylan. When she found out who he'd been in line to become...

His lungs squeezed so hard he could scarcely breathe.

When she found out he'd been lying to her all along.

He bit down into his knuckle, trying to force the bile back into his throat.

Rylan hadn't lied to Kate. Not once had he said something explicitly untrue. But that wouldn't save him. He was just as bad as her asshole of an ex, as her dad. The ones who'd made her look at a man who was extending his hand and believe he was a threat.

Rylan was that threat. He was a liar.

And he hated himself even more than he had before.

A shiver ran through him. Kate shifted, and he froze. All she did was slide her knee across his thigh, though, letting her hand rest higher on his chest.

She trusted him.

Fuck. He curled his hands up into fists, digging his nails into the meat of his palms, but it didn't help. A good man would wake her up right now and tell her everything. He'd let her make her own decisions. He'd watch her walk away.

And Rylan just...*couldn't*. Her face would crumple, and it would kill him. She'd been so skittish when she'd met him, and the idea of putting that fear in her eyes again made him want to take every single thing back. Every word and every touch. And he would never do that. Not in a million years.

What was he supposed to do?

Except be as good to her as he could.

They only had another couple of days, and if he could keep his conscience quiet, he could spend those days with her. He could shower her with all the affection and care she deserved.

Then at the end of it, she'd go, and she would never have to know. She could keep *some* kind of faith that maybe there was a guy out there who wouldn't screw her over.

He couldn't decide if it was the most selfish plan or the most selfless one he'd ever had.

Her body gave another little restless twitch, and his heart ached. But he didn't wake her. He didn't let the confessions welling up inside his chest pour out.

His decision had been made.

He'd do what he had to do. He'd stay quiet, and he'd adore her the best he could. He wouldn't hurt her. Not any more than he had to.

Picking up the remote again, he turned the television off, bathing them both in darkness. With a murmur, she turned over, and he followed, fitting his front to the curve of her spine. He buried his face against her hair and wrapped her up inside his arms, closing his eyes and breathing her in.

But sleep didn't come to him for a long, long time.

chapter TWENTY

Rylan blinked his eyes open to an early morning glow seeping in through the curtains. Blearily, he closed his eyes again. He'd never been good at getting back to sleep, but if he could just roll over and kick his feet free from the covers, he might be able to.

Beside him, Kate gave a soft moan, and just like that, a layer of fog cleared from his mind. The two of them were still spooned up together, though by some mercy, he'd managed to end up with a few inches of air separating his dick from her ass. Not that it helped much. She was sleep-warm and slack against his chest, their fingers intertwined beside her head, her breasts pressed softly to his forearm where it draped across her ribs.

His morning arousal gave a little kick, and he shifted his knees forward, sliding his shin against the back of her calf. Her skin was so smooth, felt so good against his own.

His guilt from the night before crowded in on him, though. He closed his eyes and fought the tide of want pulsing through his veins. He started to tug his arm back, but she stirred, humming and squeezing his hand. He swallowed, ready to pull away when she half turned over and snugged her ass against his hips.

Lightning flooded through him.

"Kate," he groaned, and it was strained even to his ears. He extricated his hand from hers and gripped her hip, trying to keep her still. Not pressing forward, no matter how much he was dying to, just in case she wasn't okay with this when she woke the rest of the way up.

"Hmm?"

God. She was still moving against him, probably completely unaware of what she was doing.

His voice came out raspy and low. "You're killing me." He tried to scoot away, but to no avail.

Fuck this. He shook her this time. She was all pliant and warm, stretching her arms and craning her neck and feeling so fucking sexy against him he could hardly handle it.

And then all at once she froze.

Yeah. That wasn't a gun pressed to her rear.

"Sorry," he mumbled, releasing his grip. Maybe she'd let him get away from her now. He could go rub one out in the bathroom. Or maybe take a cold shower. *Something* to keep him from losing his fucking mind with how much he wanted her.

From taking something he didn't deserve.

"No." She sounded more awake now. Reaching back, she curled a hand around his thigh, preventing him from going anywhere, and goddammit all. He wasn't made of stone.

He wrapped his arm back around her, stroking the underside of her breast and mouthing at the smooth skin of her shoulder. "Baby." He shook his head in warning. "You're playing with fire here."

"You haven't burned me yet."

She had no idea.

He squeezed her tight, fighting against the instinct to roll his hips, but it was a losing battle.

Sliding her hand higher up his leg, she pushed into his touch, and he gave up. He cupped her breast. Let himself enjoy the soft flesh pressed all along the length of him. She made a little contented sound and craned her neck. Lifting up, he caught her lips, kissing her deep and wet. She tasted like sleep and sex, and she was moving with the gentle rocking of his hips now, rubbing her thighs together.

And he'd come to a resolution last night. He'd decided to keep the status quo intact, keep all the ways he'd misled her to himself, and there'd been a good reason for it. Sure, it gave him two more days to enjoy all the light she shone into his life. But it let her hold on to this as a good memory, too. It afforded him another chance to treat her with all the care and kindness she deserved.

He could do that. He could take this pleasure for himself. And give it back to her every way he knew how.

He closed his eyes. Dropped his voice even lower as he succumbed. "Are you wet for me?"

Her only answer was a breathy whine and a shifting of her legs, and yeah. Every time he'd spoken to her like that, she'd squirmed and acted all uncertain about it, but her body'd never had any doubts at all.

Growling, he scraped his teeth against her neck. "Guess I'll have to find out for myself."

With one last tweak of her nipple, he slipped his hand down, over the smooth plane of her abdomen to the tops of her thighs, and to that soft, sweet place between.

"Oh, baby," he groaned, turning his face into the pillow. "You're soaked. Were you having naughty dreams?"

"Maybe."

What he would give to see inside her head. Barring that, he slipped his fingers over slick flesh, dipping two just inside to get them nice and wet before sliding them up to tease at her clit. She squeezed his hip, digging her nails in.

"Feel good?"

"Yeah." She moved against him, thighs parting for his exploration, teeth scraping against his bottom lip. "Do you have another condom?"

He had a whole box. Pulling his hand away from her cunt, he grabbed her wrist. Put her own fingers right where his had been, because that was okay. She had to remember that she could do that. "Keep yourself warm for me."

She must have been pretty far gone or still a little bit asleep, because there wasn't any of the reluctance from the other night. She just curled in on herself, the motions of her fingers on her flesh sounding soft and wet in the quiet room, and fuck. He could stay there, listening and watching— maybe tasting—all day.

He huffed out a breath and tore himself away. The rest of the condoms were where he'd left them in the pocket of his bag. He tore one off from the strip and opened it up. Wrapping a hand around himself, he gave a few rough tugs at his cock before rolling the latex on, then stalked back to the bed to wrap himself around her.

She hadn't stopped touching herself. He was dying to get inside, but he made himself slow down. With his knee, he nudged her top leg forward, making more space for him to get at all that sweetness. He ran his fingers along hers, through the slickness and across her clit, then down. She took two fingers easily, clenching around them, tight but not too tight. Wet and unbearably hot.

"Can I?" he asked.

"Yeah, God. Come on."

Fuck, she was close already, and what a change that was from the first night. It made a warmth that had nothing to do with sex burn through his rib cage. She was so open now, so trusting. So willing to let him see her pleasure.

It was beautiful.

He drew his hand away, reaching between them to grab a hold of himself and guide his tip into place. He groaned aloud at the easy slide into her body, and it punched a noise out of her that made him even more desperate for it. When he was all the way in, he wrapped his arm around her and bit down hard at the meat of her shoulder.

"You feel so good," he managed.

"So do you." She moved to shift her hand away, and he shook his head.

He grasped her wrist before she could get too far, bringing her fingers back to the place where they were joined. "No. Don't stop."

"But you're—" She honestly sounded confused.

"Fucking you," he finished for her. "Yeah, believe me, I know."

"So..."

"So keep touching yourself."

"You don't want to..."

He wasn't sure where she was going with that, but he shook his head all the same. "I want to fuck you while you finger that sweet little clit. Can you do that for me, Kate?"

The moan that wrung from her was a twisted mix of mortification and arousal, and it made him start to rock his hips, unable to resist the temptation to move within her. Even those short strokes had him clutching her tighter, and yeah. He wanted her mad for it. He wanted her to *remember* this.

"Can you?" he asked again. "Can you make yourself come on my cock?"

"Yeah." It was high-pitched breath of a word.

And it was all he needed to hear.

He drew back farther this time before driving back in, running his hand up and down her side. He'd always loved having sex spooned together like this—the proximity and the heat of it, all the access it afforded to a girl's clit and tits.

Here in the dim light of dawn, in this bed, with this girl, it felt even more intimate. Having to stay wrapped up tight against her back matched his mood in selfish ways. He wanted to be close. Wanted the freedom to touch her skin and kiss her ears and shoulders and neck. He wanted to give her the best sex she'd ever had, so she'd never be afraid of it again. He wanted to give her everything.

A haze of slick wanting and motion blurred his vision as he sped his hips. It was a mix of technique and instinct, and the way she seemed to bring out the best in him. He blanked his mind to the crescendo of sensation, holding out, trying to push her over.

She panted when he rubbed her nipple between his fingertips, and it only got louder when he dragged his hand up to her face and ran his thumb across her lips. It was dirty and perfect, and he pressed the pad of his finger between her teeth, only to have her suck on it hard.

"Oh, that's beautiful," he murmured. He tugged free of her mouth and rubbed wet fingers across the peak of her breast.

She twisted and fucked herself back onto his cock, hand flying between her legs. It had his balls tensing, ready to shoot, but he closed his eyes and gritted his teeth.

"Come for me. Squeeze me. Let go, Kate. Come all over me, make me come, give it up and—"

She cut him off, crying out his name, and fuck. Fuck, fuck, *fuck*, it felt even better than he'd thought it would. He sped his strokes, shifting his hand to hold her by the hip. Giving into the heat and tightness of her, the feel of her all against his front. The smell of sweetness and sex, and just *her*.

"God, Kate—"

His whole world went dark as he released himself into her, fucking forward with a few last strokes until the sensitivity got to be too much. Buried within her, he stilled, just trying to fill his lungs. After a long few breaths, he forced his fingers to uncurl, petting her flank and hoping he hadn't grabbed her hard enough to bruise.

It would be just one more thing to feel guilty about, if he'd left any marks on her skin.

As gently as he could, he wrapped his arm around her, tucking her close. They lay there together like that in silence until he started to go soft. Wishing he didn't have to, he drew back, slipping from her warmth and pressing his lips to the point of her jaw.

Before he could get any farther, though, she twisted around, lifting up a hand to touch his face, tugging him down again to meet her mouth with his. It was a soft kiss, a serious one.

He pulled back after a long moment. "You okay?"

"Yeah."

He opened his mouth to ask if she were sure, but what right did he have to press? "Okay." He leaned in for another kiss before drawing away, rolling over to the edge of the bed. Keeping his back to her, he scrubbed a hand through his hair and rose.

The sex had been amazing, and he'd done right by her. He'd given as much as he had gotten. That was the line he had to walk, these last two precious days with her. He'd hold his tongue, and he'd be so, so good to her.

Then at the end of them, he'd let her go.

"So," Rylan called from the other room. "You ready to hear my awesome plan for the day?"

Kate's hand tightened around the bottle of ink she'd been returning to her bag. In theory, she was out here getting dressed while Rylan shaved, but then she'd gotten distracted by her art supplies and by thoughts of where she might like to go to sketch this morning. His question stopped her cold.

She already had plans for the day. Good plans.

Plans designed to distract her from the twisted-up mess that had become her feelings for Rylan.

Laying herself out for him the night before had left her feeling so much lighter. She'd let him into her body and her heart and even her mind, and it had been amazing.

But it made the reality of letting him go even more impossible to bear.

"What's that?" she asked, setting the ink aside.

Kneeling beside her suitcase, she fished out the cleaner of

her two pairs of jeans. She ducked behind the bed, checking she was out of Rylan's line of sight before sucking in her stomach and tugging them on.

"Remember how I tried to talk you into going to Versailles yesterday?"

Damn, she did remember that, now that he brought it up. She frowned, pausing with her hands at her waistband.

The simple truth was, she didn't want to go to Versailles. Sure, the history of the place was appealing, but everything she'd read said it was overpriced and overcrowded. It wasn't the kind of history she was interested in anyway.

"Vaguely," she said, shaking out a shirt. She shrugged. It wasn't *too* wrinkled.

In the bathroom, the water ran, the sounds of the razor clinking against the porcelain telling her he was almost done. By the time he joined her in the main part of the room, she'd gotten the shirt on and her wet hair combed out. She tried not to stiffen when he came up behind her and put his hand on her hip.

If he noticed the tension in her body language, he didn't point it out. Instead, he wrapped his arms around her and rested his chin on her shoulder. His body was so warm. It sent a shiver through her.

"I've been thinking about it some more since then." He rocked them gently side to side. "Imagine it. Train ride out into the country. Big old fancy rich guy castle. Dinner at a little château somewhere, away from all the traffic and noise. It'll be romantic."

That was the last thing she needed. He'd swept her off her feet with the most casual of gestures. If he actually *tried* to woo her, she didn't know how she'd survive it.

She let that doubt creep into her voice. "I don't know. I only have today and tomorrow left."

It hurt just thinking about it.

"I know," he said, more serious than she'd expected. "Which is why I want to show you the best time I can. Before you go."

God. Did his voice sound as wistful as she felt?

Scolding her overeager heart, she squirmed her way out of his embrace. "Rylan..."

"You don't have to if you don't want to." He shrugged, but his smile didn't reach his eyes. "I just thought it would be nice."

He turned around and padded over to his bag, dropping the towel when he reached it. The view of him from behind was as good as from the front. Maybe better. She got lost for a second, staring, remembering herself only once he'd pulled his boxers up to cover his rear.

She snapped her gaze away, taking a couple of steps backward to fall into the chair beside the bed.

"It's just..." She worried the inside of her lip between her teeth. She couldn't tell him that she didn't want to go to Versailles; he'd just come up with another, better plan. Admitting she was afraid to spend more time with him wasn't really an option, either. Which left... "I told you all the stuff I have to figure out this week. With grad school and art and jobs and stuff."

"And I told you. You'd be crazy not to pursue what you love." He looked at her over his shoulder as he shook a pair of jeans out, his tone all matter of fact. "And what you're amazing at."

"It's not that simple."

"Why not?" He stepped into the pants and tugged them up, fastening them before turning around.

Where should she start? "It's just...not. I'll have to take out loans if I go to school, and then am I ever going to be able to pay them off? Am I just wasting my time?" Surely he had to understand that. "I have friends who did the grad school thing and ended up at ad agencies afterward anyway, but two or three years older and saddled with these massive piles of debt."

"They aren't you."

She snorted. "You make it sound so easy."

"Then let it be easy." He hopped up onto the bed and stalked across it until he was on the opposite edge, right in front of her, their knees close enough to touch. He held out his hands, and she slipped hers into them. His eyes looked so sincere. "Listen. If you really think another day of working in your sketchbook will help you figure out your future—where you should be, what you should do..." His throat bobbed, and there was another layer of meaning, one she couldn't quite grasp. "Then that's fine. Do it."

"I just..."

"But," he interrupted her. "I think you already know what you want to do. It's just battling with what you're afraid you *should* do." The stroking of his thumb across her knuckles paused, a wrinkle appearing between his brows. "What you think other people expect you to do. And all the time in the world spent thinking about it isn't going to change that." He shrugged, expression clearing. "In which case, come take a trip with me. Let me show you some pretty things and try to make out with you in inappropriate places." Squeezing her hands, he smiled. "Choice is up to you."

He had no idea which choice was killing her the most right now.

Regardless, she wasn't ready to admit defeat quite yet. She drew her hands back and let out a long sigh. "Let me finish getting ready and think about it, okay?"

He didn't seem to like that answer, but he nodded anyway. "Fine."

By the time she'd dried her hair and gotten her makeup on, she wasn't feeling any better about things. She planted her hands on the counter and stared into the bathroom mirror. Raising her voice so he would hear it, she asked, "Versailles is really expensive, isn't it?"

He popped his head around the doorframe, fully dressed and looking infuriatingly perfect. "My idea. My treat."

She frowned. "How can you afford this?"

"Don't worry about me. I can handle it." He put his hands on his hips. "Just make a decision, Kate."

Putting his insistence on treating aside for a moment—she was going to have to find some way to pay him back before she left; no chance she was letting him bankrupt himself for her—she pulled her mouth into a sideways frown, regarding herself again in the mirror. Weighing her choices. In her peripheral vision, she could see his reflection, too, though.

He looked so ready to be disappointed.

And who was she kidding, really?

"Oh, what the hell." It felt like throwing caution to the wind, like ditching class. And knowing you were probably going to get caught. She pushed the sinking feeling in her stomach aside. "I can always draw from photos when I get home, right?"

The corner of his mouth ticked up. "Yeah?"

"Sure. Why not?"

She could think of a hundred reasons, but really...he was right. She knew what she wanted to do, with her life and with him. What she *should* do, she could worry about later.

And for the moment, she could almost forget about the consequences, as the biggest, broadest smile spread across his face. Brilliant and handsome, and all of it raining down on her. He darted forward and picked her up by her waist, spinning her around. "You won't regret this."

She tried to echo his grin.

She really, really hoped that was true.

chapter TWENTY-ONE

Okay. Rylan *may* have overbuilt this in his head a little.

With a sinking feeling in his stomach, he caught Kate's eye and tipped his head toward the next room. She crossed her arms over her chest and nodded. They weaved their way past the horde of Korean tourists between them and the next doorway.

They were coming up on the most famous parts of the entire damn palace, and Kate had yet to crack a smile.

A couple more rooms and another tour group later—Japanese, this time, he was pretty sure—they spilled out into the lushest set of quarters yet. Dimly lit but glowing all the same, the bedroom was all bright gold draperies and gleaming wallpaper, every inch of it embellished by *something*, be it a fleur-de-lis or a curlicue or a sun. Hell, even the fireplace was lapis lazuli.

This was it. Louis the XIV's fucking bedroom, the centerpiece of this whole place.

He turned to Kate, hoping for something, anything. "So?"

"It's...cool?" The corners of her mouth twitched up, but he knew when he was being humored.

Fuck.

Curling his hands into fists, he tried to see the place through her eyes. It was sumptuous and lavish and dripping with wealth.

And it was useless. Hollow. Just like him.

Beside him, she made an impatient noise and stepped around one of the tourists in her way. He followed her, reaching out to grab her arm. She started, like she hadn't been expecting him to touch her, and his chest hurt.

He could fix this. He would fix this.

"Hey," he said, leaning in close. "Do you wanna get out of here?"

She looked at him in confusion. "Do you?"

"I don't know." He didn't care. So long as she smiled.

"You were the one who wanted to come here, weren't you?"

"I wanted *you* to come here. And you don't seem to be having a very good time."

He paused as a little white-haired woman tried to sneak between them. He barely managed to restrain himself from yelling at her to go around—couldn't she see they were having a moment here? Ugh. Shaking his head, he motioned toward the next room and tugged Kate along as he headed off. She didn't put up any protest, so she couldn't have been too invested in the stupid Sun King.

Of course the next room wasn't any better than the last one had been, so he kept charging past everyone. They were missing all the most well-known stuff, but he didn't care. Finally, he hit the end. He stormed down the set of stairs, only to have her wrench her arm back.

"Slow down," she hissed. She was taking the steps at half the speed that he had been, and it was a reality check.

Restraining himself from saying anything or from rushing her any further, he stayed one pace behind her until they were back in the courtyard, breathing the fresh air.

She rounded on him. "What got into you back there?"

He shrugged, looking at the building behind her. "You looked miserable."

"I told you this isn't really my thing."

"I know, I know." God, he knew. "I'm sorry, okay, this was a shitty idea."

"It could have been worse."

"How?"

The corners of her lips flirted with a grin, and it was like a weight coming off his spine. "There could have been a Russian tour group in there, too?"

He barked out a laugh. Swiping his hand across his brow, he shook his head. "Look, I wanted to show you a nice time." He'd wanted that so much. "But apparently I mucked that up."

For the first time since they'd gone into the palace, she stepped into his space. Put her hands on his chest and waited for him to look at her. "You didn't muck anything up. No, this hasn't been my favorite trip we've taken, but no one's perfect."

"This was a really long ways from perfect."

"Everywhere else you've taken me has been."

He didn't want to let go of the tension he'd been holding on to—the irrational panic, because they had so little time left, and he'd wanted to make the most of it. But when she pulled him down into a kiss, he couldn't help it. His shoulders dropped, and the rigidity of his spine melted.

"I'm sorry," he said after a minute. He spoke over her when she looked like she was going to interrupt. "Not just for talking you into coming here." He grabbed her hand and held it in his. "But for pouting like a four-year-old when you looked like you weren't enjoying yourself."

"Apology accepted." Lifting up onto tiptoes, she dragged him down to kiss his nose.

He felt so much calmer now. Letting her go, he gestured at the palace behind them. "Do you want to try to get back in there? Walk around the gardens? Anything? Or do you just want to go?"

"Were our tickets time-stamped?"

If there was one thing his family had taught him, it was how to talk people into letting him do what he wanted. Sometimes it took a greased palm, but that wasn't a problem. Still, he fished out his wallet and flipped it open, thumbing through the billfold for the tickets. He examined them for a second. "I don't see anything that says we can't go back in."

He looked up from the tickets to find her brows furrowed, and her gaze was on— He snapped his wallet shut.

The back of his neck sprung out in a cold sweat. This whole week, he'd managed to remember to pay cash wherever they went, and in small denominations, not wanting to flash around his Amex or the amount of paper money he typically carried around. He'd opened his wallet up under tables or behind the cover of his jacket or his sleeve. He'd been so damn careful about it. And now here he was, flipping the thing open in the clear light of day and right under her nose.

His pulse raced. *Play it cool.* Hanging on to the tickets, he slipped his wallet into his pocket. "So? Want to brave the crowds again?"

She just kept staring at his hands.

"Kate?"

She shook her head, snapping out of it. "Huh? Oh, um. Nah.

Though, I guess I wouldn't mind looking around the gardens? It's such a nice day, and we came all the way out here."

He had to stifle a sigh of relief. He still couldn't quite escape the feeling that she'd seen through him, but until she brought it up, he sure as hell wasn't going to. With a smile, he held out his arm for her to take. "Lead on, my lady."

She slipped her hand into the crook of his elbow readily enough. But there was something contemplative to the way she kept glancing at him as they walked. Like she was looking at him just a little bit too closely.

Lots of different credit cards looked the same.

Kate reminded herself of that on a loop, every time the niggling bit of suspicion tickled at the back of her mind. She didn't even know what a Black Amex looked like—how would she? But if it was as literal as it sounded...Well, then what else could it have been?

She snuck a peek up at him. They'd walked a decent stretch of the gardens around the palace now—hopefully enough of it to make him feel a little bit better about things. She was just starting to think about broaching the idea of heading back to the city.

He stopped her with a hand on her arm before she could turn around. "Hey." He pulled out his phone with his other hand. "Remember this trick?"

With that, he tugged her in, tucking her under his arm the way he had outside the Louvre on their very first day together.

Something nervous fluttered in her chest. "When you convinced me to take a selfie as a flimsy excuse to get your arm around me?"

"Yup. Say cheese."

She smiled the best she could, but as she did, she was looking at his phone. It was a new model. Fancy. Expensive.

She shook the thought from her head once he'd taken the shot. He let her go and flicked back to see if the picture had come out all right. When he found it, he smiled, turning the phone to show it to her. "We look good, right?"

They did. Tense but good. She nodded.

He twisted his phone around to get both thumbs on it, holding it as if to type. "You never did give me your email address, you know."

She did know that. "Oh. Right."

"Do you not want the pictures?" He raised an eyebrow.

"No, I do." It made her nervous for some reason. As if giving him a way to contact her crossed a line. Ridiculous, considering all the other lines they'd merrily waltzed past without a second glance. Fighting down the fidgety feeling, she rattled it off to him.

He typed it in and nodded. "Ta-da. Sent."

"So now I've got your address, too."

"Yup."

She hadn't checked her email since she'd left the hostel. She should probably make a point of doing that soon, just in case. Without really thinking about where she was going, she started walking again.

"So." He fell into step beside her. "Anything else you want to see here?"

She hadn't particularly wanted to see anything here in the first place. "Not really."

"May I make a suggestion?" His usual cockiness had simmered down a notch. It sounded like a real question.

"You may."

"I say we catch a train back to Paris. Have dinner. My treat."

He'd offered to treat enough times this week. She'd practically lost count.

She was counting again now. "You don't have to do that."

"I want to." He nudged her shoulder with his own. "Come on, let me apologize for... this." He waved his hand around.

This. Which he had also paid for.

Her heart was in her throat. "What did you have in mind? Dinner-wise?"

Shrugging, he steered them toward the main gates. "I haven't taken you to a real French restaurant yet. What do you say? Escargot? Cassoulet? Foie gras?" His voice lilted up, his flawless accent kicking in.

The one he'd acquired following his parents around Europe when he'd been a kid.

God. The itch of a suspicion turned into a tide of realization, her heart thumping hard against her chest. All that stuff about hostels and splitting the cost of a hotel room—had it all been a trick? If so, she'd fallen for it. He must think she was such an idiot.

"Can we just head back to the hotel first?" She needed to get her legs back under her.

Concern crossed his features. "You okay?"

"Yeah."

But when he tried to put his arm around her again, she couldn't relax into it.

All day long, ever since she'd slipped out of his bed this morning, she'd been thinking she had to protect her heart.

Maybe she should have been protecting more than that. Maybe she should have been protecting it from the start.

chapter TWENTY-TWO

Rylan managed to wait until the door of their hotel room was closing behind them before he rounded on her. And shit, he could actually feel his father's boardroom training taking over. Making him keep his distance. Making his face hard.

Just like his dad, when Rylan or his siblings or his mom had disappointed him.

What the hell else was he supposed to do, though? Kate hadn't exactly refused to touch him the whole way home, but fuck if it hadn't been the longest train ride of his life. Her, sitting right beside him, hand held loosely in his until she took it away to fidget with her nails, her hair, her bag. She forced him to reach for her when he wanted to touch her again—never offered contact herself. The entire time, they'd spoken maybe a dozen times.

Regret was eating at him, but it was slowly shifting into something angrier. He never should have pressured her into spending the day with him. He definitely shouldn't have suggested Versailles.

He should have put the tickets someplace other than his wallet.

It didn't seem like it could be that simple, but she'd gotten all closed off right after he'd flashed the damn thing in front of her. He didn't need to be a detective to figure it out.

He closed his eyes and curled his hands into fists, taking three deep breaths before staring across the room at her. Last night, everything had seemed perfect. And now it had come to this.

Fuck it.

"Say it." He tore his jacket off and tossed it in the corner with the rest of his things. "Whatever you're thinking. Just say it."

She'd been facing away from him, rummaging through her bag, but at the harsh sound of his voice, she shoved the thing aside, sending it clattering to the floor. The violence of it startled him, and his heart squeezed as she set her hands on the edge of the desk. Dropped her head and drew her shoulders up.

"Who are you?" She didn't look at him until the question was out of her mouth, and even then, she didn't turn. Just twisted her neck to gaze at him with dark, sad eyes.

His heart rose up into his throat. "What do you mean?"

The whole thing was choking him, the irony making it hard to breathe. Yes, he'd hidden the details of his life from her. But in these spare handful of days, he'd shown her all these other things. Parts of himself that people who knew a lot more of the facts had never seen. Parts he'd never shown to anyone before.

"I mean," she said slowly, "who are you?"

"You know."

"No." Her mouth drew into a tight line. "That's the problem. I don't."

For a moment that felt like an age, he stood there, waiting for the blow.

Finally, Kate turned around, her gaze level. Her voice quiet but strong. "Let me see your wallet."

And there it was. Not a physical impact, but a punch to the gut all the same. "Kate..."

Negotiate. Dodge around the subject. Turn the tables.

She held out her hand. "Give it to me."

He tried to joke, "If you needed money, you could have just said—"

"That's not what I need. That's the last thing I want from you." Her throat bobbed, and her eyes were far too bright. "Don't you know that?"

There wasn't any negotiating with that—with the way she was looking right through him. She'd seen his heart; all these days and nights, he'd showed it to her again and again. But she didn't want that. She wanted the shell.

And it was all his fault. He'd set himself up for this right from the start.

"I can explain everything," he tried, but she shook her head. "Just let me see."

He wished he'd gotten a chance to kiss her one last time.

Resigned, he reached into his pocket and pulled the damn thing out. Really, if she'd been paying attention, just the brand and the suppleness of the leather gave him away. A hundred tiny details all gave him away, from the watch he'd been wearing that very first day to his patterns of speech to the shape of his father's ring. But she hadn't wanted to see. Hadn't wanted to hear.

And now he had to tell her the truth.

"It's funny," he said, handing his wallet over. The world seemed to shiver, a low sense of vertigo making everything sway. "I told you my last name when we were at the Musée d'Orsay. You didn't flinch."

"Should I have?"

"A lot of Americans do."

She opened the billfold and counted out the five hundred odd euros he had left in there. Then with unsteady hands, she pulled out the Black Amex. The membership to the VIP fitness club attached to his mother's apartment building. Each card as damning as the last, and when she looked up at him, her expression was bereft.

"Theodore Rylan Bellamy the third," he said, like he were introducing himself for the first time. It was a weight lifting off his shoulders and an anchor sinking him to the bottom of the sea. "Firstborn son of Theodore and Felicienne Bellamy."

She repeated the name, pronouncing it slowly, recognition a distant but approaching hollowness to her eyes. "Theodore Bellamy."

"I'm surprised you don't remember it, if you go to school in New York. It was in all the papers last year. He embezzled half the earnings out of Bellamy International." He couldn't help grasping the ring through his shirt. "Within five years, it went from one of the biggest IPOs of the decade to a cautionary tale."

Her gaze followed the motion of his hand as he tightened his grip on that little slip of gold. "Your father who went to prison."

"Currently starting the second of a fifteen-year sentence."

"I don't remember—" She cut herself off. "I was in school. I didn't pay that much attention to the news."

"There's not much more to tell. Well, unless you skip to the gossip pages. Then there's his society wife who was having dalliances with half the young men in Europe. She had her own assets, so when Dad went away, she started over again. Somewhere. I imagine she's doing well."

"And your assets?"

"My father lost almost everything, but we each had trust funds predating the crimes. The courts couldn't touch them."

Looking faint, she sunk down to sit on the edge of the bed and dropped her head into her hands. "Trust fund. You have a trust fund."

Of course that was what she keyed in on.

"I never lied to you, Kate." Spoken aloud, it sounded just as empty as it had when he'd thought it in his head the night before.

She look up at him, eyes blazing, and *fuck*. Apparently, it sounded even worse than that.

And then she laughed, the sound ugly and wrong and bordering on hysterical. "No," she choked out amidst it all. "No, of course you didn't. Stupid me just made assumptions about you being a normal guy. Stupid me suggested you'd been staying in as terrible of a hostel as I was."

"I should have corrected you."

"Damn right you should have. Crap." She buried a hand in her hair and tugged. It looked painful—made him want to cross the room to her and stop her, or soothe the ache with his touch. "Shit, you must think I'm such an idiot."

"No. Not at all." He went so far as to reach out, but she recoiled, standing and stepping back, putting as much space between their bodies as the room could afford.

It was a slap in the face. One he deserved, but one that

took him by surprise. It hurt even more when she wrapped her arms around herself.

Her expression was lost. "You lied to me. I trusted you, and you lied to me. After everything I let you do, after everything I told you last night..."

"I wanted to tell you..." His excuses and his plans seems so pathetic now.

She shook her head. "With that kind of money, you can have anything, do anything you want. Stay at the nicest place in the city. And yet you're here."

"I thought you'd be more comfortable—"

"What? Someplace cheap?"

This was all spinning out of his control so fast. "Someplace..." The word stuck in his throat. "Normal."

Because that was what he'd been stealing here, what he'd been squirrelling away in this pocket of time. The chance to be *normal*. To have a normal life instead of having to be...him.

It had been exactly the wrong thing to say.

"Normal." The corner of her lips twitched downward. "Ordinary, right?"

She was the furthest possible thing from ordinary. "No!" He planted his feet, raked his hand through his hair. "You're twisting everything I say."

"Because you lied." She said it so quietly. "I asked you who you were, so many times, and you lied."

"Not about the things that mattered."

Something in her eyes broke. "But they were things that mattered to me."

And what could he say to that?

He wasn't sorry. She never would have touched him had

she known, and he wouldn't give up what they'd had for all the money in the world. Even with how much this hurt right now. He wouldn't give it up.

"Tell me how to fix this."

Shaking her head, she looked away. "I don't think you can." She swiped a hand under her eyes and turned, picking her purse up off the floor.

Reaching for her suitcase.

Everything in him screamed. She wasn't really leaving. Not without giving him some kind of a chance to make this right. "What are you doing?"

"Packing."

"And where are you going to go?"

"I don't know. Back to the hostel. A different hostel. I don't care."

"No. No way."

"I'm sorry, but you don't get to tell me what to do."

His throat ached. "You're really going to throw this all away? Just like that?"

She twisted to look over her shoulder at him. "Throw what away? This was never going to last." And there was something bitter there. "Even if—even if you hadn't... It was a fling. I live in New York and you live here. Even if I were in your league—"

"Don't you ever say that." He steamrolled right over her. She could say a lot of things, but she could *not* say that.

"Please," she scoffed. She looked away again, but not before he saw the redness in her eyes. "I'm this naïve, broke art student, and you're..."

The word came out before he could stop it. "Lost." With her, he'd felt found for the first time in months. In years. "You weren't wrong, that day in Montmartre. When you asked me what I was running away from. I may have more resources—"

"And more experience, and all these..." She waved her hand, flustered. "...moves. Your pickup crap."

"My pickup crap never worked on you."

She shook her head. "It worked so much better than you ever would have imagined. I just pretended it didn't because—"

He gave her a beat before asking, "What?"

"Because I knew you were going to break my heart."

God.

"Kate..."

"No." She grabbed the couple of things she'd spread out on her nightstand and shoved them into one of the pockets on her bag. "It doesn't matter."

Two could play at that game. "It matters to me."

She snorted, clambering over the bed to avoid touching him on her way to the bathroom. The second she stepped away, he headed over to her bag and started taking things out again. She came back, her toiletry and makeup bags in her hands, and glared at him.

"I'm not letting this go without a fight," he promised. "After everything. All the places we went, and the..." His gaze drifted to their bed. The one where she'd let him strip her bare. Let him taste her and touch her and put himself inside her. He squeezed his hands into fists. "After everything we've done together." His heart dropped another inch. "After I posed for you."

He'd shown her his fucking soul, and now it was all worth nothing to her? Because he'd told a couple of little half truths?

She paused, breathing slower, and for a brief instant, he

let himself harbor a hope. She surveyed the tiny space where they'd touched and kissed, and dammit, made love.

And then she gave him the most watery, awful smile. "Maybe it's better this way."

"Better?"

She stepped around him, placing her things into her bag. Swallowing hard, she grabbed his hands, and it felt so fucking good just to have her touch him. Right up until she took the shirt he had balled up in his fist and pried his fingers away.

She repacked it, along with the other items he'd removed. "If this had gone on—if I'd left feeling the way I felt yesterday..." Her voice cracked, and just the sound of it had his own eyes burning. "I would have held a torch for you forever. I always would have wondered."

He would never, ever stop wondering.

"And now?" He barely dared ask.

She zipped her bag, and it sounded like the end of the world. "Now I can go home knowing it was never meant to be."

He took a step back. She was done. Really, truly done, and he didn't have any more illusions about changing her mind. Besides, it wasn't right. He'd told her, that first night she'd let him make her come: Anything she didn't want to happen—he would never force it. That hadn't just been about sex.

It was her choice. He could respect that. He *had* to respect that.

She raised the handle of her suitcase and turned toward the door.

Oh, goddammit. Fuck decorum and fuck respect. "You know," he said, stopping her. "The only reason I didn't tell you the truth right off the bat." It was a weakness, admitting this. It rankled, but who cared? He'd already given her everything else. "It wasn't to deceive you, or to seduce you."

She paused.

It was his only chance.

"You were beautiful, and smart, and you saw right through my bullshit." He took a deep breath. "And I thought—I thought you saw something more than just that superficial stuff. Like you *wanted* to see more than that. And I wanted it. I wanted it so fucking bad, though I didn't know it at the time. The idea that a girl might like me not because of my name, or who my parents are, or because I've got some money." Because of all the things that had been beyond his control. His lungs felt hollow in his ribs. "I wanted you to like me for who I was."

"Oh, Rylan." Her gaze met his. "I would have liked you for who you were regardless." The corner of her lip wobbled. "But you were the one who wouldn't show me who that was."

He had to look away.

When he turned to her again, her eyes were glassy and her cheeks splotched, but her shoulders were back. She lifted her chin.

"You told me—" She cut herself off and started again. "This morning, you said you thought I already knew what I wanted. I just had to stop worrying about what I *should* do and go for it. You're right. You were right about me." She shook her head. "I hope you figure out what *you* want, Rylan. I hope you can be honest about it, at least to yourself, when you do." She shot him a shaky smile. "Because I'm not the only one you've been lying to this week."

With that, she let go of the handle of her suitcase and came over to him. She put two hands on his shoulders, but he knew what this was.

The kiss when it came was hard and angry and sad. It tasted like good-bye.

"Don't go," he said, sounding broken to his own ears. "If you want me to leave, I will, but stay. Take the room." *It's yours anyway.*

With a wistful little smile, she said, "I like to pay my own way."

And that was it.

She made it all the way to the door before he gave in and stopped her one last time. It was fucking masochistic, dragging it out like this, but he couldn't let this one thing go unsaid. "I never lied about how amazing you are." There was more, too, about how he hoped she pursued her art and her dreams, because she was so damn *good.* She made the world a more beautiful place.

But before he could reopen his mouth, she said, "Neither did I." She didn't look back.

The door opened and closed behind her. It sounded like a death knell. All the energy going out of him at once, he collapsed into the empty chair in the empty, empty room.

Just like that, she was gone.

chapter TWENTY-THREE

Oh God.

Kate just barely made it to the elevator bay before she broke down, smacking the button over and over while the dam burst inside her. She heaved out her first rough sob while still mashing at the button, waiting for the freaking doors to open. She had to get this under control—there could be someone in the lift, Rylan could decide to chase after her, hell, a maid might stumble by—but it wasn't any use. She'd managed to hold it together that whole time in Rylan's room, and now it was all crashing over her.

She'd walked out on him. He'd lied to her, had been pretending to be someone he thought she'd like. The entire time, when he'd touched her and when he'd told her she deserved more. It had all been one big lie.

The doors of the elevator slid open, revealing an empty car, thank God. Dragging her suitcase along after her, she stepped in and pressed the button for the lobby, letting out a whole new fresh torrent of tears with the closing of the doors.

Alone in that contained space, she shuddered and buried

her face in her hands. She'd loved him so much. It had been too soon to feel so strongly, but she had. None of it had been real, though, and she'd been such an idiot to let him in in the first place. More of one to fall so fast and so hard. He was probably laughing at her right now.

Except she'd seen the look on his face. The devastation. He was a damn good actor, she knew, but was he that good? Did she care?

The elevator dinged as it arrived at the ground floor, and she scrubbed at her eyes. As if that would help.

She had practical things to worry about. She needed to find a place to stay for her last couple of nights. Rylan probably wouldn't come looking for her, but there weren't any guarantees about that, so she needed to find a different hostel than the one she'd started out in. He had her email address, but no other contact information for her. She was probably safe.

She shoved her hair back from her face and squared her shoulders before stepping out. The little details—the ones she'd somehow managed to ignore every time they'd strode through here in the past—stuck out to her like sore thumbs now. Gilded edges on mirrors and a marble bust beside the door. Thick draperies and gleaming tile. Of course this place cost more than he'd said. Lying *liar*.

Shaking her head, she marched up to the desk and dug through her purse until she found her keycard. She placed it down on the counter and slid it across to the woman standing there.

Who of course asked her a question in French.

Shit. She'd gotten way too dependent on Rylan handling all of their transactions this past week. She blinked a couple of times, all her high school French flying out of her mind, deserting her.

"English?" she asked weakly.

"But of course. Are you checking out, mademoiselle?"

"No. No, I—the other person I was staying with. He can keep the room." It was his anyway. She bit her lip. Maybe she should offer to pay her half of the bill for the past few days. As if there was any chance she could afford it. "It's just me who's leaving."

"I see." She took the keycard and fixed her with a sympathetic look, and Kate wanted to melt right into the tile and disappear. "There is a water closet." She pointed to the left, down a hallway, then gestured at her own face. "If you would like to freshen up, I can hold your bag."

How much of a mess did she look like?

She nodded. "Thanks." She rolled her suitcase to the end of the desk, where the woman tucked it under the counter.

Her cheeks burned as she rounded the corner to the bathroom, hauling the door open and stepping inside. At least there wasn't anybody else there to witness her humiliation. She stepped up to the mirror and took a good, long look at herself.

It was worse than she'd thought.

Her eyes and nose were red, heartache written across every inch of her. In despair, she grabbed a wad of paper towels and ran them under the tap.

The goddamn gold-filigree tap.

God*damm*it.

She squeezed the sodden mess in her fist and threw it away, turning off the tap and running to lock herself into a stall. Her head hit the back of the door, and her eyes blurred and burned. Hot tears made tracks down her face. Their room had been just as nice, the fixtures had shone just as brightly.

She felt so *stupid*, and not just for missing the signs.

Her mother's voice kept coming back to her, telling her that people weren't always who they said they were. Kate hadn't learned from her mother's mistakes, and now she hadn't even learned from her own. After her last breakup, she'd sworn she'd learn to stand on her own, that she'd never let anyone lure her in with pretty words again.

Rylan's words had been pretty all right.

Another choking sob tore itself free from her throat. He'd made her feel special, and so she'd let down her defenses, convinced that he was *different*.

She took a deep, shaking breath and blew it out, opening her eyes. She tore off a couple of handfuls of toilet paper and wiped her eyes and blew her nose.

This time, she'd learned her lesson. Letting people in was a mistake, believing any of the things they told her to get her in bed. It was all a mistake.

One she was never, ever going to make again.

Rylan wanted to throw something. He eyed his phone, the lamp, half the contents of his suitcase. Reared back and started to take a swing at the wall itself but drew himself up short.

He could see the headline in the gossip page: BELLAMY HEIR TRASHES HOTEL ROOM. He didn't need that shit.

He didn't need any of this.

Threading his hand through his hair, he gave it a good

hard tug and turned around to look at the fucking empty room he'd been left with. She'd only stalked out a few minutes ago. If he ran he could catch her. For a few euros, the doorman would probably be happy to tell him which way she'd gone.

But no. Fuck, no. He'd already made his case. He'd stopped her ten times on her way out. Nothing he could say would change anything. It would probably just make things worse. He couldn't go after her.

He couldn't stay here, alone, either.

Jaw gritted, barely restrained violence still thrumming through his limbs, he gathered up what little of his stuff he'd let get strewn across the room and shoved it into his bag. Out of habit, he opened all the drawers and checked the closet. Even lifted up the bed skirt—

Only to find a book there.

A sketchbook.

Fuck.

It suddenly seemed impossible to breathe through the tightness of his chest. He flipped it open, and he had to close his eyes. Had to stop himself from crinkling the paper in the stone of his fist.

They were the pictures of him, of course. A dozen pages of his face and his eyes and his hands. All of him, spread nude across that bed.

He'd shown her so much. He'd hidden things he shouldn't have, but his ribs were clawing at him with the anger boiling in his chest.

Well, fuck her. Fuck that and fuck everything. He grasped the pages in his fist and moved to tear them out and—

And he couldn't. It was all he had of hers.

Faltering, eyes hot, he closed the book and laid it on top of all the other crap in his bag. He'd find a way to get it back to her. That would be the right thing to do.

With that, he zipped up the bag and slung it over his shoulder.

He took the stairs down to the lower level. When he slid his card across the counter to the woman at the desk, she raised one eyebrow and asked, "Vous partez?" *Are you checking out?*

That had been his plan, but..."Non." He'd booked the room through the end of her stay.

And he might be livid with her now, but if she couldn't find someplace else...she could always come back here. He wouldn't take that option away from her.

The woman furrowed her brow as she scanned the card. "Une clé nous a déjà été rendue pour cette chambre." *I've already had another key returned for this room.* She looked up from her screen, and the expression on her face was damning.

Kate had dropped her key off when she'd left. It made him even angrier, that she would have left herself without recourse. What if she couldn't find someplace? Her options had to be limited on her budget, and hostels sometimes sold out.

"Oh." He blinked a couple of times. Dammit all. Refusing to be judged, he asked to add another name to the reservation.

Kate wouldn't come back. Her pride wouldn't let her. But if she had to...he'd make sure she was taken care of.

It was too little too late. But it was all he had left that he could do.

* * *

Of course the only open bunk was a top one, smack-dab in the middle of the room.

Kate put her bravest face on. She was lucky to have found a place to stay, and to have been able to afford it. Forget that it had no privacy, or that she was probably going to fall and break her neck if she had to go to the bathroom in the middle of the night.

She shook her head and rolled her suitcase up to the wall beside the bunk. She was lucky to be here, and it was only two nights. Two nights alone in a tiny bed, sharing a room with five strangers.

But it was fine. The best she could have hoped for, considering.

Grabbing her purse, she climbed the ladder up to her bed. At least the ceiling was high enough that she could sort of sit up without bumping her head. Sighing, she dug through her bag until she found her travel guide. It was already well into the evening, so there wasn't much point going out, but she could figure out what to do with the rest of her trip. Not everything was lost. She had one more day here in Paris, and she had the freedom to spend it any way she wanted to. No negotiating about when to meet up with anyone for dinner. No smoldering, pleading eyes staring at her. No gorgeous man entreating her to stay in bed.

Just her and her sketchpad. Exactly how she'd wanted it to be.

But it wasn't what she wanted anymore.

The idea of exploring museums on her own hurt her heart. Eating meals in cafés alone, reading a book when she could be snuggled up in bed, watching weird TV while listening to the translation being whispered, warm against her ear. It all *hurt*.

The cover of the book blurred as her vision went damp. She'd had so many ideas about what this trip would be, and all of them had been wrong.

She had one more day to see everything left she had to see.

And all she wanted to do was go home.

The door to the apartment banged against the wall as Rylan slammed it open. Shoving the thing closed behind him, he dropped his bag in the foyer and stormed into the kitchen.

The mess he'd left behind had all been cleared away, but the foul, stifling feeling in the air still lingered. No cleaning crew would ever be able to contend with that. He laughed darkly at himself.

Reaching up into the cabinet, he pulled down a highball glass. The good liquor was stashed behind the bar in the living room. Seemed a pity to waste thirty-year-old scotch on a mood as poisonous as the one he was choking on right now, but that was the benefit of his life, right? His stupid, pointless life.

Gripping the glass, he headed to the bar, not bothering to turn on the lights. He'd left the curtains open, so Paris's glow was seeping in. He popped the top off one of the crystal decanters and poured himself a couple of fingers. The whiskey went down nice and smooth as he knocked it back.

He slapped the glass down on the top of the bar, then braced his arms and let his head hang.

A week. He'd had one fucking week with Kate. After

spending a year essentially alone, it should have been nothing. A drop in the bucket. But it had been everything.

One week had been all it had taken to make the rest of his life look so hollow.

He raised his head a fraction, and his gaze focused in on the vase sitting on the corner of the bar. It was pink porcelain. Probably cost a fortune.

He *hated* the fucking thing.

He hated all the time he'd spent staring at it, hated the color of it, hated the idea that his mother—his *mom* had left it here along with all the other things she didn't need. Left it here to rot.

The violence that had shaken his limbs at the hotel came rumbling back with a vengeance. Before he knew what he was doing, he'd picked the vase up and drawn his arm back. And he put all his force and all his anger into hurling it as hard as he could.

The vase hit the wall with a crash, shattering into ruin. A rain of jagged porcelain shards, crumbling into the carpet, and fuck. Just *fuck*.

He'd made such a mess of everything.

"Was that really necessary?" a voice asked out of nowhere.

He jerked his head up, flailing his arm to the side, getting his hand around a stray corkscrew that'd been left out. A figure was sitting up on the couch—the very one he'd just flung a vase over. Pulse rocketing, he reached behind himself, feeling along the wall for a light, flicking it up when his fingers connected with the switch.

He blinked hard against the sudden brightness, willing his vision to adjust. Once it had, he gaped. Set the corkscrew back down on the counter.

What the hell?

"Lexie?"

His sister arched her back, letting out an enormous yawn. "Long time no see, brother dearest." She paused for a minute and sat up straighter. She blinked, then cocked her head to the side. "Dude. You look like shit."

chapter TWENTY-FOUR

"Seriously, what happened to you?"

Rylan wanted to bang his head against the table, but he managed to restrain himself. Barely. "Could we maybe focus first on what the hell you think you're doing here?"

"What"— Lexie looked around innocently—"in the dining room? Where else am I supposed to eat my dinner? Midnight snack? Is it closer to midnight in this time zone? I'm not sure."

He rolled his eyes.

Once he'd more or less recovered from the heart attack she'd given him by showing up in his living room, he'd stormed off to the bedroom he'd been using as his own to wash his face and try to get himself under control. His sister had apparently taken advantage of the pause in conversation to order take-out.

Now she sat at the big, fancy dining room table he never used, dark hair tied in a knot on top of her head, bright pink pajamas making his already sore eyes hurt.

He gestured toward the croissant and lox and fruit she'd

unpacked from the brown paper sack it had arrived at their door in. "Who even delivers croissants?"

She shrugged. "Beats me. Jerome can get you anything you want, though. Night or day."

"Jerome." The concierge down in the lobby. "How do you know Jerome?"

She gave him a look like he was an idiot. It wasn't an expression he'd had directed at him in a while, but it was painfully familiar. "Mother and Evan and I killed an entire summer here one year." She waved a hand at him. "But you wouldn't remember. You decided to stay at Exeter or something, I think."

Of course he had. He'd taken any excuse he could get not to go home back then. "You were, what? Fifteen?"

"Fourteen."

"And Jerome was getting you anything you wanted, huh?"

"Within moderation." Her eyebrow twitched upward. "Some things I preferred to handle internally."

Rylan really didn't even want to know.

He gave her a second as she tore off a piece of croissant, topped it with a bit of the salmon, and popped it into her mouth. The noise she made was borderline obscene. "You cannot get a croissant like this outside of Paris."

Of course you could. There were five places he could name in New York alone. "Lex," he finally said, out of patience. He'd come back here to lick his wounds, dammit, not deal with his sister. "What are you doing here?"

"Well, I was trying to take a nap, right up until you decided you didn't like Mom's interior decorating."

He didn't take the bait. "Aren't you supposed to be at school?"

She rolled her eyes. "I graduated two weeks ago. If you read your email you'd know that."

"So, what, you decided to celebrate with a trip to Paris? Here to find yourself or something?" The question came out sneering, but it threatened to strangle him.

"Ha-ha. Not all of us have time to travel for pleasure, you know." She stabbed a bit of her fruit, then set her fork aside, narrowing her eyes as she stared at him. "Look, Thomas has been trying to call you. I've been trying to call you. The one time you actually pick up, you brush me off within about three seconds. It's been a year, Teddy."

"Don't call me that."

"I'll call you whatever I want. Family gets to do that."

He snorted. "Family."

"Yup. Like it or not, that's what we are."

"And we're supposed to, what? Band together and pick up the pieces our disgraced patriarch left for us?"

"Basically."

"Well, I don't want to." He rose from his seat, feeling too caged in there at the fancy table in this ugly, fancy room. Feeling too caged in this conversation. Rubbing a hand over his face, he paced over to the wall, then flipped, putting his back to the plaster. "I wash my hands of the whole damn thing."

"You washing your hands of me and Evan, too?"

"Evan doesn't give a shit about any of this."

"He will, someday, when he wakes up from the hippy dreamland he's living in."

That *hippy dreamland* being art school. Anger rose up in Rylan's throat. "Why do you always have to dismiss what he wants to do with his life?"

"Because it's not a real life! He should be part of the family business—"

"Not everybody wants to be you!"

Fuck. First it had been Kate, thinking about throwing away her passion because of whatever imaginary pressures she was facing to conform, and now it was this. It had always been this.

It had always been Lexie, striving so damn hard to be their father. Only their father hadn't wanted a daughter for a CEO. He'd wanted a son. Evan had been too sensitive—too drawn into other things.

So Rylan had been the one to step up. He'd done what he had to do, for the family and the company, and for Lexie and Evan, too. Fighting for Lexie's right to a seat at the table. For Evan's chance to study whatever he wanted to at school. Fighting for everyone except himself, and he was tired, goddammit all.

He was done.

He glanced up at Lexie to find her staring at him, face stricken.

"Fuck it," he mumbled under his breath. She'd never understood anyone who hadn't had her drive.

He was almost to the door before she spoke.

"I don't want anyone to be me." Her voice was unusually soft. Just a little bit shaky.

He didn't turn around, facing the hall as he said, "But you expect us all to want the same things you do."

"I don't. I just want you to care."

"Well, I don't. Not anymore."

"Just because Dad got caught—"

"He didn't just get caught. Christ, Lex, don't you get it?"

All the things he never talked about—the things he never even let himself so much as *think* about—were rising up, sticking in the back of his throat and dripping poison into his gut.

She threw her hands up. "No! I don't, okay? I don't get it. The whole thing made you so damn butt-hurt—"

"They took everything." Fuck, fuck, *fuck*. He smacked his fist against the archway of the door and closed his eyes, pressing his brow to the back of his hand. "I gave my whole fucking life to Dad's ambition." His breath went short, his lungs tightening. "It was all I had, okay? Dad's name and Dad's company and Dad's dirty money, and the name's worthless now. Our family is worthless. The company is in ruins. All I have left is the money."

He'd thought there'd been something else there. With Kate, when she hadn't known who he was or what he brought to the table. She'd looked at him like he was something more.

But in the end, after she'd found out...

It still hadn't been enough.

He squeezed his eyes shut tighter and gritted out, "Without it, I'm nothing."

A long beat of silence followed, deafening even over the roaring in his ears.

"Teddy..."

He cut her off right there. Pushing off the wall, he opened his eyes and squared his shoulders. "If you're still here in the morning, the coffee's—"

"In the jar next to the fridge."

"Right." He took another step forward.

Her voice followed. "You're not nothing."

"Sure."

"And you know you can't run forever."

He clenched his hands into fists and kept walking.

Only in the silence of his room, with the door closed, did he whisper, "Watch me."

Kate knelt beside her suitcase the following morning, gathering her things as she got ready to head out. Her heart still ached every time she let herself think about what had happened the day before, but she was done with that. *Done.*

She'd given into the temptation to be a self-pitying lump the night before, but this morning, Paris was her oyster. She was going to do all the things she'd been too caught up in her whirlwind romance to take the time for. There were a couple of sights she still wanted to see, and she was getting back to the Louvre if it killed her. All she needed were her pencils and charcoals, maybe that lonely little bottle of ink. Her new sketchbook . . .

Her heart pounded in her chest as she turned the contents of her suitcase over a second time. Her sketchbook.

It wasn't there.

The metal structure of the bunk behind her creaked as one of her still-sleeping roommates turned over in her bed. Kate bit her lip. She felt like a heel to be making so much noise, but she needed that book. Professionally if nothing else. Those sketches she'd done had documented the new style she was developing. She could've used them for reference for when she wanted to—

She stopped herself, an ugly bubble of laughter getting caught in her throat.

For when she wanted to what, *draw* him?

And suddenly, she wanted to do just that. Not the lovesick paintings she'd imagined she'd labor over while she nursed her broken heart, but angry ones. She wanted to take him apart, lay him out with furious brushstrokes and flay him to pieces with a palette knife. Expose him as a liar and a thief and—

A thief.

A new, colder rage slipped like ice into her veins. Did he *steal* her book? He would've had the opportunity. While she'd been in the bathroom, when he'd started to unpack her stuff in an effort to get her to stay. He'd already stolen her secrets and her story and her body. Taking her art would've been just one more violation.

Maybe he'd done it to get her to contact him. He was so good at saying all the right things. He'd lured her into his bed once already, and he'd been damn close to convincing her to stay and hear him out yesterday. Maybe this had all been another trick to rob her of her time, or convince her to let him fuck her again before she left.

Maybe she should do just that.

He had told her that she deserved pleasure and sex, and clearly he knew how to give it to her. She could get in touch with him and ask him if he'd found her sketchbook and go back to the mansion he probably lived in and get him to put his mouth on her again. Take what she wanted from him this time.

And then leave. Go home with all kinds of lessons learned.

About what she could ask for in bed and what happened to her when she let it become more than that. More than just sex.

But no. Crawling back to him after everything she'd said—she wouldn't give him the satisfaction.

She couldn't afford to take the risk. Rage might be fueling her blood right now, but her heart was still too tender. Too bruised. She didn't trust it enough.

It—and she—needed time to harden up before she tried getting close to anyone again.

Hands shaking, she repacked her suitcase and stowed it, then checked over her purse. She'd swing by the hotel where she and Rylan had stayed on the off chance that housekeeping had found her book. That she'd just left it there by mistake.

If it wasn't there, she'd write it off as a loss. She'd put it behind her.

She'd move on.

Lexie was still there when Rylan woke up. She'd traded the pajamas for one of her usual ensembles, a black and white and pink top with jeans she'd probably paid a grand to have look like they'd been casually worn in. She'd done her hair and makeup, too, though he had no idea who for.

He stopped at the threshold of the living room to blink the sleep from his eyes.

Jesus, when had she started to look so much like their mother?

Scrubbing at his face, he stumbled past the couch where it looked like she'd decided to crash for the night, pillows and folded-up blankets stacked up neatly on the floor beside it. He mumbled out a low grunt of a greeting as he passed her.

"You seem chipper."

He grunted again and poured himself some coffee. Lexie must have made it earlier. At least having her around was good for something.

It was early yet. By his own ridiculous standards, he'd slept in the past few mornings with Kate, but waking up alone had apparently reverted him back to his usual habits. And he was exhausted.

"What're you doing up?" He poured some cream in his coffee and took a sip.

"Jet lag is a bitch. I got a nap in, but that was about it."

"You could have used one of the bedrooms."

"You're in the one I always used to stay in. And Mother's room..."

Yeah. That was the last place he wanted to sleep, too.

"There's always a hotel."

"Like the one you've been staying at the past few days?"

That woke him up. "Excuse me?"

"You left the bill on the entryway table. You still have the place for another night, you realize."

"That's not for me." Not anymore.

"And the duffel bag by the door is just one you keep full of dirty laundry all the time?"

He didn't have an answer for that. Flipping her off was close enough, though.

"Very mature." She turned off the TV and crossed the room to him, empty coffee mug in hand. "You know, you never did tell me what was wrong last night."

There wasn't much point denying that something had been bothering him. The shattered vase in the corner kind of gave him away. "I don't want to talk about it."

"Ooh, it must be good, then." She refilled her cup and put her back to the counter. "Come on." Her voice went teasing. "I can braid your hair and you can tell me all your secrets."

He gave her an appraising look. She was trying just a

little too hard here. But then again, she also decidedly wasn't pressing him about going back to New York to save the company. Or giving him shit about his outburst from the night before.

So he went with it, letting the one corner of his mouth curl up. "The hair-braiding thing only ever worked on Evan and you know it."

She hummed in agreement. "He had such nice hair, before Dad made him cut it off."

"It's probably grown back by now."

"It was still short the last time I saw him."

"Which was when?"

"Six months ago, maybe? He came and stayed with me for Christmas."

While Rylan had stayed here, staring out a window at a Paris that was lit up like a tree.

"Teddddyyyyyy," she whined. "Tell me."

The name and the question made every hair on the back of his neck stand up.

"It's nothing." He gripped his mug tighter. "Just—just a girl."

"I knew it!"

"Please."

"What's her name? What does she do? Is she French? I bet she's French."

"It doesn't matter." He set his mug down before he could break it. "She's gone now." He put his hands on the counter and faced away from her. Fuck, this hurt to admit. "It's over."

He tried to remind himself: It had been over before it had begun.

*　　*　　*

Kate hesitated, standing at the base of a set of white marble steps. It was one of her very favorite parts of the Louvre. Above her loomed *Winged Victory*, the huge statue she'd seen with Rylan that very first day, when he'd taken her here to try to earn her trust. This was the path they had taken. Just a few more twists and turns and she'd be back in the rooms where he'd charmed her, looking at beautiful, enormous paintings. Waxed philosophical about Greek mythology and told her about his family. If any of that had even been true. Bitterness welled up at the back of her throat.

But then she hesitated. His tales about the rich, socialite mother who'd taken him to art museums when the family visited Paris on business—they fit with the confessions he'd made once she'd figured him out. So maybe not every story he'd sucked her in with had been a lie. Just the majority of them.

If only she could go back in time and *shake* her former self. Open her eyes and save herself so much heartache. All the signs had been there. She was the idiot who'd refused to read them.

She dug her nails into her palm. And he'd been the asshole to let her believe what she wanted to.

She was blocking up the flow of traffic, standing where she was. Sighing at herself, she changed direction and headed away from the stairs, back toward the gallery she'd just been through. There were entire sections of the museum they hadn't made it to. She was going to hit as many of them as she could.

This was what she'd come to Paris for in the first place, after all. Not to have some torrid love affair, or to fall head over heels for a beautiful, tousle-haired, blue-eyed boy.

A rich, lying, confused, sad man.

She was here for art and beauty and culture. To find her muse, and she'd found it all right. She'd happened upon a whole new style of drawing that she was going to take home with her, and into whatever was next for her life.

She didn't need him to make the art come to life. Didn't have to conjure the feeling of him at her spine to get her drawings to come out right. She didn't.

She wouldn't.

The next morning, Lexie slammed a briefcase down on the coffee table.

Rylan looked at it for a long second, then turned his attention back to his phone. "Nice. But I prefer black leather. Brown snakeskin is a little feminine."

"You asshole."

"Yes, dear?"

It was pointless, but he tapped the refresh icon on his email again. When nothing happened, his throat threatened to close on him.

There were so many things he'd never asked Kate about. He didn't know where in New York she lived or what her parents' names were. He knew she'd gotten into Columbia for graduate school, but he didn't know if she'd take the offer, and if she didn't, he didn't know where she'd end up working.

He knew that she was leaving the country today, at some unspecified time, on some unspecified flight. He hadn't expected her to contact him, and the same restraint that had kept him from running after her when she'd walked out of their hotel room had stopped him from sending a message of his own.

But she was leaving. Soon. It already felt like she was a little bit farther away.

Lexie shoved the briefcase closer. "These are all of the reports you're legally entitled to as Dad's proxy."

"Wonderful. I needed some kindling."

"Goddammit, Teddy."

He snapped his head up. "I told you not to call me that."

"And I told you to come home." For a second her mouth wavered, real emotion in those cool, distant eyes.

It made him pause. "Lex…"

"Please. I can't do this without you. Legally, I'm not allowed to." She took a deep breath and dropped her arms to her side. "I don't want to do this alone. Dad built this company from nothing. It's all we have left."

"He should have given it all to you."

"Yeah." She said it unironically. "After the way you flaked, he should have. But he didn't." She looked him right in the eye. "Please. Rylan." Her voice shivered as she gave in and used his actual name. "I know he fucked you over. Him and Mom, both. They fucked us all over, up, down, and sideways. But we can make something of it."

"Like what?"

"A life? A family?" Her half attempt at a smile crumpled. "I don't know. Maybe it's a stupid idea. But it matters to me. And you being okay matters to me, too."

He leaned back against the couch. "I'm always all right."

"No. You're not." She crossed the room to the bag he'd

somehow failed to notice her packing. She put on her jacket and lifted the handle of the suitcase. "I told you before. You can't run forever."

"Is that a challenge?"

"A fact." She shook her head. "I can't tell you what to do. Obviously. But I'm worried about you. I'm mad at them, too, but I want to make something of what they left us. If you change your mind . . ."

"You'll be the first to know."

"Please, Rylan. If you won't leave with me today . . . the next board of directors meeting is in a few months." Her expression went pleading. "It's our last chance."

His chest constricted, his throat catching.

One of the emails he hadn't replied to had warned him they were coming up on the date. Ninety days out from the sentencing, the now provisional board had taken over, with a one-year mandate of stewardship. Once that year was up, the Bellamy family had a final chance to restake their claim, and then that was it. Everything his father had built and destroyed—everything he himself had helped build . . .

He'd get to watch it all be swept away. A silent shareholder with a front-row seat to witness his legacy as it burned.

He should have laughed. Should have been delighted to watch it go.

But there was something. This quiet voice in his heart, one Kate had awoken.

It told him he was better than sitting here idly. He could make something of his life.

He pushed it down and returned his gaze to his phone. He could go back there, all right. But if he did, his life would never be his own.

With a sigh, Lexie rolled her suitcase across the carpet to him. Bending at the waist, she dipped to press a kiss to his cheek. "Come home. Help me fix this."

He grabbed her hand and squeezed it.

But he couldn't promise her any of that.

Letting go, he said, "Have a safe trip back, Lex."

Something in her face fell. She turned around without saying anything else.

He didn't watch her walk away from him, luggage in hand. He'd had enough of that to last him a lifetime this week. Instead, he buried his gaze in the screen of his phone.

And he hit refresh. Again.

Kate heaved out a sigh as she plunked herself down in the lone free chair at the airport internet café. Around her, people were moving, wheeling around their tiny suitcases and checking their passports. She tucked her own boarding pass and travel documents into the front pocket of her purse, her security wallet relegated to the bottom of her carry-on at last.

With an hour and a half left before her flight took off, and her gate only a flight of stairs away, she let herself relax. It hadn't been easy, getting herself packed up and checked out of her hostel, or carrying her things down to the Metro, or enduring the long ride out to Charles de Gaulle. But she'd done it by herself, and now it was over.

Her trip was over.

She wiggled the mouse to dismiss the screen saver. A window popped up, asking for her payment information before it'd let her log on and actually use the thing. She hesitated.

She wasn't unwilling to spend the couple of euros, extortionate though the price might be. But she wanted to get her head on straight before she started burning time.

She'd come here for a reason. Both to Paris and to this café.

Swallowing hard, she rummaged through her bag and pulled out her sketchbooks. She flipped through the one she'd finished, forcing herself to really acknowledge the progression in the images flicking past her. More than a year's worth of drawings, more than a year's worth of trying to figure out who she was.

When she got to the one she'd done from the top of Montmartre, she ran her thumb across the bottom of the page. It was good. Really good. A nice capstone to all the other styles she'd tried on over the past year—one drawing done in a style that felt like her own.

She'd *found* something that day. The whole trip was worth it, just for that. No matter how much the rest of it hurt.

Refusing to dwell, she closed that book and opened up the one she'd started yesterday. She'd filled a dozen pages with studies of statuary in the Louvre, and views of the Arc de Triomphe and the Seine. They didn't have the same quality to them as the ones she'd done before things with Rylan had fallen apart. But that was okay. She could recapture that with time. After a few days alone to lick her wounds.

Nodding to herself, she turned back to the computer screen and entered in her information. Once she was in, she opened up a web browser and fired up her email. She glanced at the clock, giving herself exactly five minutes to indulge herself.

The snapshots Rylan had sent her took a few seconds to load, and she watched the screen with her heart in her throat.

When they appeared, the sight of them was a punch to the gut. God. That first day, with the two of them outside the museum, him looking so debonair, her with a smile that seemed about to crumble right off her face. Brittle and wary. She'd had no idea what she was getting herself into.

And then their last day together, when she was a whole different kind of miserable.

He looked . . . fragile in this picture. Like he knew, and had accepted it, and was waiting for the blow.

Well, she'd delivered it. He deserved even worse for how he'd used her and lied to her and betrayed her trust. But at least she could hold her head high. She'd figured him out, and this time she hadn't hesitated. She wasn't her mom, and she wasn't her old self, either.

She deserved better. And she was finally starting to demand it.

As much as part of her wanted to forget their whole time together, that was one thing she could be grateful for. Rylan's voice had joined her own in drowning out her father's. He'd told her that her artwork was amazing, and it hadn't just been simple praise. He'd really looked at the work she'd done, and with a considering eye. He'd always taken a moment to think before making his pronouncement.

He'd told her that it was she herself who was special. Her way of seeing. The pieces of herself that she let bloom across the page.

He'd told her she already knew what she wanted to do.

There were still a couple of minutes left of the five she'd budgeted for wallowing, but she minimized the window with the images, returning to her inbox.

It only took a moment to pull up the messages that had

been haunting her this entire time. She brought each one up in a new window and arranged them side by side.

Grad school or a real job. Risk or safety. Dreams or security.

She'd come to Paris chasing a dream. She'd followed a different one, one about love and sex and the ideal of a man who might treat her with honesty and care.

That one had turned out to be a fantasy.

But the other one...

Rylan might have been a fantasy. But he'd told her some things she'd needed to hear.

Without another thought, she clicked on the message from the admissions office.

She typed out her acceptance with shaking hands. This might be crazy, but if she didn't take the chance, she'd regret it always.

Her reply declining the job offer was even quicker and easier to write. Once you knew what you were doing with your life, everything seemed to flow.

She hit send on both messages, then closed the windows.

Before logging out of the terminal, she brought up the photos of her and Rylan again. Every moment since she'd left him, she'd been torn between wanting to punch his teeth in and wanting to contact him. She didn't know what she'd say, but things felt somehow unfinished between them.

Just in case, she checked her inbox one last time. Her chest deflated when there wasn't a message from him. A tiny part of her was still hoping for some kind of overture, some kind of apology.

Just as well.

With her time on the computer running out, and with only an hour until her flight, she took one last look at his face on the screen. She was still angry, but there was more there, too.

She pressed her fingers to her lips and then grazed them across the screen.

"Thank you," she whispered. "You asshole. For everything."

She ended her session and gathered her things.

It was time to leave Paris—and Rylan—behind.

chapter TWENTY-FIVE

Three months later

The stool next to Rylan's made an ugly, scraping noise as it was dragged against the floor. He furrowed his brow. He hadn't thought he'd been quite that unaware of what was going on around him. But shit happened. He looked up from his paper to take in the girl settling herself in beside him.

Smooth, caramel-colored skin, tight curls. One of those weird teardrop-shaped bags.

Shorts. Converse.

He folded his paper over and shot her a halfhearted grin, feeling a little sick at himself as he did. God. It was like muscle memory or a reflex, the way he flirted. No wonder he didn't come across as the kind of guy to trust.

The girl smiled back and held up her hand to try to get the bartender's attention. The man came over and glanced between the two of them.

Rylan tapped at his own empty glass. The man looked at the girl expectantly as he reached for Rylan's whiskey.

"Anglais?" the girl asked. *English?*

Fuck it. Rylan was bored. Holding up a hand to stall the

bartender, he turned to her. "Allow me. What would you like?"

She raised an eyebrow. "Red wine. Dry. Local would be nice."

Rylan knew just the thing. He rattled off her order to the barkeep. While the bartender was pouring, Rylan held out his hand to the girl. "Rylan."

She took it, her grip warm and firm. "Naya."

"Nice to meet you."

"You, too."

Her wine appeared in front of her. Dropping her hand, Rylan plucked his own glass off the bar and held it up. She clinked obligingly and they each took a sip.

It was a promising start, if a tired one. There were more than enough free stools at this particular bar this early in the evening. She didn't have to pick the one right next to his. He didn't have to buy her a drink. And yet she did and he did.

A handful of months ago, he'd have considered it ideal. Now it was just another way to pass the time.

"Traveling by yourself?" he asked. Creepy as conversational openers went, but he didn't really care. This wasn't going anywhere.

"Nah. My girlfriends ditched me for a club. Not my speed."

He hummed and took a sip of his drink. "And what is your speed?"

"Quiet bars. Dark, mysterious strangers." Her elbow nudged his, and God. A handful of months ago, he'd have considered this a *dream*.

Today, he shook his head, grinning wryly. "What else?"

At least the girl could take a hint. She shifted her arm

away. But she didn't pick up her drink and go. "I don't know." She shrugged. "Art museums, I guess."

She said it so casually, as if they were just another thing she'd get around to while she was in town. Not the way Kate had said it, voice warm with reverence. Like those shrines to old, dead masters were exactly that. Sacred.

Still, he lifted his gaze, his flagging interest recaptured. "Yeah? Which ones have you been to so far?"

"Hit the Louvre today. Musée d'Orsay is on tap for tomorrow."

Rylan twisted in his seat to face her more fully. "You're going to love it. They—" He paused, the back of his throat suddenly dry. "They have an amazing collection of Cézannes."

"I'll be sure to keep an eye out for them." Her gaze raked him up and down. "And what's your speed?"

Nope. Not happening. He shook his head. "Don't worry about me." He turned his glass in his hands, feeling that tight ball of wistfulness unfurling in his chest. "I'm just a guy."

Just a part of the scenery.

He didn't know why he was still here.

He slammed his fifth glass of whiskey down.

She pulled out her sketchbook.

He ordered another.

"Whoa, you okay there?"

Rylan listed in his chair, frowning unhappily at his empty glass. "I'm fine," he lied. "Just fine."

The girl paused, lifting her pencil from the paper.

Squinting, he tilted his head to the side. "You know who you remind me of?"

"Who?"

His smile felt like it would break. Just like his ribs.

Just like his heart.

He opened his mouth to answer—

Rylan woke the next morning to the sound of his phone. His head throbbed dimly, and vague flashes from the night before skipped through his mind as he struggled to sit up, reaching for his nightstand where he always plugged the damn thing in. Only it wasn't there—

Only it wasn't even his bed he was lying in. Jesus, he'd passed out on the couch again. A quick pat-down of his pockets and he found his phone. Holding it up to his face, he saw his sister's name. Mashing the button to ignore the call, he tossed his phone aside. With a groan, he lay back down.

He hadn't forgotten about her fucking board meeting, thank you very much. As if he could forget that the whole future of the company was riding on him tucking his tail between his legs and letting himself get sucked right back into the life he'd finally escaped. The one full of mandates and guilt trips and his father always breathing down his goddamn neck. High-stakes negotiations with clients and business partners, wining and dining, and the blood-heating rush of adrenaline, of power when you got what you wanted.

The satisfaction of a job well done.

He thunked his head back against the arm of the couch and instantly regretted it. A shock of pain burst through his skull.

Wincing, he squeezed his eyes shut tighter and gripped the top of his head.

See? Why would he need his old life back? Here, he had an uncomfortable designer sofa. An empty apartment and empty days and an empty fucking heart.

And a hangover from hell.

What the hell had he done to himself last night? He'd dragged himself home at least, but he'd slept in the living room, in his clothes, and he smelled like the bottom of an ashtray.

Like perfume.

Fuck. There had been a girl. An artist. She'd tried to pick him up, and he'd said no. He'd *definitely* said no. He knew how that kind of thing ended now.

Kate had left and Lexie had left, and he had stayed, and he had *tried* to go back to his routine. To his distractions. But no one was Kate.

This girl hadn't been Kate, either.

She'd still tried to draw him, though.

His stomach gave a protesting lurch as it started to come back to him.

The girl had waited until he was pretty hosed before she'd asked if she could do a sketch of him, and he'd tried to decline. But the girl hadn't given up. Eventually, he'd closed his eyes and let her do her worst, and it had *hurt.* Deep inside, in a place that liquor could never touch, no matter how hard he tried, it ached.

Because he remembered that. He remembered being as naked as a person could be, lying back and letting a woman see every part of him. Letting her capture it on a page.

Only to have her walk out the door the very next day.

At some point, the girl had finished. She'd shown him her sketch despite his protests, and it hadn't been like it'd been with Kate. The image staring back at him had looked as ugly as he had felt. In the very center of it had been the gap of his shirt. The glint of his father's ring against his chest.

His hand darted up to his neck, to the chain draped over his collarbones. And it burned. He'd been wearing the thing for years now, and why? When it just reminded him of his father, how he threw everything away. He'd thrown away their mother for being as faithless as he was. Had thrown away Lexie for being a girl and Evan for wanting more, and Rylan . . .

Bile filled the back of his throat.

Rylan he'd kept, but only the parts of him that served. Anything else Rylan had wanted for his life had been discarded like so much trash. Like he'd tried to discard the ring itself.

Only for Rylan to save it. To hold on to it and wear it above his heart.

Just like that, Rylan was back in his father's office, the day the papers had been signed on the divorce. He'd watched his father rip the band from his finger and hold it over the garbage bin. And Rylan said, "Stop."

The world threatened to swim, and it wasn't the low ripple of nausea or the way last night's bad decisions still throbbed through his brain.

Kate had worked her way under his skin because she'd looked at the world differently. She'd looked at *him* differently.

And the sudden twist of vertigo was him seeing his life in a whole different kind of light.

Clutching the top of his head against the lingering ache there, he shoved himself off the couch and stumbled down the hall toward his room. He caught himself in the doorframe for a second, then made his way to the wardrobe in the corner. He tugged on the handle of the drawer he never let himself open.

Kate's sketchbook was sitting there. Right where it always was.

He reached out a hand for it. Gripping the spine as delicately as he could, he pulled out the book and dropped backward, bracing himself as his ass connected with the floor. He winced at the impact, clasping his head a little tighter before letting go. Crossing his legs, he cradled the book on his lap and brushed his fingertips over the cover. And then he flipped it open. Past the cover where she'd written her name and her address, past her warm-ups, to the image of his body, naked on a bed for her.

Without even really thinking about it, he gripped his father's ring. It stood out in Kate's drawing, the chain darkly shaded against the bare skin of his chest. He'd kept it on him when he'd stripped everything else of himself away, and Kate had rendered it as if it were a part of him. Maybe it was.

Their very first day together, Kate had shown him this little sliver of her world, reminding him of art and beauty and all the things his father had taught him there wasn't room for in his life. He'd wanted to give her something back, and it hadn't even occurred to him at the time, as he'd led her into a deserted museum wing...

He hadn't just been showing her a painting he'd once been fond of. He'd been showing her a sliver of himself, from before. When he'd still had hope.

Hope for Zeus and Hera and hope for his parents' marriage. A vain hope, because he knew they both ended in ruin, but still. A hope that maybe, from all that pain and awfulness, there was something worth saving.

He raked a hand through his hair, tugging at the scalp until the ache lit up into a fierce, splitting pain.

Rylan had been so eager to believe the best about his parents' lives, and about the lives of ancient, fictional gods.

But not about his own.

When he'd first gotten to Paris, he'd felt like hell itself was on his heels. The trial had still been fresh, the loss stinging. He'd thrown himself into wasting his life with gusto, and he'd done a damn good job of it, too. The time had flown by, right up until it hadn't. Even then, the restlessness had only driven him to pursue his diversions more intensely.

Until, one day, a beautiful girl with eyes that saw the world in a way he'd never managed to before had walked into a coffee shop. She'd reminded him that there were parts of his life worth not throwing away.

And then he'd done what he'd been doing all year. He'd denied his past. God, but he'd deserved it when she'd left him.

Every day since then had felt like a year. He had no idea what he was doing anymore. Casual sex was ruined; sightseeing and chatting up tourists and exploring the city—they were all ruined.

He flipped to the page where Kate had drawn just his face.

It was such a contrast from what the girl last night had drawn.

It looked like the man he wanted to be.

His vision went blurry, his fingers curling in on themselves. Before he could destroy anything else, he closed Kate's sketchbook and pushed it away across the floor.

Right before she'd left, Kate had told him that he needed to figure out what he wanted. That he had to stop lying. To her, to himself.

Maybe he already knew. Maybe he just had to get past the things that were stopping him, too.

Around him, everything went still. He held his breath.

With unsteady hands, he reached for the back of his neck. He fumbled with the clasp of the chain. One, two tries, and then it was slipping from around his throat.

Nothing happened. No music played, and his life didn't suddenly change, but he felt lighter somehow. Dropping the ring into his open palm, he stared at the dull gleam of it.

Fucking off to France had felt like a way of saying to hell with everything and everyone. His father and all the ways he'd betrayed him; his mother and her distance, her abandonment. But all the while, he'd worn this symbol around his neck. He'd kept this reminder that even in the midst of an awful defeat, there had once, at its core, been something good.

Something worth not giving up on.

He'd done a lot of giving up of late.

He'd given up on Kate, had let her go without a fight.

He'd given up on his life and his family, on the company he'd helped build—and so what if it hadn't been his choice? He was the one who'd let himself be corralled down his father's path.

He was the one who could salvage something from its ashes.

But he'd given up on himself, too.

With his blood roaring in his ears, he took his father's ring, and he set it down. Let the chain that had tethered it to him for years fall by its side, and then he stared at them both on the ground.

It was time to stop romanticizing people who'd been too flawed to save themselves.

There was something worth saving. In his life. In his work.

And with the girl who'd opened his eyes to all of it.

With Kate.

It didn't seem to matter how hard Kate tried. Nothing was working.

Her frugality was the only thing keeping her from tossing the stupid canvas in the trash—or better, lighting it up. Well, her frugality and her vague goal of trying to come across as sane to the others in her program. Pulling her earbuds from her ears, she glanced around the studio. No one else was paying her any attention. Still, she suppressed her groan of frustration as she dropped her brushes in the turpentine and covered her face with her hands.

The semester had only just begun, and she was already starting to wonder if she'd made the wrong decision.

No. That was her father talking again.

She mentally slapped herself, pulling the brushes out of the soup and swabbing them off on her wad of paper toweling. Stabbing a little harder at it than was really a good idea for the health of the bristles, but whatever.

She belonged here, dammit all. She was as good as the rest of the students in her cohort, and she'd worked just as hard for her spot. Sacrificed as much, if not more. She was just in a rut, was all. A big Rylan-shaped rut.

Her heart gave a little pang, and she tightened her grip on the paint-soaked towels.

Three months it had been since she'd left him. Since she'd walked away from him and all the amazing, incredible things he'd done for her life and her confidence. He'd made her body and her art come alive. And then he'd torn her damned heart out.

She'd tried to paint him. Tried to process the mess he'd left of her chest in charcoal and oil. Working from grainy cell phone photographs and out-of-focus candids she'd snuck while he wasn't looking, she'd traced the outlines of his face. And every time she'd tried to sketch in those lips or those soulful eyes, she'd just about broken down.

She'd tried to destroy him, in her paintings. Taken him apart in a completely different way from how she had in that perfect hotel room on that perfect afternoon. Sliced streaks of crimson and black through the lying lines of his smile, blocked out the hollow of an eye and scrawled her anger across his ear as if that could make him hear her.

Once or twice, she'd tried to worship him, too. Lovingly rendered the details of his brow line and his jaw. But that hadn't worked for her, either.

She hated him and she loved him, and if she spent another second dwelling on either, she'd never make it out of this mess she'd made for herself. She needed to move on. Maybe she'd made the right decision, refusing to even so much as hear him out, and maybe she hadn't. But she'd made her choice, and she had to live with it now.

And so here she was. Even her pictures of the rest of Paris had been soured by her memories, but New York...New York was home. Intent on embracing what she had instead of mourning what she'd lost, she'd taken her crappy point-and-shoot to all the corners of the city and tried to capture it. The people and the dirt and the beauty of the place. She'd tried to *see* it, the way she'd learned to on her trip.

Facing her canvas again, she sighed. The city street looked dull, the line work she'd been so close to *getting somewhere* with in Paris contrived and stupid and pointless.

She dragged her wrist across her brow.

Then she picked out a brush. Squeezed a little more cerulean out onto her palette and dabbed the bristles into the paint. She closed one eye and regarded the image.

Returning her headphones to her ears, she stepped in closer to the canvas again.

She'd given up on Rylan, but she wasn't giving up on this. Time healed all wounds, and soon enough, with enough hard work, she'd find her muse again.

She'd find her *self* again. Here. On her own. At home.

chapter TWENTY-SIX

Home. Rylan turned the word over in his mind as he stared through tinted glass at the streets he'd left behind some fifteen long, pointless months ago.

At the time, he hadn't given a shit if he ever saw them again. He'd boarded a plane with his proverbial middle fingers up and washed the taste of the trial and his father and his wasted life away with the burn of airline whiskey. He'd left with the clothes on his back and a couple of books in a knapsack, and he wasn't returning with a whole lot more. A single suitcase and Lexi's briefcase.

Kate's sketchbook.

Swallowing hard, he ran his thumb across the cover one last time before tucking it safely back away. He'd have his chance to face that particular bit of smoldering landscape later. First, he had a different set of fires to put out—ones he'd once thought he'd just let burn.

But not anymore.

Smooth as could be, the car made the turn onto Sixth Avenue, and he worked his jaw, leaning forward to brace his elbows on his knees. Closing his eyes, he ran through his talking points in his mind.

It was his first time entering the lion's den on his own, and that alone made his pulse beat faster. If his father were here, he'd be drilling Rylan, checking with him over and over that he understood the plan. Rylan would've stared out the window as he nodded, silently stewing all the while.

He'd put in the time. Earned the degree his father had demanded of him, worked the long hours and sacrificed everything else. The least he could ask was to be trusted to know how to do his job.

There was no one telling him he had to be here now. Well. There'd been Lexie's entreaties and the board's demands, but at the end of the day, this was Rylan's decision.

The first one he'd made about his life in so long.

At last, the car slowed, and he took a deep breath, opening his eyes. There it was. Bellamy International. His goddamn name in big red letters on the side of a hundred-story building, and it made something squeeze in his chest.

No matter how much his father had ruined, this remained. It bore his name, so it was his.

It was well past time he acted like it.

As the driver came around to get the door, Rylan checked his watch. Five minutes to spare. Exactly as he'd planned.

Grabbing Lexie's briefcase, he adjusted his tie and his cuff links. Did up the button on the jacket of his suit.

Showtime. The door swung open. And he stepped out onto the sidewalk not just Rylan, but Theodore R. Bellamy III. And like it or not, he was home.

*   *   *

The whispers started before he'd made it halfway across the lobby. Tightening his grip on Lexie's briefcase, he ate up the marble-tiled space with long, measured strides, gaze forward. He recognized one of the girls at the visitors' desk and gave her a nod, holding a finger to his lips when she did a double take and reached for the phone. He didn't need to be greeted, and he sure as hell didn't want to be announced. She narrowed her eyes at him but moved her hand away from the receiver. Good girl.

At the executive elevator, he got a whole different sort of a look from the operator. "Mr. Bellamy. We weren't expecting you today."

He raised a brow and stepped into the waiting elevator car. "Good to see you, too, Marcus."

"Didn't say it wasn't good to see you, sir." Marcus pressed the button to close the doors. His reflection in the mirror smiled. "Just didn't know I'd get the pleasure."

"Ninety-fifth floor, if you would."

"Sure thing."

Rylan's ears finally popped around floor eighty-two. When the doors slid open, he gave Marcus a salute. He waited until the elevator was gone before turning around to face the hall.

Because if he hadn't, he might've stepped right back into that car.

Jesus, but it was his dad's tastes personified. Red carpet and dark wood and all the little tricks he swore reminded your visitors that they were on your turf now.

It was the furthest thing from home Rylan could imagine. But considering the closest he'd gotten to having one in the last ten years had been a tiny hotel room on a bread-scented *rue* in Paris, maybe that wasn't saying much.

Squaring his shoulders, he took the first step forward.

By the time he reached the conference room, it was two p.m. on the dot. The door stood all but closed, just a crack of space revealing the room within. Silently, he nudged it wider and peeked inside.

The scene was familiar enough. Spread out around the giant oak table were men old enough to be his father. There, at the head, was that bastard McConnell. Meanwhile, Thomas had been relegated to a seat maybe two-thirds of the way down. Rylan noted a half dozen other friendly faces and a couple of new ones. More than a couple of unfriendly ones, too. He cast his gaze wider, taking in the rest of the room. Behind the board members, in chairs pulled up to but not quite *at* the table, were their bevy of secretaries and PAs, and—

And Rylan had always known it looked bad. But in the past, he'd been at the table himself, not looking in.

Not seeing his crazy, fierce-as-hell sister sitting all alone in the corner of the room, lacking even an old white guy of her own to justify her presence there.

A nonvoting member. That was the status Lexie had been relegated to. The shortsighted assholes. The day she came of age or Rylan figured out a way to work around the charter to get her a spot on the board, they were going to be wishing they'd never pissed her off. Because she was going to *own* them.

Literally.

Only . . . only, she didn't look entirely her imperious self right now. Rylan tilted his head to the side, watching. Her gaze went from her notes to the head of the table, then to the clock and back again. Her chin was lifted high, her posture straight, because she wasn't giving an inch of ground,

SEVEN NIGHTS TO SURRENDER

oh no. But there was something resigned about her. Not even disappointed, but like disappointment were a foregone conclusion. Like she'd already been disappointed so many times before.

But today, she wouldn't be. At least not by him.

Up at the front of the room, McConnell cleared his throat. "What do you say, gentlemen? Time we got started?"

That was probably Rylan's cue to make his presence known, but he smirked as he leaned against the doorframe, folding his arms across his chest. Biding his time. Never let it be said he didn't know how to make an entrance.

"Let's come to order then. Let the record show that this meeting of the board of directors of Bellamy International began at 2:02. Members in attendance include..." McConnell rattled off the names of all the gray-haireds at the table. He swept his gaze around the room, purposely passing Lexie over. "Is there a representative of the Bellamy family?"

And *there* it was. He paused to the count of three, just long enough for Lex to grit her teeth and open her mouth. But before she could get the first word out, Rylan pushed the door open.

"Why yes, there is." He projected his voice across the room as he swept into it. A dozen heads swung around to gawk at him, and he took them all in at once. Caught the split-second of surprise on McConnell's face before he schooled his expression. Caught Lexie's grimace turning into what was, for her, in this room, the closest thing to a shit-eating grin Rylan had ever seen. "Two of them, actually," he said, raising a hand in greeting to her. "Hey, sis."

She nodded back, eyes triumphant but smile restrained. "Theodore."

Ugh. He'd get her back for that later.

Putting a little extra swagger in his step, he headed straight for the front of the room, lifting an eyebrow at the guy who'd been presumptive enough to sit in his seat. The dude went red in the face, a battle clearly going on inside him about whether or not to budge. Thomas added the weight of his stare, and the chair-stealer finally caved. Leaving his PA to pick up his stuff, he scooted a few feet down, and Rylan dropped himself into the open spot.

Opening the briefcase, he pulled out a folder and set it on the table.

Ever since the day his father'd been led away in handcuffs, Rylan had been fighting who he was and where he came from, afraid he'd gone too far in becoming the man his father had wanted him to be. Into a copy of himself. But in that moment, there at that table, he remembered. The rush of it washed over him. He was good at this. He'd trained at it all his life.

He let the energy of confrontation fill him up, and then he banked it. With his posture that of a man completely at his leisure, he leaned back in his chair, twirling his pen and nodding along as McConnell fought to recover his balance and start working his way through the agenda. One by one, the other board members got over his unexpected appearance in their midst.

Right up until he asked his first question. Then all the heads in the room turned as one.

"What?" He pointed to the part of the document they'd been discussing. "I did the reading."

McConnell made a strangled-sounding noise with his throat.

Fortunately, Thomas jumped in before McConnell's eyes could actually pop out of his head. "Mr. Bellamy does bring up a good point."

Rylan swiveled back and forth in his chair as the discussion shifted. Over the course of the next hour, he left the running of the meeting to the people who'd been there all along, but he managed to keep things pointed in the direction he wanted them to go.

The direction Lexie had laid out for him.

He looked over at her as the tide started to turn in their favor, quirking one eyebrow in a silent question. *Good enough for you?*

She made a show of heaving her shoulders as she sighed, but her smile belied it all.

After what felt like about a million years, the meeting neared its close. Just one item left on the agenda.

McConnell looked around the room, and Rylan could see him counting in his head. Well, Rylan had done his counting, too. "As for the matter of reversion of the Bellamy family's controlling interest..." His gaze went to Rylan.

The bastard wasn't sure he had the votes to stay in control. Honestly, Rylan wasn't sure he had enough support, either.

But there was one motion he was sure he could get through.

Rylan cleared his throat and stood. "I'd like to call for a ninety-day grace period before the vote."

Relief fairly rippled through the room. McConnell's shoulders even lowered a fraction. "The motion stands," he said. "Simple majority."

Hands went up in the air to the tune of aye, and Rylan sank back into his seat.

Ninety days. Ninety days to shore up support, to devise a strategy.

To decide exactly how far he wanted this all to go, and whether or not he was prepared to take the helm.

The meeting adjourned shortly after, and Rylan stretched his arms over his head with a sense of satisfaction. There was still a lot to figure out, but he'd taken the first step, at least. He'd shown up. Claimed his place. And declined to let Rome burn.

Standing, Rylan packed up the briefcase, holding off the couple of folks who seemed to want to strike up a conversation by nodding toward his sister. He made his way over to her while she was still finishing her notes.

"So?" he asked. "How'd I do?"

"There's room for improvement." She closed her folio and set her pen down. "But I think you've got potential."

He smirked. She'd begrudged him his father's favor for so long. Even that admission felt like a triumph. "Glad to hear it."

Rising, she crossed her arms in front of her chest. "You cut it a little close there with the timing."

The corner of his lip threatened to twitch up, but he held steady, expression blank. "Sorry. Traffic across the Atlantic Ocean was a bitch."

"Asshole." Her frown held for another few beats. Then all at once, it fell away and she held out her arms.

He stepped into the hug, scooping her up.

"Thanks for coming," she said into his chest.

"Thanks for the push."

He held her close for a long minute. There weren't going to be any big emotional declarations here. Hell, already they'd said more than they usually did. That was how they worked. But all the same, it was apology and forgiveness. Approval and acceptance.

Letting her go, he stepped away.

"So," she started, slinging her bag over her shoulder. "You want to grab a drink or something? Dinner at Ai Fiori's? I can probably call in and get Dad's table. God knows he's not using it."

He jerked his thumb toward the door. "Nah. Just got into town this afternoon, and there are some things I need to do."

"*Pfft.* It's been a year. No one's going to care if you put them off another day."

"But I will."

She gave him an appraising look, and not for the first time, he felt like she could see right through him. After a second, she glanced away and shrugged. "If you say so. You have a place to stay?"

God, he hoped he did. "I'll figure something out."

"Well, if you don't..."

He shook his head. "Thanks for the offer, but I think I'm good."

"Suit yourself. Later this week, though, let's catch up. We need to talk strategy going forward for handling all of this." She gestured at the board table.

"Sure." He half turned away, one foot already edging toward the exit.

She stopped him before he could go. "Rylan?"

"Yeah?"

"I'm glad you're home."

His heart did something strange and complicated inside his chest at that word. *Home.* "Yeah."

"It's just—I don't have a lot of people left who I can count on. Who I can trust. It's nice to know you're one of them."

He swallowed down the things he wanted to say to that. Managing the barest excuse for a smile, he touched the outside pocket of the briefcase. Felt the spiral binding of the sketchbook he had placed there through the leather.

The fact that he still had it said he wasn't worthy of anybody's trust.

But he was trying to be.

Nodding, he turned his back on Lexie, on the room as a whole.

At his father's insistence, he'd sacrificed the parts of his life that happened beyond this building, but not anymore. He had other responsibilities, other apologies to make.

He just had to pray that they'd be heard.

chapter TWENTY-SEVEN

"I didn't peg you for a Brooklyn girl."

Kate startled and whipped around, managing to yank her headphones out of her ears and knock over a brush in the process. As she fumbled for them both, she darted her gaze up. Liam, one of the guys from her program, stood behind her, looking way too amused at having caught her unawares. If the streaks of paint on his jeans and in the front of his messy, sandy hair were anything to go by, he'd been in the studio for a while. She must've really been out of it not to have noticed him until now.

As she ducked to retrieve her brush, she smiled. It wasn't that she hadn't made other friends among the students here, but Liam was the one who made a point of saying hi to her, of offering to grab her a coffee when he went on a caffeine run. She wasn't under any illusions. The niceness was probably flirtiness, but that wasn't the worst thing in the world.

If there was one thing she had learned from the mess this summer, it was how to handle a guy who wanted to get in her pants.

The slow flicker of a smile on her lips faded and died. She faltered as she stood back up. This summer…Well, she'd learned a lot of things, and most of them the hard way. But that was fine. Time healed all wounds, after all. The scars Rylan had left on her heart weren't gone yet, but they were slowly closing over, leaving her stronger than she had ever been.

Slowly but steadily, she was recovering.

Now if she could only say the same about her art.

With a grimace, she glanced over her shoulder at the painting she'd been working on. Liam had recognized it at least, so that was something.

"What's wrong with Brooklyn?" she asked.

"Nothing. Well, unless you're talking about Park Slope, in which case only everything." Liam grinned. "But Bushwick is pretty legit." He nodded toward the photo she had tacked up beside her easel. "That's where you took that?"

"Yeah." She'd been scouring a bunch of local neighborhoods, taking pictures, looking for different sorts of architecture, different types of cityscapes. She just couldn't seem to connect to them the way she had the sights in Paris. Trying to paint from them didn't feel the same.

"You're not happy with it?"

She sighed. "It's a process." That was what they all said when they were struggling.

"Maybe you've been staring at it for too long?"

"Nah, I've only been here for…" She wiped her hand on her pants and pulled out her phone and did a double take. How the hell had it gotten so late? "…okay, a *lot* of hours." Maybe it was time for a break. Right on cue, her stomach made a groan of protest. Between covering the breakfast shift at the diner and running to her seminar class and then losing track of time completely here, she hadn't exactly had a chance to eat. Or sit down. Or anything, honestly.

"You definitely need to get out of here." His tone shifted, going just a little bit too casual. "You wanna go grab a bite or something? I know a couple of good places."

The invitation made her pause. She half turned away, swirling her brushes through the turpentine to buy herself a second.

She'd just acknowledged to herself the fact that he might be flirting some thirty seconds ago, so it shouldn't be a surprise that he was making an overture. And yet she hadn't been sure—she still wasn't, honestly.

Lying liar that he was, at least Rylan had been upfront about his intentions.

Whatever Liam was trying for, she really didn't have the energy right now. "Actually, I'm pretty beat. I think I might just head home."

His eyes fell, but if he was too disappointed, he kept it under wraps. "You sure?"

"Yeah. Maybe some other time."

"Okay." That seemed to lift his spirits. "I think I'm going to go." He pointed his thumb toward the door. "But you want me to wait for you? Walk you to the subway? Or whatever."

She shook her head. "It's going to take me a while to get this all cleaned up."

He didn't linger for long after that, and she couldn't decide if she was relieved about it or not.

It was the first time someone had really made a pass at her since this summer, and it had unsettled her more than she would've expected it to. As she went about the work of washing her brushes and wrapping up her palette, she kept replaying it in her mind.

What was the worst that could've happened if she'd said yes? She and Liam were friends, sure, but they'd only known each other a little while. Even if their quasi date had tanked, they probably would've been able to get past it. *She* would've been able to get past it.

Her conviction about that much solidified as she tugged on her jacket and made her way down to the subway.

Being with Rylan this summer had taught her a lot of things. She knew now, in a way she hadn't before, that she had a right to ask for what she wanted, to tell a potential partner what felt good and when he was leaving her cold. Or worse, hurting her. Sex was sex, and love was something else entirely, something that had burned her yet again. She'd gotten too attached too fast.

But she hadn't made the same mistake with Rylan that she had with Aaron. The one her mother had made with her father. At the very first hint of Rylan's deception, she hadn't stayed to hear his excuses or let him sweet-talk her into giving him another shot. She'd packed her bags.

Maybe, just maybe, she could try again with someone else. Learn from this mistake the same way she had from her last one. She could find a guy, be it Liam or whomever, and she could get all the touching and kissing and bone-melting sex she'd had the barest taste of in her week with Rylan, except this time without all the pain. If she guarded her heart, it might even work. She could keep it casual and keep her feelings and her secrets to herself. She could give herself a chance.

Maybe she was ready, at least for that much. For a fresh start.

By the time she finally made it to her stop and trudged the last few blocks home, she'd just about managed to convince herself that this time, really, she was ready to move on. Crossing the street, she dug around in her bag for her keys, only to find the door to her building had been propped open anyway. Ugh. People locked their doors around here for a reason. She kicked the doorstop out of the way before checking her mail and heading for the stairs.

At the top of the second flight, she turned in the direction of her apartment, fumbling with her keys again. Once she'd found the one she needed, she lifted her gaze from them. And froze.

Her knees shook, and she gripped the strap of her bag hard enough to make her knuckles hurt. A half dozen times, she blinked, but nothing about the vision before her changed. It was there. *Real.*

Her worst nightmare and her most infuriating, shameful fantasy.

The figure sitting on the ancient carpet outside her door—the one dressed in a fucking three-piece suit, gorgeous hair a finger-combed mess, jaw as sharp as it had ever been—was Rylan. Beside him was a suitcase.

And in his hands lay her sketchbook.

chapter TWENTY-EIGHT

It was the tiniest sound. The faintest hint of a whimper, but it was as loud as gunfire in that quiet hall. Rylan jerked his head up from his near-meditative consideration of the cracks in the plaster wall in front of him. The ones he'd been staring at for hours now. So long that if it hadn't been for her name beside the buzzer at the door, he might've worried he had the wrong place.

But all that waiting, it'd been worth it. He would've waited the rest of the night if he'd had to, and still would've called it a fair deal.

There she was. Kate. For a minute, all he could do was drink her in. Her cheeks were flushed, her eyes bright and hair a mess. She was wearing the most unappealing, awful, shapeless pair of paint-streaked jeans he'd ever seen, and *fuck*. He wanted her. Not just in his bed and in his arms but in his *life*.

Her name rose to his lips, but before he could so much as get it out, all the words he'd planned, the ones he'd rehearsed for this very moment, evaporated in his mouth. Moving slowly, as if not to spook a skittish horse, he dusted off his slacks and climbed to his feet. The distance between them pulsed. In the silence, he willed the words to come.

Then finally, quietly, she said, "Rylan."

He nodded.

"You're here."

His face cracked, a smile stealing over him, and he found his voice. "Yeah."

She didn't move, and he didn't, either. Their very first conversation rose to his mind. That first cup of coffee in a bustling French café. She'd been suspicious, and he'd been overconfident, and every single word he'd dragged out of her had been hard-won. A softness crept over him just thinking about it. His Kate.

Well, he could do the conversational heavy lifting here, too. He opened his mouth.

But she cut him off before he could speak. "What the hell do you think you're doing here?"

The soft haze of memory evaporated. The sharpness in her tone and the anger in her eyes slid like a knife between his ribs.

Right. This wasn't a cozy nook in a coffee shop, and they weren't two tentative prospective lovers, feeling each other out. She wasn't the same quietly cautious girl. He wasn't that brazen, bored, angry man.

Her gaze grew more pointed, and his chest squeezed. He would've denied it, if anyone had pressed him on it, but there'd been this piece of him that had clung to the hope that she might welcome him with open arms. Even after everything he'd done and all the ways he'd hurt her. All his illusions crumbled to the ground.

It wasn't quite like being in front of the firing squad of the boardroom, but he found himself drawing up straighter all the same, bracing himself for whatever defenses he might have to construct. Grounding himself.

She wasn't going to throw herself at him? Fine. But he wasn't going to let her walk away this time without hearing him out.

"I..." He worked his jaw. Where did he even start? Gripping the spiral binding tighter, he lifted her sketchbook. "I found this."

Her brows rose. "And? Are all the postal workers in France on strike?" He faltered, but she didn't miss a beat. She let out a harsh, sad bark of a laugh. "I mean, I know the economy is rough, but if billionaire moguls have to resort to taking courier jobs—"

"Kate—"

"No." She lifted a hand up in front of herself, and he stopped in his tracks, held back from the step he'd been about to unconsciously take forward.

Because she was here. Real and beautiful and everything he'd ever wanted and been too much of a fool to keep back when he might've had a chance, and he needed to touch her so badly it ached.

"Kate," he tried again, "you have to know—"

"No, I don't *have to know* anything." If it was possible, her posture went even more closed.

He took that single step forward. Threw his arms wide, ready to throw her sketchbook, too, if it weren't the most important thing he had. "You have to know, I came here for you. To see you. This is yours. I found it in our room after you left. It was selfish of me to keep it for so long—"

"For three *months*. Three months, Rylan. You can't just walk back into someone's life after that kind of time."

"But I've spent every second, every moment of it thinking about you."

She rounded on him, her cheeks flushed, hands curled tightly into fists. "Like I haven't spent it thinking about you? About what an idiot I was for you? You used me."

"Never," he said, and he spat the word. He'd come here to apologize, but not for that. Anger boiled low in his gut, taking up some of the space that had been nothing but regret and hurt. "I didn't take anything from you that I wasn't prepared to give back a hundredfold."

"Except my trust." Her face scrunched up, her eyes shining, and it was the first glimmer of anything except disgust. Her voice wavered. "Except my heart."

His own shuddered. He took a deep breath.

He'd always wondered, deep down where he'd nursed the ache she had left in her wake. To get as angry as she had, to have acted so betrayed. She must have felt something for him. His stunted heart that hadn't dared to feel anything for so damn long had grown three sizes for her, and maybe she wasn't as attached as he was. But she had—she'd cared. At some point.

And fuck guardedness and fuck silence. They'd had enough of that these past few endless months. He edged even closer, hands in front of himself in a gesture of supplication. He licked his lips. "Like I said. Nothing I wasn't ready to give right back to you."

Her eyes snapped wide, her whole body going still, and something inside of him ached. If he could just reach out to her, just bridge this gap. There was something here. She'd admitted it. Something worth salvaging, if only she'd let him.

In the distance, a door on one of the lower floors creaked open and slammed shut. The muffled sounds of footfalls and the jangling of keys. It knocked Rylan out of his trance.

Jesus. They were in a public space here. Anyone could walk by. People in every apartment around them were probably listening in.

He shook his head and leaned forward that final inch. His hand closing around her arm was a jolt of electricity, the warmth of contact that soothed him even as it seemed to set Kate further on edge. He stroked the point of her wrist with his thumb, feeling her tremor through her clothes. He caught her gaze and held it, pitching his tone lower. No one else needed to hear this.

"You told me—before you left. You said I had a lot of things to figure out for myself, and I've been trying. I've been trying so damn hard." Gulping, throat dry, he hauled her hand up to his chest, slotting it underneath his tie, pressing her palm flat to the muscle underneath. To where the absence of his father's ring hung like its own kind of weight.

Did she understand him? He was freer now. He wasn't running away, not from who he was or from the possibility of being known. And he'd never hide who he was from her again.

"There's a lot of stuff I'm still working on," he said, "but there are two things I'm certain of. I'm a better man now. And I'm a better man because of you."

"Rylan…" Her gaze flickered down, to the rise of his chest. To his heart beneath her hand.

"I'm sorry. For everything. But please." He wasn't above

begging. Glancing meaningfully at the doors around them, he pled, "Please just let me come inside. Talk to me."

Her eyes drifted closed, her head shaking ever so slightly, and his stomach plummeted into his knees. But she didn't pull back. "Do you have any idea how angry I am with you?"

"I think I'm starting to, actually, yeah."

She curled her fingers in the fabric of his shirt, and it was so wrong, so inappropriate, but even as he was waiting for the verdict that would send him to the gallows, heat flooded his skin. His sex drive, nearly MIA these past few months, gave a kick.

When she lifted her gaze back to his eyes, it was with a new kind of uncertainty, one he himself had put there, and damn if he wasn't prepared to spend the rest of his life working to take it away.

"Me inviting you in doesn't mean I'm any less pissed."

The sudden rebound of his gut snapping back into place left him dizzy. Relief, pure and simple, felt like the first breath he'd taken since he'd let her go.

"I can work with that."

"I know you can," she muttered.

And it struck him that maybe, just maybe, he had a shot.

Pulling her hand from his chest, she turned toward her apartment. The center of his ribs felt cold without her touch, his eyes sore without the vision of her face as she bent to get the lock. But none of that mattered, because a second later, she was opening the door, and stepping inside, and instead of slamming the door between them, she held it open wide.

She twisted around to look at him and asked, "Well? Are you coming in or not?"

* * *

Never, not in the two years she'd been living in it, had Kate's tiny shoebox of an apartment ever felt so small.

Mechanically, she undid the buttons of her jacket, then dropped her keys into the bowl on the little table beside the door—the one she had literally picked up on the side of the road. All the while, her eyes stayed glued to Rylan's form.

She'd never seen him dressed anything but casually in their time together in Paris, but damn could the man fill out the lines of a suit. Expensive and perfectly tailored, it made him look even taller than she remembered, more handsome. Her eyes burned.

She wanted to give in to the trembling in her hands and in her knees. Run over to him and kiss him and beg him take her, hard, on her bed or on the floor or against the wall. It took all of her restraint not to.

She wanted to slap him.

It was like he sucked all the air out of the room, leaving none of it for her, and her lungs went tight. He took up so much *space*. Moved into it with hardly more than a by-your-leave. Entered it and dominated it, the same way he'd pushed his way into her vacation and then her thoughts and her life.

And, God, but how dare he? Three long months after she'd found him out, after she'd done the hardest thing she'd ever had to do in her life and walked away from him. After she'd spent all this time getting over him—and it had been working, too. She'd been so close.

Now she was going to have to start all over again.

What the hell was he even doing here? What was *she* doing here?

Shaking it off, she set her bag down and hung her coat up. She didn't let herself look at him again as she made her way into her cramped little kitchen. "Anything you have to say can wait until I eat."

"Do you want to go somewhere? I don't know many places in this neighborhood, but..."

"Nope." If someone had told her this morning she'd be turning down not one but two invitations to dinner today, she'd have laughed herself hoarse. Forget that dinner out for once sounded amazing. If Rylan was coming all the way out to the boroughs for her, coming into her home, he could deal with her food. Her terrible, terrible food.

She tugged open a cabinet and surveyed the prospects. She hauled out a packet of noodles with a sigh.

"Are you hungry?" she asked. It'd be a hit to her budget, but she was pretty sure she could spare the seventeen cents to feed a guest.

"I could eat."

She bet he could. She grabbed a second pack and closed the cabinet. "I hope you like ramen."

"Can't say I've tried it."

She dug her fingers into the counter hard enough to bruise. Slow and steady, she forced herself to take a couple of nice deep breaths. She unclenched her hands and turned her head.

He was there. Rylan, the guy who had stolen her heart this summer and then ripped it to shreds. He was standing there, his back to her, in that perfect, expensive suit, with his perfect hair, not even knowing what ramen was. And he was in her apartment, looking at her stuff. Looking at her *life*.

Her vision swam for a second as her focus shifted. She'd tried so hard, on a limited budget and with limited time, to make her home a sanctuary. Dove-gray walls to make a crowded space a cozy one, her friends' art on display, an eclectic mix of things she'd found at flea markets and rummage sales all over the city giving the place character.

And it all looked so cheap.

If she'd known he was coming, she could have at least picked up a little. Her easel set up in the corner had another failure of a painting on it, and there were more awful drawings spread out on the floor. Every flat surface was covered in papers or books or art supplies, and her paint-streaked clothes threatened to spill out of her hamper. Worse, the ones that stank of fryer grease from the diner were piled on top of them.

And she was even more of a mess. She had pigment on her sleeves and probably splashed across her face. Her hair was all windblown. This man had been the one to make her really believe that she could be beautiful, but letting him see her like this, while he looked like that...

Her breath caught, a choked sound sneaking past her throat.

Fuck him for ambushing her. Fuck him for stealing the higher ground and for making her *want* him again.

"Kate?" He'd turned around to stare right at her, and she couldn't stand it. Not for another second.

The tightness in her throat threatened to choke her. "Can you go to the bathroom or something for a minute?"

"Excuse me?"

How could she explain? "I just need..." She needed him to be somewhere else and she needed to fix this all. Take control of it. She needed to *think*.

Frowning, he narrowed his eyes at her, and he must've seen some fragment of how unhinged she felt. "All right." He set her sketchbook down, and that right there—that he still had it, whether he'd stolen it or found it or what—that was a whole other can of worms, and her frayed nerves came one step closer to snapping.

She pointed at the right door; there were only two of them, a tiny closet and a tinier bathroom—it wasn't as if he could miss it. He slipped inside, lingering briefly, watching her as if he knew precisely the kind of time bomb he was dealing with.

She waited until the door clicked closed and the sound of the fan came on to bury her head in her hands and turn around. With her back to the counter, she let herself slide down until her butt hit the ground.

Until there was no farther down to fall.

Okay. This was not how Rylan had seen this going.

While instant forgiveness followed by enthusiastic reunion sex had been his secret, dark-horse favorite for how this might turn out, he'd never discounted screaming, door slamming, and an invitation to go fuck himself. He'd even imagined a couple of potential middle grounds.

Sitting on the edge of her bathtub, idly scanning the ingredients on her toiletries, had not been among them.

How long, precisely, was he supposed to wait in here?

The drone of the exhaust fan muted any noises that might be coming from outside, but he hadn't heard much of anything. He strained, listening harder, clenching his hand into a fist. She wouldn't have left, right? If she didn't want to deal with him, it would've made more sense to kick him out, not ask him to go sit in her bathroom while she escaped.

His heart squeezed. He was trying to keep his expectations low, but he'd been waiting so long to see her. If he could just get her to talk to him. To give him a chance.

Finally, he couldn't take it anymore. He checked his watch and it'd been a solid ten minutes. With his phone long past run out of batteries and his patience about as empty, he sat up. Checked himself in the mirror. Then took a deep breath and cracked the door open.

"Kate?" What exactly was he supposed to say? *Do I have your permission to come out of the bathroom now?* He rolled his eyes at himself. "You still out there?"

"In the kitchen," she called, and it shouldn't have been such a relief, just hearing her voice.

And oh hell. He nudged the door a little wider and tried to peer through the gap. "Not that I'm not enjoying the décor in here, but…"

The sound of metal clinking on metal carried through the space, followed by a sigh. She grumbled something he couldn't make out, then, louder, "Come on out, I guess."

He poked his head out first, surveying the room. From his angle, he couldn't see into the kitchen, which was a wonder. He'd lived in houses with closets larger than this entire place.

And yet he liked her apartment better than any of them. It hadn't been some designer putting her home together for her. There was no feng shui or flow. Just art. Just *life*, where there had been so little of it in the mansions he'd been told to call home before.

Stepping out, he furrowed his brow. It was subtle, but the place was different than it had been before she'd banished him. Neater. He drew the one side of his mouth up, ready to tell her she really hadn't needed to scoop her underwear off the floor for him, but then he paused. That wasn't the only bit of tidying she'd done.

All the paintings, all of her artwork, were gone. Not *gone* gone, there wasn't close to room enough in this place for her to disappear them completely, but the one on the easel—it had been of a bridge, maybe? She'd tucked it behind her dresser, leaving only the edge of it peeking out. The rows of pictures that had been lined up against the wall had all been turned. Staring at the blank backsides of canvases, he frowned.

The second day he'd met her, he'd gotten her to show him her sketchbook. Only the last few pictures, sure, but she'd barely hesitated before baring her soul to him that way. He'd treated it with the respect it deserved, really looking at her work before passing judgment or commenting, and the next time, she'd granted him even greater access. She'd let him flip through months' or maybe years' worth of drawings.

She'd let him see himself through her eyes, his hollow places filled in by the tender touch of her hand as she'd studied him and captured him on a page.

Now, he wasn't allowed to look.

He worked his jaw against the ache it gave him. He'd lost so much when she'd walked out that door. More than he'd even realized at the time.

God, he hoped she gave him the chance to earn it back.

Squaring his shoulders, he turned to face the kitchen. If she'd been watching him, she buried her gaze back in the pot bubbling away on the stove. Didn't spare a single glance at him.

"Dinner's almost ready."

He swallowed a couple of times, because that was the last of his concerns. "Sounds good."

She snorted. "I promise you, it's not."

"All right..."

Shaking her head at him, she flipped the burner off and stepped to the side. She grabbed one mug from a dish drainer beside the sink, then dug around in a cabinet until she came up with another, larger one in a different color. She sprinkled something from a couple of little foil packets into the pot and stirred, then unceremoniously dumped whatever concoction she'd made into the mugs. Tugging open a drawer, she came up with two mismatched spoons and dropped one in each. "Here you go." She gestured at the soup as if to say *go ahead*.

He had to admit. He was intrigued.

Expecting her to step back, he darted forward, and his skin prickled with heat when she refused to yield an inch. It was the closest they'd been since she'd let him inside, nearly as close as when he'd grabbed her wrist. Only this time she wasn't staring him down or yelling at him. He saw his opening. Ever so slowly, he put his hand to her waist, molding to the soft curve of her frame. Her breath stuttered, and his heart pounded, and maybe this wasn't a lost cause after all. He breathed her in for a moment, the faint scent of still-wet paint weaving together with the roses and vanilla of her hair, drawing him closer.

And he almost leaned in. Very nearly reached forward to take the kiss he'd been aching for these past three months. But for all that her body spoke of invitation, her eyes were terrified, the line of her mouth hard.

He schooled his reaction and reminded himself: This girl was worth playing the long game for.

Holding her gaze, he reached beyond her to take the closest cup by its handle. With it firmly in his grasp, he let go of her side.

She stared at him, dazed, as he stepped back. Every inch of space he put between them hurt, but he could be patient. He could wait.

There wasn't a table or any place to sit in her kitchen, so he turned toward the main room. He didn't find much better options there. The lone chair she appeared to own was a rolling one, pulled up beside a little painted white desk tucked into a corner beside her easel. If he sat there, she'd be worlds away from him.

It was a calculated risk. But after a moment's thought, he crossed the space to her bed. A double, barely big enough for two—not that he'd mind. If she ever let him take her to it, he'd never want to let her go. Having to sleep pressed tight against her... He couldn't think of anything better.

He cast one look over his shoulder at her before dropping down to sit on the edge of her mattress. It barely gave at all, but it would do. Soft, worn-looking purple sheets slipped beneath his hand as he stroked the material. Maybe she'd join him here. Sit beside him.

But instead, she hovered in the doorway, mug clutched tightly enough her knuckles went white.

For the first time, he directed his attention to his own cup, and he had to stop himself from frowning. Its contents were... well, brown. A curly mass of noodles in a murky broth. He poked at it with his spoon and raised a brow. Across the room from him, Kate brought a spoonful to her mouth and blew on it, rosy lips puckering, and he lost the thread for a second, just watching the shape of her mouth.

Then she gestured for him to go ahead. His haze receded, and he regarded his mug again. Her gaze sat like a weight on him as he gathered up some noodles, anticipation like a shiver through his skin.

Shrugging, he took a bite.

This was not a test. If pressed, Kate would swear up, down, and sideways that it wasn't. She honestly didn't have anything else in the house to offer him.

And yet, as he closed his mouth around his spoon, she held her breath.

He'd said so many things, their final day in Paris together. She'd been blind with fury and betrayal, shoving her things into her suitcase and barely able to see through the threat of tears. And he'd talked. Told her his regrets, told her how he'd only lied to her because he wanted her so much.

He'd wanted to be normal. To have this little slice of normalcy, there, in that room, with her. And she had so very, very nearly turned around.

The problem was, he didn't even know what normal *was*. It didn't matter how torn up she was over seeing him, bouncing between elation and rage and every possible emotion in between—if he couldn't handle cheap, terrible noodles—if he couldn't manage to get them down without lying to her . . . then they were doomed.

He pulled the spoon from between those soft, too-kissable lips, and his shoulders stiffened, his expression going impassive. It took him a hell of a long time to swallow.

"So?" she asked.

His throat bobbed as he managed to get his mouthful down. "Well..."

"Don't lie." And it was supposed to come out light, even teasing. But there was too much history between them. It was too loaded of a statement. Her throat felt raw.

His gaze snapped up to hers, something dark and sharp passing behind his eyes.

Of course he knew this was a test.

Moving ever so slowly, he reached to the side and set his mug down on her bedside table. She stared at the bright red handle of the thing, a stupid freebie she'd picked up in the student union for signing up for something, and she was serving fucking ramen to some society heir in it. Her eyes prickled.

And then he was in her space, warm hands closing around hers, and she'd nearly forgotten how good it felt to be touched. To have this man, the one who could have any woman he wanted—and who probably had—to have him touching her...

Don't. Her mind screamed at her. Don't trust him, don't let him in, don't let him touch you again. But her body went rigid. Frozen.

He coaxed her fingers to unclench, gently prying her mug from her. Twisted to set it on the counter behind her, and that put them even closer. She felt unbearably brittle, like any little thing could cause her to shatter, but the heat of him, the proximity of his body hovering over hers, it melted the edges of her. Fused them together with this vague, impossible promise that he could make her whole.

Taking her face between his palms, he tilted her head up until she had no choice but to look at him. The dazzling blue of his eyes stared back at her, and she'd loved this man so much. For one perfect week, she had.

But she couldn't trust him.

"I'm sorry," he said. "I'm so sorry. For every single thing I did that caused you pain."

She shook her head within his grasp, vision going blurry. Wasn't that exactly what she wanted him to say? What she'd always wanted all the men in her life who had hurt her to say?

His gaze went deeper. "If you don't want me to lie to you about how oversalted and unappealing that soup is, then I won't. I can promise you, I will never, ever lie to you again. Not about anything that matters, and not about your cooking, either, if that's what you want."

A snort of laughter broke through her closed-up throat. "I'd hardly call it cooking."

He didn't let her change the subject or digress. "Whatever you want to call it, then. I won't lie about it."

She gazed back up into his eyes. "Would you have told me the truth about it, though?" Because that had been the problem. When she'd called him out on all his not-quite truths in Paris, he'd sworn he'd never lied to her, not outright, and maybe he hadn't been wrong about that. But he'd kept his silences, muttered vague agreements that dodged all around the questions she'd really been asking him. "Or would you have just said nothing? Just let me believe what I wanted to?"

He stroked his thumbs across her cheeks. "We're not arguing about your soup here."

"No. I guess we aren't."

Sighing, an aching sadness to him, he took one of his hands and braced it on the wall behind her. "So talk to me about something besides soup."

Like all of her strings had been cut, she sagged, leaning back into the wall. It would be so easy to let her head fall forward onto his shoulder, to rest there for a moment. He was clearly ready to give her whatever comfort she wanted, but it wouldn't fix anything. Him showing up here, making promises he'd given her no reason to believe up until this point—it didn't solve *anything*.

"Rylan." She placed her hand over his and pulled it gently from her cheek. "What are you doing here? Really."

"I already told you. I came here for you."

"But why?" And this wasn't the same insecurity from their first night together, eating crepes in the open air on a Paris night. She had some kind of hold over him, there was no denying that at this point. But "Why here? Why now?"

He turned his hand over in hers, tangling their fingers together, and it felt too easy to let him do it. She squeezed his palm, stilling him. Because this was important.

When he spoke again, his voice pitched lower, and his Adam's apple bobbed. "It's funny, you know. I was in Paris for a year before I met you, and the whole time, I was never lonely. I was too angry, too—" He cut himself off with a harsh breath of a laugh. "I felt too betrayed. I'd gone there running from this shitstorm my father had left for us, and I couldn't see anything beyond that. Not even how unhappy I was. I knew my life was empty, but...it was like it almost seemed better that way."

And she had seen that, hadn't she? It'd been lurking in the corners of her vision, all that time they'd spent together shadowed by it. There'd been a restlessness to him, a dissatisfaction he never would've admitted to but which she could all but taste. How else did a man like him get so caught up in something the way he had? How else did he change all of his plans for an entire week, and for what? A girl?

She didn't want to sell herself short, but it didn't make any kind of sense.

"That still doesn't explain—" she started.

"And then you walked into my life, and you were anything but empty. You cared so much about life and art, and you let me touch you..." He trailed off, gaze darting down the center of her body, leaving a low trail of warmth everywhere it went. "And I didn't feel hollow for the first time in so long."

"And so you lied."

"And so I glossed over the details of my life. Because for that moment, that handful of days, I wanted to live in yours. By the time I realized how much I needed you—that I had to come clean with you...it was too late." His mouth twisted up into a painful shadow of a smile. "I thought I was doing the right thing. I'd already fucked it up, so there was no way I could keep you, but I couldn't—I couldn't do it. Couldn't be another guy who'd hurt you."

Her eyes blurred. But she wasn't going to let him see her shake. "You understand the irony of that statement, don't you?"

"There is nothing I regret more than hurting you."

"But you did." There was no invective left to throw behind the words. They were simply there, true and awful and bare. "You broke my heart. Because I let myself think you were different. You only let me see these little glimmers of yourself—"

"I showed you more than I've ever shown anybody else."

Dizziness swept over her, because he believed that. The way he was looking at her, a fierceness to his gaze, he had to.

"I know I showed you more, because it was more than I'd shown myself." He took her hand in both of his. "After you left, I had to face it. There wasn't any pretending anymore. I tried. God, I tried. But none of it was the same."

"So what? You've just been wasting away without me these past few months?"

He shrugged, but he missed casual by a mile. "Essentially, yes."

And that was it. The intensity of his gaze was too much. She suddenly couldn't breathe, and she twisted, tugging her hand away and squirming out from under his arm.

"I'm just a girl," she insisted, retreating. It was a couple of feet worth of distance, but it felt like the world.

"No." His voice broke. "Don't you get it? You're *the* girl. The one who opened my eyes. Before you, Kate, I—" He turned, taking her place with his back to the wall. It seemed like it was the only thing keeping him up. "I was running. I wouldn't let anyone get close to me. And you barreled right through that." He lifted his head. "Two days ago, I took off my father's ring."

A shiver ran down her spine. Right. He'd pressed her hand to the center of his ribs until she'd felt that absence. The place where that band of gold used to be.

"I came here. To New York, to a board of directors meeting to save my father's company, because I'm tired of acting like I don't have any choices anymore. *You* made me want to take my life back again. To find some good in it." His eyes went bright. "I'm tired of living in my father's shadow. I want to be here. I want to fix things with my family. I want to fix things with you."

Her lip quivered. "But what if you can't?"

"Then I'll die trying?"

She laughed, but it came out with a sniffle. "Melodramatic much?"

"Hardly." He licked his lips. "Kate..." He trailed off, hands twitching at his sides like he wanted to reach out again. She took an unconscious step backward. And then another.

Her apartment was such a shoebox, it only took her a half dozen more for her knees to hit the edge of her bed, and she sat back against it heavily.

"This is crazy." The thought finally made it past her lips. "You barely know me, you barely let me know you. We had just—what? A week together?"

"We were supposed to have seven nights."

"And we didn't even get that far." How could they hope to get any farther? "And now you want to uproot your whole life because of me? It's too much."

"It's barely the half of what you make me want." Rough, he said, "What we had, it might not have lasted long, but it changed me. I think it changed you, too."

It had. In so many ways.

"When you let me touch you, when you let me inside you, it meant something." His words sent molten heat to the center of her. But the sex wasn't the problem. Before she could open her mouth to protest, he swallowed, throat bobbing, eyes darkening. "I still think about it. All the time. How sweet you tasted, how it felt to put my hands on you..."

"Don't." She raised a hand as if that could stop him. Her insides trembled. God, it had been a long three months, with nothing to sate her. He'd started this fire within her from the barest kindling, and she'd had no way to put it out. Only the time to let it burn. Three words from him, and the smolder-ing embers of it threatened to consume her whole.

"I still have the toys we bought. I'd love to put them inside you again. Make you come over and over—"

It felt like a blow, the wave of need that threatened to knock her over. She shook her head even as she clenched her thighs.

"We *had* something. Something I've never had before, and I was a fool to let it go without a fight last time. Hell if I'm going to do it again. Isn't it at least worth something? All I'm asking is for you to let us try. Let me try, to win you back, to earn your trust."

And just like that, it all bubbled over. The anger and the hurt and the betrayal, and it was so mixed up with how much she had loved him, how much she still wanted him. How much she didn't know if she could ever trust him again. "I don't know you!"

She'd thought she had, but he'd hidden himself at every turn, and so everything he claimed they'd had was ash, scat-tering at the faintest wind. He'd been just like her father, just like Aaron, pretending to be one thing while deep down he was someone else. Just waiting to turn on her.

He was the reason she'd hardened her heart. She'd learned her lesson, thanks to him, that opening yourself up only led to pain.

She dug her nails into her palms, blinking back tears.

If she let him in again and he hurt her, she'd never forgive herself.

But if she threw him out. If she didn't give him this chance. Would she regret that just as much someday?

She closed her eyes for a long moment, fighting to catch

her breath. She should throw him out. Even if it was only for the night. Having this all tossed back in her face just as the wound had been starting to heal had her reeling. She had to catch her balance—needed time to think.

When she opened her eyes again, though, he was closer. The sight of him on his knees a scant few feet from her...It sucked the air from her lungs all over again.

He worked his jaw, the sharp, perfect point of it flexing as if with a contained strength, a coiled need. "You know me," he gritted out. "Better than anyone in the world. I showed you my fucking soul. I let you draw me. And if that isn't enough..."

She finally heard the undercurrent. *If I'm not enough...*

He shook his head. "Let me prove to you that I'm the man I said I was, deep down. I'll show you the rest of it, too, if you want. The money, my family. Everything. But it won't change anything. The man who made love to you in Paris. That's me. That's all the important parts of me."

A hardness, a tight muscle that had been aching inside her all these months, gave beneath the pressure. Softening. "How?" she asked.

He paused, blinking for a moment. Then as if hit by sudden inspiration, his gaze brightened. Still on his knees, he shuffled closer, reaching out to take her hands, and by God, she let him.

"Seven nights. That's what we were supposed to have in Paris."

"Yes..."

"So give me seven nights more, here, in New York. If by the end of that, I haven't shown you, if I haven't proven to you that I am who I say I am...if you still don't think you can trust me..." He worked his jaw back and forth. "Well, I can't promise I'll go quietly, but I'll go."

She couldn't decide if it was the most ridiculous idea she'd ever heard or the best. "Rylan..."

"Kate. I'm—" The words seemed to choke him, but he got them out all the same. "I'm begging you. Please. Give me a chance. I promise, I will be so good to you." That heat crept back into his tone, making it richer. Deeper. "Remember how good we were?"

The problem was, she did. The summer had been a disaster because of him, but it had had these shining moments she'd remember forever. Standing next to him in a museum, telling him what she saw in a Cézanne, and listening to him break down and start to tell her about his family.

Moments when she lay under him, when his mouth had been on her, when he'd filled her and made her body spark with pleasure in a way she hadn't even known it could.

She was an idiot for even considering it, and even more of one for the way a part of her, a part that had gone unsatisfied for so long, wanted to give in to it right now.

If she was going to think about it, she should *think* about it. Take a day and mull it over. Definitely not let him keep rubbing warmth into her hands, pressing broad fingertips to the skin of her wrists.

She shouldn't be turning her palm over in his to grasp him back. It shouldn't feel this *good*.

As if to clinch it, he dipped his head to kiss her knuckles. "Please."

Really, what were seven nights? She could guard her heart for that long, and take from him all the pleasure he himself had taught her she could ask for from a man. And when it

inevitably fell apart, she could let him go without any lingering doubts in her mind. She'd never have to look back on this
moment and wonder *what if?*

Shakily, she said, "Seven nights."

"It's not so much to ask."

"Does that include tonight?" It was another not-quite test,
because she was exhausted from all of this. Hungry, and not
just for the dinner she'd barely managed to eat half of.

Hungry for connection and touch and to just give in for a
while. To surrender.

"I suppose that depends."

"On what?"

She held her breath as he drifted his hand up her arm, to
her shoulder and her throat before letting it fall down the
center of her body. He stopped it with his palm between
her breasts, every inch of contact throwing sparks. All the
supplication from before disappeared, replaced by the quiet,
commanding confidence he'd always shown when they were
like this. When he was about to prove to her that he could
teach her body to do so much more.

"On whether or not you'll let me lay you out on this
bed. On whether you'll let me remind you just how good
we can be."

"Seven nights," she said one last time, already dizzy with it.

"Starting with this one." His other hand slipped to her
thigh, edging upward with every exhalation.

A beat passed and then another. And maybe she was a fool.
But she'd be more of one not to take this.

It was what he'd been trying to show her all along, after
all. She deserved pleasure. She had the right to accept it
from him.

Swallowing down her nerves, steeling her heart, she placed her hands over his. She gave in to the heat surging through her from this simple touch. To the tiny piece of her that was willing to give this a shot.

Leaning forward, she let her mouth hover just above his. "Then you had better make it count."

Rylan will stop at nothing to win back
Kate's trust—and heart.

Don't miss the stunning sequel to
Seven Nights to Surrender:

eight ways to
ECSTASY

Available Spring 2016